IMPOSSIBLE INCORPORATED

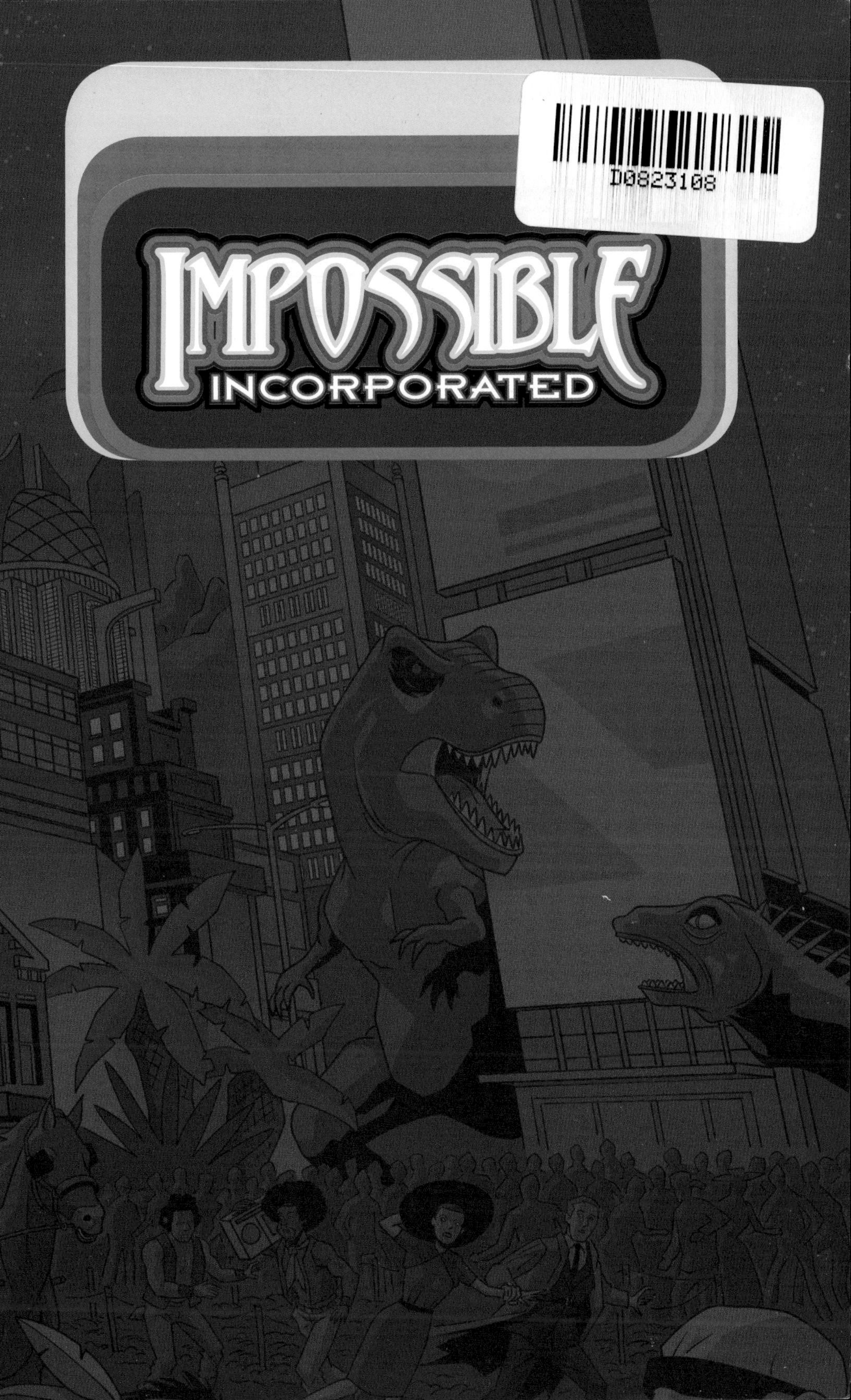

Facebook: **facebook.com/idwpublishing**
Twitter: **@idwpublishing**
YouTube: **youtube.com/idwpublishing**
Tumblr: **tumblr.idwpublishing.com**
Instagram: **instagram.com/idwpublishing**

ISBN: 978-1-68405-435-0   22 21 20 19   1 2 3 4

COVER ARTIST
MIKE CAVALLARO

LETTERER
TOM B. LONG

SERIES ASSISTANT EDITORS
CHASE MAROTZ
& MEGAN BROWN

SERIES EDITOR
DAVID HEDGECOCK

COLLECTION EDITORS
JUSTIN EISINGER
& ALONZO SIMON

COLLECTION DESIGNER
CLYDE GRAPA

Chris Ryall, President, Publisher, and CCO

John Barber, Editor-In-Chief

Robbie Robbins, EVP/Sr. Art Director

Cara Morrison, Chief Financial Officer

Matt Ruzicka, Chief Accounting Officer

David Hedgecock, Associate Publisher

Jerry Bennington, VP of New Product Development

Lorelei Bunjes, VP of Digital Services

Justin Eisinger, Editorial Director, Graphic Novels & Collections

Eric Moss, Senior Director, Licensing and Business Development

Ted Adams, IDW Founder

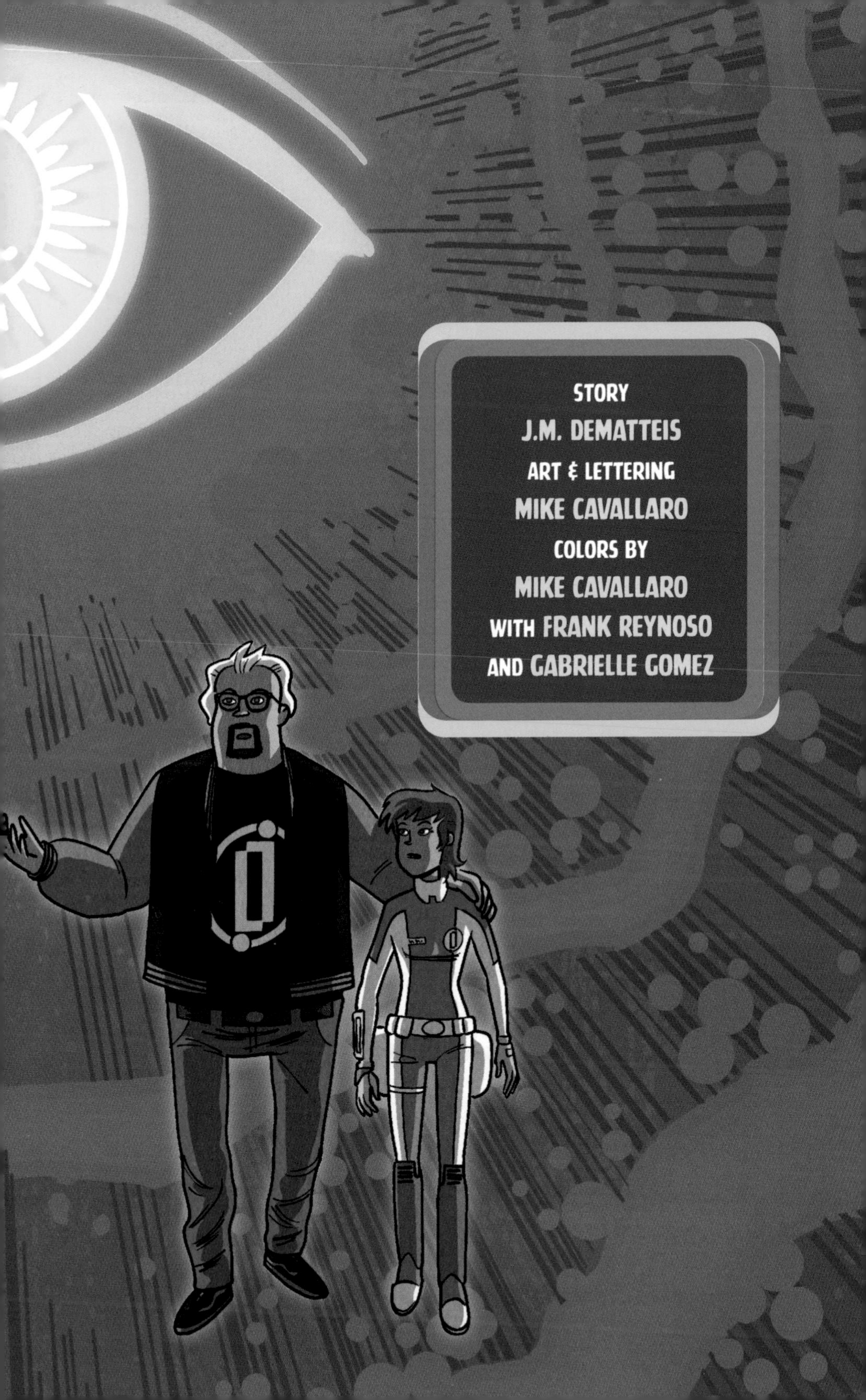
STORY
J.M. DEMATTEIS
ART & LETTERING
MIKE CAVALLARO
COLORS BY
MIKE CAVALLARO
WITH FRANK REYNOSO
AND GABRIELLE GOMEZ

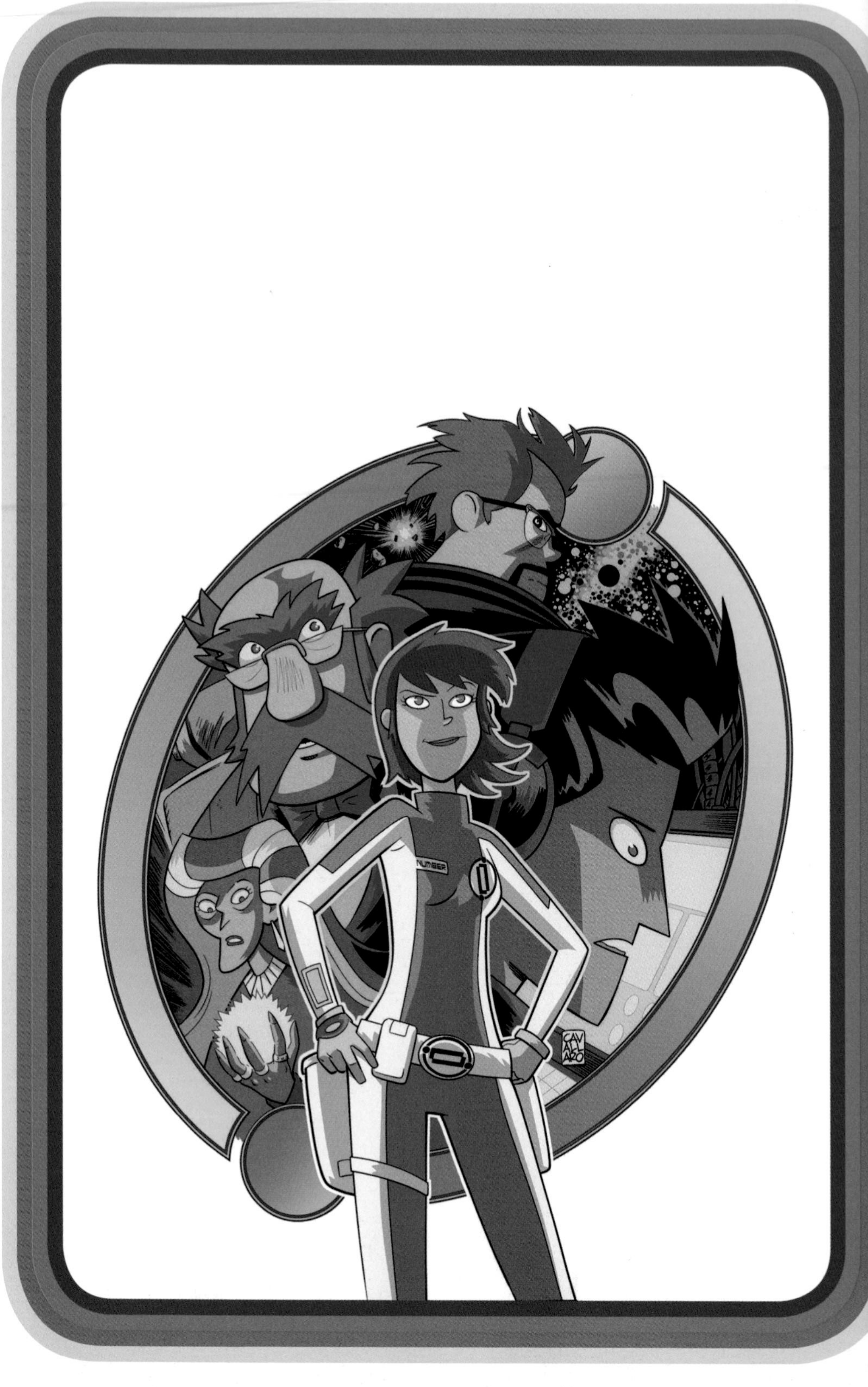
NUMBER
CAV
ALL
ARO

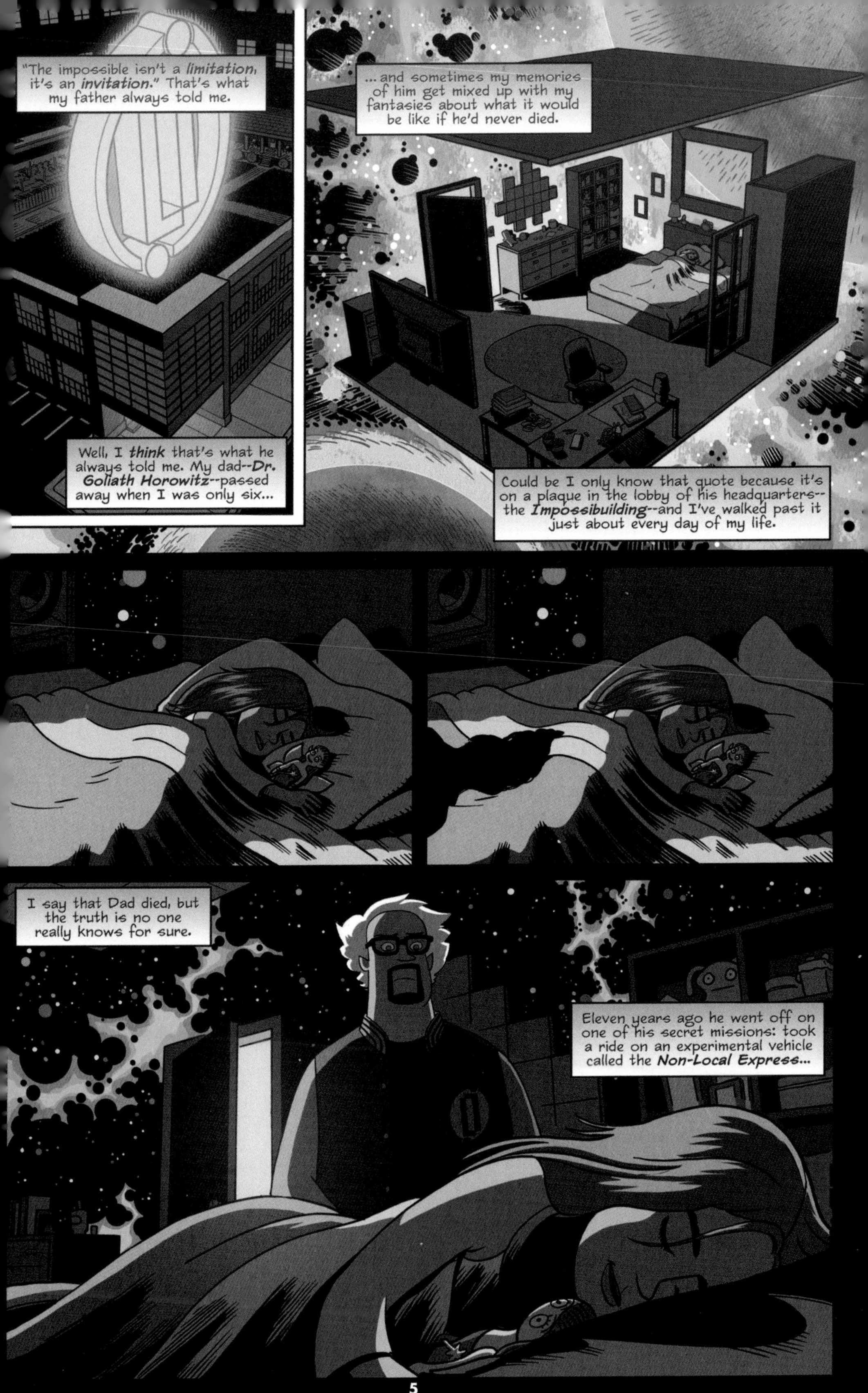
"The impossible isn't a *limitation*, it's an *invitation*." That's what my father always told me.
...and sometimes my memories of him get mixed up with my fantasies about what it would be like if he'd never died.
Well, I *think* that's what he always told me. My dad--**Dr. Goliath Horowitz**--passed away when I was only six...
Could be I only know that quote because it's on a plaque in the lobby of his headquarters--the ***Impossibuilding***--and I've walked past it just about every day of my life.
I say that Dad died, but the truth is no one really knows for sure.
Eleven years ago he went off on one of his secret missions: took a ride on an experimental vehicle called the ***Non-Local Express***...

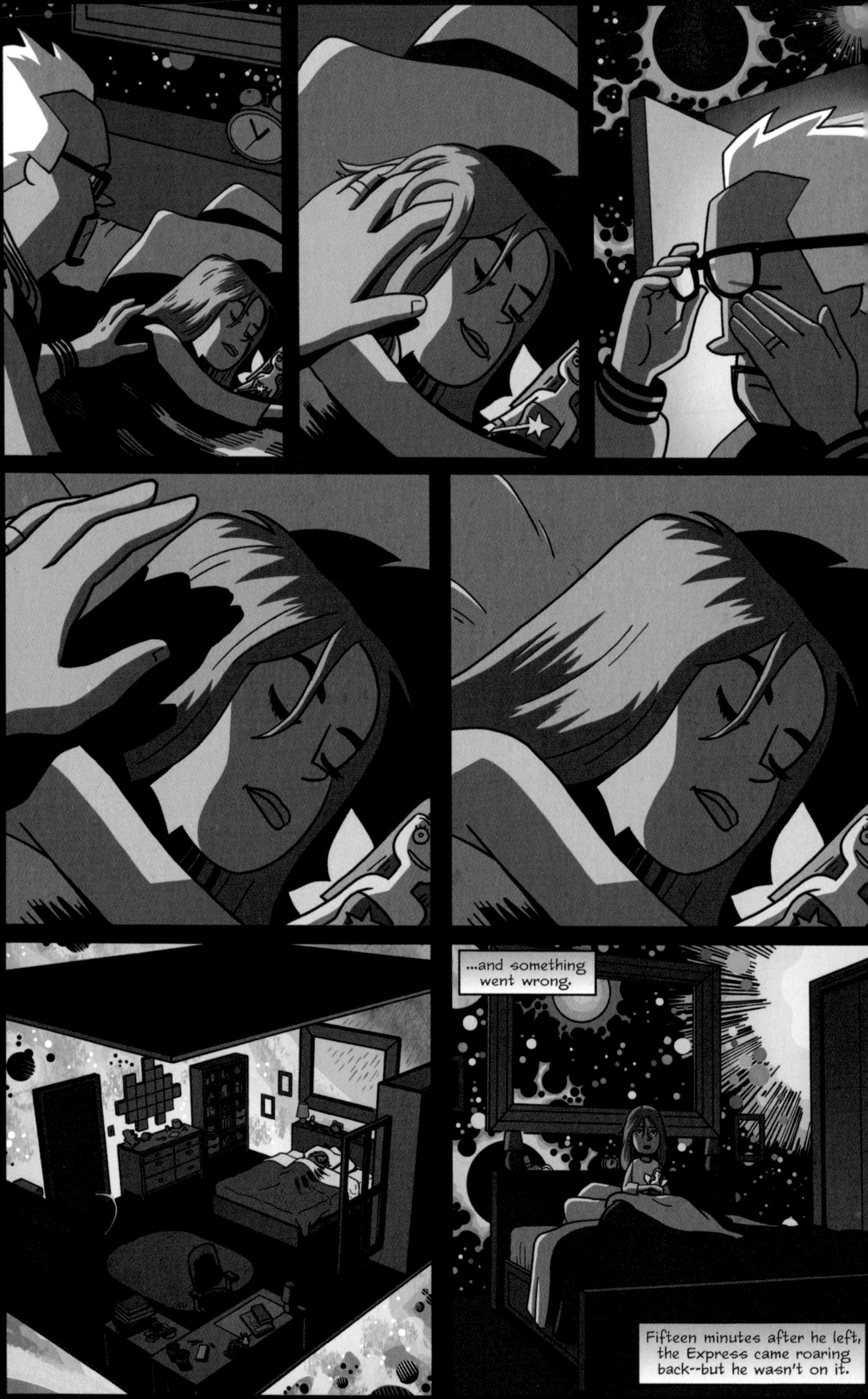
...and something went wrong.
Fifteen minutes after he left, the Express came roaring back--but he wasn't on it.

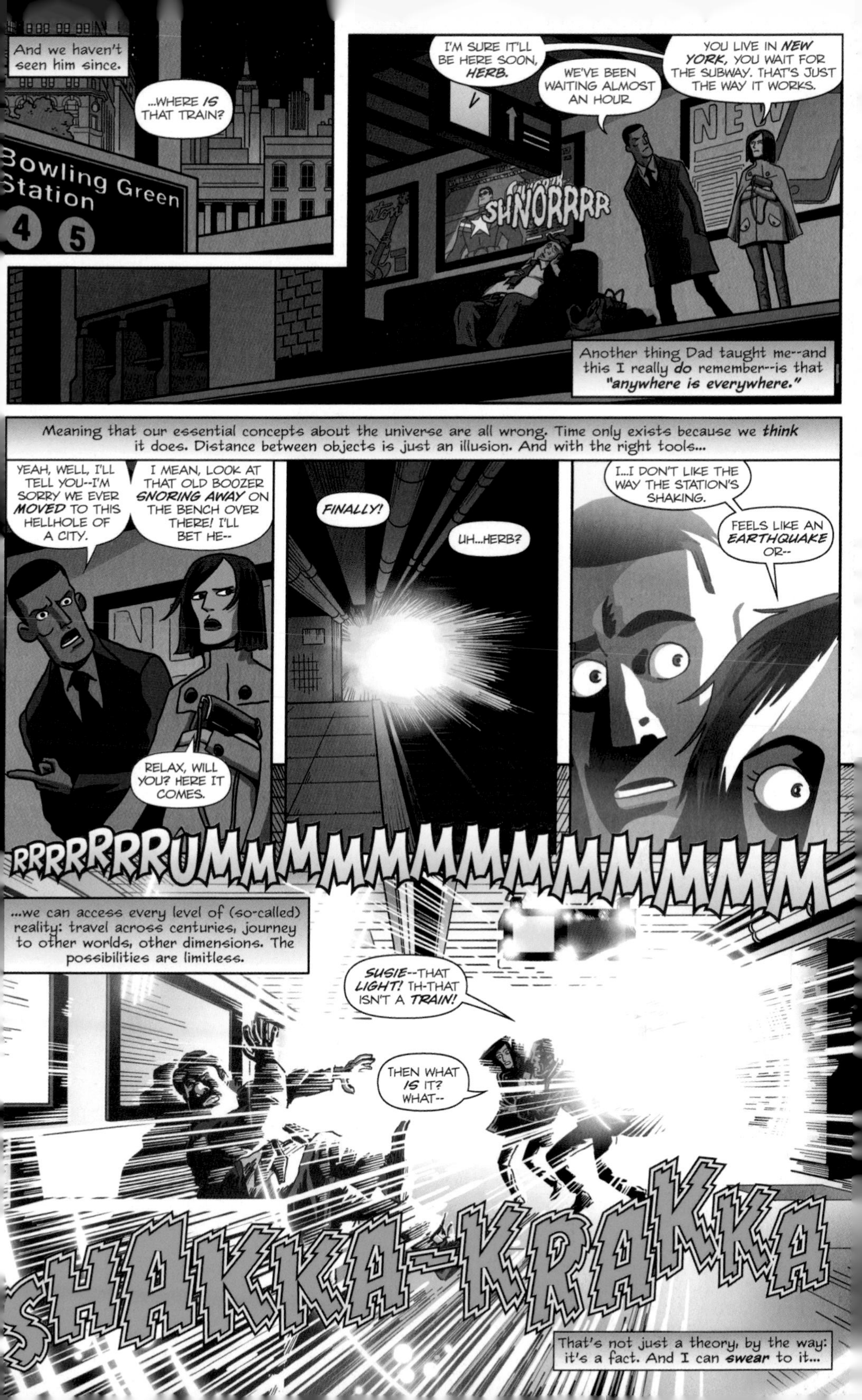

And we haven't seen him since.
...WHERE IS THAT TRAIN?
Bowling Green Station
4
5
I'M SURE IT'LL BE HERE SOON, HERB.
WE'VE BEEN WAITING ALMOST AN HOUR.
YOU LIVE IN NEW YORK, YOU WAIT FOR THE SUBWAY. THAT'S JUST THE WAY IT WORKS.
SHNORRRR
Another thing Dad taught me--and this I really do remember--is that "anywhere is everywhere."
Meaning that our essential concepts about the universe are all wrong. Time only exists because we think it does. Distance between objects is just an illusion. And with the right tools...
YEAH, WELL, I'LL TELL YOU--I'M SORRY WE EVER MOVED TO THIS HELLHOLE OF A CITY.
I MEAN, LOOK AT THAT OLD BOOZER SNORING AWAY ON THE BENCH OVER THERE! I'LL BET HE--
RELAX, WILL YOU? HERE IT COMES.
FINALLY!
UH...HERB?
I...I DON'T LIKE THE WAY THE STATION'S SHAKING.
FEELS LIKE AN EARTHQUAKE OR--
RRRRRRUMMMMMMMMMMMMMMM
...we can access every level of (so-called) reality: travel across centuries, journey to other worlds, other dimensions. The possibilities are limitless.
SUSIE--THAT LIGHT! TH-THAT ISN'T A TRAIN!
THEN WHAT IS IT? WHAT--
SHAKKA-KRAKKA
That's not just a theory, by the way: it's a fact. And I can swear to it...

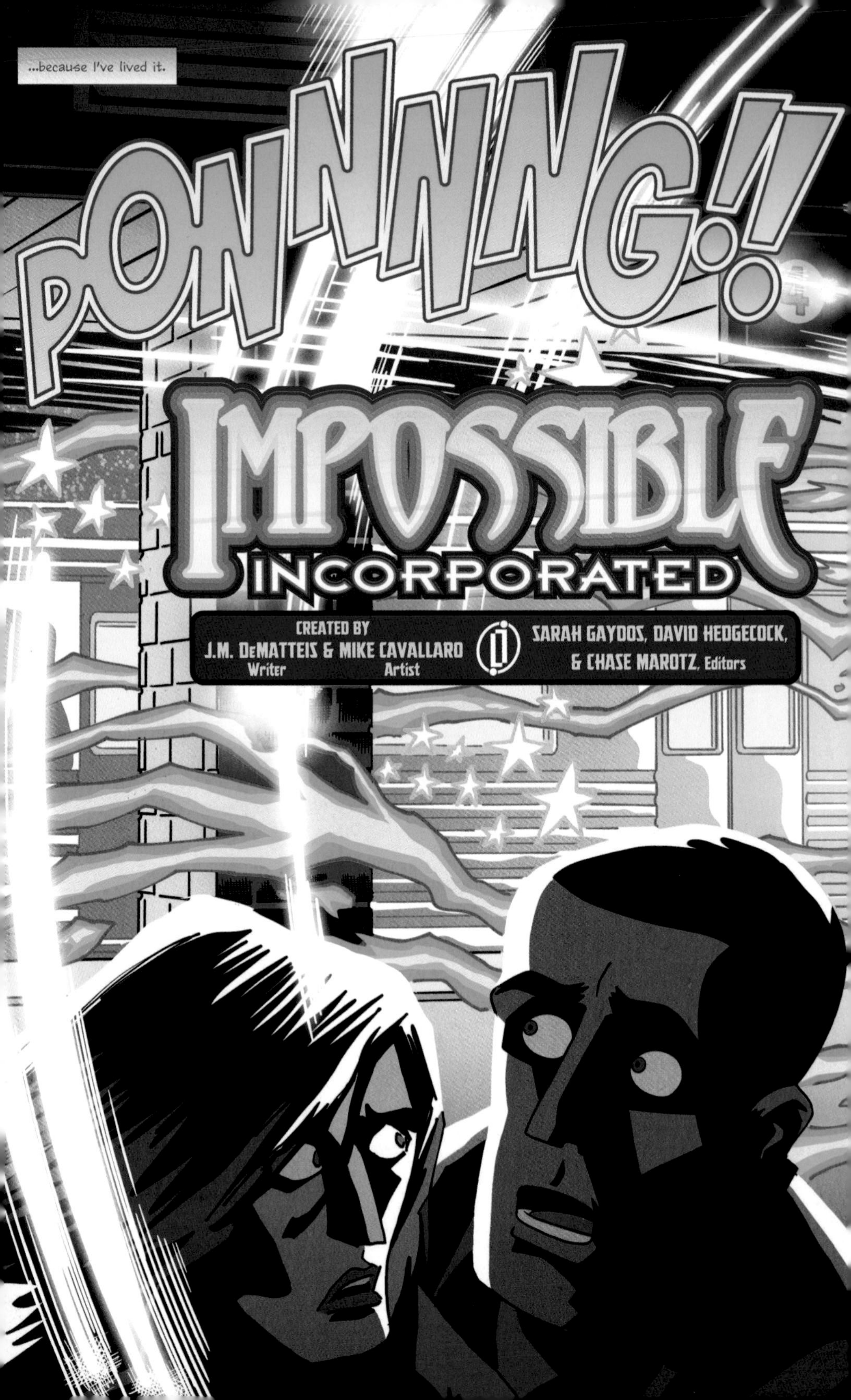

...because I've lived it.
PONNNNG!!
IMPOSSIBLE INCORPORATED
CREATED BY
J.M. DeMATTEIS & MIKE CAVALLARO
Writer Artist
SARAH GAYDOS, DAVID HEDGECOCK, & CHASE MAROTZ, Editors

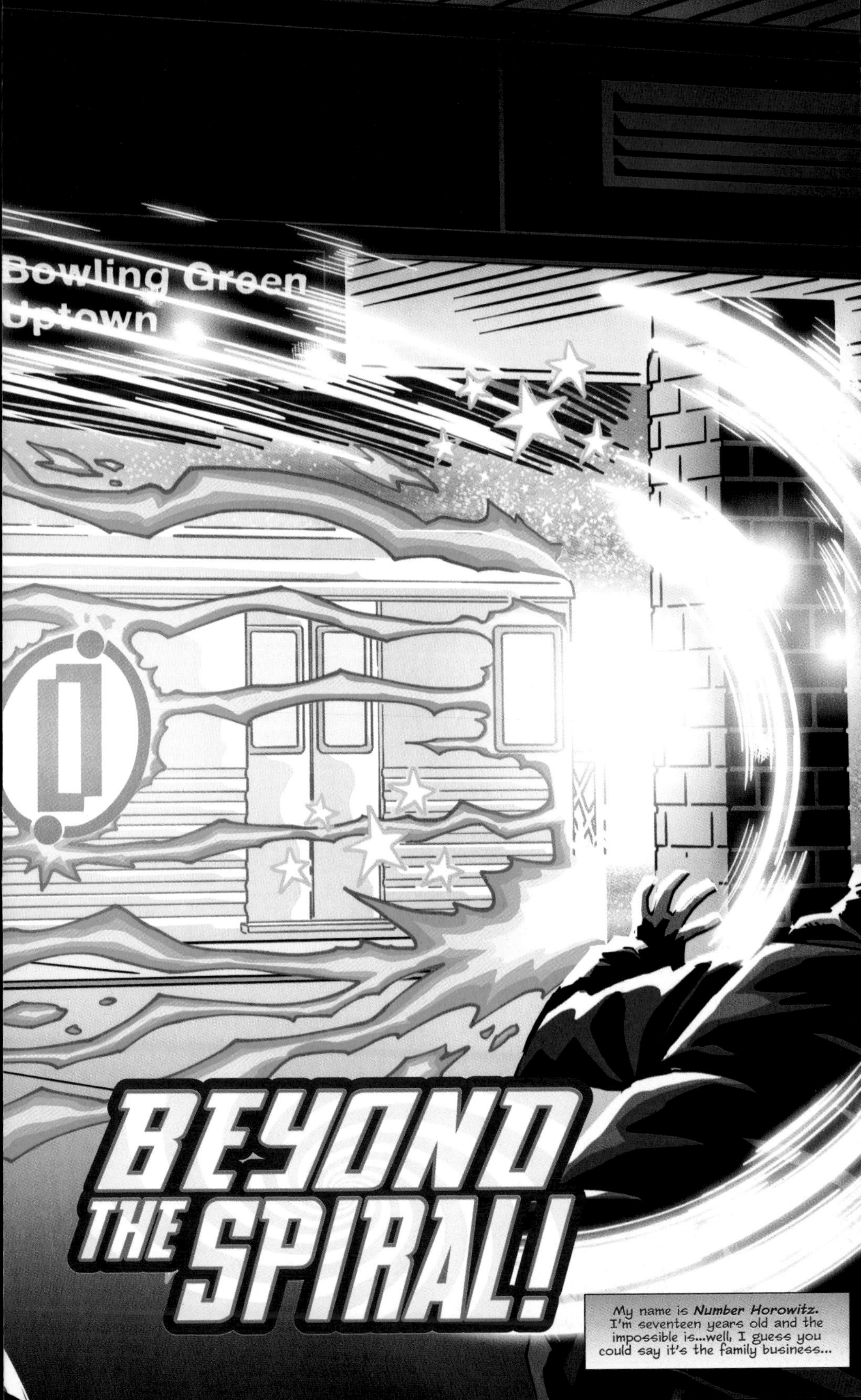
Bowling Green
Uptown
BEYOND THE SPIRAL!
My name is Number Horowitz. I'm seventeen years old and the impossible is...well, I guess you could say it's the family business...

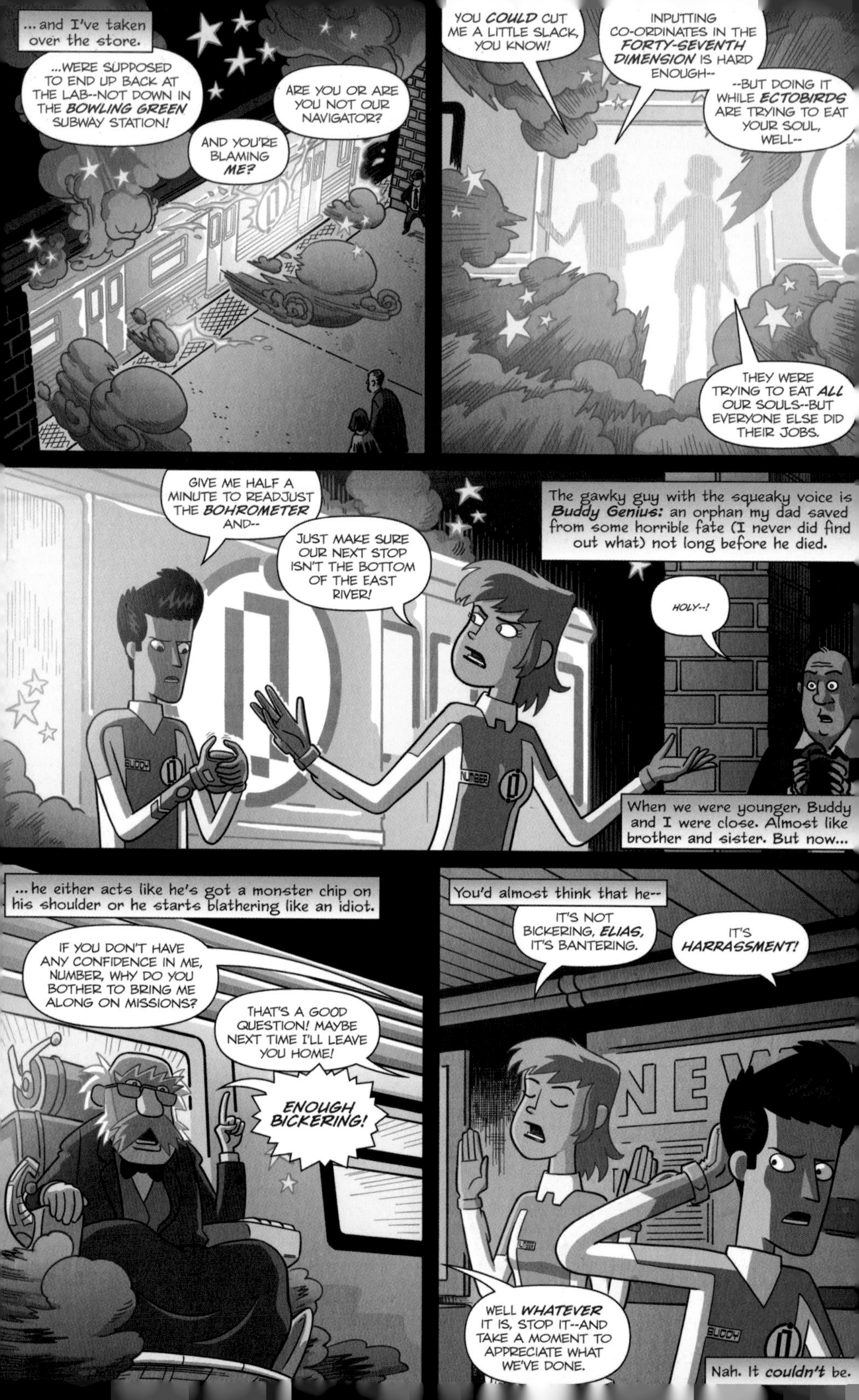
...and I've taken over the store.
...WERE SUPPOSED TO END UP BACK AT THE LAB--NOT DOWN IN THE BOWLING GREEN SUBWAY STATION!
AND YOU'RE BLAMING ME?
ARE YOU OR ARE YOU NOT OUR NAVIGATOR?
YOU COULD CUT ME A LITTLE SLACK, YOU KNOW!
INPUTTING CO-ORDINATES IN THE FORTY-SEVENTH DIMENSION IS HARD ENOUGH--
--BUT DOING IT WHILE ECTOBIRDS ARE TRYING TO EAT YOUR SOUL, WELL--
THEY WERE TRYING TO EAT ALL OUR SOULS--BUT EVERYONE ELSE DID THEIR JOBS.
GIVE ME HALF A MINUTE TO READJUST THE BOHROMETER AND--
JUST MAKE SURE OUR NEXT STOP ISN'T THE BOTTOM OF THE EAST RIVER!
The gawky guy with the squeaky voice is Buddy Genius: an orphan my dad saved from some horrible fate (I never did find out what) not long before he died.
HOLY--!
BUDDY
NUMBER
When we were younger, Buddy and I were close. Almost like brother and sister. But now...
...he either acts like he's got a monster chip on his shoulder or he starts blathering like an idiot.
IF YOU DON'T HAVE ANY CONFIDENCE IN ME, NUMBER, WHY DO YOU BOTHER TO BRING ME ALONG ON MISSIONS?
THAT'S A GOOD QUESTION! MAYBE NEXT TIME I'LL LEAVE YOU HOME!
ENOUGH BICKERING!
You'd almost think that he--
IT'S NOT BICKERING, ELIAS, IT'S BANTERING.
IT'S HARRASSMENT!
NEW
WELL WHATEVER IT IS, STOP IT--AND TAKE A MOMENT TO APPRECIATE WHAT WE'VE DONE.
BUDDY
Nah. It couldn't be.

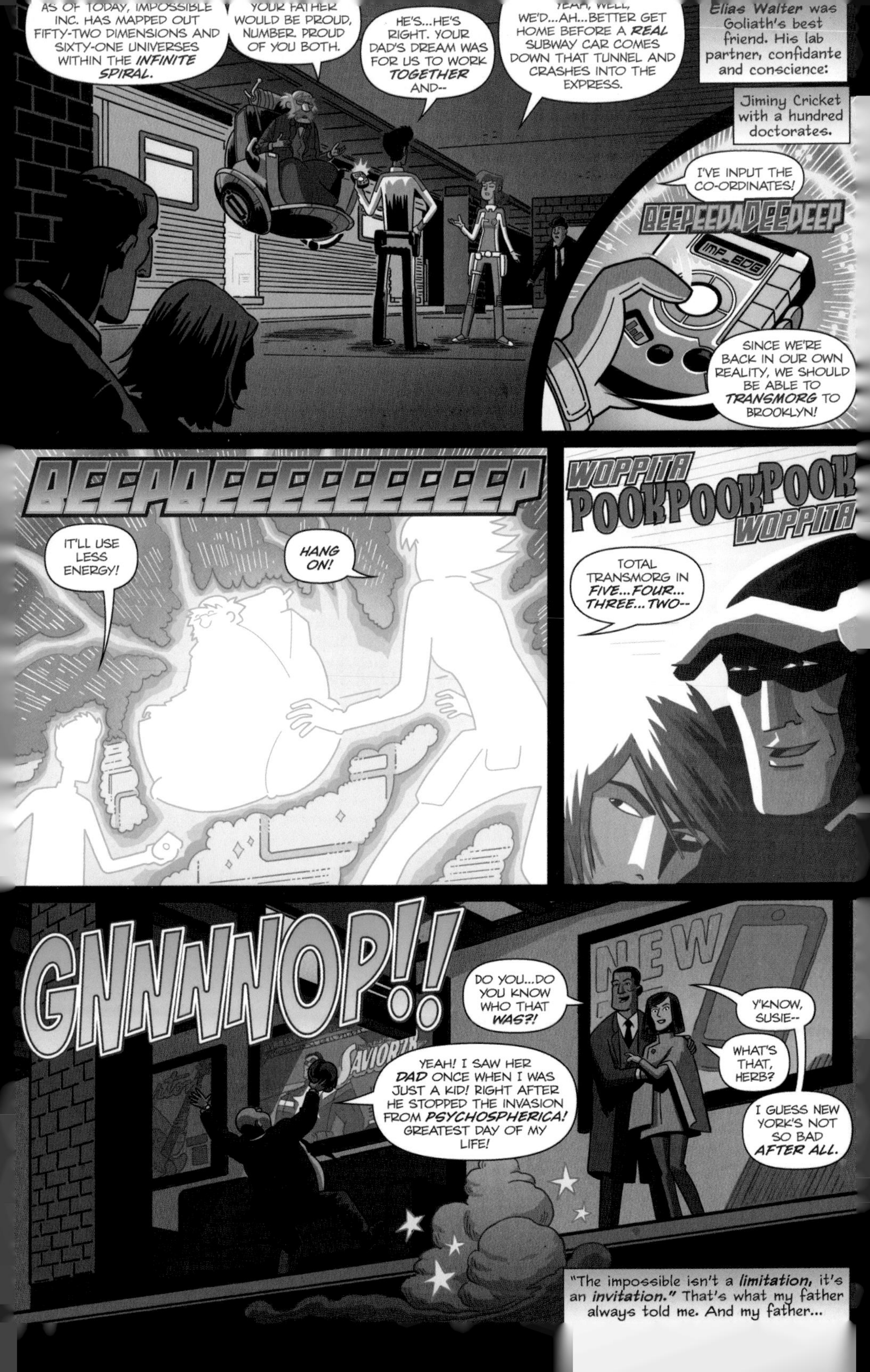
AS OF TODAY, IMPOSSIBLE INC. HAS MAPPED OUT FIFTY-TWO DIMENSIONS AND SIXTY-ONE UNIVERSES WITHIN THE INFINITE SPIRAL.
YOUR FATHER WOULD BE PROUD, NUMBER. PROUD OF YOU BOTH.
HE'S...HE'S RIGHT. YOUR DAD'S DREAM WAS FOR US TO WORK TOGETHER AND--
YEAH, WELL, WE'D...AH...BETTER GET HOME BEFORE A REAL SUBWAY CAR COMES DOWN THAT TUNNEL AND CRASHES INTO THE EXPRESS.
Elias Walter was Goliath's best friend. His lab partner, confidante and conscience:
Jiminy Cricket with a hundred doctorates.
I'VE INPUT THE CO-ORDINATES!
BEEPEEDADEEDEEP
IMP_BDG
SINCE WE'RE BACK IN OUR OWN REALITY, WE SHOULD BE ABLE TO TRANSMORG TO BROOKLYN!
BEEPBEEEEEEEEEEEP
IT'LL USE LESS ENERGY!
HANG ON!
WOPPITA POOKPOOKPOOK WOPPITA
TOTAL TRANSMORG IN FIVE...FOUR... THREE...TWO--
GNNNNOP!!
DO YOU...DO YOU KNOW WHO THAT WAS?!
YEAH! I SAW HER DAD ONCE WHEN I WAS JUST A KID! RIGHT AFTER HE STOPPED THE INVASION FROM PSYCHOSPHERICA! GREATEST DAY OF MY LIFE!
NEW
SAVIOR
Y'KNOW, SUSIE--
WHAT'S THAT, HERB?
I GUESS NEW YORK'S NOT SO BAD AFTER ALL.
"The impossible isn't a limitation, it's an invitation." That's what my father always told me. And my father...

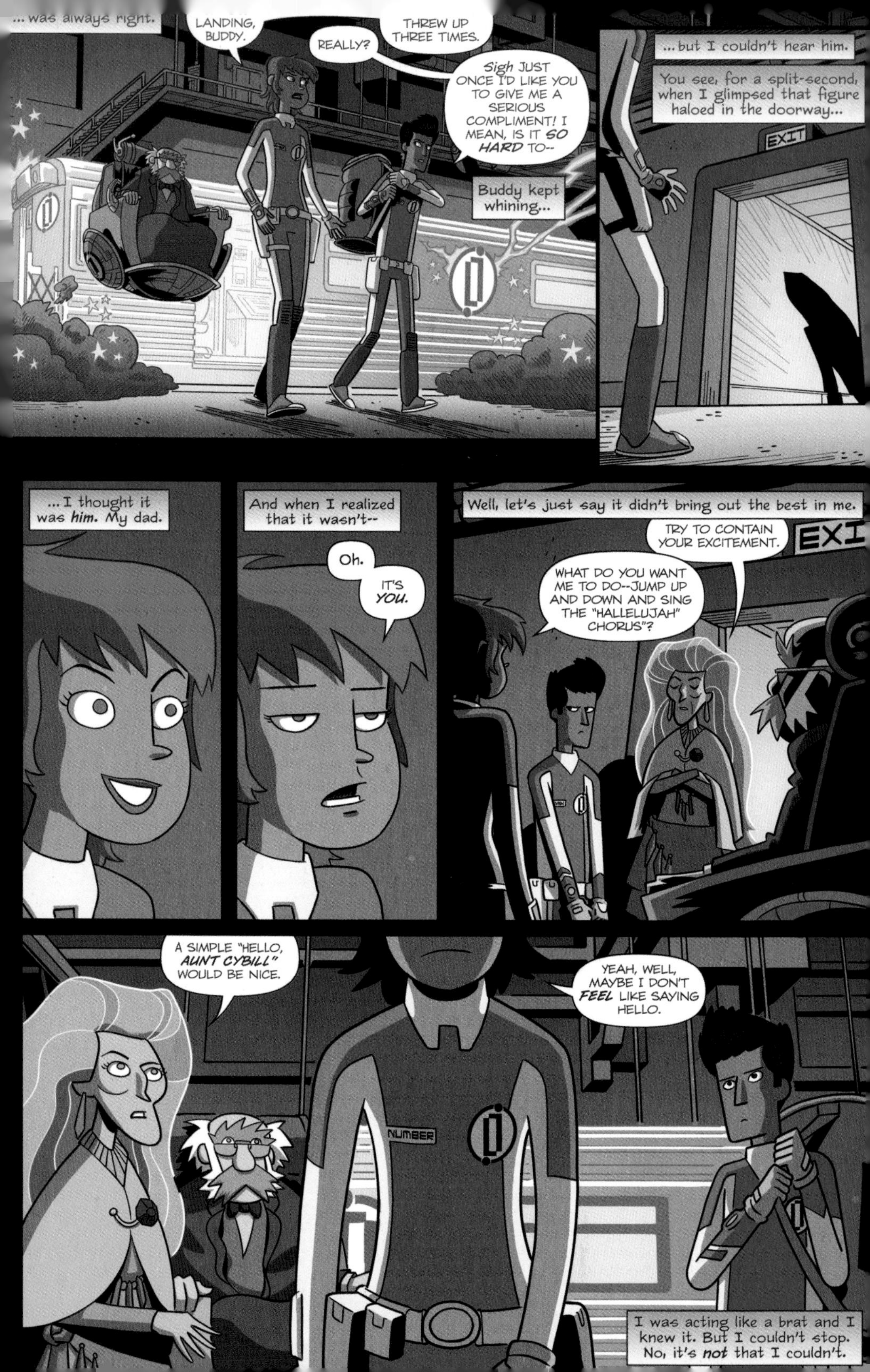

...was always right.
LANDING, BUDDY.
THREW UP THREE TIMES.
REALLY?
Sigh JUST ONCE I'D LIKE YOU TO GIVE ME A SERIOUS COMPLIMENT! I MEAN, IS IT SO HARD TO--
Buddy kept whining...
...but I couldn't hear him.
You see, for a split-second, when I glimpsed that figure haloed in the doorway...
EXIT
...I thought it was him. My dad.
And when I realized that it wasn't--
Oh.
IT'S YOU.
Well, let's just say it didn't bring out the best in me.
TRY TO CONTAIN YOUR EXCITEMENT.
WHAT DO YOU WANT ME TO DO--JUMP UP AND DOWN AND SING THE "HALLELUJAH" CHORUS"?
A SIMPLE "HELLO, AUNT CYBILL" WOULD BE NICE.
YEAH, WELL, MAYBE I DON'T FEEL LIKE SAYING HELLO.
NUMBER
I was acting like a brat and I knew it. But I couldn't stop. No, it's not that I couldn't.

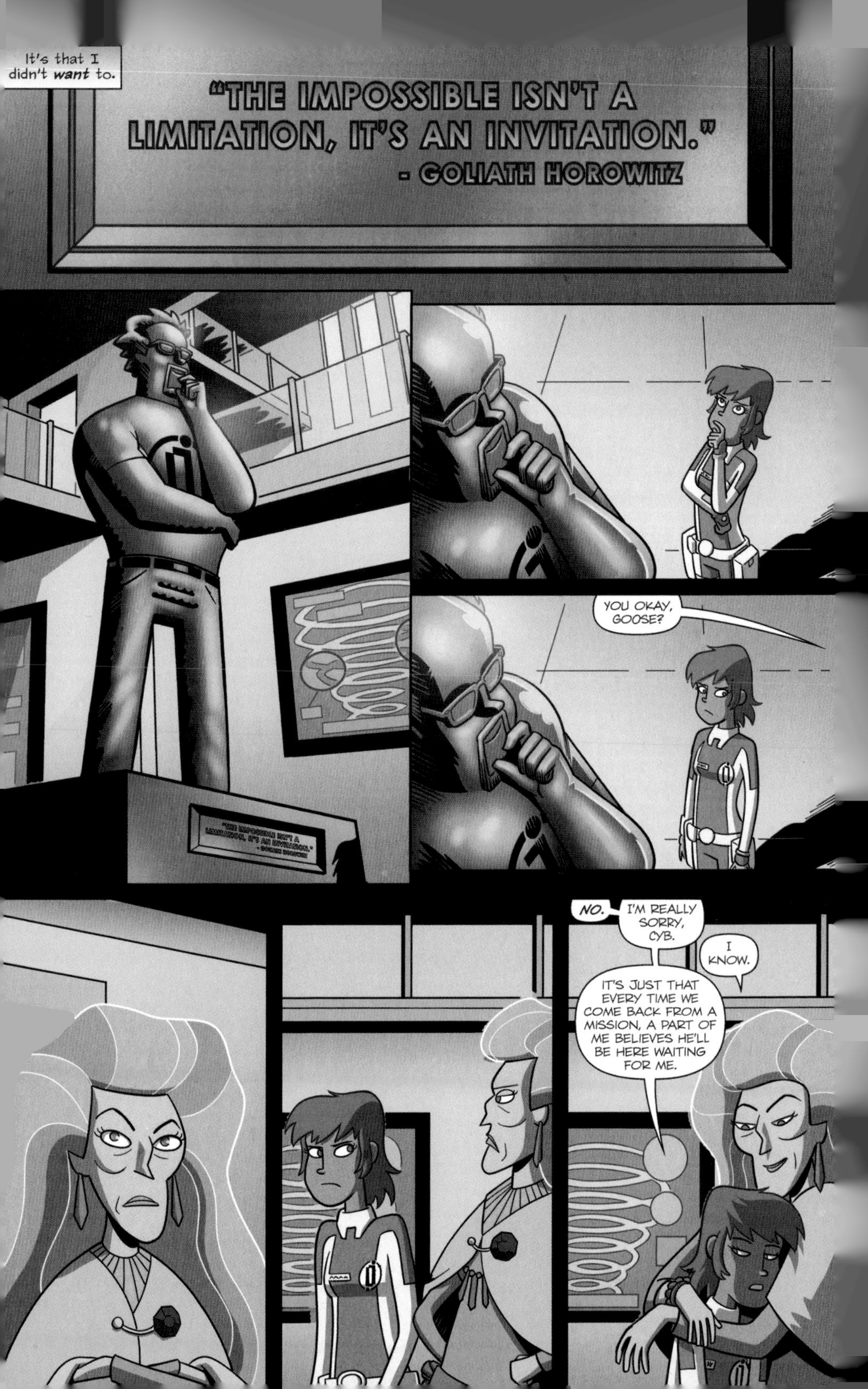
It's that I didn't *want* to.
"THE IMPOSSIBLE ISN'T A LIMITATION, IT'S AN INVITATION."
- GOLIATH HOROWITZ
YOU OKAY, GOOSE?
NO.
I'M REALLY SORRY, CYB.
IT'S JUST THAT EVERY TIME WE COME BACK FROM A MISSION, A PART OF ME BELIEVES HE'LL BE HERE WAITING FOR ME.
I KNOW.

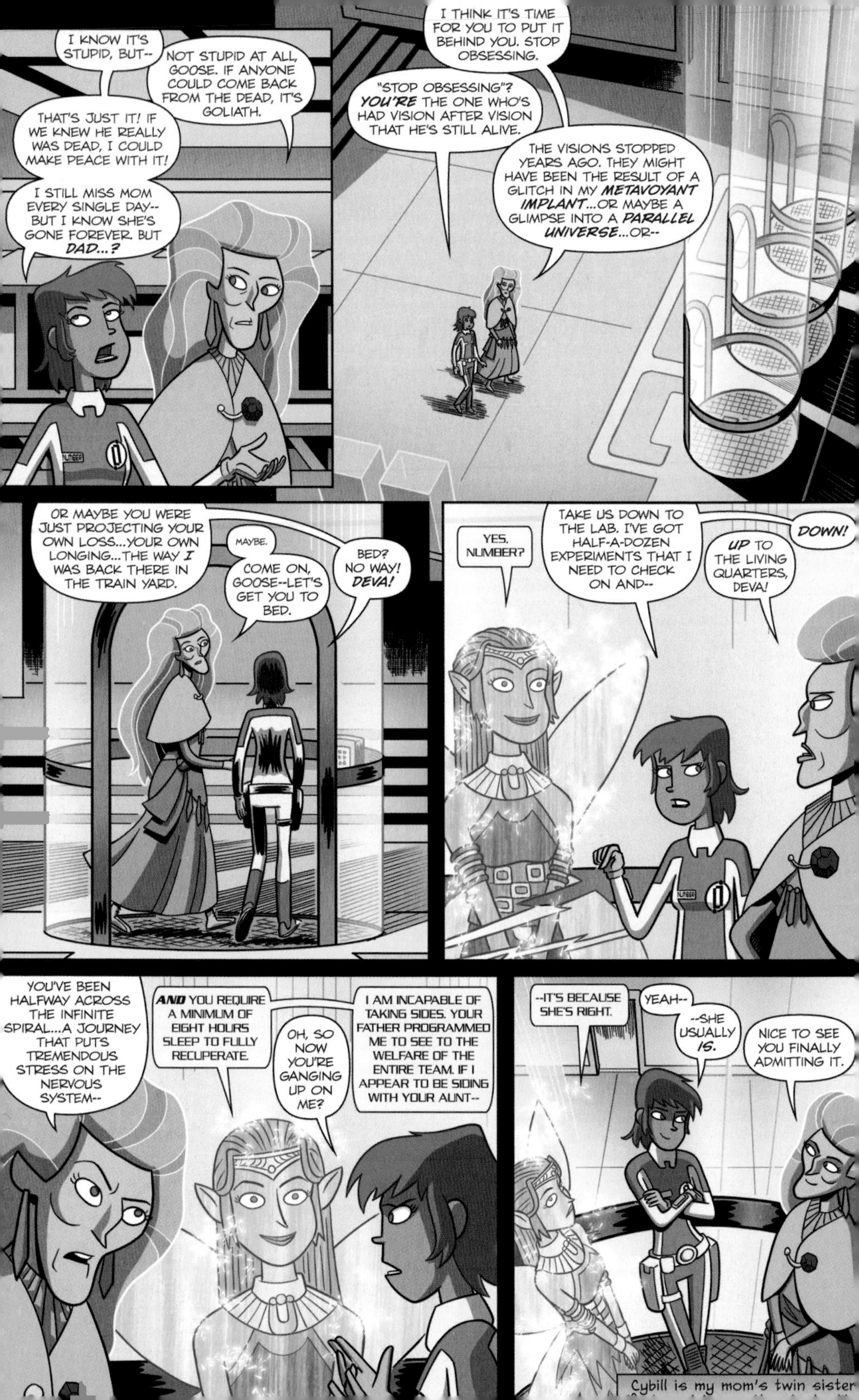
I KNOW IT'S STUPID, BUT--
NOT STUPID AT ALL, GOOSE. IF ANYONE COULD COME BACK FROM THE DEAD, IT'S GOLIATH.
THAT'S JUST IT! IF WE KNEW HE REALLY WAS DEAD, I COULD MAKE PEACE WITH IT!
I STILL MISS MOM EVERY SINGLE DAY-- BUT I KNOW SHE'S GONE FOREVER. BUT DAD...?
I THINK IT'S TIME FOR YOU TO PUT IT BEHIND YOU. STOP OBSESSING.
"STOP OBSESSING"? YOU'RE THE ONE WHO'S HAD VISION AFTER VISION THAT HE'S STILL ALIVE.
THE VISIONS STOPPED YEARS AGO. THEY MIGHT HAVE BEEN THE RESULT OF A GLITCH IN MY METAVOYANT IMPLANT...OR MAYBE A GLIMPSE INTO A PARALLEL UNIVERSE...OR--
OR MAYBE YOU WERE JUST PROJECTING YOUR OWN LOSS...YOUR OWN LONGING...THE WAY I WAS BACK THERE IN THE TRAIN YARD.
MAYBE.
COME ON, GOOSE--LET'S GET YOU TO BED.
BED? NO WAY! DEVA!
YES, NUMBER?
TAKE US DOWN TO THE LAB. I'VE GOT HALF-A-DOZEN EXPERIMENTS THAT I NEED TO CHECK ON AND--
DOWN!
UP TO THE LIVING QUARTERS, DEVA!
YOU'VE BEEN HALFWAY ACROSS THE INFINITE SPIRAL...A JOURNEY THAT PUTS TREMENDOUS STRESS ON THE NERVOUS SYSTEM--
AND YOU REQUIRE A MINIMUM OF EIGHT HOURS SLEEP TO FULLY RECUPERATE.
OH, SO NOW YOU'RE GANGING UP ON ME?
I AM INCAPABLE OF TAKING SIDES. YOUR FATHER PROGRAMMED ME TO SEE TO THE WELFARE OF THE ENTIRE TEAM. IF I APPEAR TO BE SIDING WITH YOUR AUNT--
--IT'S BECAUSE SHE'S RIGHT.
YEAH--
--SHE USUALLY IS.
NICE TO SEE YOU FINALLY ADMITTING IT.
Cybill is my mom's twin sister

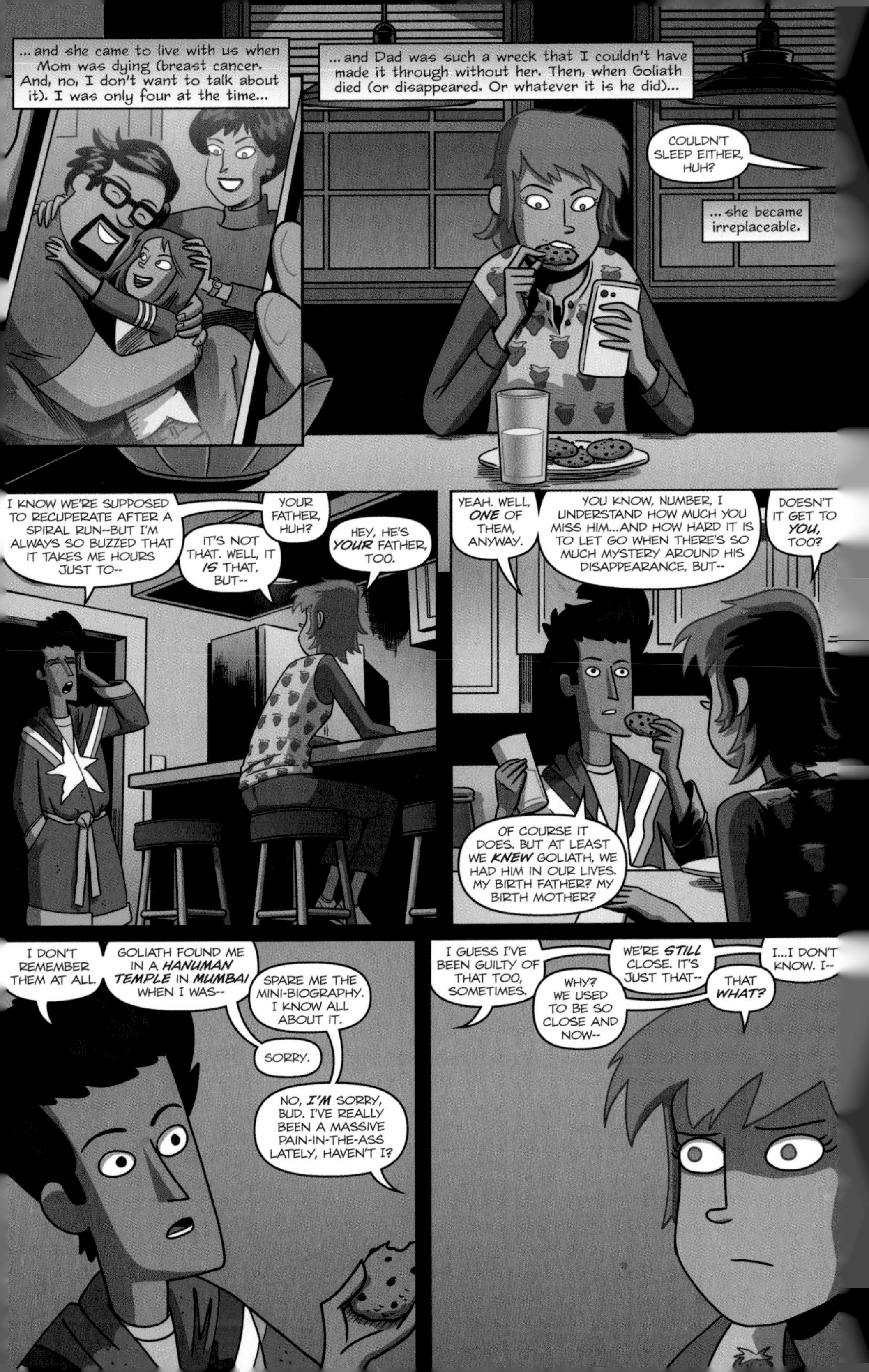
...and she came to live with us when Mom was dying (breast cancer. And, no, I don't want to talk about it). I was only four at the time...
...and Dad was such a wreck that I couldn't have made it through without her. Then, when Goliath died (or disappeared. Or whatever it is he did)...
COULDN'T SLEEP EITHER, HUH?
...she became irreplaceable.
I KNOW WE'RE SUPPOSED TO RECUPERATE AFTER A SPIRAL RUN--BUT I'M ALWAYS SO BUZZED THAT IT TAKES ME HOURS JUST TO--
YOUR FATHER, HUH?
IT'S NOT THAT. WELL, IT IS THAT, BUT--
HEY, HE'S YOUR FATHER, TOO.
YEAH. WELL, ONE OF THEM, ANYWAY.
YOU KNOW, NUMBER, I UNDERSTAND HOW MUCH YOU MISS HIM...AND HOW HARD IT IS TO LET GO WHEN THERE'S SO MUCH MYSTERY AROUND HIS DISAPPEARANCE, BUT--
DOESN'T IT GET TO YOU, TOO?
OF COURSE IT DOES. BUT AT LEAST WE KNEW GOLIATH, WE HAD HIM IN OUR LIVES. MY BIRTH FATHER? MY BIRTH MOTHER?
I DON'T REMEMBER THEM AT ALL.
GOLIATH FOUND ME IN A HANUMAN TEMPLE IN MUMBAI WHEN I WAS--
SPARE ME THE MINI-BIOGRAPHY. I KNOW ALL ABOUT IT.
SORRY.
NO, I'M SORRY, BUD. I'VE REALLY BEEN A MASSIVE PAIN-IN-THE-ASS LATELY, HAVEN'T I?
I GUESS I'VE BEEN GUILTY OF THAT TOO, SOMETIMES.
WHY? WE USED TO BE SO CLOSE AND NOW--
WE'RE STILL CLOSE. IT'S JUST THAT--
THAT WHAT?
I...I DON'T KNOW. I--

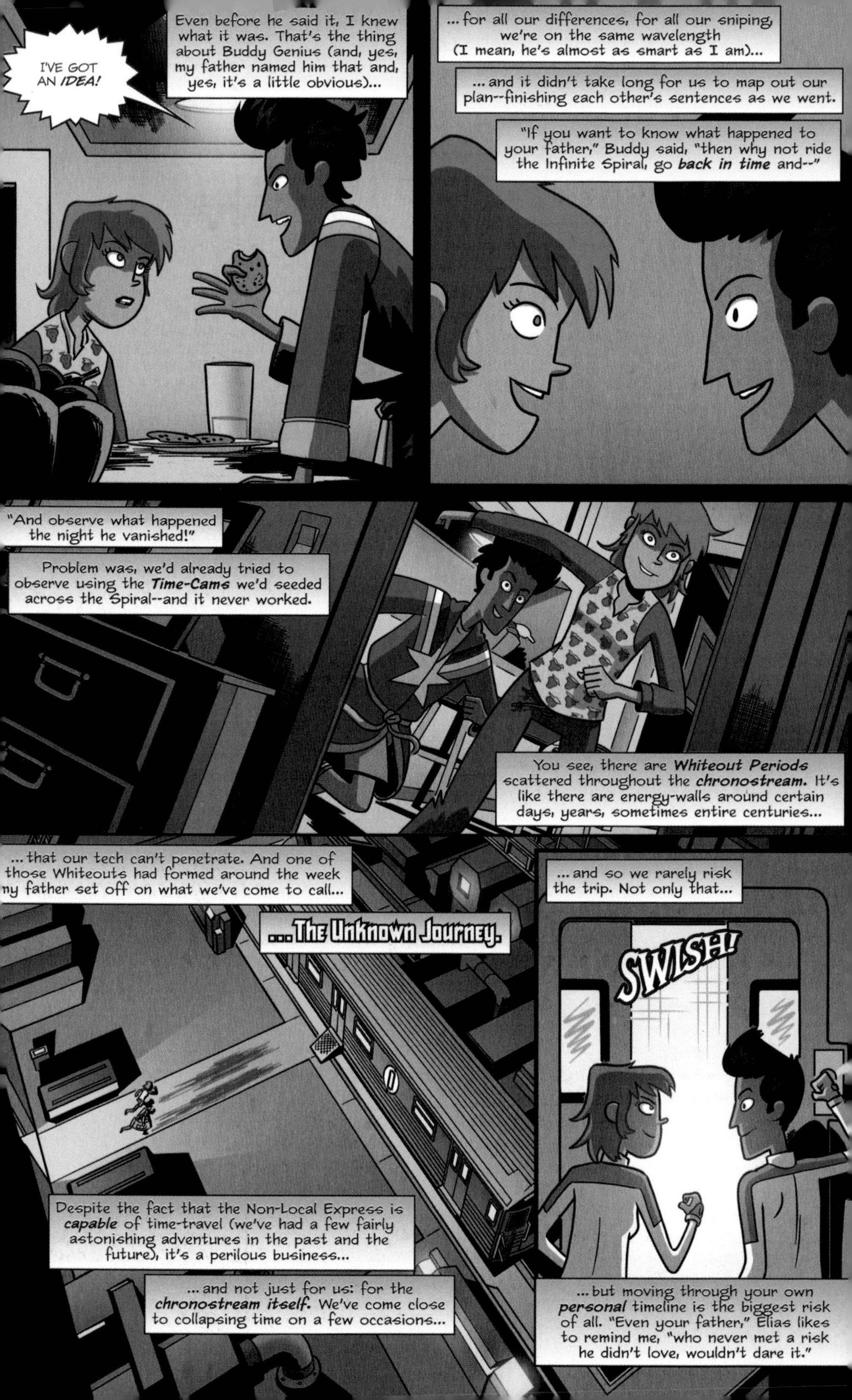
I'VE GOT AN *IDEA!*
Even before he said it, I knew what it was. That's the thing about Buddy Genius (and, yes, my father named him that and, yes, it's a little obvious)...
... for all our differences, for all our sniping, we're on the same wavelength (I mean, he's almost as smart as I am)...
... and it didn't take long for us to map out our plan--finishing each other's sentences as we went.
"If you want to know what happened to your father," Buddy said, "then why not ride the Infinite Spiral, go ***back in time*** and--"
"And observe what happened the night he vanished!"
Problem was, we'd already tried to observe using the ***Time-Cams*** we'd seeded across the Spiral--and it never worked.
You see, there are ***Whiteout Periods*** scattered throughout the ***chronostream.*** It's like there are energy-walls around certain days, years, sometimes entire centuries...
... that our tech can't penetrate. And one of those Whiteouts had formed around the week my father set off on what we've come to call...
...The Unknown Journey.
Despite the fact that the Non-Local Express is *capable* of time-travel (we've had a few fairly astonishing adventures in the past and the future), it's a perilous business...
... and not just for us: for the ***chronostream itself.*** We've come close to collapsing time on a few occasions...
... and so we rarely risk the trip. Not only that...
SWISH!
... but moving through your own ***personal*** timeline is the biggest risk of all. "Even your father," Elias likes to remind me, "who never met a risk he didn't love, wouldn't dare it."

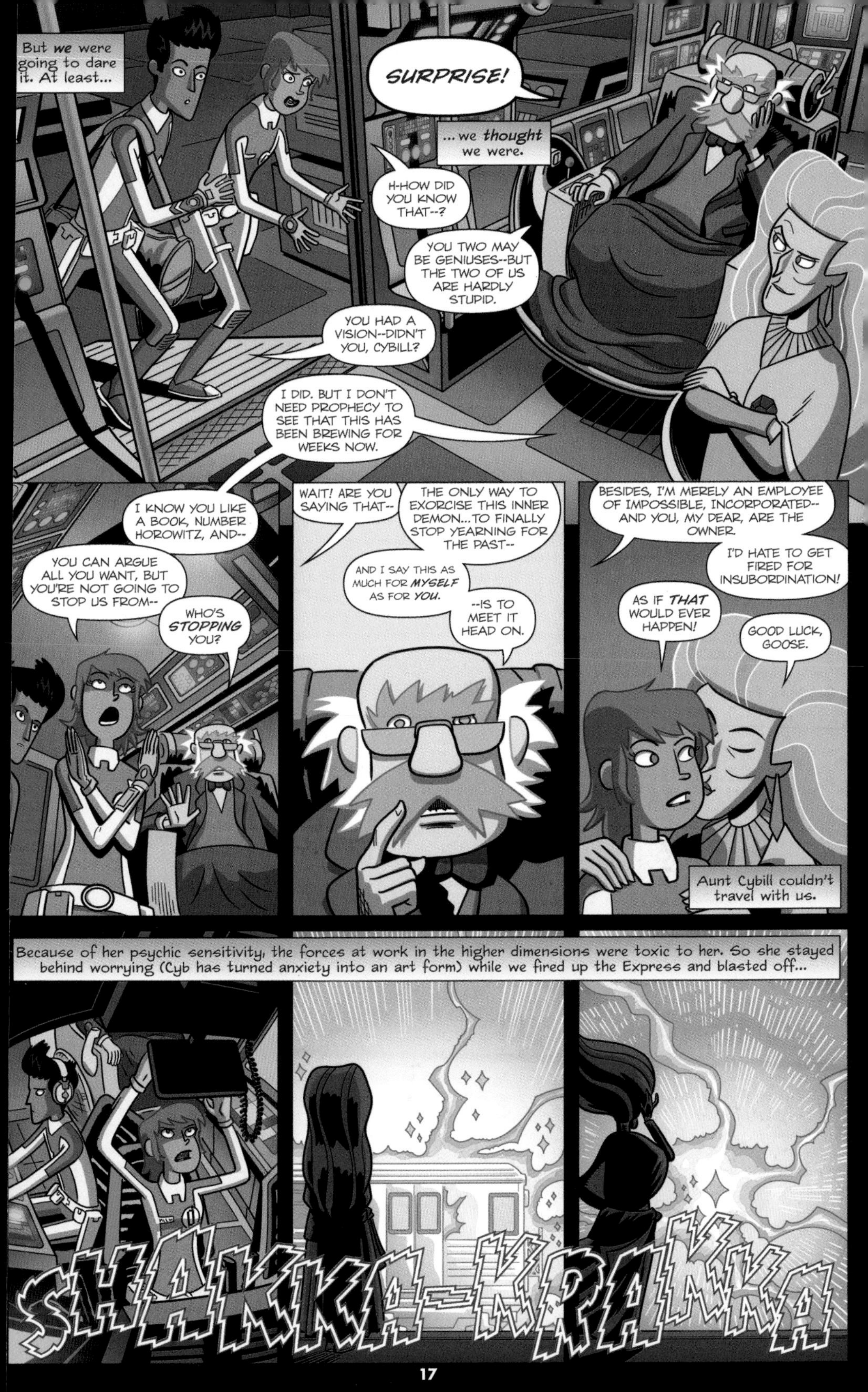
But we were going to dare it. At least...
SURPRISE!
...we thought we were.
H-HOW DID YOU KNOW THAT--?
YOU TWO MAY BE GENIUSES--BUT THE TWO OF US ARE HARDLY STUPID.
YOU HAD A VISION--DIDN'T YOU, CYBILL?
I DID. BUT I DON'T NEED PROPHECY TO SEE THAT THIS HAS BEEN BREWING FOR WEEKS NOW.
I KNOW YOU LIKE A BOOK, NUMBER HOROWITZ, AND--
YOU CAN ARGUE ALL YOU WANT, BUT YOU'RE NOT GOING TO STOP US FROM--
WHO'S STOPPING YOU?
WAIT! ARE YOU SAYING THAT--
THE ONLY WAY TO EXORCISE THIS INNER DEMON...TO FINALLY STOP YEARNING FOR THE PAST--
AND I SAY THIS AS MUCH FOR MYSELF AS FOR YOU.
--IS TO MEET IT HEAD ON.
BESIDES, I'M MERELY AN EMPLOYEE OF IMPOSSIBLE, INCORPORATED--AND YOU, MY DEAR, ARE THE OWNER.
I'D HATE TO GET FIRED FOR INSUBORDINATION!
AS IF THAT WOULD EVER HAPPEN!
GOOD LUCK, GOOSE.
Aunt Cybill couldn't travel with us.
Because of her psychic sensitivity, the forces at work in the higher dimensions were toxic to her. So she stayed behind worrying (Cyb has turned anxiety into an art form) while we fired up the Express and blasted off...
SHAKKA-KRAKKA

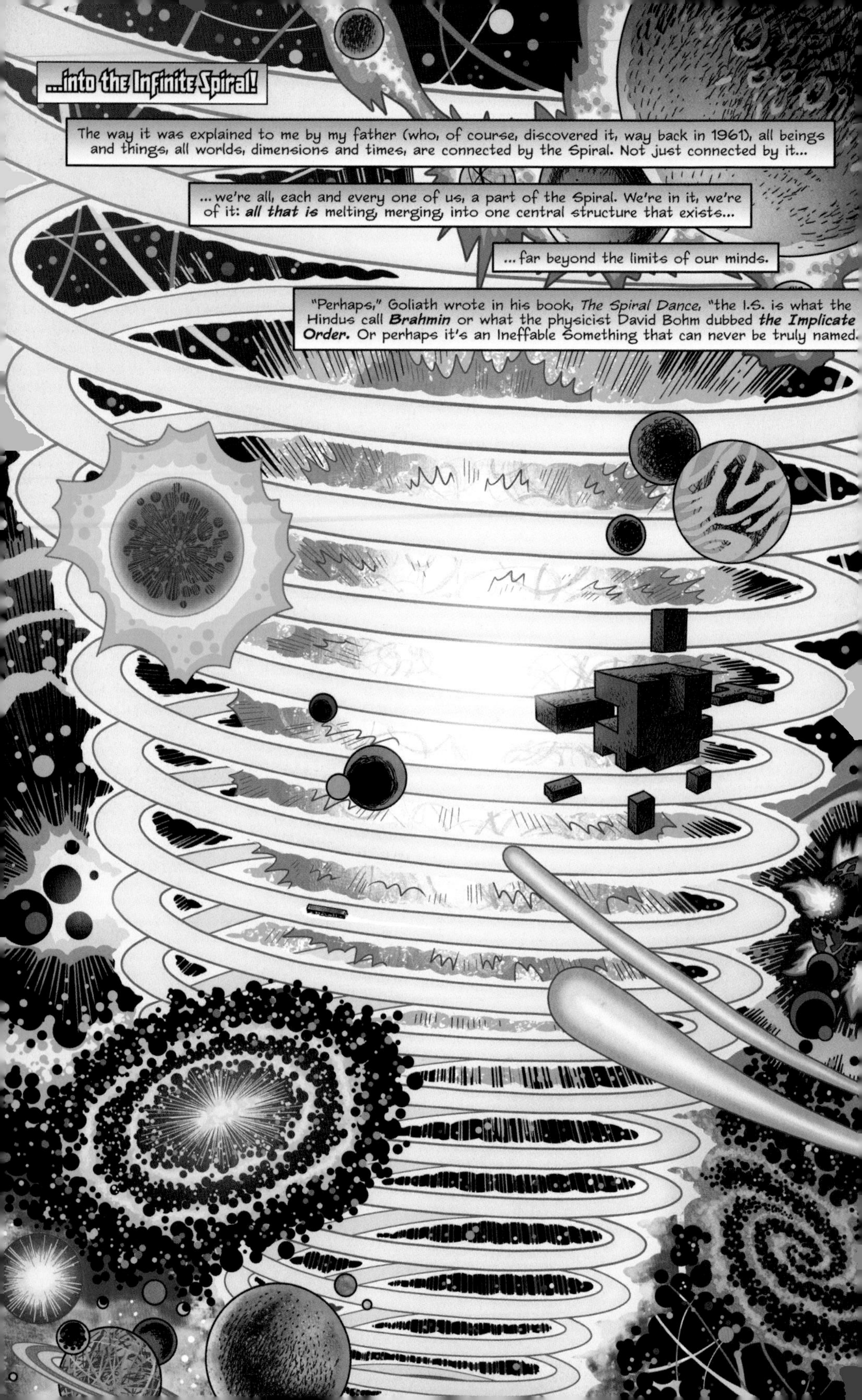
...into the Infinite Spiral!
The way it was explained to me by my father (who, of course, discovered it, way back in 1961), all beings and things, all worlds, dimensions and times, are connected by the Spiral. Not just connected by it...
...we're all, each and every one of us, a part of the Spiral. We're in it, we're of it: all that is melting, merging, into one central structure that exists...
...far beyond the limits of our minds.
"Perhaps," Goliath wrote in his book, The Spiral Dance, "the I.S. is what the Hindus call Brahmin or what the physicist David Bohm dubbed the Implicate Order. Or perhaps it's an Ineffable Something that can never be truly named.

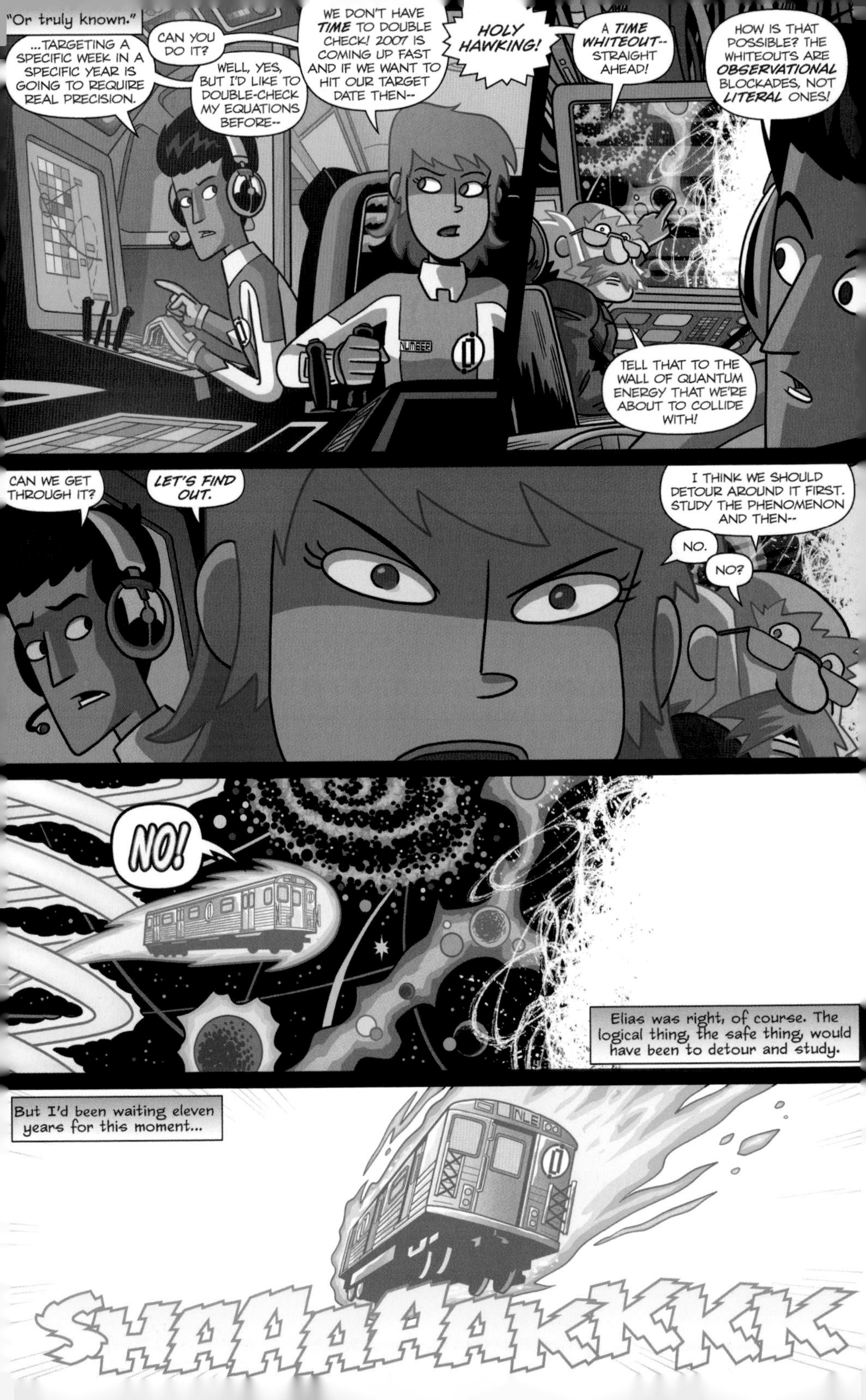
"Or truly known."
...TARGETING A SPECIFIC WEEK IN A SPECIFIC YEAR IS GOING TO REQUIRE REAL PRECISION.
CAN YOU DO IT?
WELL, YES, BUT I'D LIKE TO DOUBLE-CHECK MY EQUATIONS BEFORE--
WE DON'T HAVE TIME TO DOUBLE CHECK! 2007 IS COMING UP FAST AND IF WE WANT TO HIT OUR TARGET DATE THEN--
HOLY HAWKING!
A TIME WHITEOUT-- STRAIGHT AHEAD!
HOW IS THAT POSSIBLE? THE WHITEOUTS ARE OBSERVATIONAL BLOCKADES, NOT LITERAL ONES!
TELL THAT TO THE WALL OF QUANTUM ENERGY THAT WE'RE ABOUT TO COLLIDE WITH!
CAN WE GET THROUGH IT?
LET'S FIND OUT.
I THINK WE SHOULD DETOUR AROUND IT FIRST. STUDY THE PHENOMENON AND THEN--
NO.
NO?
NO!
Elias was right, of course. The logical thing, the safe thing, would have been to detour and study.
But I'd been waiting eleven years for this moment...
SHAAAAKKKK

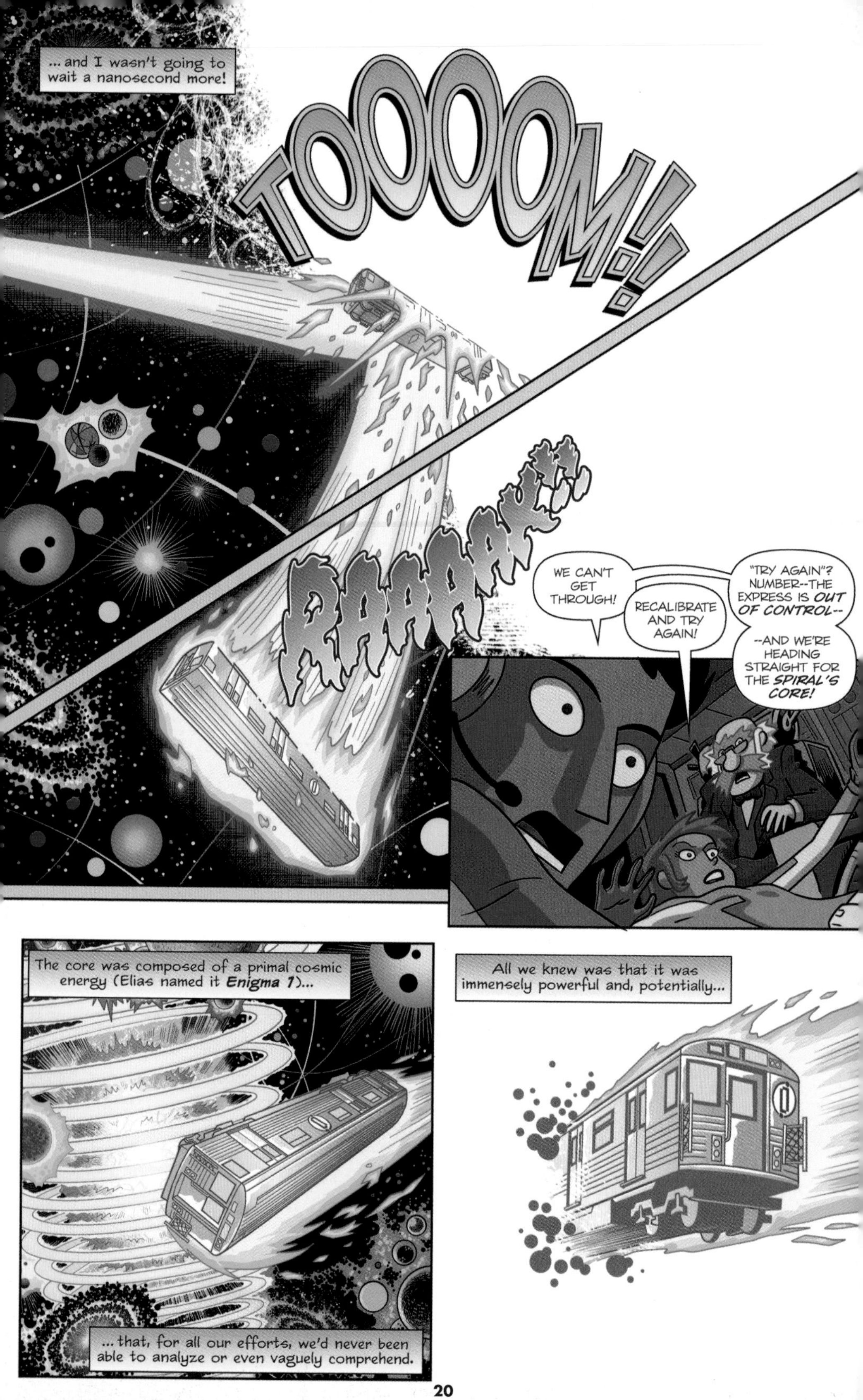

...and I wasn't going to wait a nanosecond more!
TOOOOM!!
RAAAK!!
WE CAN'T GET THROUGH!
RECALIBRATE AND TRY AGAIN!
"TRY AGAIN"? NUMBER--THE EXPRESS IS OUT OF CONTROL--
--AND WE'RE HEADING STRAIGHT FOR THE SPIRAL'S CORE!
The core was composed of a primal cosmic energy (Elias named it Enigma 1)...
...that, for all our efforts, we'd never been able to analyze or even vaguely comprehend.
All we knew was that it was immensely powerful and, potentially...

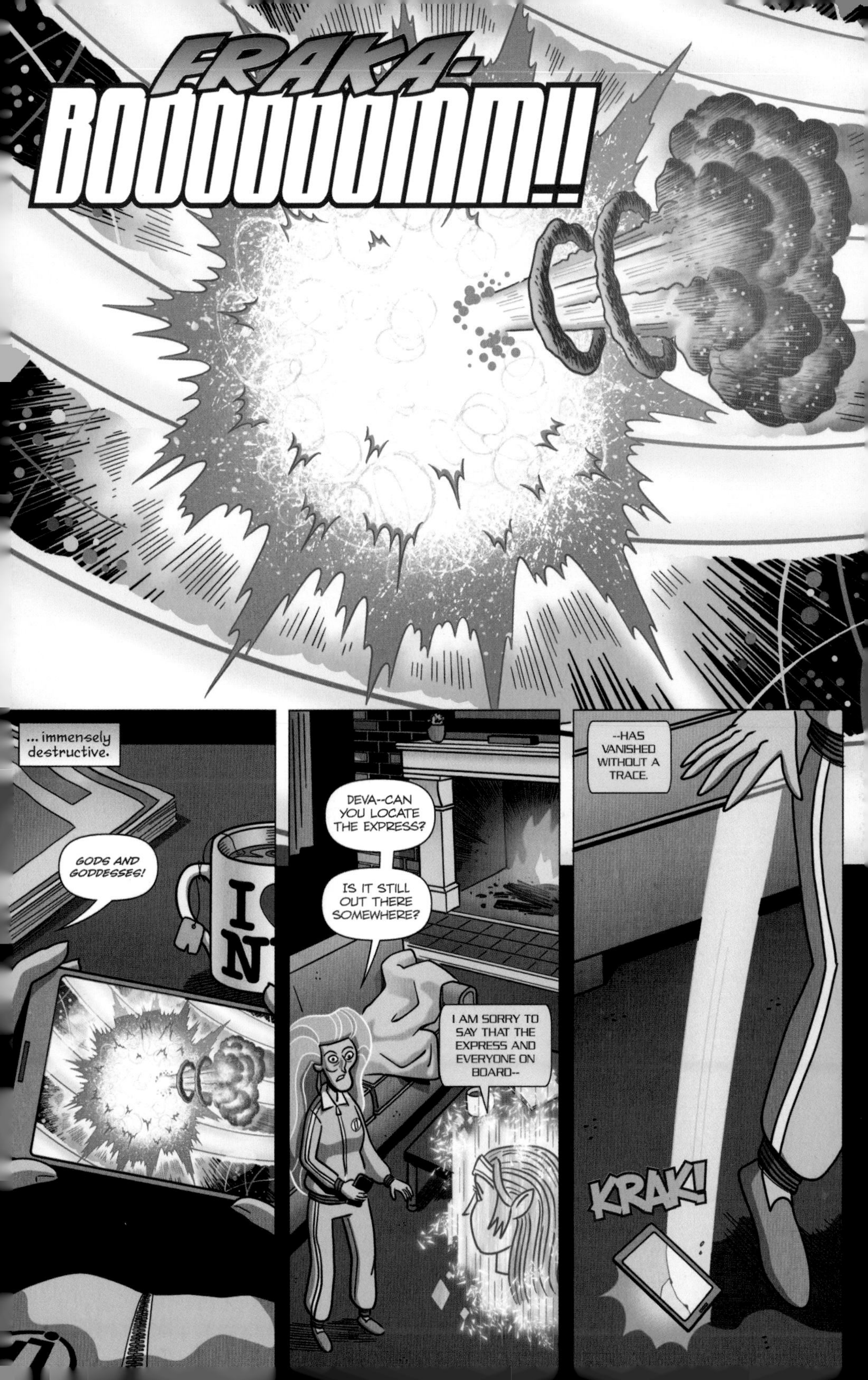

FRAKA-BOOOOOOOMM!!
... immensely destructive.
GODS AND GODDESSES!
DEVA--CAN YOU LOCATE THE EXPRESS?
IS IT STILL OUT THERE SOMEWHERE?
I AM SORRY TO SAY THAT THE EXPRESS AND EVERYONE ON BOARD--
--HAS VANISHED WITHOUT A TRACE.
KRAK!

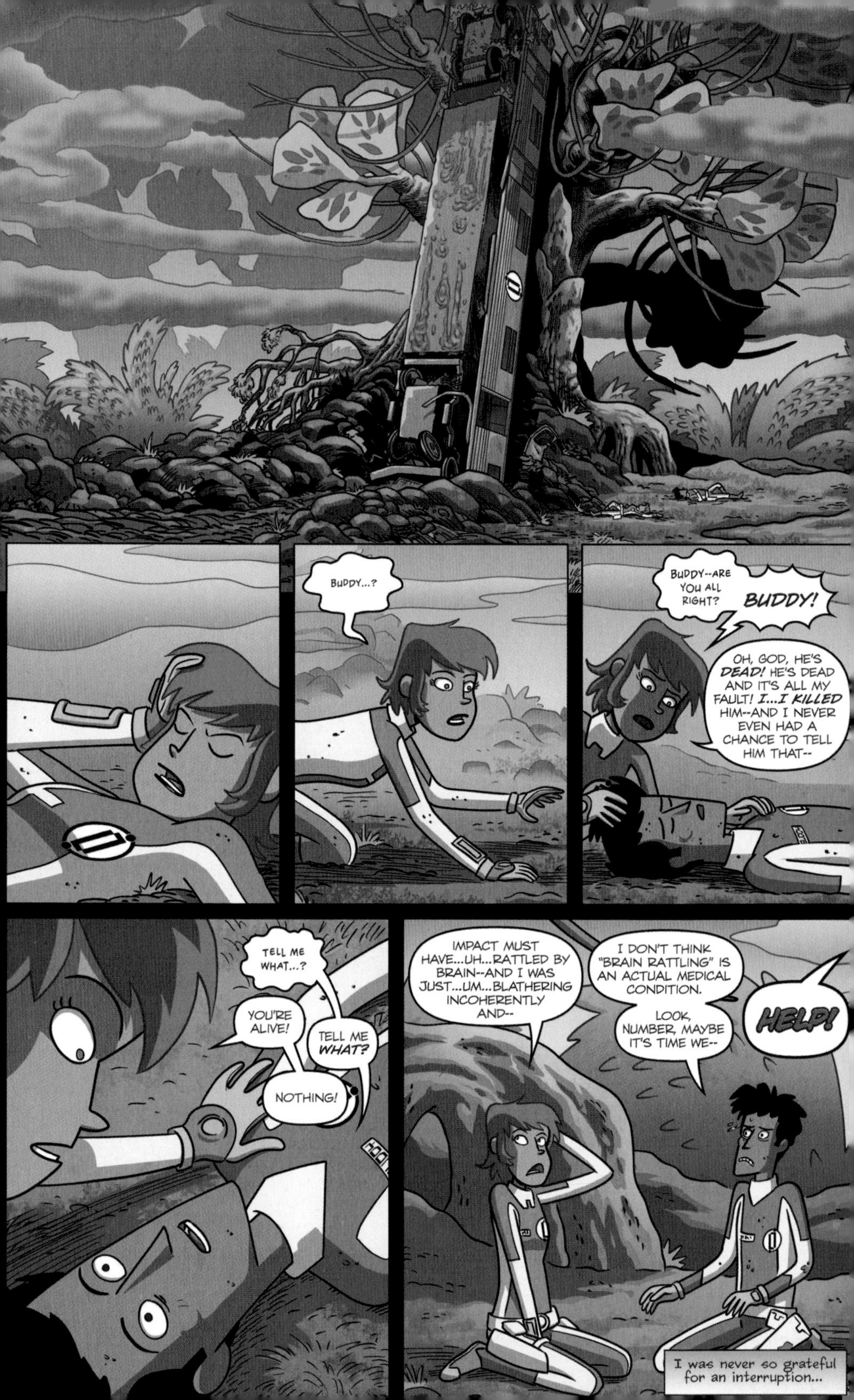
BUDDY...?
BUDDY--ARE YOU ALL RIGHT?
BUDDY!
OH, GOD, HE'S DEAD! HE'S DEAD AND IT'S ALL MY FAULT! I...I KILLED HIM--AND I NEVER EVEN HAD A CHANCE TO TELL HIM THAT--
TELL ME WHAT...?
YOU'RE ALIVE!
TELL ME WHAT?
NOTHING!
IMPACT MUST HAVE...UH...RATTLED BY BRAIN--AND I WAS JUST...UM...BLATHERING INCOHERENTLY AND--
I DON'T THINK "BRAIN RATTLING" IS AN ACTUAL MEDICAL CONDITION.
LOOK, NUMBER, MAYBE IT'S TIME WE--
HELP!
I was never so grateful for an interruption...

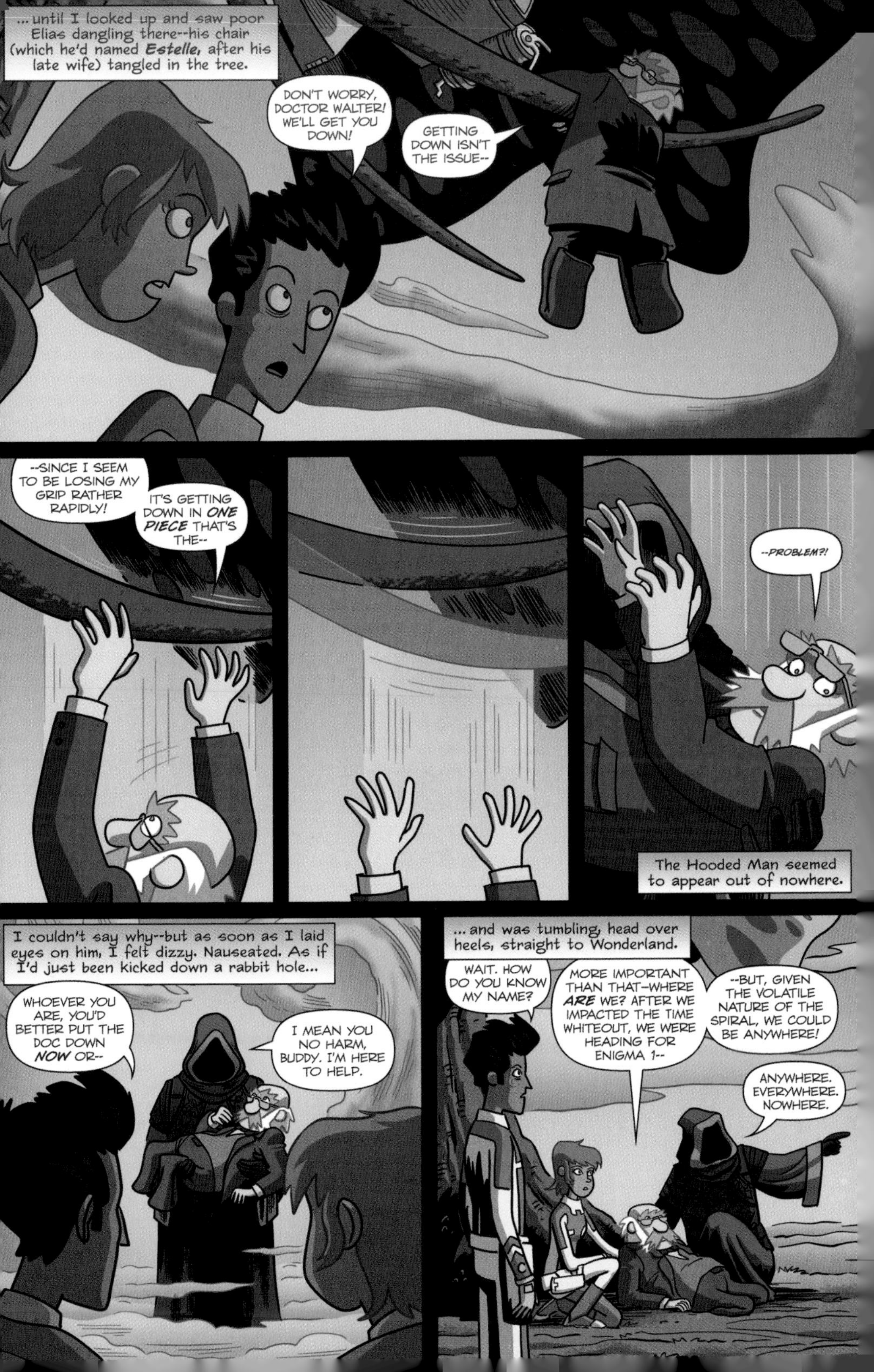
...until I looked up and saw poor Elias dangling there--his chair (which he'd named Estelle, after his late wife) tangled in the tree.
DON'T WORRY, DOCTOR WALTER! WE'LL GET YOU DOWN!
GETTING DOWN ISN'T THE ISSUE--
--SINCE I SEEM TO BE LOSING MY GRIP RATHER RAPIDLY!
IT'S GETTING DOWN IN ONE PIECE THAT'S THE--
--PROBLEM?!
The Hooded Man seemed to appear out of nowhere.
I couldn't say why--but as soon as I laid eyes on him, I felt dizzy. Nauseated. As if I'd just been kicked down a rabbit hole...
WHOEVER YOU ARE, YOU'D BETTER PUT THE DOC DOWN NOW OR--
I MEAN YOU NO HARM, BUDDY. I'M HERE TO HELP.
...and was tumbling, head over heels, straight to Wonderland.
WAIT. HOW DO YOU KNOW MY NAME?
MORE IMPORTANT THAN THAT—WHERE ARE WE? AFTER WE IMPACTED THE TIME WHITEOUT, WE WERE HEADING FOR ENIGMA 1--
--BUT, GIVEN THE VOLATILE NATURE OF THE SPIRAL, WE COULD BE ANYWHERE!
ANYWHERE. EVERYWHERE. NOWHERE.

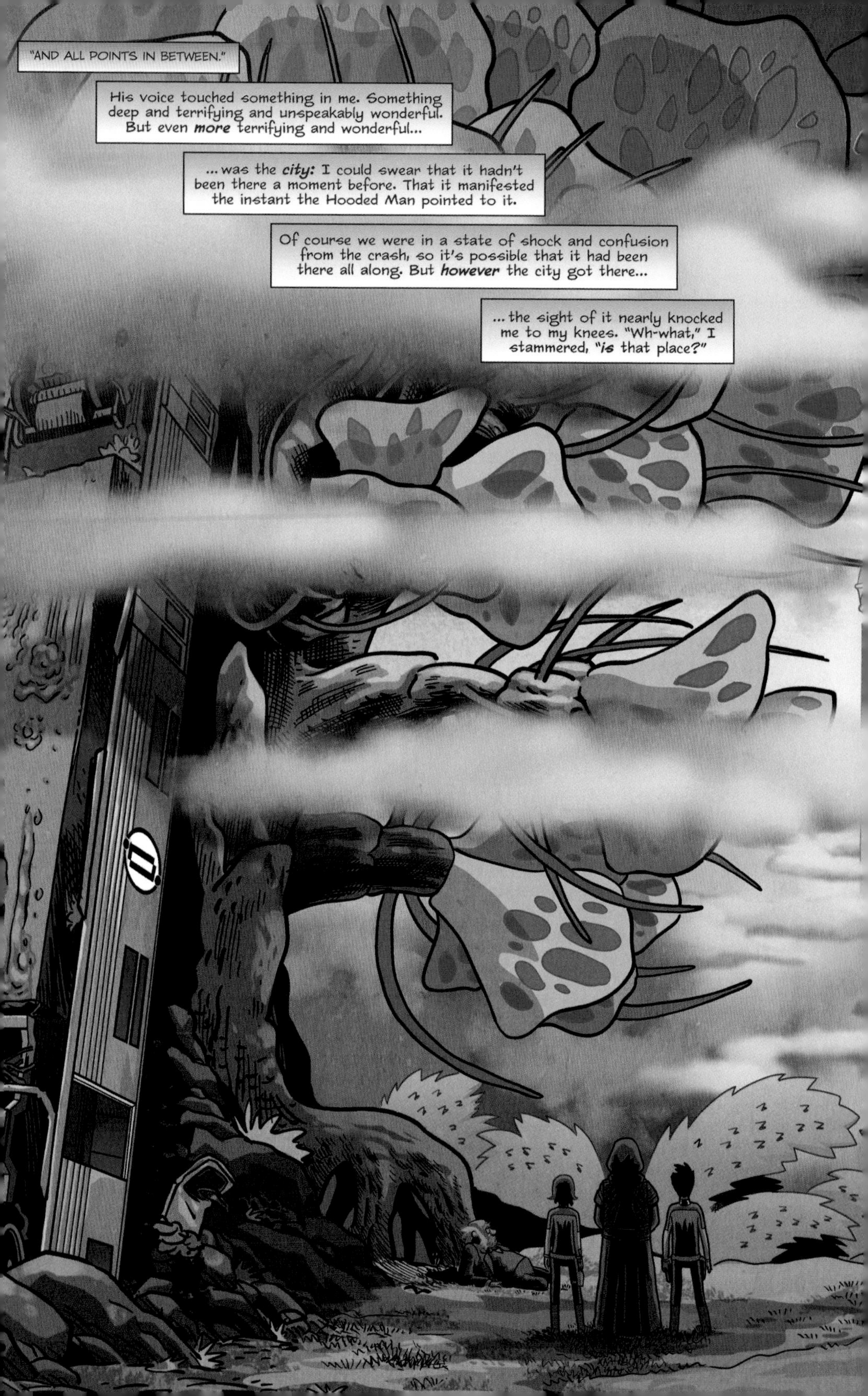
"AND ALL POINTS IN BETWEEN."
His voice touched something in me. Something deep and terrifying and unspeakably wonderful. But even **more** terrifying and wonderful...
...was the **city:** I could swear that it hadn't been there a moment before. That it manifested the instant the Hooded Man pointed to it.
Of course we were in a state of shock and confusion from the crash, so it's possible that it had been there all along. But **however** the city got there...
...the sight of it nearly knocked me to my knees. "Wh-what," I stammered, "**is** that place?"

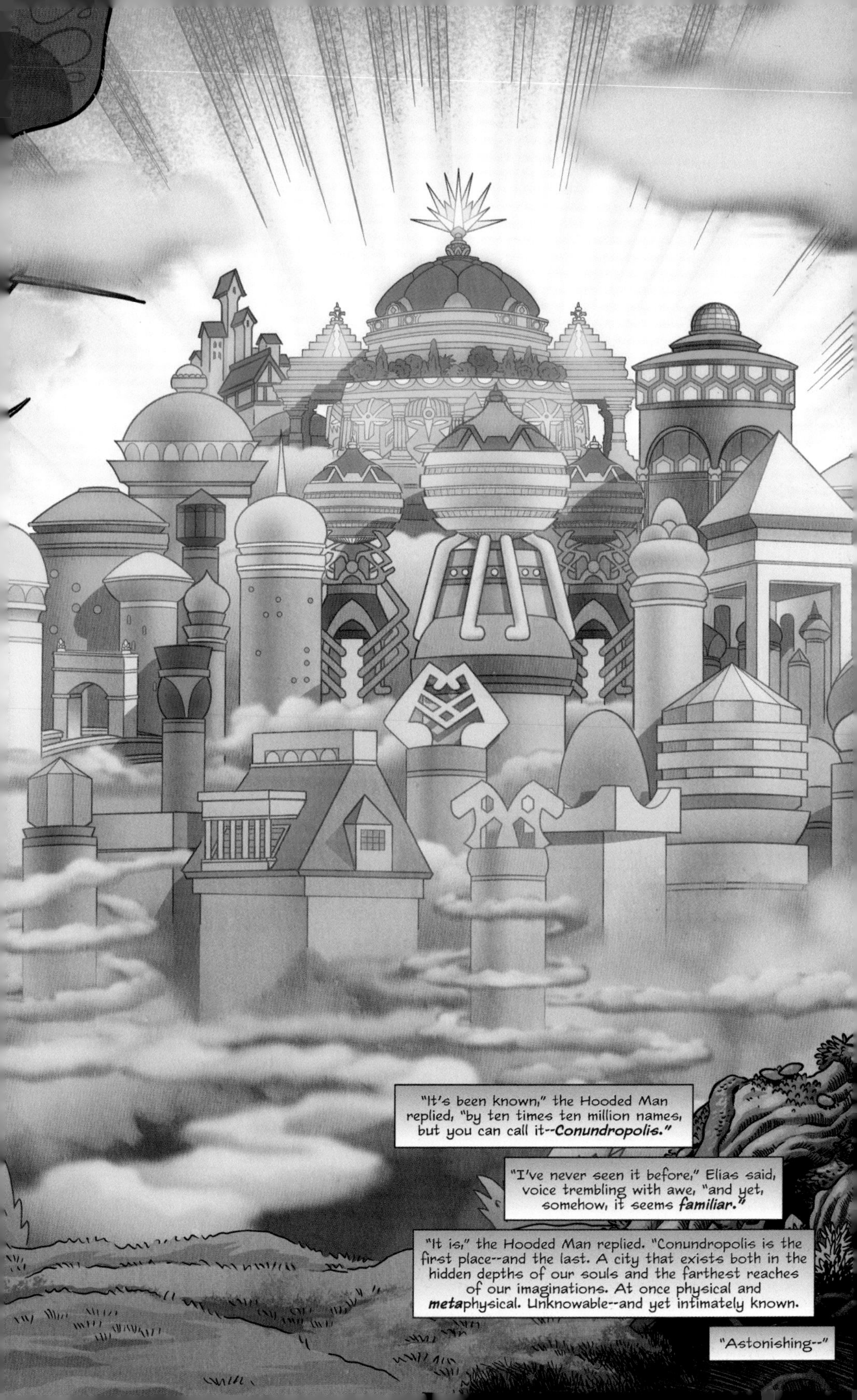
"It's been known," the Hooded Man replied, "by ten times ten million names, but you can call it--*Conundropolis.*"
"I've never seen it before," Elias said, voice trembling with awe, "and yet, somehow, it seems *familiar.*"
"It is," the Hooded Man replied. "Conundropolis is the first place--and the last. A city that exists both in the hidden depths of our souls and the farthest reaches of our imaginations. At once physical and ***meta***physical. Unknowable--and yet intimately known.
"Astonishing--"

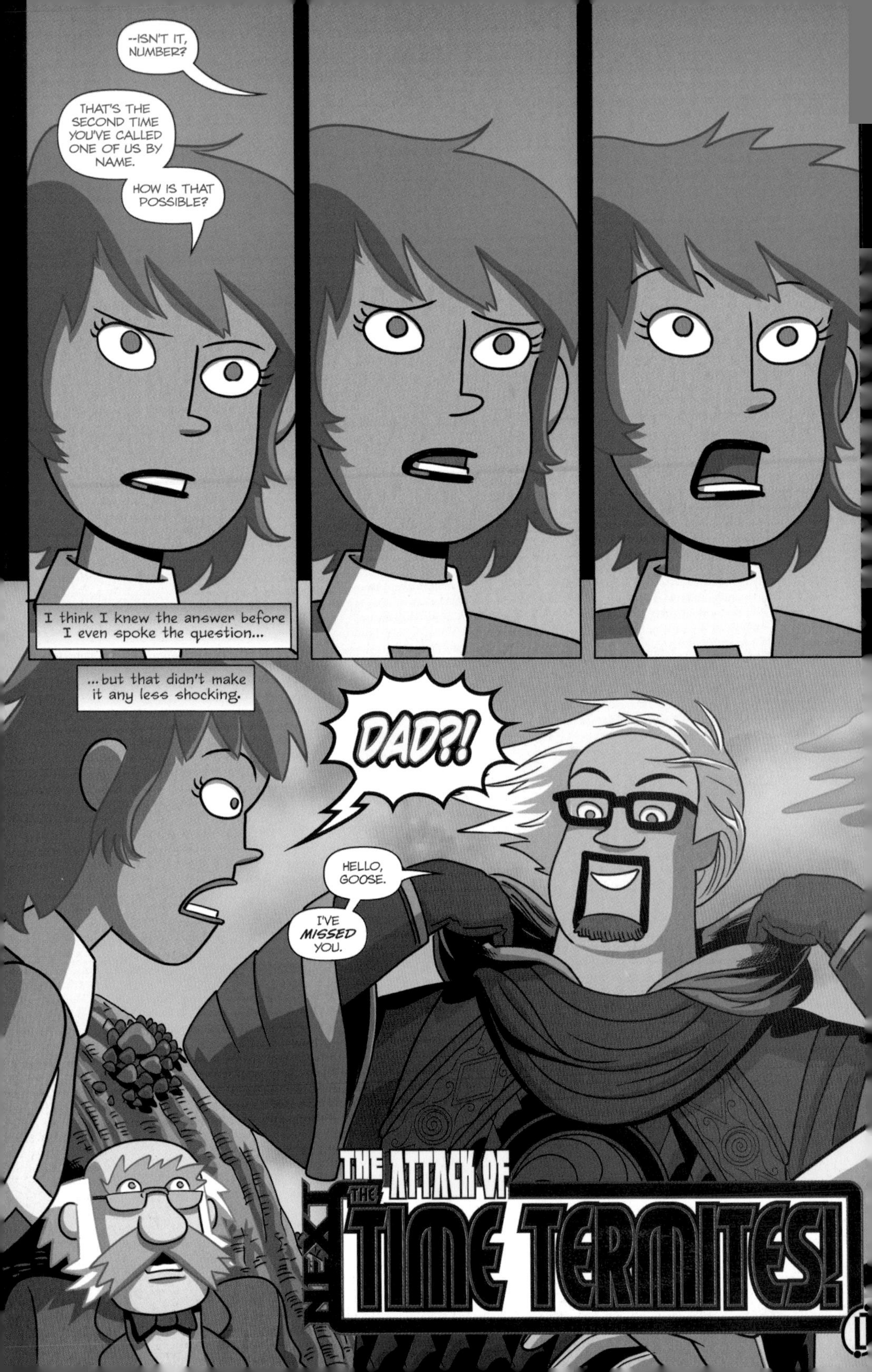
--ISN'T IT, NUMBER?
THAT'S THE SECOND TIME YOU'VE CALLED ONE OF US BY NAME.
HOW IS THAT POSSIBLE?
I think I knew the answer before I even spoke the question...
...but that didn't make it any less shocking.
DAD?!
HELLO, GOOSE.
I'VE MISSED YOU.
NEXT
THE ATTACK OF THE TIME TERMITES!

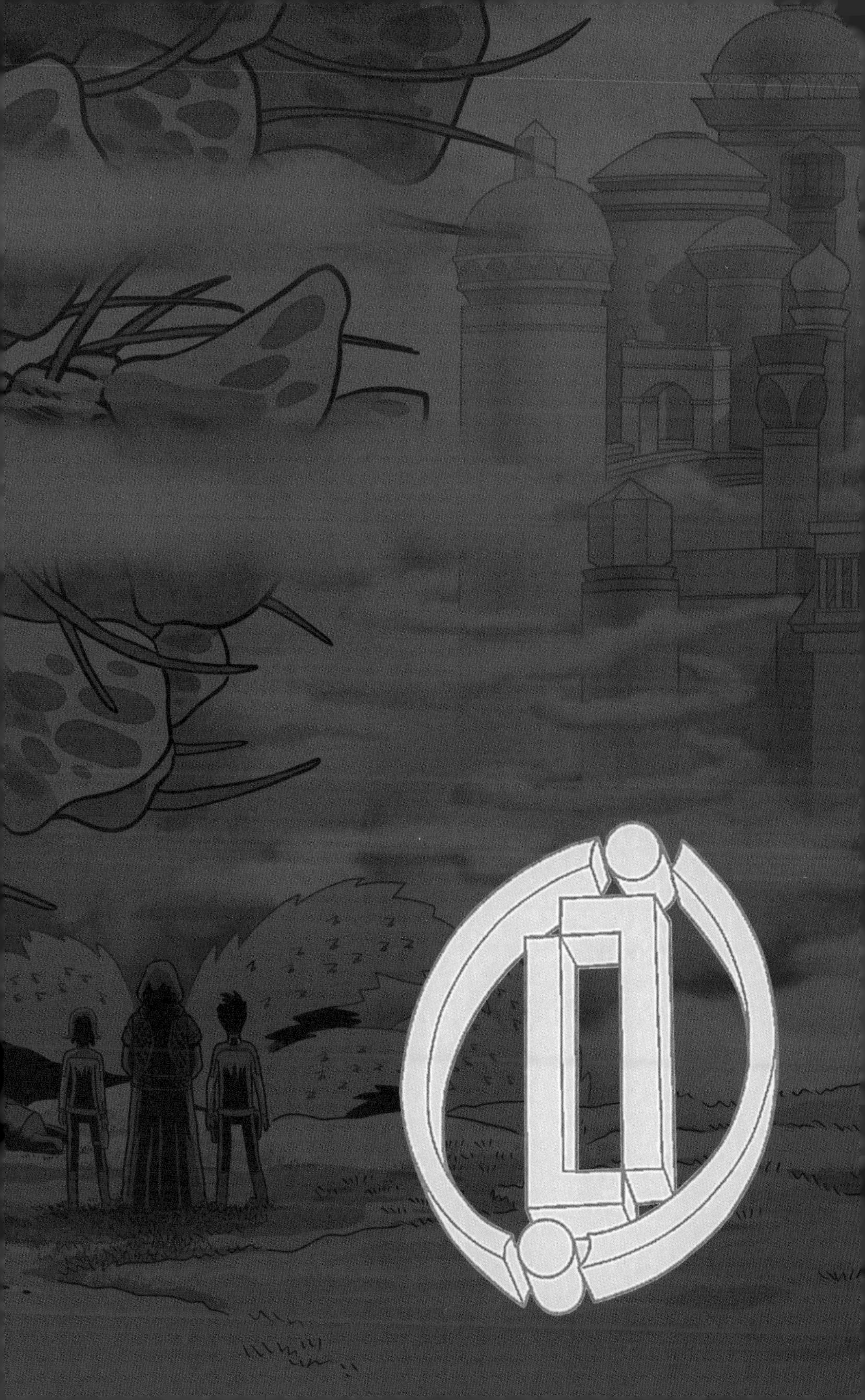

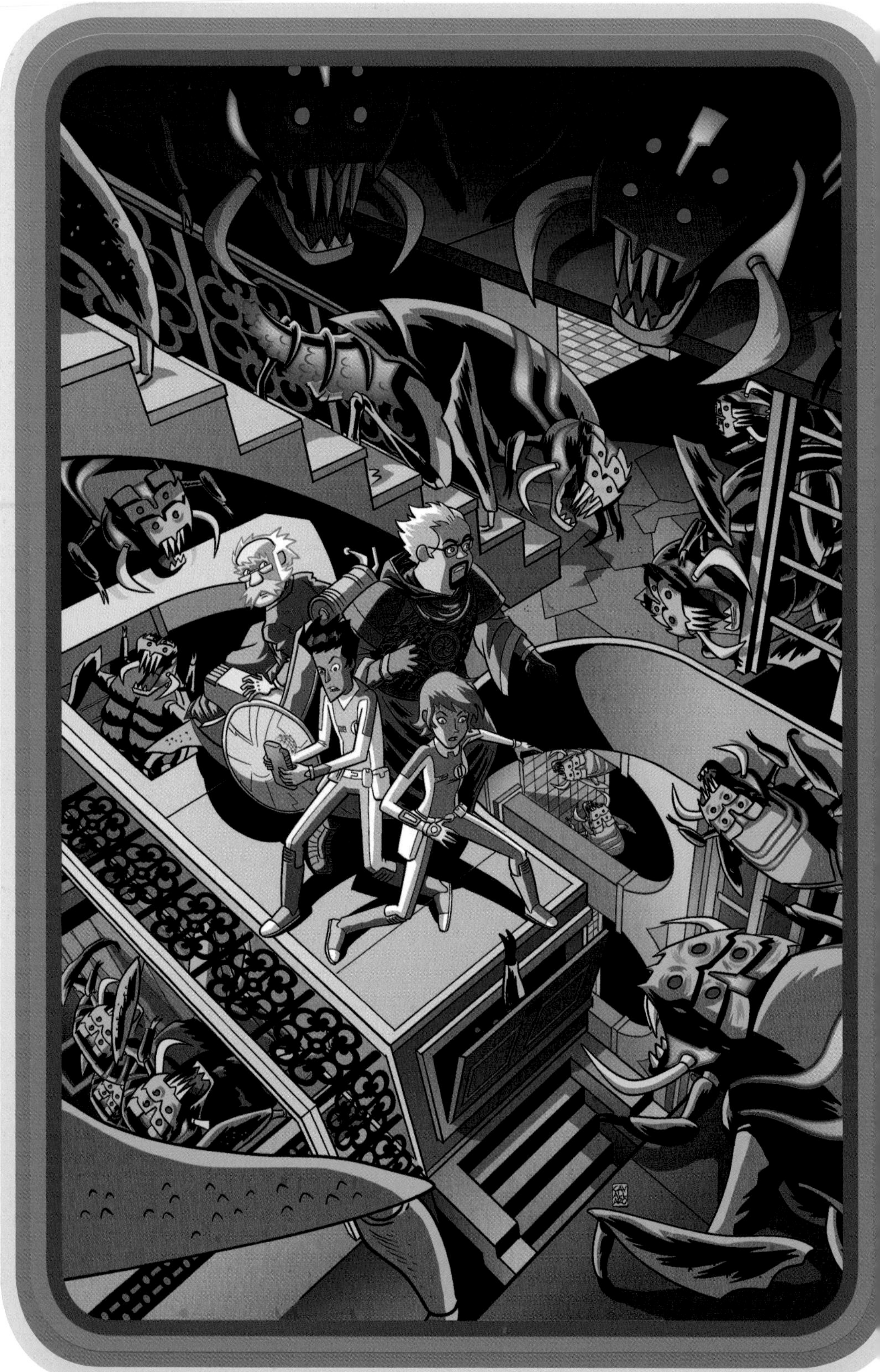

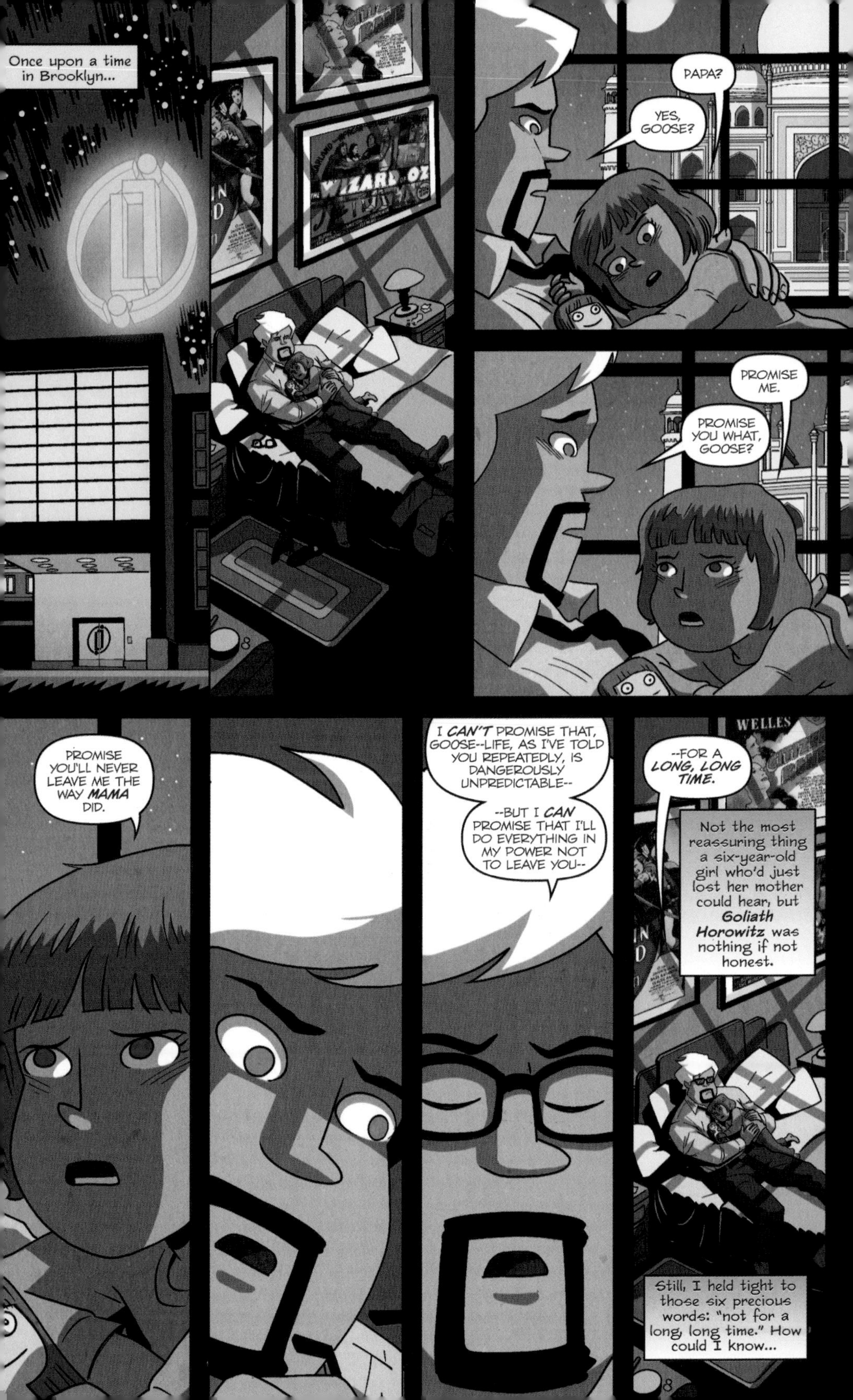
Once upon a time in Brooklyn...
PAPA?
YES, GOOSE?
PROMISE ME.
PROMISE YOU WHAT, GOOSE?
PROMISE YOU'LL NEVER LEAVE ME THE WAY MAMA DID.
I CAN'T PROMISE THAT, GOOSE--LIFE, AS I'VE TOLD YOU REPEATEDLY, IS DANGEROUSLY UNPREDICTABLE--
--BUT I CAN PROMISE THAT I'LL DO EVERYTHING IN MY POWER NOT TO LEAVE YOU--
--FOR A LONG, LONG TIME.
Not the most reassuring thing a six-year-old girl who'd just lost her mother could hear, but Goliath Horowitz was nothing if not honest.
Still, I held tight to those six precious words: "not for a long, long time." How could I know...

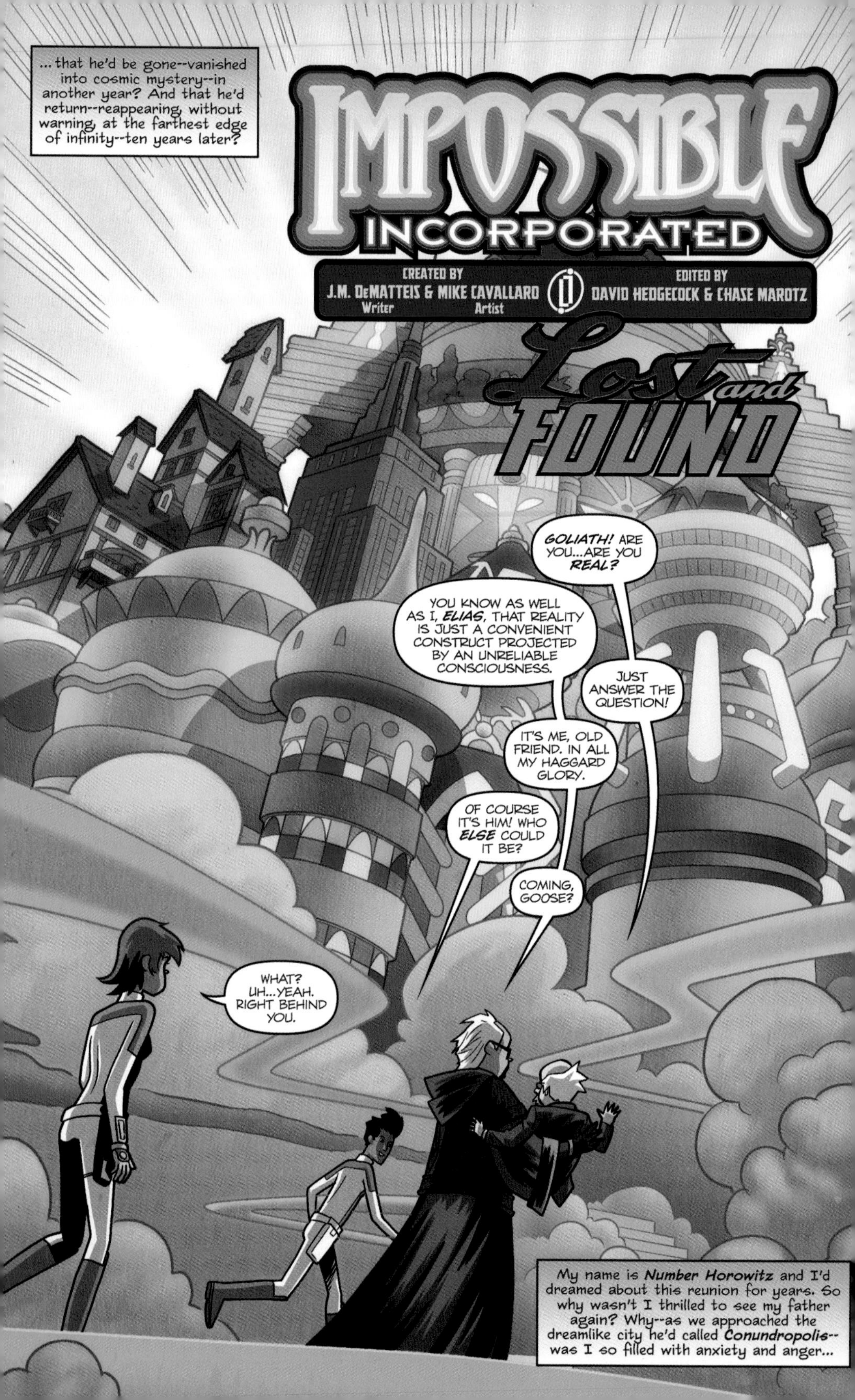
...that he'd be gone--vanished into cosmic mystery--in another year? And that he'd return--reappearing, without warning, at the farthest edge of infinity--ten years later?
IMPOSSIBLE INCORPORATED
CREATED BY J.M. DeMATTEIS & MIKE CAVALLARO Writer Artist
EDITED BY DAVID HEDGECOCK & CHASE MAROTZ
Lost and FOUND
GOLIATH! ARE YOU...ARE YOU REAL?
YOU KNOW AS WELL AS I, ELIAS, THAT REALITY IS JUST A CONVENIENT CONSTRUCT PROJECTED BY AN UNRELIABLE CONSCIOUSNESS.
JUST ANSWER THE QUESTION!
IT'S ME, OLD FRIEND. IN ALL MY HAGGARD GLORY.
OF COURSE IT'S HIM! WHO ELSE COULD IT BE?
COMING, GOOSE?
WHAT? UH...YEAH. RIGHT BEHIND YOU.
My name is Number Horowitz and I'd dreamed about this reunion for years. So why wasn't I thrilled to see my father again? Why--as we approached the dreamlike city he'd called Conundropolis--was I so filled with anxiety and anger...

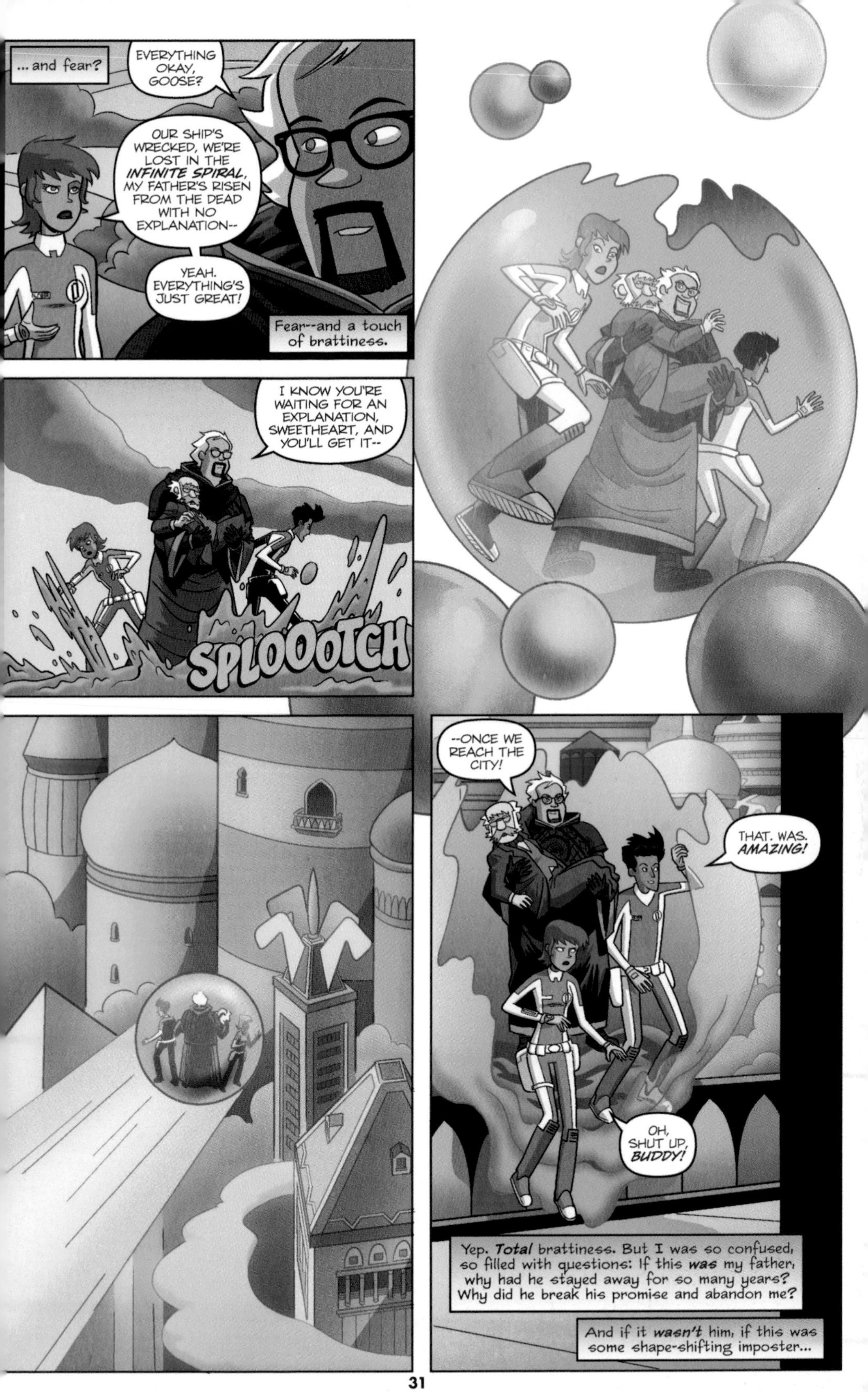

... and fear?
EVERYTHING OKAY, GOOSE?
OUR SHIP'S WRECKED, WE'RE LOST IN THE ***INFINITE SPIRAL***, MY FATHER'S RISEN FROM THE DEAD WITH NO EXPLANATION--
YEAH. EVERYTHING'S JUST GREAT!
Fear--and a touch of brattiness.
I KNOW YOU'RE WAITING FOR AN EXPLANATION, SWEETHEART, AND YOU'LL GET IT--
SPLOOOTCH
--ONCE WE REACH THE CITY!
THAT. WAS. ***AMAZING!***
OH, SHUT UP, ***BUDDY!***
Yep. ***Total*** brattiness. But I was so confused, so filled with questions: If this ***was*** my father, why had he stayed away for so many years? Why did he break his promise and abandon me?
And if it ***wasn't*** him, if this was some shape-shifting imposter...

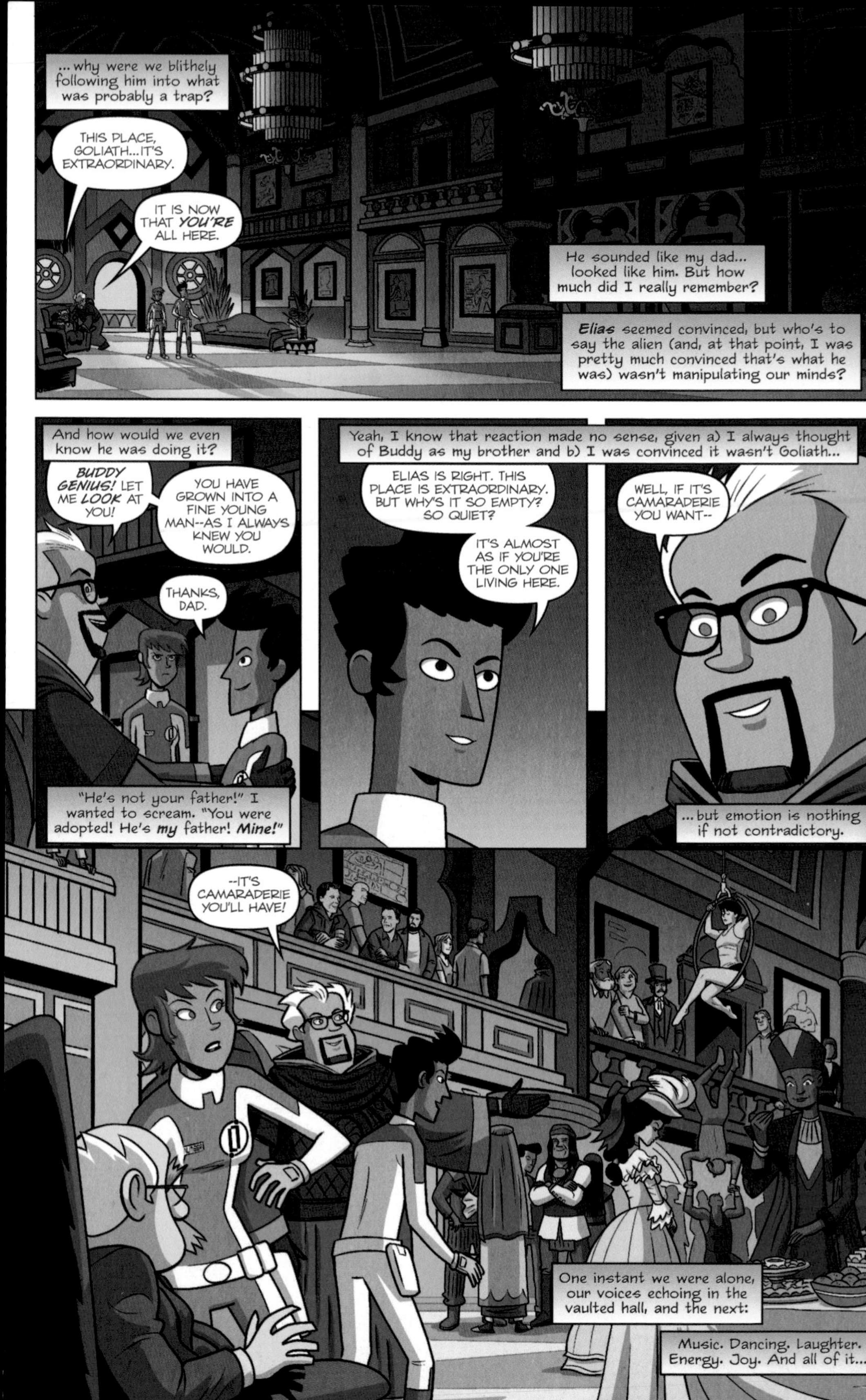

...why were we blithely following him into what was probably a trap?
THIS PLACE, GOLIATH...IT'S EXTRAORDINARY.
IT IS NOW THAT YOU'RE ALL HERE.
He sounded like my dad... looked like him. But how much did I really remember?
Elias seemed convinced, but who's to say the alien (and, at that point, I was pretty much convinced that's what he was) wasn't manipulating our minds?
And how would we even know he was doing it?
BUDDY GENIUS! LET ME LOOK AT YOU!
YOU HAVE GROWN INTO A FINE YOUNG MAN--AS I ALWAYS KNEW YOU WOULD.
THANKS, DAD.
"He's not your father!" I wanted to scream. "You were adopted! He's my father! Mine!"
Yeah, I know that reaction made no sense, given a) I always thought of Buddy as my brother and b) I was convinced it wasn't Goliath...
ELIAS IS RIGHT. THIS PLACE IS EXTRAORDINARY. BUT WHY'S IT SO EMPTY? SO QUIET?
IT'S ALMOST AS IF YOU'RE THE ONLY ONE LIVING HERE.
WELL, IF IT'S CAMARADERIE YOU WANT--
...but emotion is nothing if not contradictory.
--IT'S CAMARADERIE YOU'LL HAVE!
One instant we were alone, our voices echoing in the vaulted hall, and the next:
Music. Dancing. Laughter. Energy. Joy. And all of it...

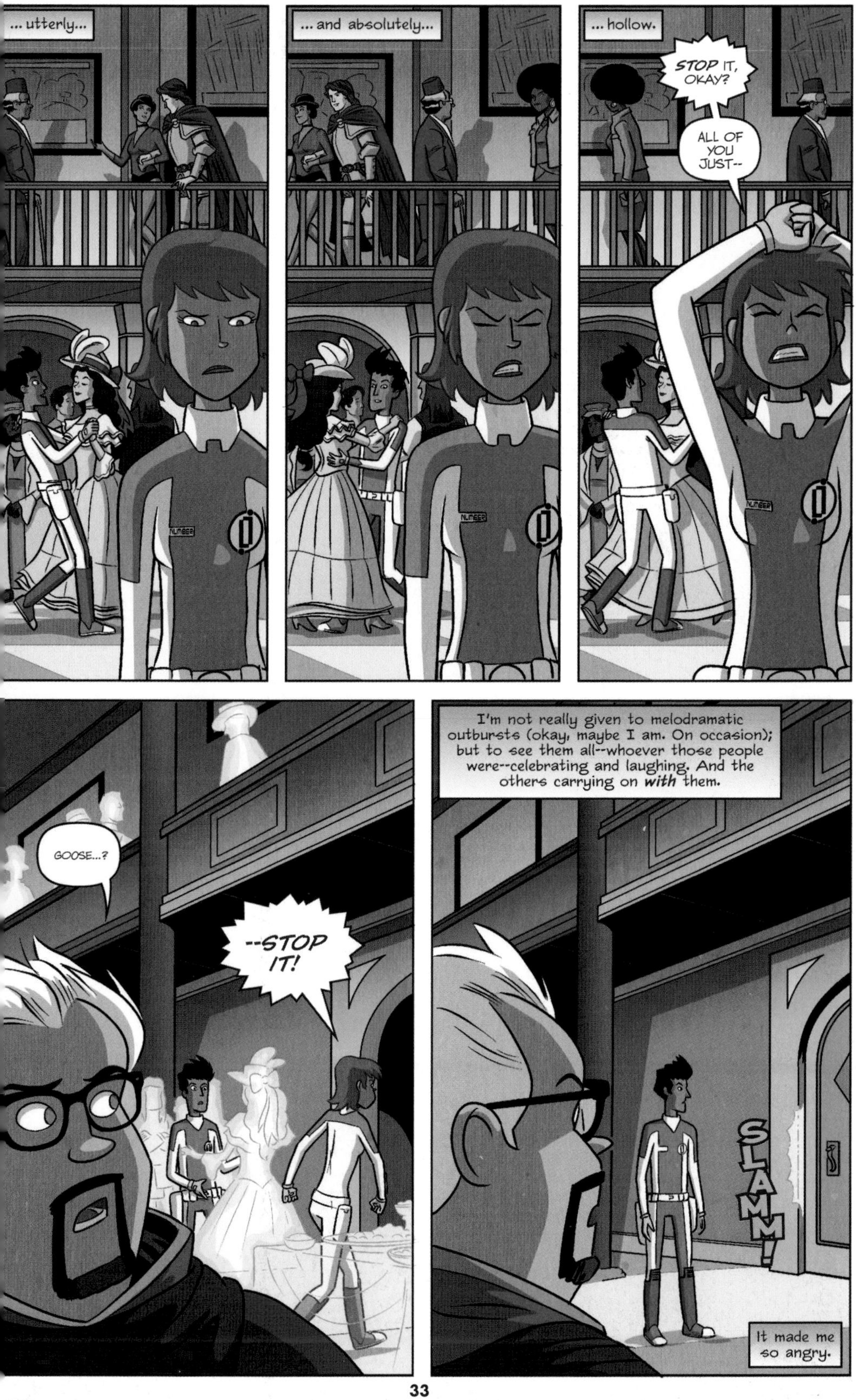
... utterly...
... and absolutely...
... hollow.
STOP IT, OKAY?
ALL OF YOU JUST--
GOOSE...?
--STOP IT!
I'm not really given to melodramatic outbursts (okay, maybe I am. On occasion); but to see them all--whoever those people were--celebrating and laughing. And the others carrying on with them.
SLAMM!
It made me so angry.

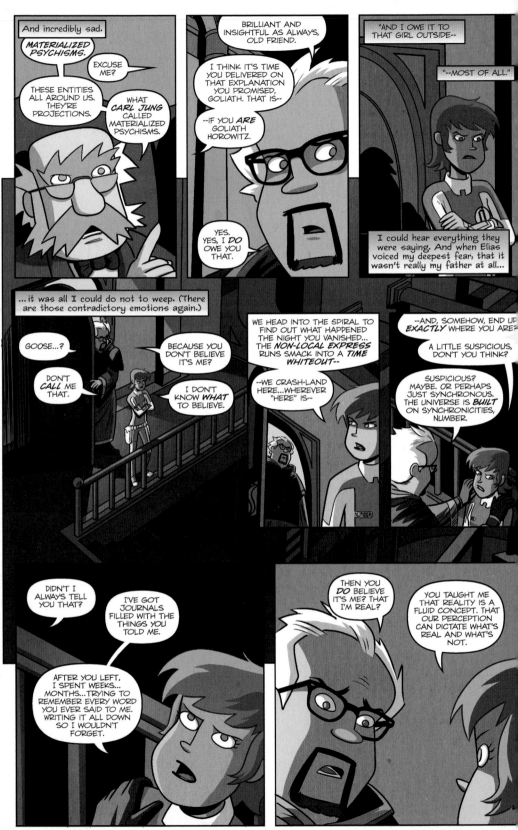

And incredibly sad.

MATERIALIZED PSYCHISMS.

EXCUSE ME?

THESE ENTITIES ALL AROUND US. THEY'RE PROJECTIONS.

WHAT CARL JUNG CALLED MATERIALIZED PSYCHISMS.

BRILLIANT AND INSIGHTFUL AS ALWAYS, OLD FRIEND.

I THINK IT'S TIME YOU DELIVERED ON THAT EXPLANATION YOU PROMISED, GOLIATH. THAT IS--

--IF YOU ARE GOLIATH HOROWITZ.

YES. YES, I DO OWE YOU THAT.

"AND I OWE IT TO THAT GIRL OUTSIDE--

"--MOST OF ALL."

I could hear everything they were saying. And when Elias voiced my deepest fear, that it wasn't really my father at all...

...it was all I could do not to weep. (There are those contradictory emotions again.)

GOOSE...?

DON'T CALL ME THAT.

BECAUSE YOU DON'T BELIEVE IT'S ME?

I DON'T KNOW WHAT TO BELIEVE.

WE HEAD INTO THE SPIRAL TO FIND OUT WHAT HAPPENED THE NIGHT YOU VANISHED... THE NON-LOCAL EXPRESS RUNS SMACK INTO A TIME WHITEOUT--

--WE CRASH-LAND HERE...WHEREVER "HERE" IS--

--AND, SOMEHOW, END UP EXACTLY WHERE YOU ARE?

A LITTLE SUSPICIOUS, DON'T YOU THINK?

SUSPICIOUS? MAYBE. OR PERHAPS JUST SYNCHRONOUS. THE UNIVERSE IS BUILT ON SYNCHRONICITIES, NUMBER

DIDN'T I ALWAYS TELL YOU THAT?

I'VE GOT JOURNALS FILLED WITH THE THINGS YOU TOLD ME.

AFTER YOU LEFT, I SPENT WEEKS... MONTHS...TRYING TO REMEMBER EVERY WORD YOU EVER SAID TO ME. WRITING IT ALL DOWN SO I WOULDN'T FORGET.

THEN YOU DO BELIEVE IT'S ME? THAT I'M REAL?

YOU TAUGHT ME THAT REALITY IS A FLUID CONCEPT. THAT OUR PERCEPTION CAN DICTATE WHAT'S REAL AND WHAT'S NOT.

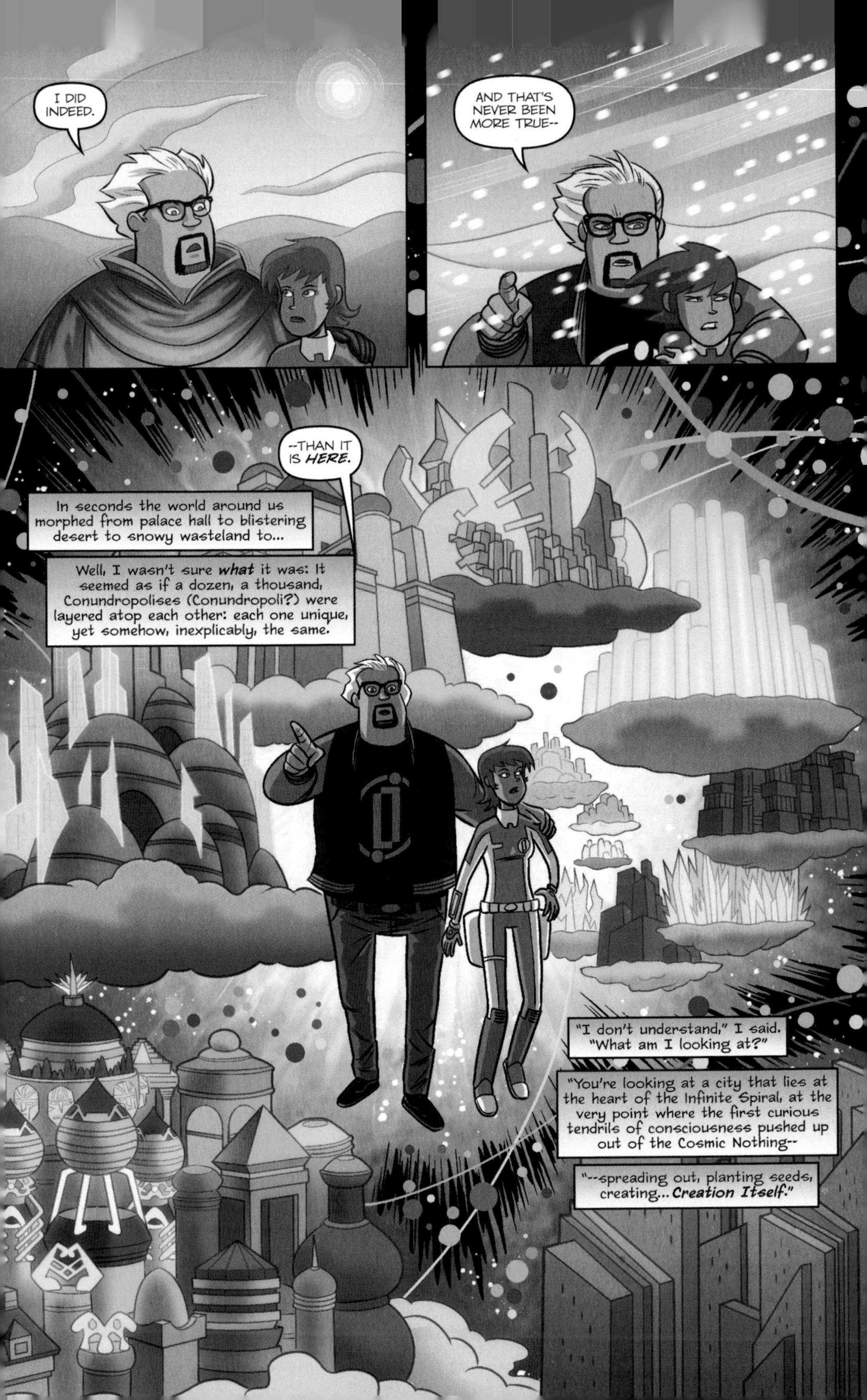
I DID INDEED.
AND THAT'S NEVER BEEN MORE TRUE--
--THAN IT IS *HERE*.
In seconds the world around us morphed from palace hall to blistering desert to snowy wasteland to...
Well, I wasn't sure *what* it was: It seemed as if a dozen, a thousand, Conundropolises (Conundropoli?) were layered atop each other: each one unique, yet somehow, inexplicably, the same.
"I don't understand," I said. "What am I looking at?"
"You're looking at a city that lies at the heart of the Infinite Spiral, at the very point where the first curious tendrils of consciousness pushed up out of the Cosmic Nothing--
"--spreading out, planting seeds, creating... *Creation Itself*."

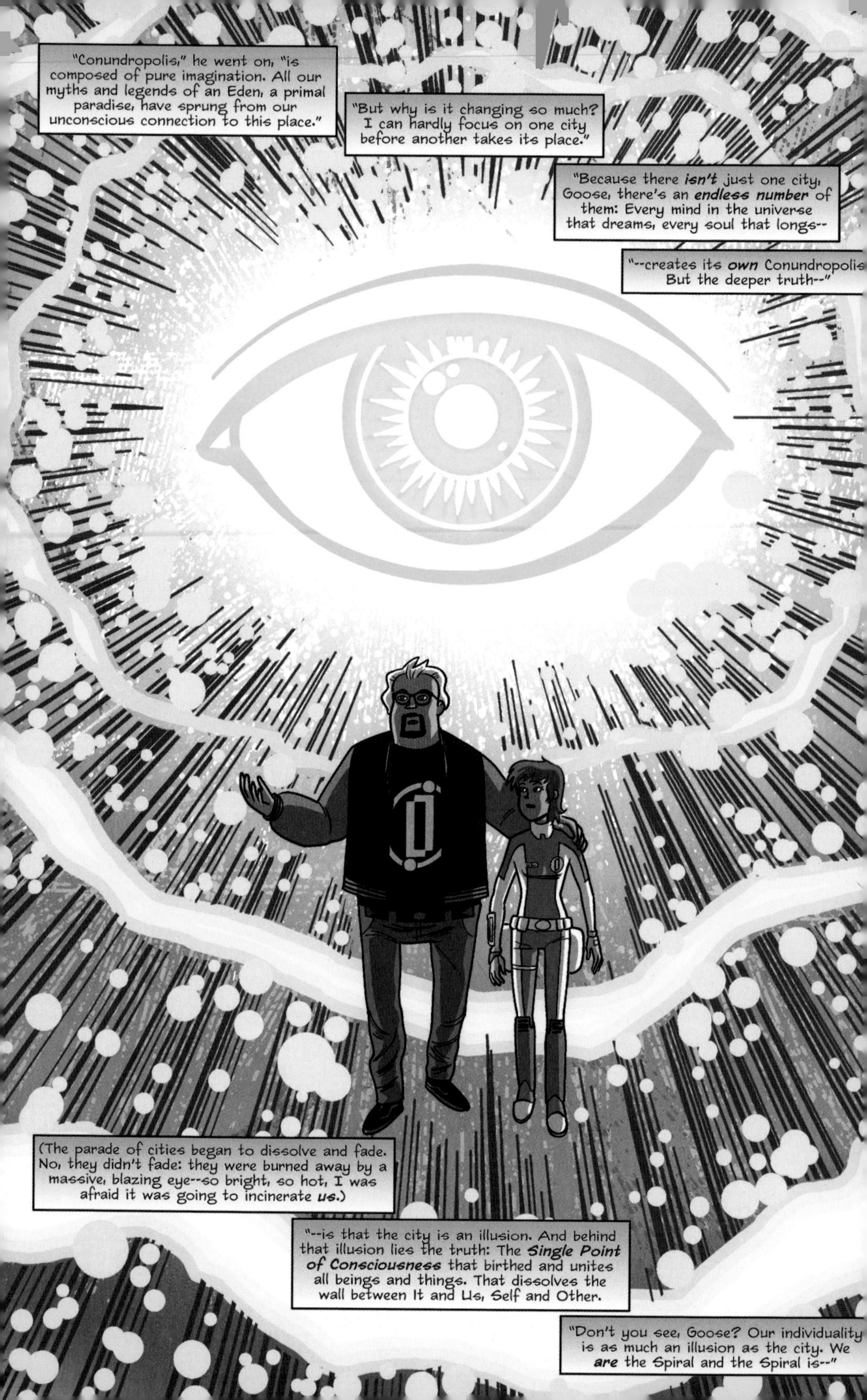
"Conundropolis," he went on, "is composed of pure imagination. All our myths and legends of an Eden, a primal paradise, have sprung from our unconscious connection to this place."
"But why is it changing so much? I can hardly focus on one city before another takes its place."
"Because there isn't just one city, Goose, there's an endless number of them: Every mind in the universe that dreams, every soul that longs--
"--creates its own Conundropolis. But the deeper truth--"
(The parade of cities began to dissolve and fade. No, they didn't fade: they were burned away by a massive, blazing eye--so bright, so hot, I was afraid it was going to incinerate us.)
"--is that the city is an illusion. And behind that illusion lies the truth: The Single Point of Consciousness that birthed and unites all beings and things. That dissolves the wall between It and Us, Self and Other.
"Don't you see, Goose? Our individuality is as much an illusion as the city. We are the Spiral and the Spiral is--"

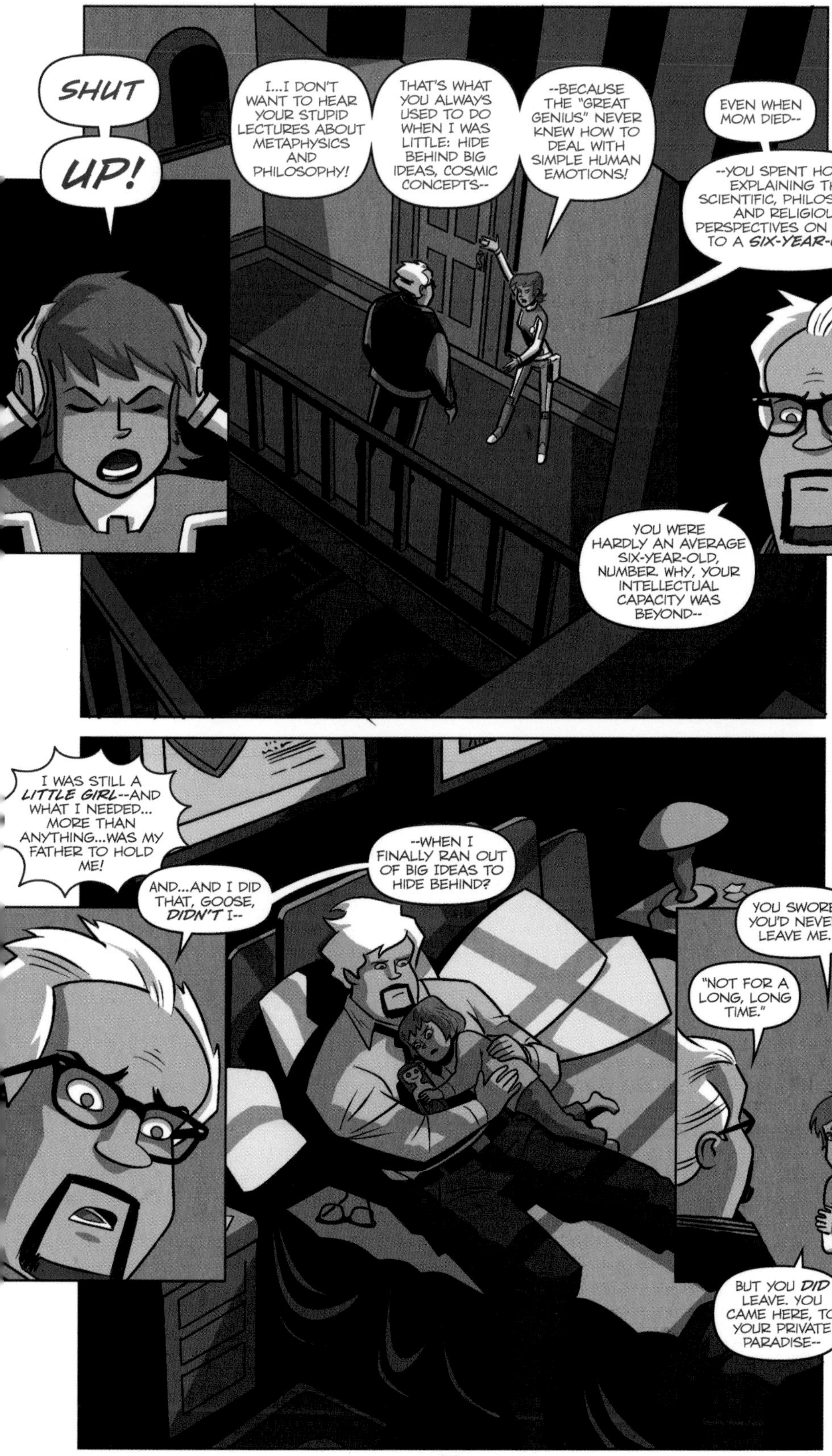
SHUT UP!
I...I DON'T WANT TO HEAR YOUR STUPID LECTURES ABOUT METAPHYSICS AND PHILOSOPHY!
THAT'S WHAT YOU ALWAYS USED TO DO WHEN I WAS LITTLE: HIDE BEHIND BIG IDEAS, COSMIC CONCEPTS--
--BECAUSE THE "GREAT GENIUS" NEVER KNEW HOW TO DEAL WITH SIMPLE HUMAN EMOTIONS!
EVEN WHEN MOM DIED--
--YOU SPENT HOURS EXPLAINING THE SCIENTIFIC, PHILOSOPHIC AND RELIGIOUS PERSPECTIVES ON DEATH. TO A SIX-YEAR-OLD!
YOU WERE HARDLY AN AVERAGE SIX-YEAR-OLD, NUMBER WHY, YOUR INTELLECTUAL CAPACITY WAS BEYOND--
I WAS STILL A LITTLE GIRL--AND WHAT I NEEDED... MORE THAN ANYTHING...WAS MY FATHER TO HOLD ME!
AND...AND I DID THAT, GOOSE, DIDN'T I--
--WHEN I FINALLY RAN OUT OF BIG IDEAS TO HIDE BEHIND?
YOU SWORE YOU'D NEVER LEAVE ME.
"NOT FOR A LONG, LONG TIME."
BUT YOU DID LEAVE. YOU CAME HERE, TO YOUR PRIVATE PARADISE--

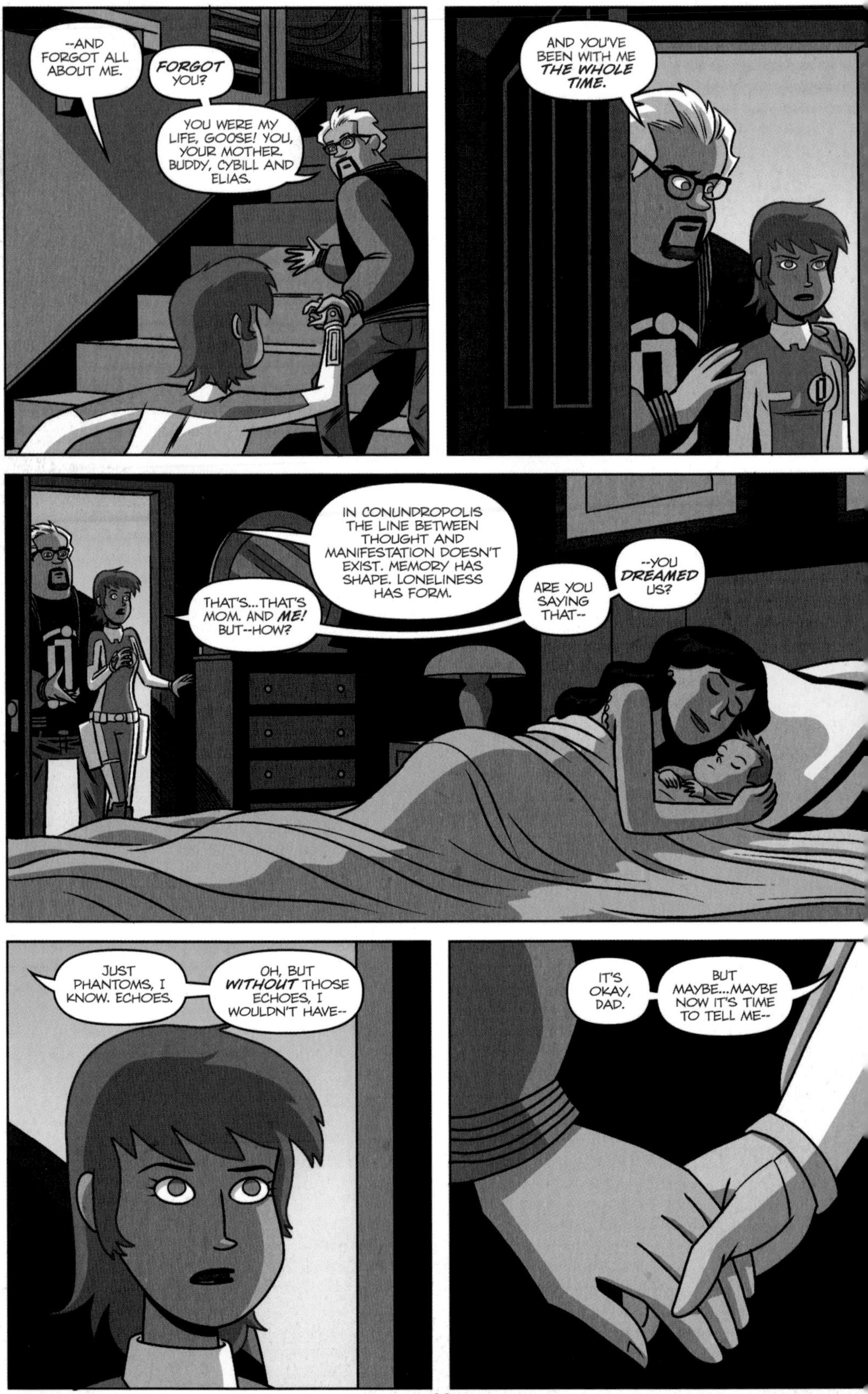
--AND FORGOT ALL ABOUT ME.
FORGOT YOU?
YOU WERE MY LIFE, GOOSE! YOU, YOUR MOTHER. BUDDY, CYBILL AND ELIAS.
AND YOU'VE BEEN WITH ME THE WHOLE TIME.
IN CONUNDROPOLIS THE LINE BETWEEN THOUGHT AND MANIFESTATION DOESN'T EXIST. MEMORY HAS SHAPE. LONELINESS HAS FORM.
THAT'S...THAT'S MOM. AND ME! BUT--HOW?
ARE YOU SAYING THAT--
--YOU DREAMED US?
JUST PHANTOMS, I KNOW. ECHOES.
OH, BUT WITHOUT THOSE ECHOES, I WOULDN'T HAVE--
IT'S OKAY, DAD.
BUT MAYBE...MAYBE NOW IT'S TIME TO TELL ME--

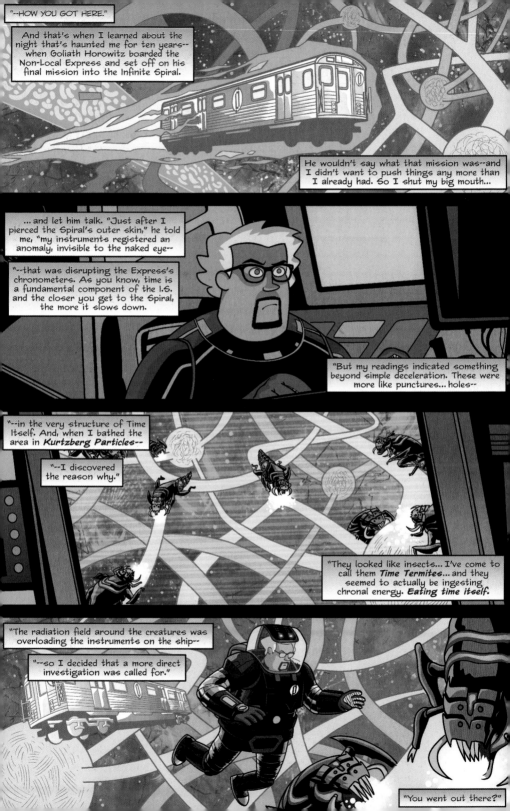

"--HOW YOU GOT HERE."

And that's when I learned about the night that's haunted me for ten years-- when Goliath Horowitz boarded the Non-Local Express and set off on his final mission into the Infinite Spiral.

He wouldn't say what that mission was--and I didn't want to push things any more than I already had. So I shut my big mouth...

... and let him talk. "Just after I pierced the Spiral's outer skin," he told me, "my instruments registered an anomaly, invisible to the naked eye--

"--that was disrupting the Express's chronometers. As you know, time is a fundamental component of the I.S. and the closer you get to the Spiral, the more it slows down.

"But my readings indicated something beyond simple deceleration. These were more like punctures... holes--

"--in the very structure of Time Itself. And, when I bathed the area in *Kurtzberg Particles*--

"--I discovered the reason why."

"They looked like insects... I've come to call them *Time Termites*... and they seemed to actually be ingesting chronal energy. *Eating time itself.*

"The radiation field around the creatures was overloading the instruments on the ship--

"--so I decided that a more direct investigation was called for."

"You went out there?"

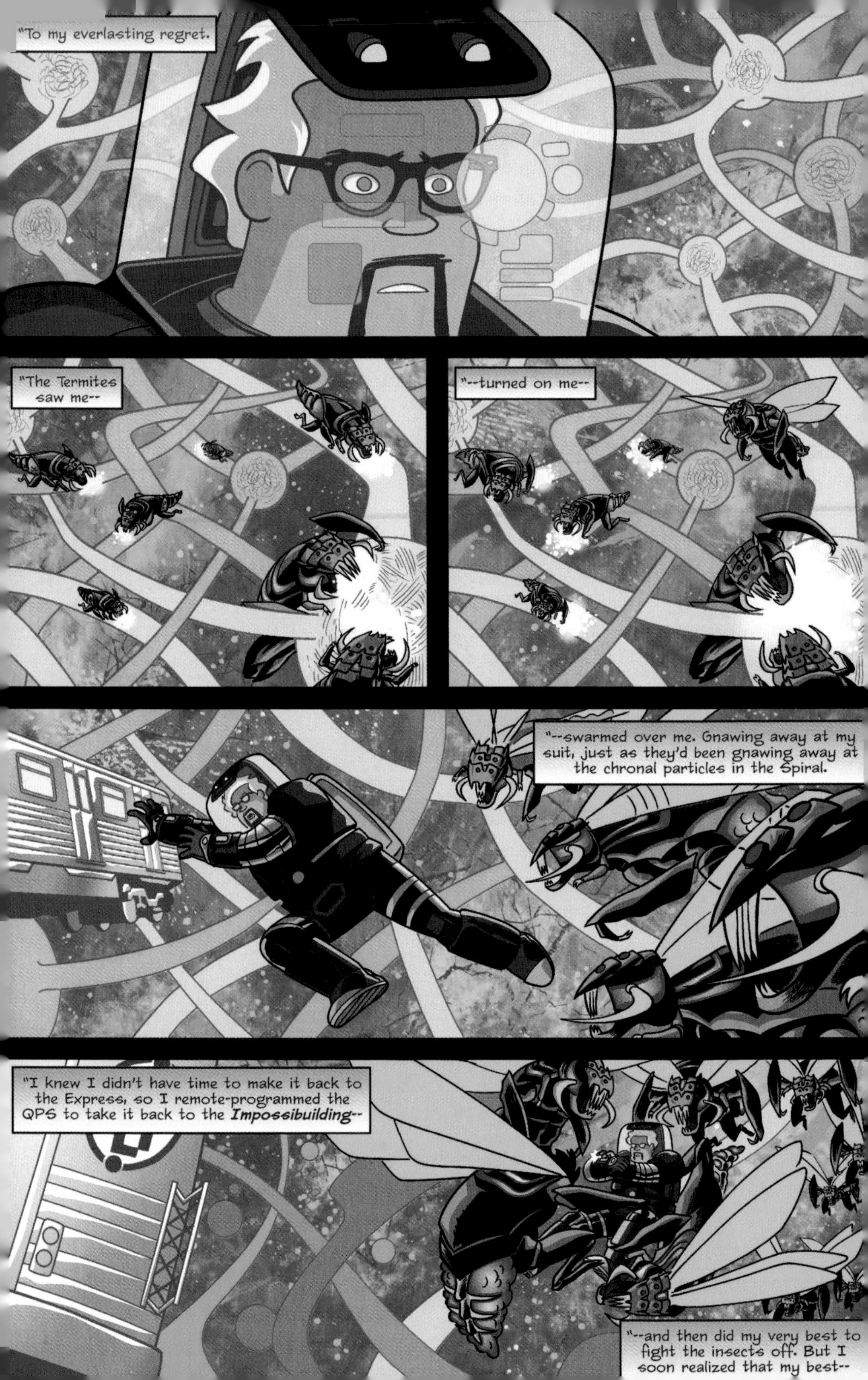
"To my everlasting regret.
"The Termites saw me--
"--turned on me--
"--swarmed over me. Gnawing away at my suit, just as they'd been gnawing away at the chronal particles in the Spiral.
"I knew I didn't have time to make it back to the Express, so I remote-programmed the QPS to take it back to the *Impossibuilding*--
"--and then did my very best to fight the insects off. But I soon realized that my best--

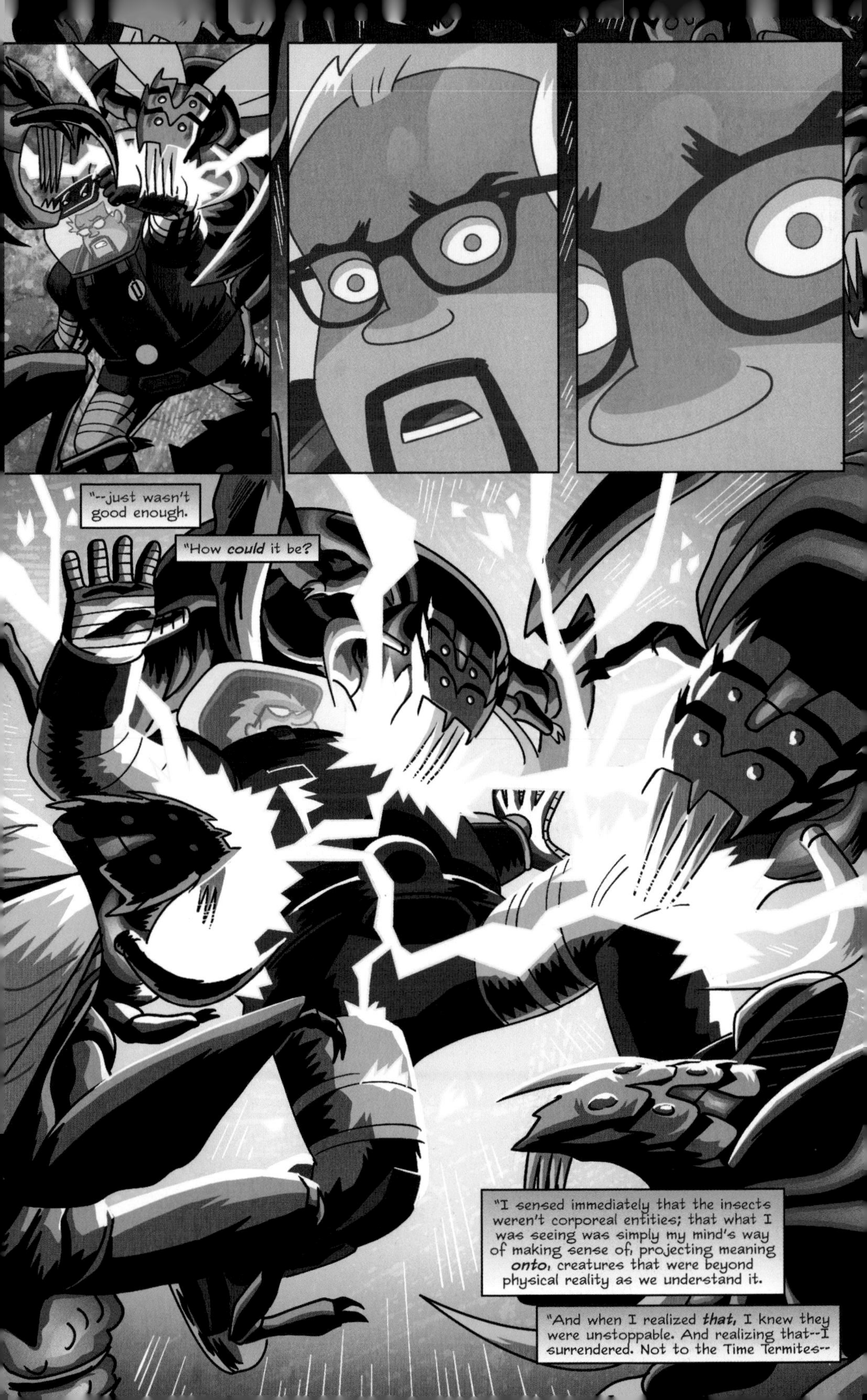
"--just wasn't good enough.
"How *could* it be?
"I sensed immediately that the insects weren't corporeal entities; that what I was seeing was simply my mind's way of making sense of, projecting meaning *onto*, creatures that were beyond physical reality as we understand it.
"And when I realized *that*, I knew they were unstoppable. And realizing that--I surrendered. Not to the Time Termites--

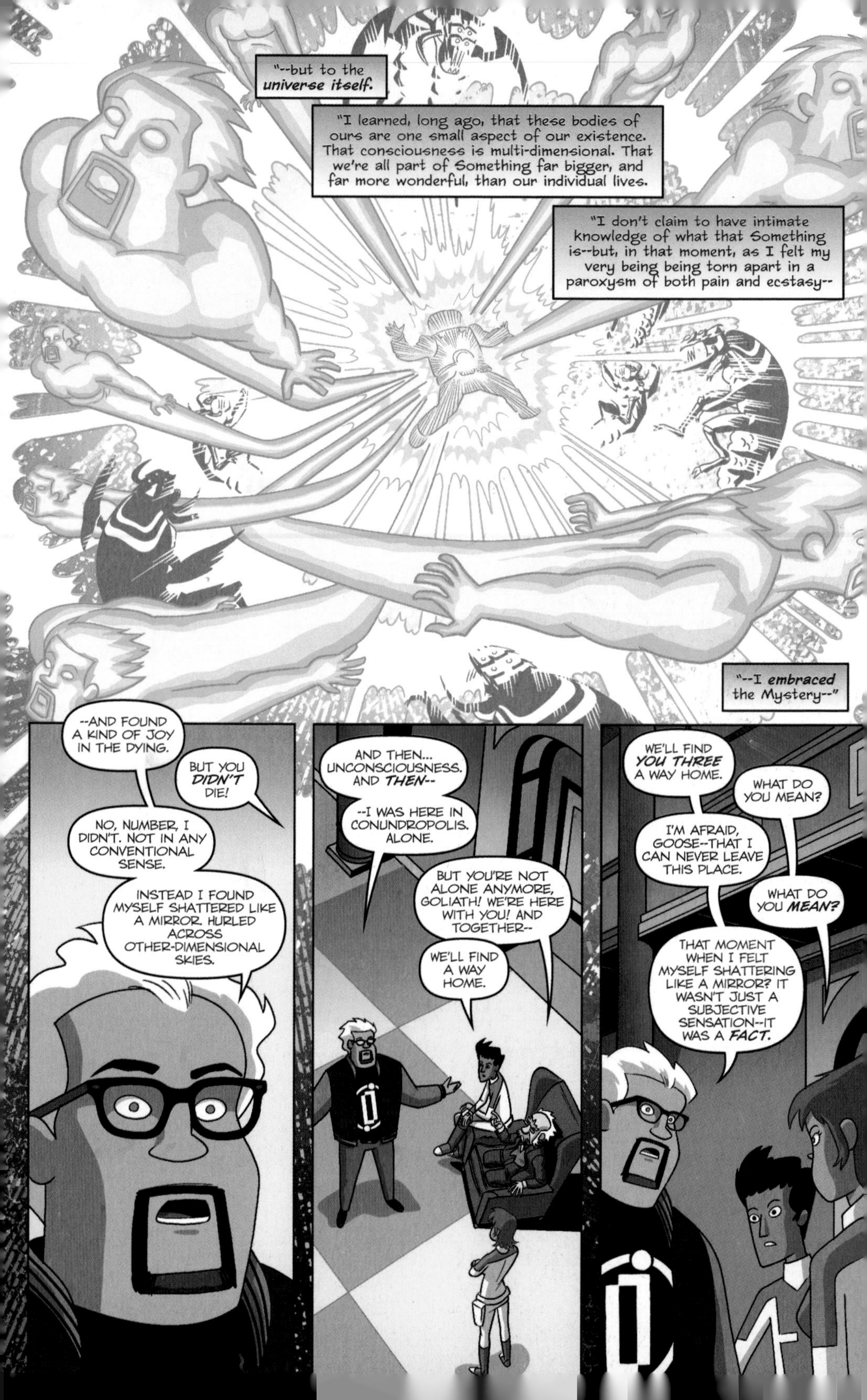
"--but to the *universe itself.*
"I learned, long ago, that these bodies of ours are one small aspect of our existence. That consciousness is multi-dimensional. That we're all part of Something far bigger, and far more wonderful, than our individual lives.
"I don't claim to have intimate knowledge of what that Something is--but, in that moment, as I felt my very being being torn apart in a paroxysm of both pain and ecstasy--
"--I *embraced* the Mystery--"
--AND FOUND A KIND OF JOY IN THE DYING.
BUT YOU *DIDN'T* DIE!
NO, NUMBER, I DIDN'T. NOT IN ANY CONVENTIONAL SENSE.
INSTEAD I FOUND MYSELF SHATTERED LIKE A MIRROR. HURLED ACROSS OTHER-DIMENSIONAL SKIES.
AND THEN... UNCONSCIOUSNESS. AND *THEN*--
--I WAS HERE IN CONUNDROPOLIS. ALONE.
BUT YOU'RE NOT ALONE ANYMORE, GOLIATH! WE'RE HERE WITH YOU! AND TOGETHER--
WE'LL FIND A WAY HOME.
WE'LL FIND *YOU THREE* A WAY HOME.
WHAT DO YOU MEAN?
I'M AFRAID, GOOSE--THAT I CAN NEVER LEAVE THIS PLACE.
WHAT DO YOU *MEAN?*
THAT MOMENT WHEN I FELT MYSELF SHATTERING LIKE A MIRROR? IT WASN'T JUST A SUBJECTIVE SENSATION--IT WAS A *FACT.*

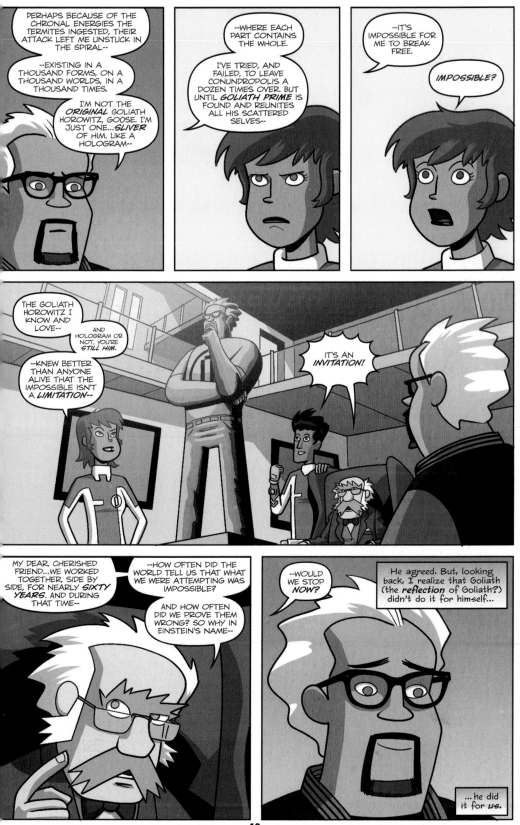

PERHAPS BECAUSE OF THE CHRONAL ENERGIES THE TERMITES INGESTED, THEIR ATTACK LEFT ME UNSTUCK IN THE SPIRAL--

--EXISTING IN A THOUSAND FORMS, ON A THOUSAND WORLDS, IN A THOUSAND TIMES.

I'M NOT THE *ORIGINAL* GOLIATH HOROWITZ, GOOSE. I'M JUST ONE...*SLIVER* OF HIM. LIKE A HOLOGRAM--

--WHERE EACH PART CONTAINS THE WHOLE.

I'VE TRIED, AND FAILED, TO LEAVE CONUNDROPOLIS A DOZEN TIMES OVER BUT UNTIL *GOLIATH PRIME* IS FOUND AND REUNITES ALL HIS SCATTERED SELVES--

--IT'S IMPOSSIBLE FOR ME TO BREAK FREE.

IMPOSSIBLE?

THE GOLIATH HOROWITZ I KNOW AND LOVE--

AND HOLOGRAM OR NOT, YOU'RE *STILL HIM.*

--KNEW BETTER THAN ANYONE ALIVE THAT THE IMPOSSIBLE ISN'T A *LIMITATION*--

IT'S AN *INVITATION!*

MY DEAR, CHERISHED FRIEND...WE WORKED TOGETHER, SIDE BY SIDE, FOR NEARLY *SIXTY YEARS*. AND DURING THAT TIME--

--HOW OFTEN DID THE WORLD TELL US THAT WHAT WE WERE ATTEMPTING WAS IMPOSSIBLE?

AND HOW OFTEN DID WE PROVE THEM WRONG? SO WHY IN EINSTEIN'S NAME--

--WOULD WE STOP *NOW?*

He agreed. But, looking back, I realize that Goliath (the *reflection* of Goliath?) didn't do it for himself...

... he did it for *us.*

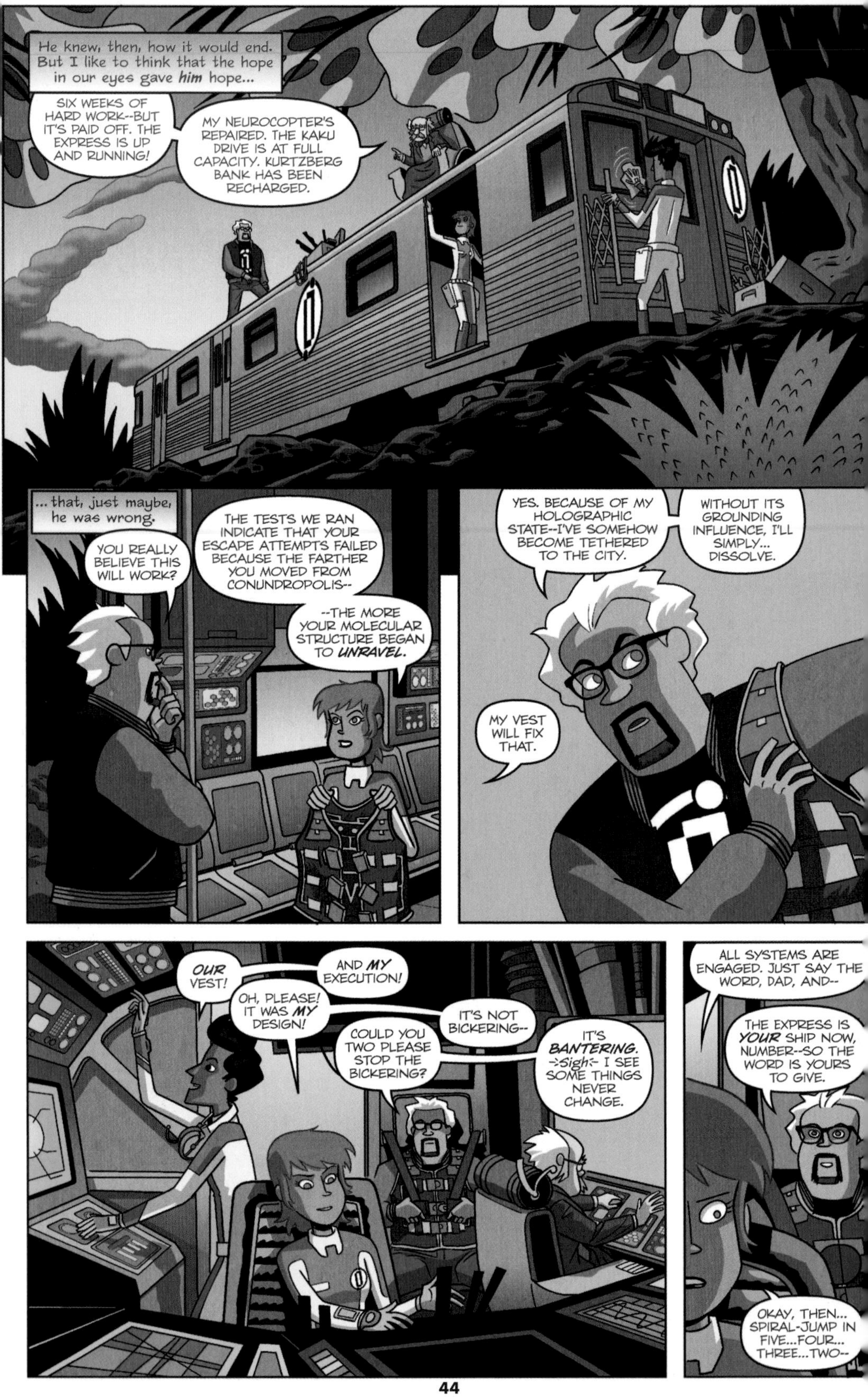
He knew, then, how it would end. But I like to think that the hope in our eyes gave *him* hope...
SIX WEEKS OF HARD WORK--BUT IT'S PAID OFF. THE EXPRESS IS UP AND RUNNING!
MY NEUROCOPTER'S REPAIRED. THE KAKU DRIVE IS AT FULL CAPACITY. KURTZBERG BANK HAS BEEN RECHARGED.
... that, just maybe, he was wrong.
YOU REALLY BELIEVE THIS WILL WORK?
THE TESTS WE RAN INDICATE THAT YOUR ESCAPE ATTEMPTS FAILED BECAUSE THE FARTHER YOU MOVED FROM CONUNDROPOLIS--
--THE MORE YOUR MOLECULAR STRUCTURE BEGAN TO *UNRAVEL.*
YES. BECAUSE OF MY HOLOGRAPHIC STATE--I'VE SOMEHOW BECOME TETHERED TO THE CITY.
WITHOUT ITS GROUNDING INFLUENCE, I'LL SIMPLY... DISSOLVE.
MY VEST WILL FIX THAT.
OUR VEST!
AND *MY* EXECUTION!
OH, PLEASE! IT WAS *MY* DESIGN!
COULD YOU TWO PLEASE STOP THE BICKERING?
IT'S NOT BICKERING--
IT'S *BANTERING.* *-sigh-* I SEE SOME THINGS NEVER CHANGE.
ALL SYSTEMS ARE ENGAGED. JUST SAY THE WORD, DAD, AND--
THE EXPRESS IS *YOUR* SHIP NOW, NUMBER--SO THE WORD IS YOURS TO GIVE.
OKAY, THEN... SPIRAL-JUMP IN FIVE...FOUR... THREE...TWO--

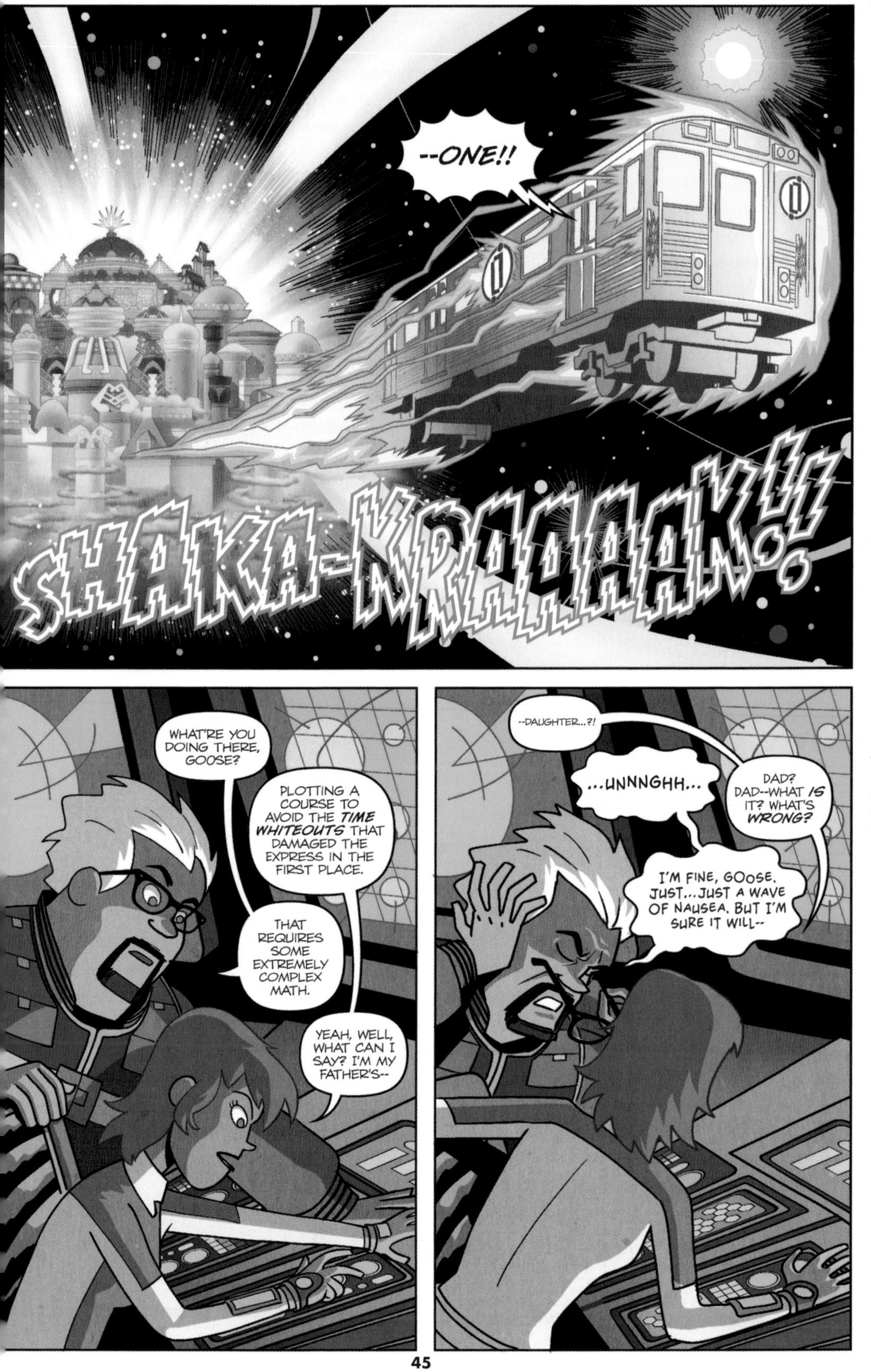
--ONE!!
SHAKA-KRAAAAK!!
WHAT'RE YOU DOING THERE, GOOSE?
PLOTTING A COURSE TO AVOID THE *TIME WHITEOUTS* THAT DAMAGED THE EXPRESS IN THE FIRST PLACE.
THAT REQUIRES SOME EXTREMELY COMPLEX MATH.
YEAH, WELL, WHAT CAN I SAY? I'M MY FATHER'S--
--DAUGHTER...?!
...UNNNGHH...
DAD? DAD--WHAT *IS* IT? WHAT'S *WRONG?*
I'M FINE, GOOSE. JUST...JUST A WAVE OF NAUSEA. BUT I'M SURE IT WILL--

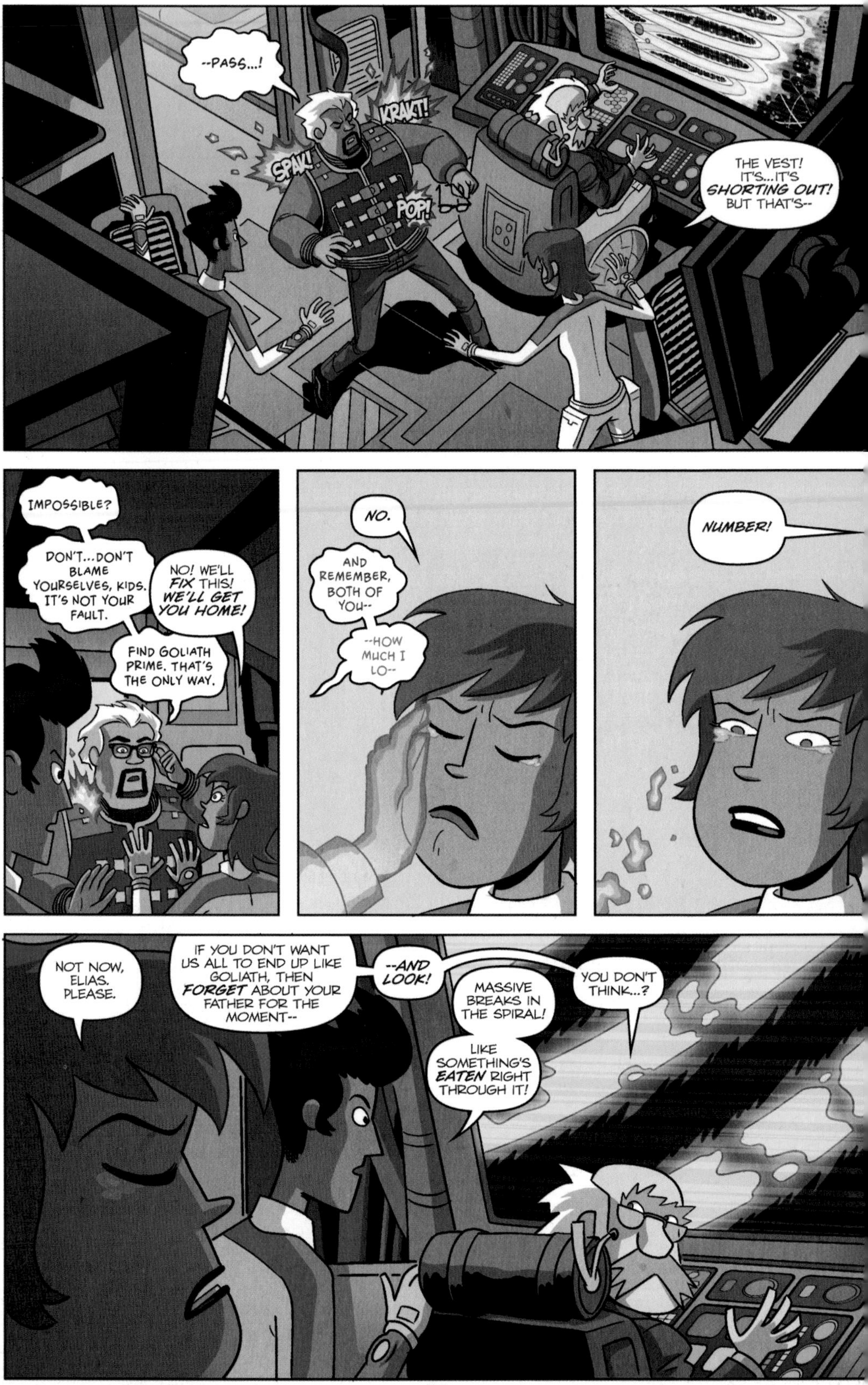
--PASS...!
KRAKT!
SPAK!
POP!
THE VEST! IT'S...IT'S SHORTING OUT! BUT THAT'S--
IMPOSSIBLE?
DON'T...DON'T BLAME YOURSELVES, KIDS. IT'S NOT YOUR FAULT.
NO! WE'LL FIX THIS! WE'LL GET YOU HOME!
FIND GOLIATH PRIME. THAT'S THE ONLY WAY.
NO.
AND REMEMBER, BOTH OF YOU--
--HOW MUCH I LO--
NUMBER!
NOT NOW, ELIAS. PLEASE.
IF YOU DON'T WANT US ALL TO END UP LIKE GOLIATH, THEN FORGET ABOUT YOUR FATHER FOR THE MOMENT--
--AND LOOK!
YOU DON'T THINK...?
MASSIVE BREAKS IN THE SPIRAL!
LIKE SOMETHING'S EATEN RIGHT THROUGH IT!

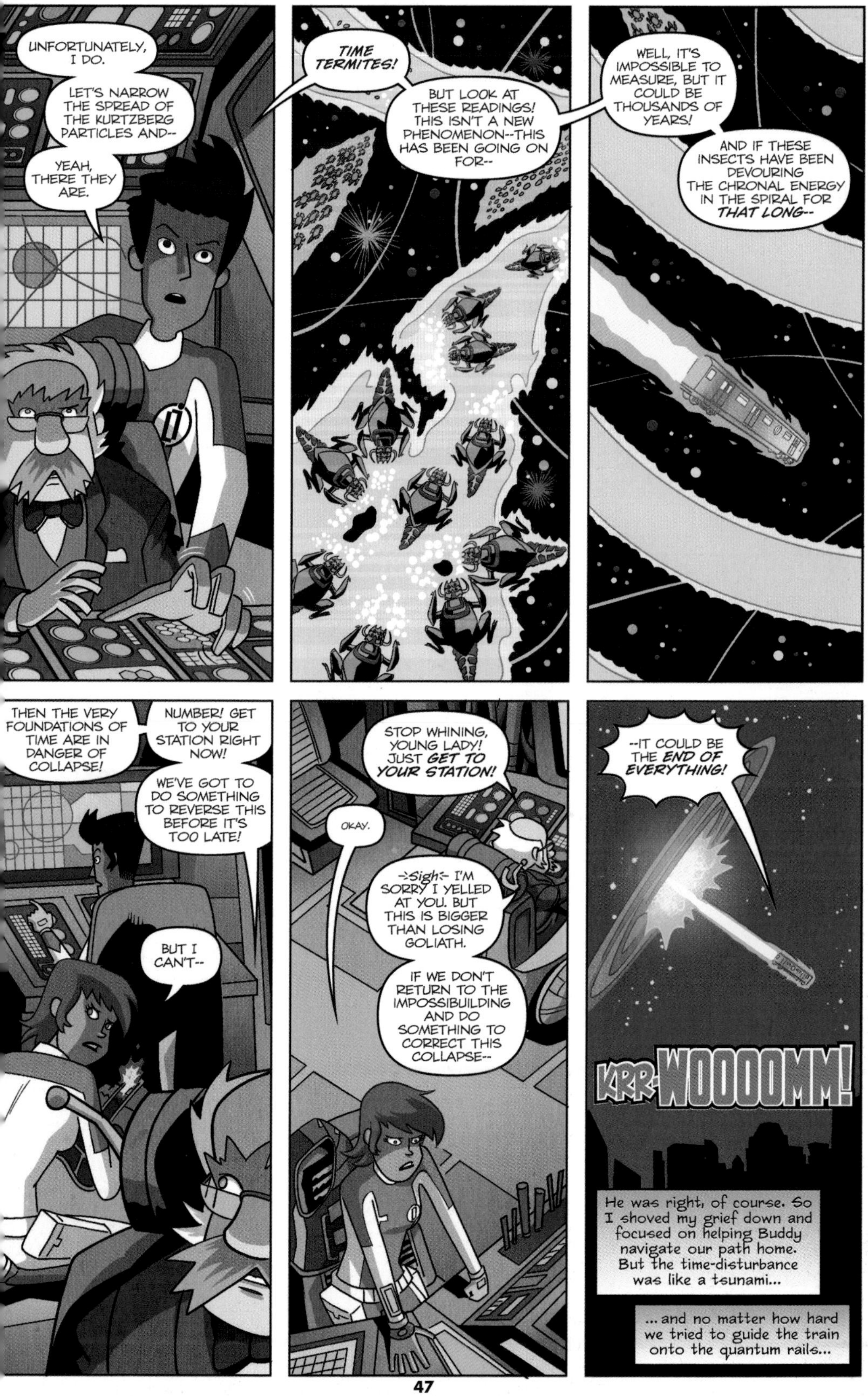
UNFORTUNATELY, I DO.
LET'S NARROW THE SPREAD OF THE KURTZBERG PARTICLES AND--
YEAH, THERE THEY ARE.
TIME TERMITES!
BUT LOOK AT THESE READINGS! THIS ISN'T A NEW PHENOMENON--THIS HAS BEEN GOING ON FOR--
WELL, IT'S IMPOSSIBLE TO MEASURE, BUT IT COULD BE THOUSANDS OF YEARS!
AND IF THESE INSECTS HAVE BEEN DEVOURING THE CHRONAL ENERGY IN THE SPIRAL FOR THAT LONG--
THEN THE VERY FOUNDATIONS OF TIME ARE IN DANGER OF COLLAPSE!
NUMBER! GET TO YOUR STATION RIGHT NOW!
WE'VE GOT TO DO SOMETHING TO REVERSE THIS BEFORE IT'S TOO LATE!
BUT I CAN'T--
STOP WHINING, YOUNG LADY! JUST GET TO YOUR STATION!
OKAY.
-Sigh- I'M SORRY I YELLED AT YOU. BUT THIS IS BIGGER THAN LOSING GOLIATH.
IF WE DON'T RETURN TO THE IMPOSSIBUILDING AND DO SOMETHING TO CORRECT THIS COLLAPSE--
--IT COULD BE THE END OF EVERYTHING!
KRR-WOOOOMM!
He was right, of course. So I shoved my grief down and focused on helping Buddy navigate our path home. But the time-disturbance was like a tsunami...
... and no matter how hard we tried to guide the train onto the quantum rails...

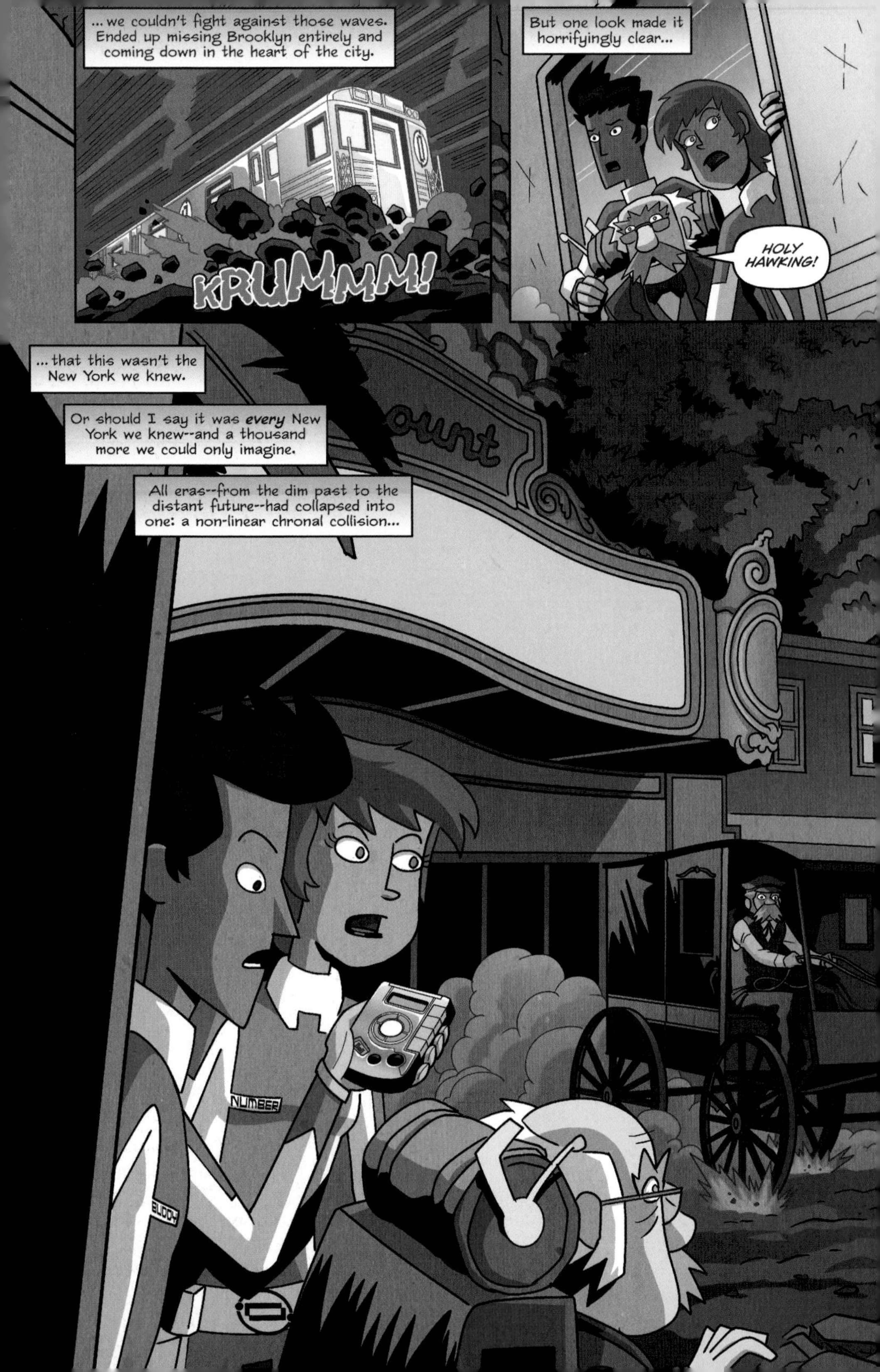
...we couldn't fight against those waves. Ended up missing Brooklyn entirely and coming down in the heart of the city.
KRUMMM!
But one look made it horrifyingly clear...
HOLY HAWKING!
...that this wasn't the New York we knew.
Or should I say it was *every* New York we knew--and a thousand more we could only imagine.
All eras--from the dim past to the distant future--had collapsed into one: a non-linear chronal collision...
ount
NUMBER
BUDDY

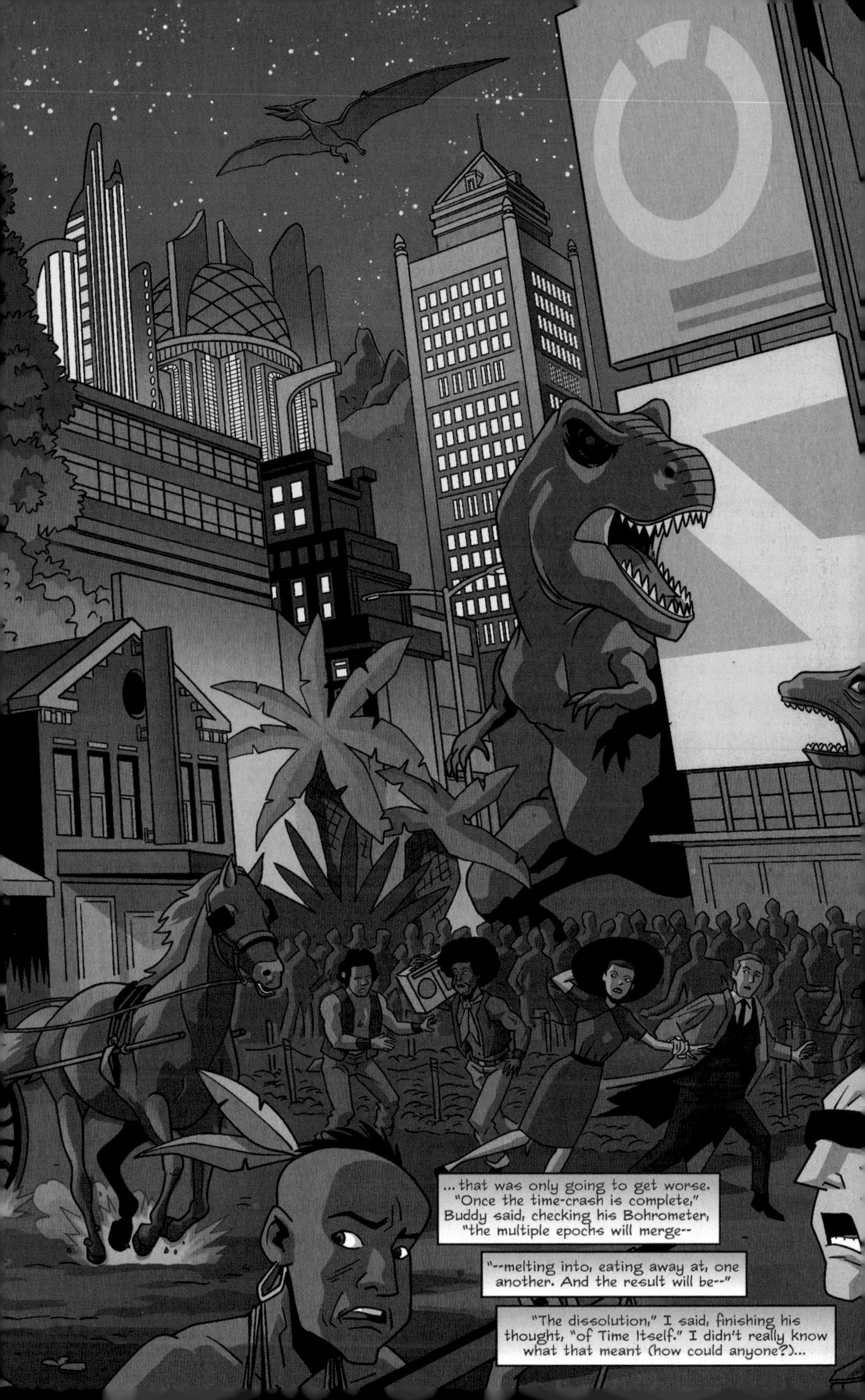
...that was only going to get worse. "Once the time-crash is complete," Buddy said, checking his Bohrometer, "the multiple epochs will merge--
"--melting into, eating away at, one another. And the result will be--"
"The dissolution," I said, finishing his thought, "of Time Itself." I didn't really know what that meant (how could anyone?)...

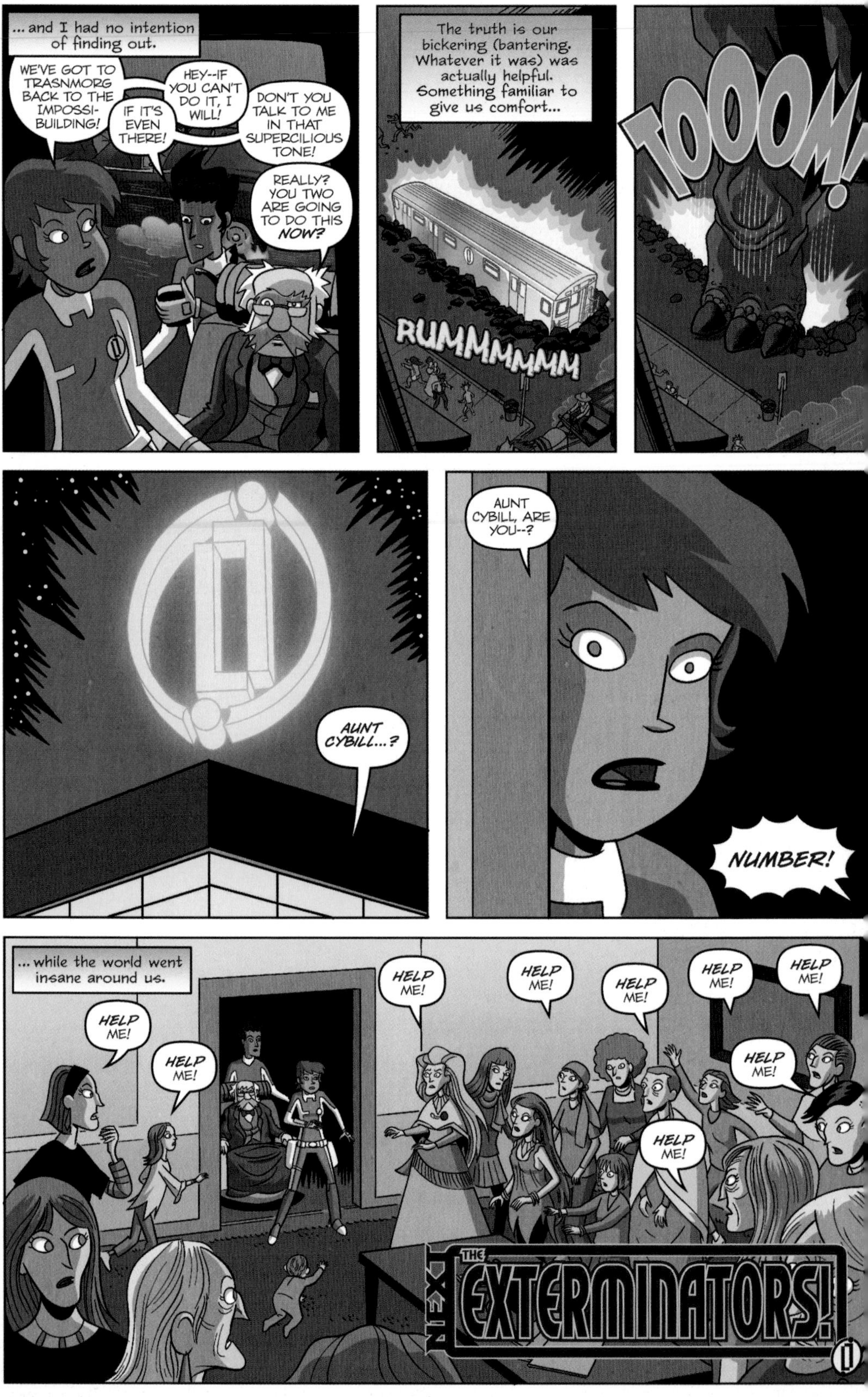

... and I had no intention of finding out.
WE'VE GOT TO TRASNMORG BACK TO THE IMPOSSI-BUILDING!
IF IT'S EVEN THERE!
HEY--IF YOU CAN'T DO IT, I WILL!
DON'T YOU TALK TO ME IN THAT SUPERCILIOUS TONE!
REALLY? YOU TWO ARE GOING TO DO THIS NOW?
The truth is our bickering (bantering. Whatever it was) was actually helpful. Something familiar to give us comfort...
RUMMMMMMM
TOOOM!
AUNT CYBILL...?
AUNT CYBILL, ARE YOU--?
NUMBER!
... while the world went insane around us.
HELP ME!
HELP ME!
HELP ME!
HELP ME!
HELP ME!
HELP ME!
HELP ME!
HELP ME!
HELP ME!
NEXT THE EXTERMINATORS!

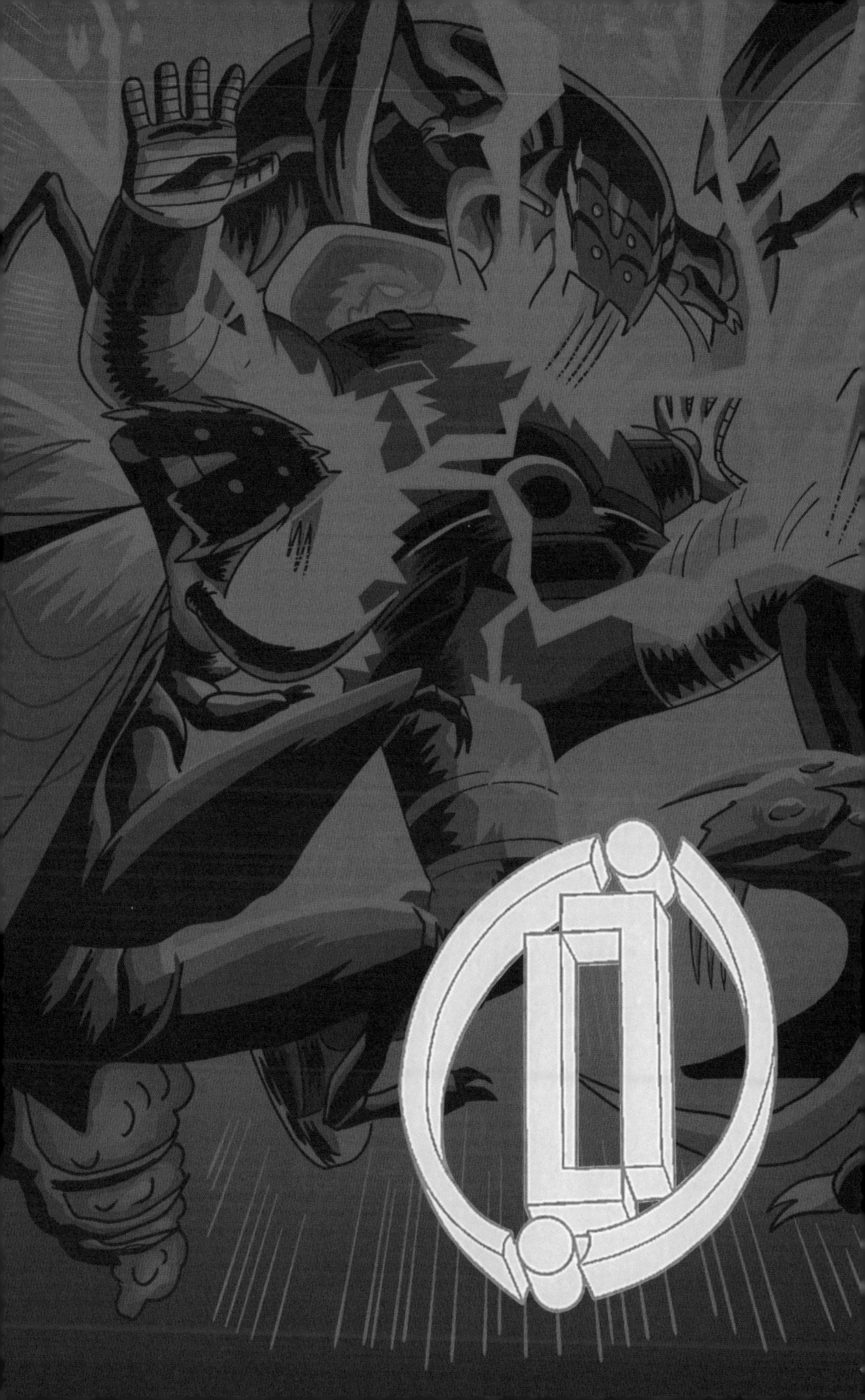

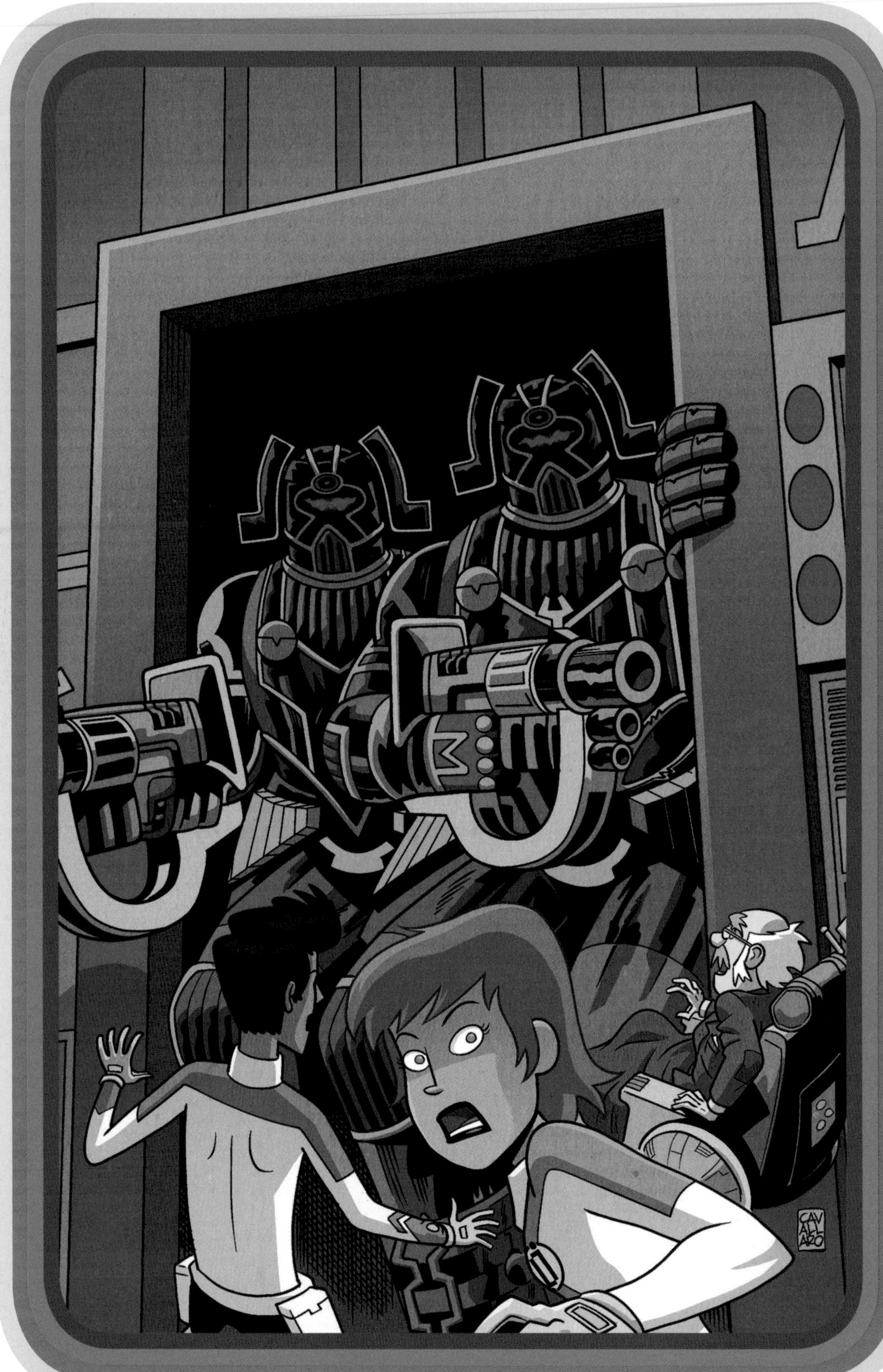
CAV
ALL
ARO

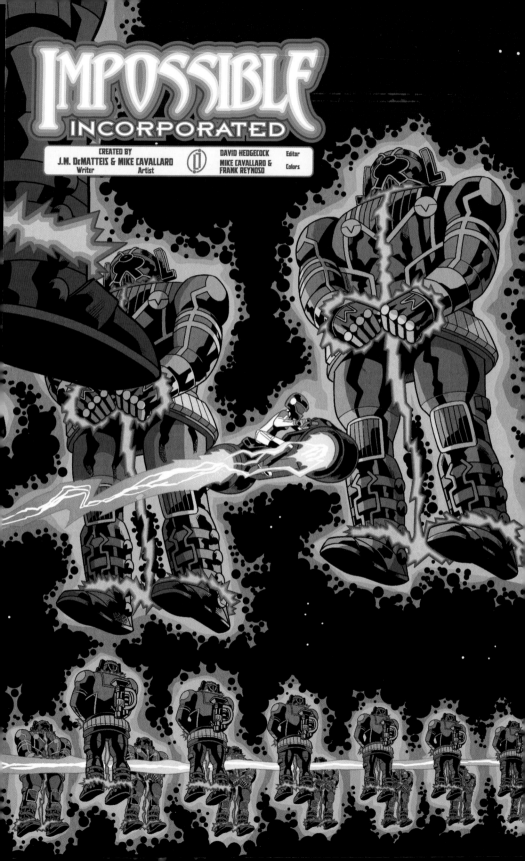

IMPOSSIBLE
INCORPORATED

CREATED BY
J.M. DeMATTEIS & **MIKE CAVALLARO**
Writer   Artist

DAVID HEDGECOCK   Editor

MIKE CAVALLARO &   Colors
FRANK REYNOSO

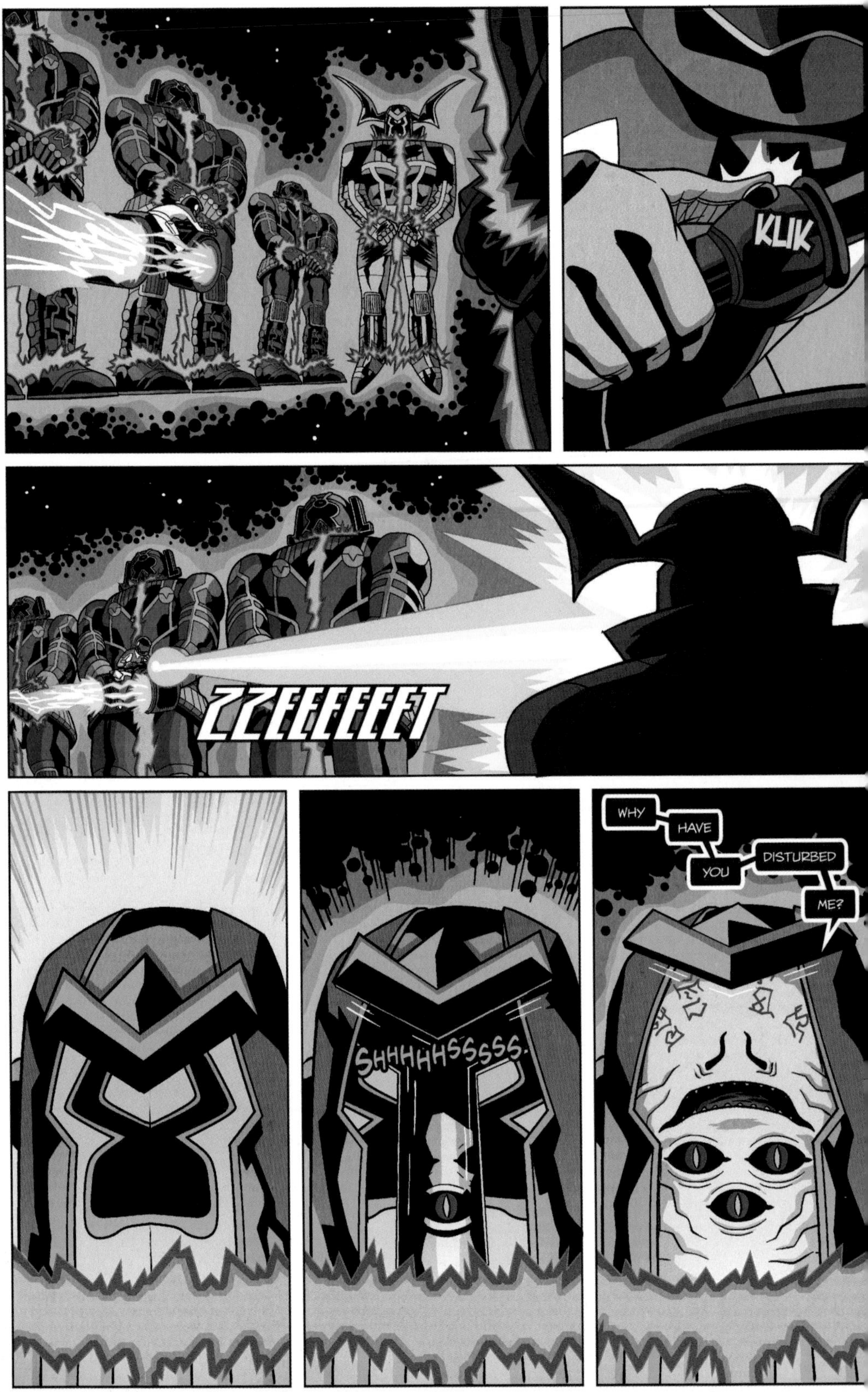
KLIK
ZZEEEEEEET
SHHHHHSSSSS
WHY
HAVE
YOU
DISTURBED
ME?

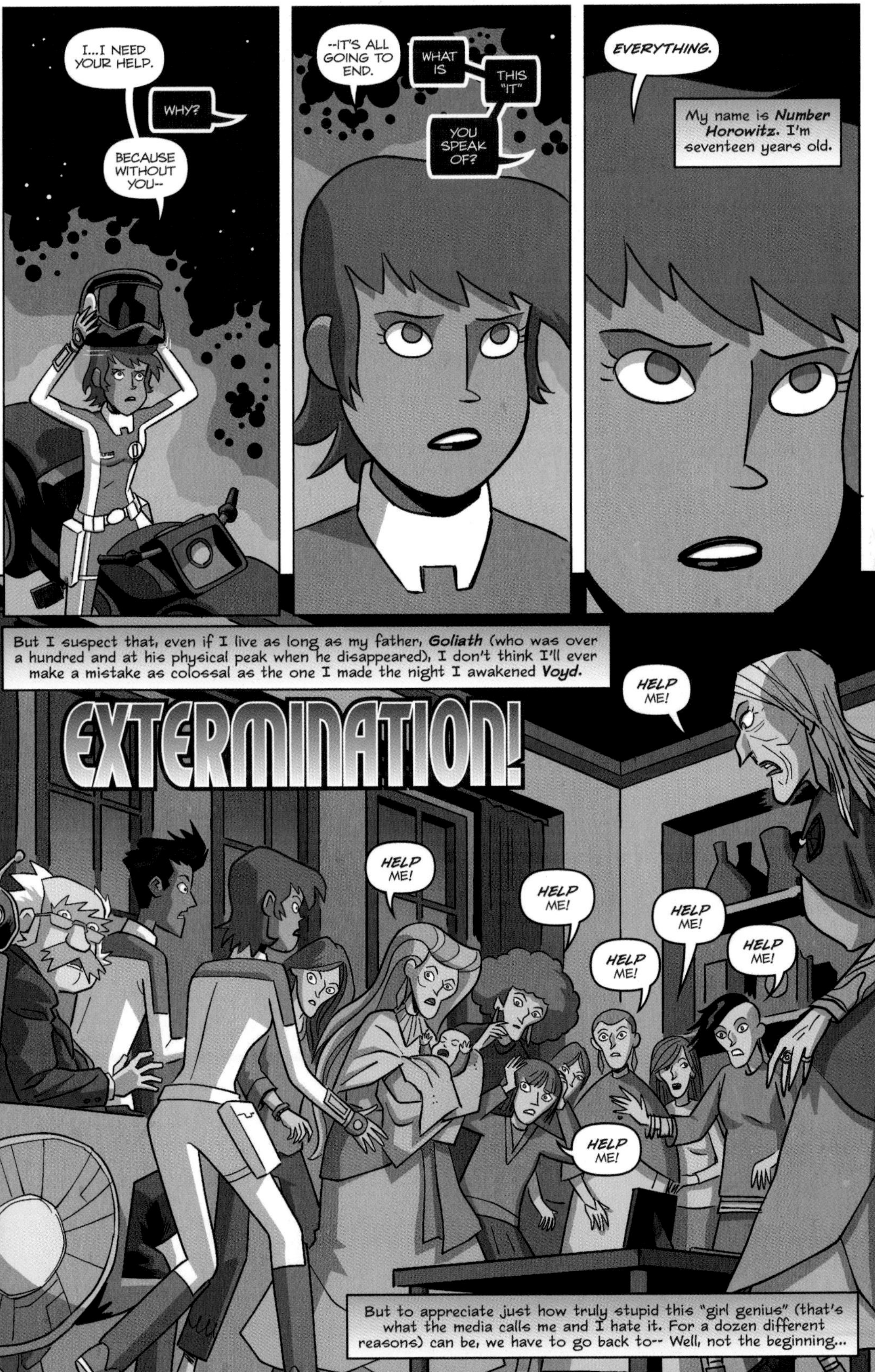
I...I NEED YOUR HELP.
WHY?
BECAUSE WITHOUT YOU--
--IT'S ALL GOING TO END.
WHAT IS
THIS "IT"
YOU SPEAK OF?
EVERYTHING.
My name is Number Horowitz. I'm seventeen years old.
But I suspect that, even if I live as long as my father, Goliath (who was over a hundred and at his physical peak when he disappeared), I don't think I'll ever make a mistake as colossal as the one I made the night I awakened Voyd.
HELP ME!
EXTERMINATION!
HELP ME!
HELP ME!
HELP ME!
HELP ME!
HELP ME!
HELP ME!
But to appreciate just how truly stupid this "girl genius" (that's what the media calls me and I hate it. For a dozen different reasons) can be, we have to go back to-- Well, not the beginning...

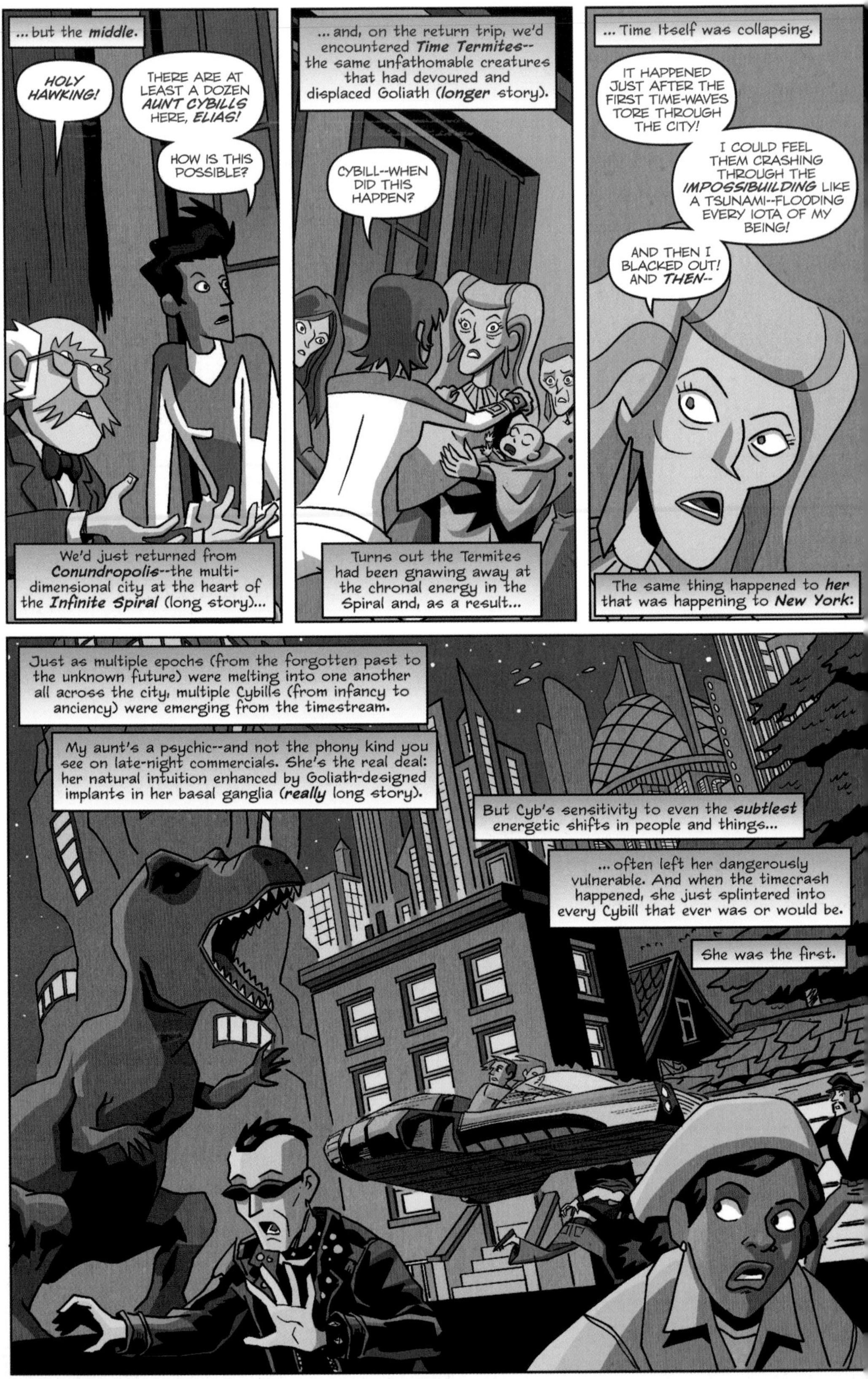

...but the middle.
HOLY HAWKING!
THERE ARE AT LEAST A DOZEN AUNT CYBILLS HERE, ELIAS!
HOW IS THIS POSSIBLE?
We'd just returned from Conundropolis--the multi-dimensional city at the heart of the Infinite Spiral (long story)...
...and, on the return trip, we'd encountered Time Termites--the same unfathomable creatures that had devoured and displaced Goliath (longer story).
CYBILL--WHEN DID THIS HAPPEN?
Turns out the Termites had been gnawing away at the chronal energy in the Spiral and, as a result...
...Time itself was collapsing.
IT HAPPENED JUST AFTER THE FIRST TIME-WAVES TORE THROUGH THE CITY!
I COULD FEEL THEM CRASHING THROUGH THE IMPOSSIBUILDING LIKE A TSUNAMI--FLOODING EVERY IOTA OF MY BEING!
AND THEN I BLACKED OUT! AND THEN--
The same thing happened to her that was happening to New York:
Just as multiple epochs (from the forgotten past to the unknown future) were melting into one another all across the city, multiple Cybills (from infancy to anciency) were emerging from the timestream.
My aunt's a psychic--and not the phony kind you see on late-night commercials. She's the real deal: her natural intuition enhanced by Goliath-designed implants in her basal ganglia (really long story).
But Cyb's sensitivity to even the subtlest energetic shifts in people and things...
...often left her dangerously vulnerable. And when the timecrash happened, she just splintered into every Cybill that ever was or would be.
She was the first.

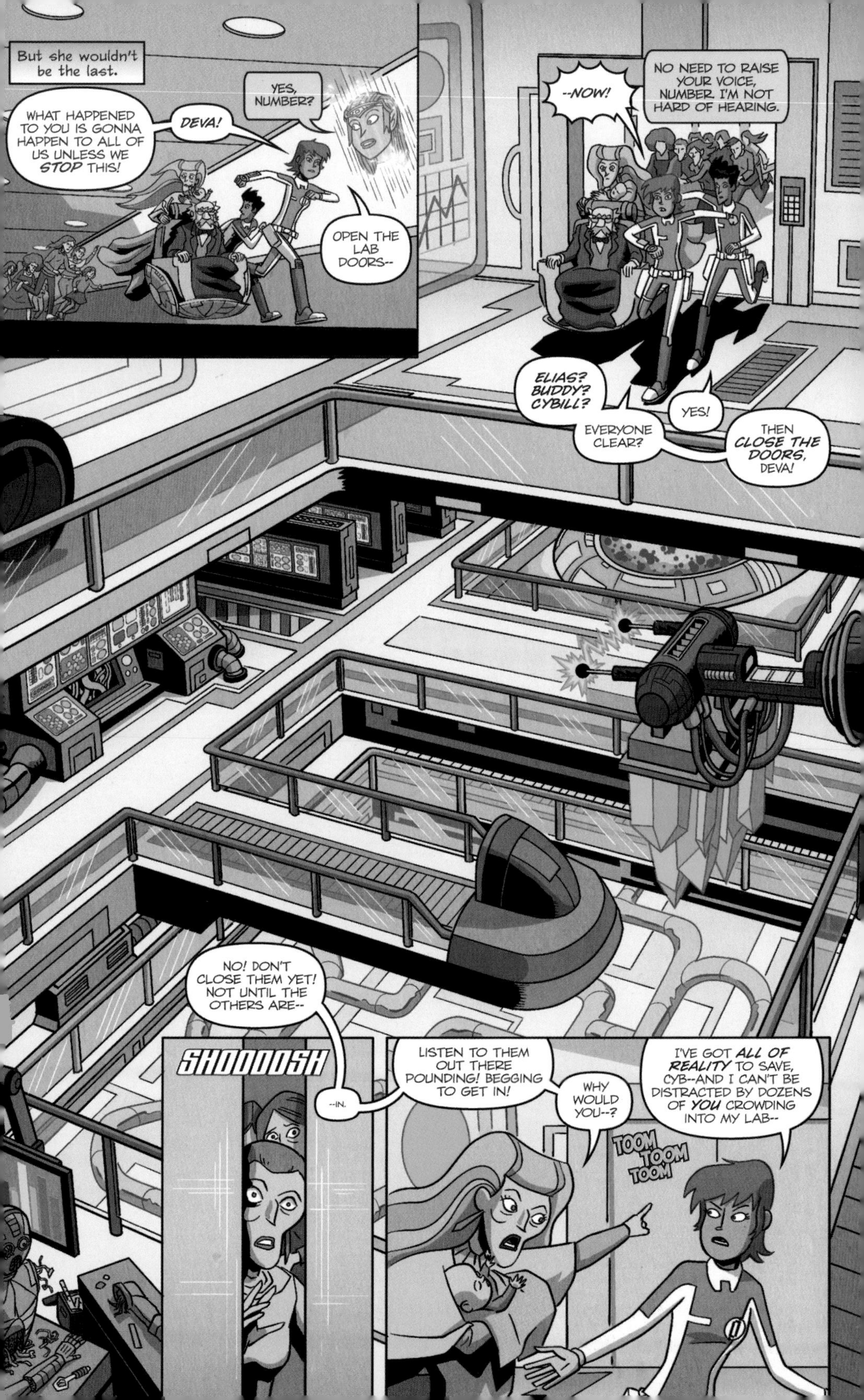

But she wouldn't be the last.
WHAT HAPPENED TO YOU IS GONNA HAPPEN TO ALL OF US UNLESS WE STOP THIS!
DEVA!
YES, NUMBER?
OPEN THE LAB DOORS--
--NOW!
NO NEED TO RAISE YOUR VOICE, NUMBER. I'M NOT HARD OF HEARING.
ELIAS? BUDDY? CYBILL?
EVERYONE CLEAR?
YES!
THEN CLOSE THE DOORS, DEVA!
NO! DON'T CLOSE THEM YET! NOT UNTIL THE OTHERS ARE--
SHOOOOSH
--IN.
LISTEN TO THEM OUT THERE POUNDING! BEGGING TO GET IN!
WHY WOULD YOU--?
TOOM TOOM TOOM
I'VE GOT ALL OF REALITY TO SAVE, CYB--AND I CAN'T BE DISTRACTED BY DOZENS OF YOU CROWDING INTO MY LAB--

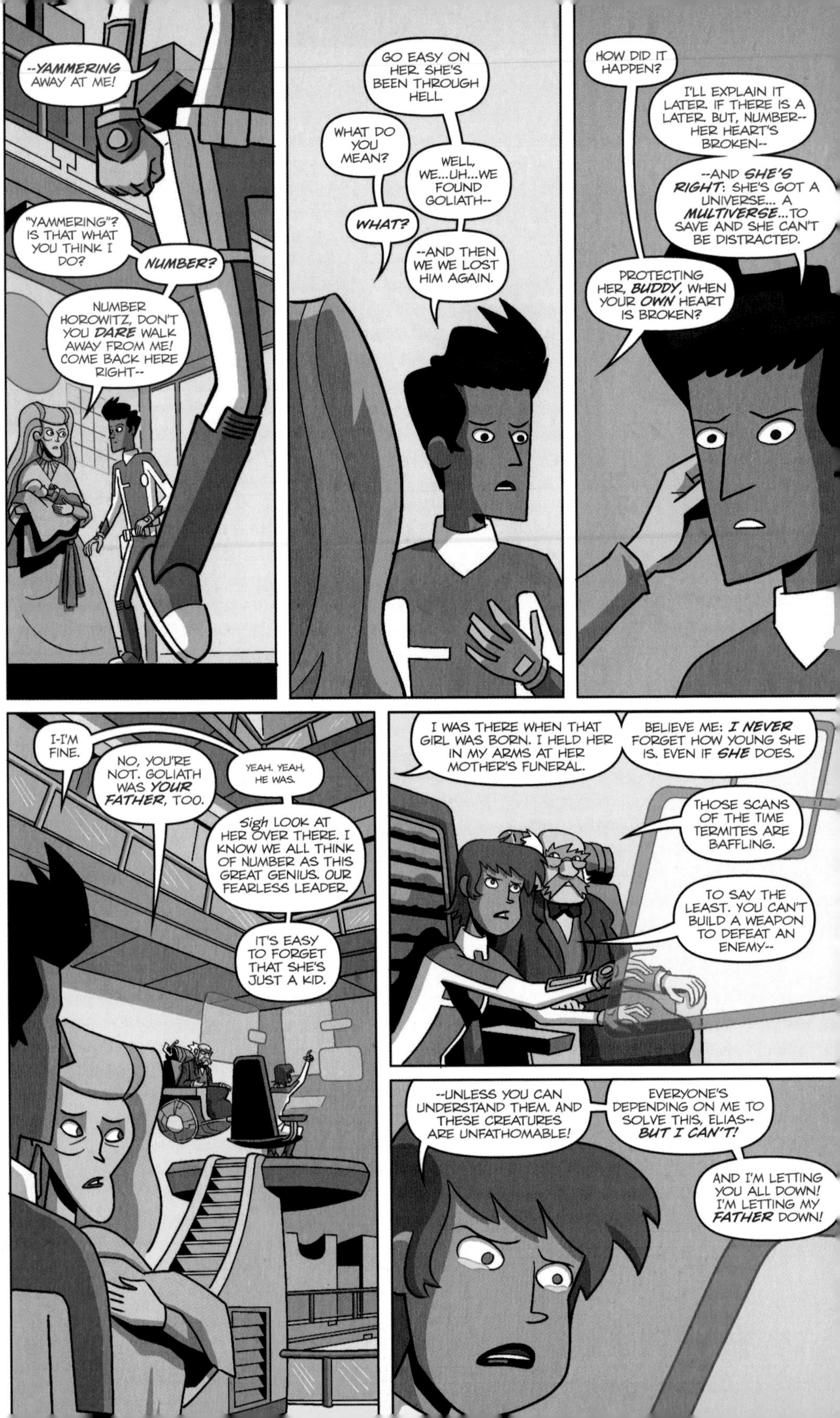
--YAMMERING AWAY AT ME!
"YAMMERING"? IS THAT WHAT YOU THINK I DO?
NUMBER?
NUMBER HOROWITZ, DON'T YOU DARE WALK AWAY FROM ME! COME BACK HERE RIGHT--
GO EASY ON HER. SHE'S BEEN THROUGH HELL.
WHAT DO YOU MEAN?
WELL, WE...UH...WE FOUND GOLIATH--
WHAT?
--AND THEN WE WE LOST HIM AGAIN.
HOW DID IT HAPPEN?
I'LL EXPLAIN IT LATER. IF THERE IS A LATER. BUT, NUMBER-- HER HEART'S BROKEN--
--AND SHE'S RIGHT: SHE'S GOT A UNIVERSE... A MULTIVERSE...TO SAVE AND SHE CAN'T BE DISTRACTED.
PROTECTING HER, BUDDY, WHEN YOUR OWN HEART IS BROKEN?
I-I'M FINE.
NO, YOU'RE NOT. GOLIATH WAS YOUR FATHER, TOO.
YEAH. YEAH, HE WAS.
Sigh LOOK AT HER OVER THERE. I KNOW WE ALL THINK OF NUMBER AS THIS GREAT GENIUS. OUR FEARLESS LEADER.
IT'S EASY TO FORGET THAT SHE'S JUST A KID.
I WAS THERE WHEN THAT GIRL WAS BORN. I HELD HER IN MY ARMS AT HER MOTHER'S FUNERAL.
BELIEVE ME: I NEVER FORGET HOW YOUNG SHE IS. EVEN IF SHE DOES.
THOSE SCANS OF THE TIME TERMITES ARE BAFFLING.
TO SAY THE LEAST. YOU CAN'T BUILD A WEAPON TO DEFEAT AN ENEMY--
--UNLESS YOU CAN UNDERSTAND THEM. AND THESE CREATURES ARE UNFATHOMABLE!
EVERYONE'S DEPENDING ON ME TO SOLVE THIS, ELIAS-- BUT I CAN'T!
AND I'M LETTING YOU ALL DOWN! I'M LETTING MY FATHER DOWN!

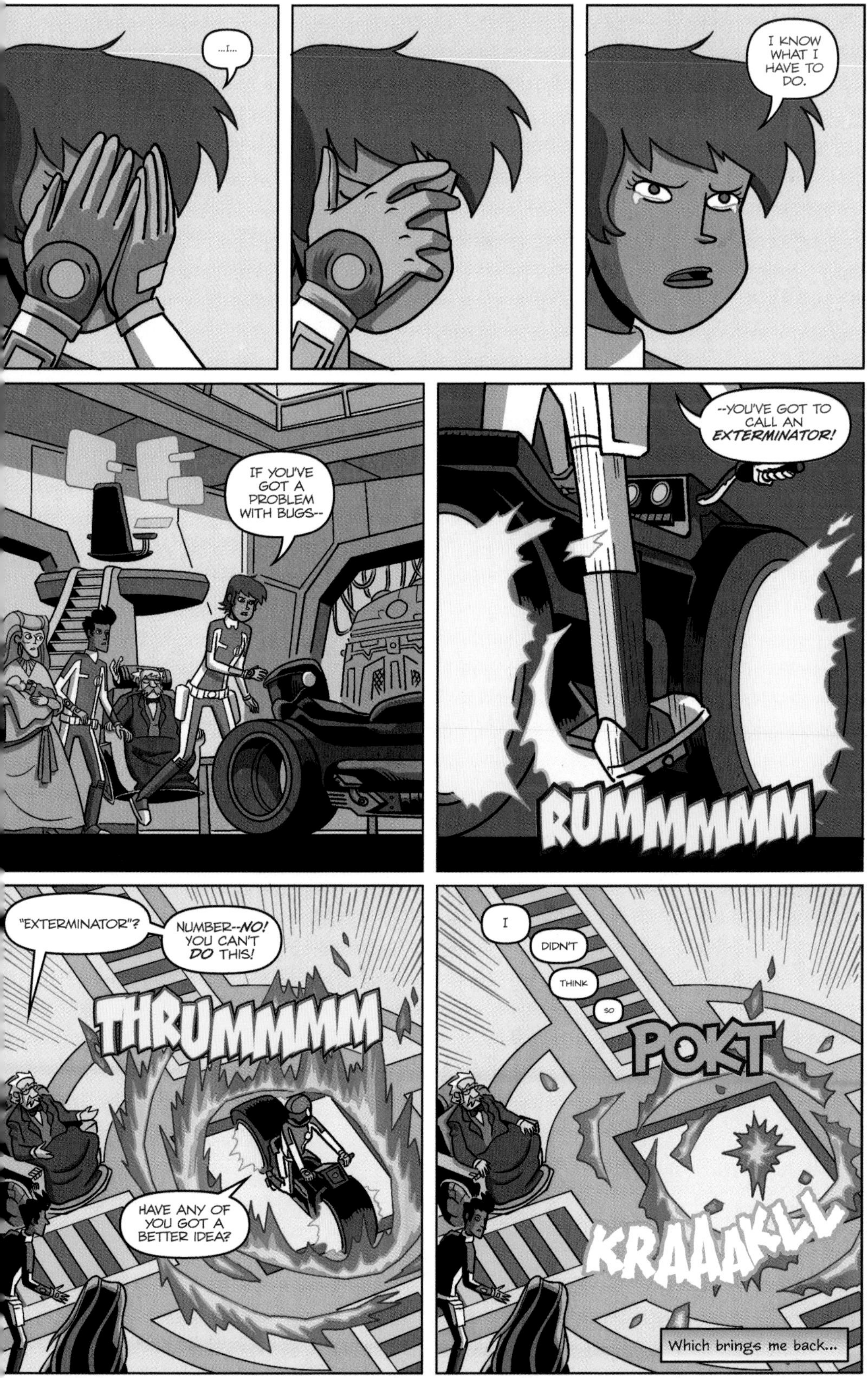
...I...
I KNOW WHAT I HAVE TO DO.
IF YOU'VE GOT A PROBLEM WITH BUGS--
--YOU'VE GOT TO CALL AN EXTERMINATOR!
RUMMMMMM
"EXTERMINATOR"?
NUMBER--NO! YOU CAN'T DO THIS!
THRUMMMMM
HAVE ANY OF YOU GOT A BETTER IDEA?
I
DIDN'T
THINK
SO
POKT
KRAAAKLL
Which brings me back...

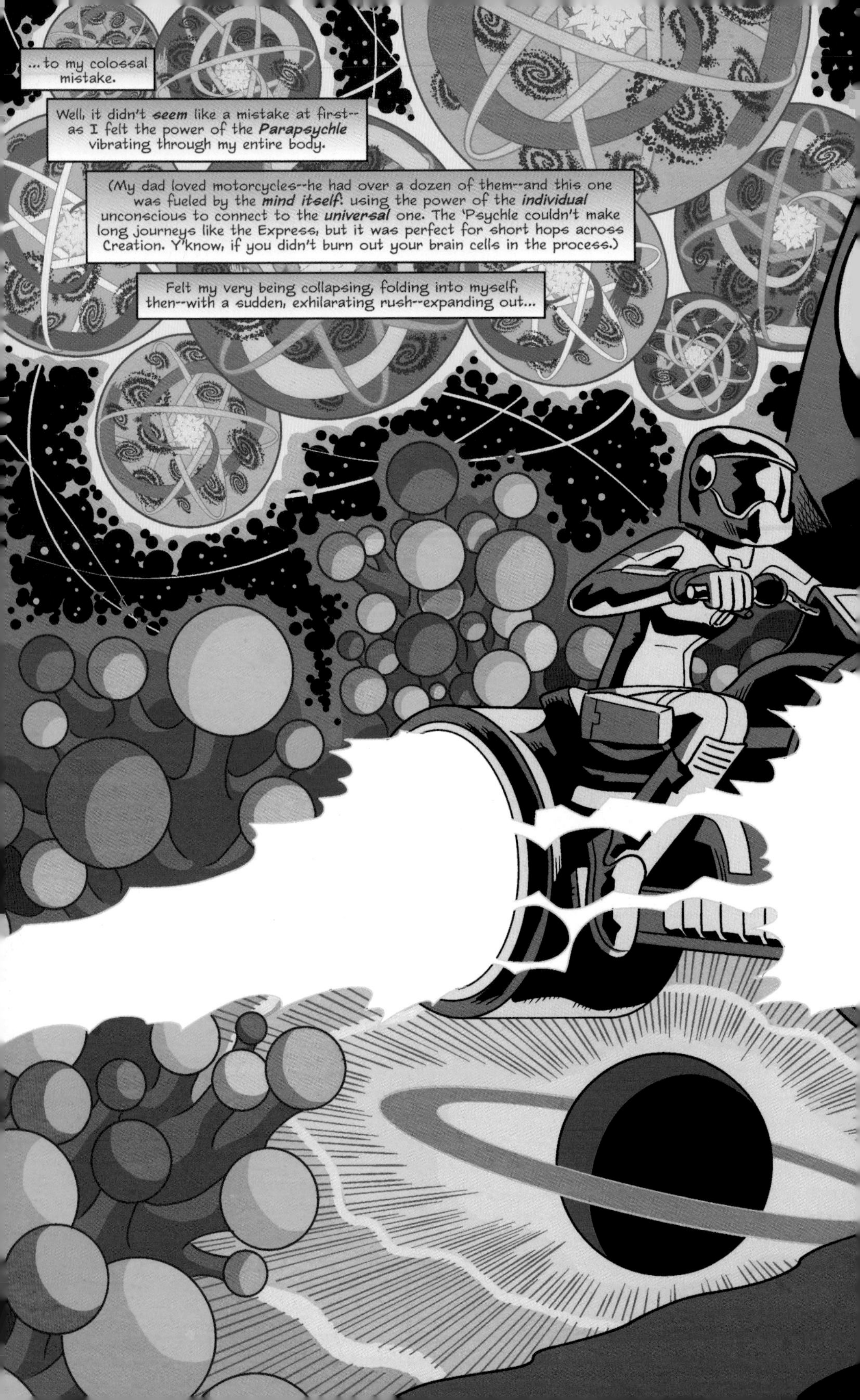
...to my colossal mistake.
Well, it didn't *seem* like a mistake at first--as I felt the power of the *Parapsychle* vibrating through my entire body.
(My dad loved motorcycles--he had over a dozen of them--and this one was fueled by the *mind itself*: using the power of the *individual* unconscious to connect to the *universal* one. The 'Psychle couldn't make long journeys like the Express, but it was perfect for short hops across Creation. Y'know, if you didn't burn out your brain cells in the process.)
Felt my very being collapsing, folding into myself, then--with a sudden, exhilarating rush--expanding out...

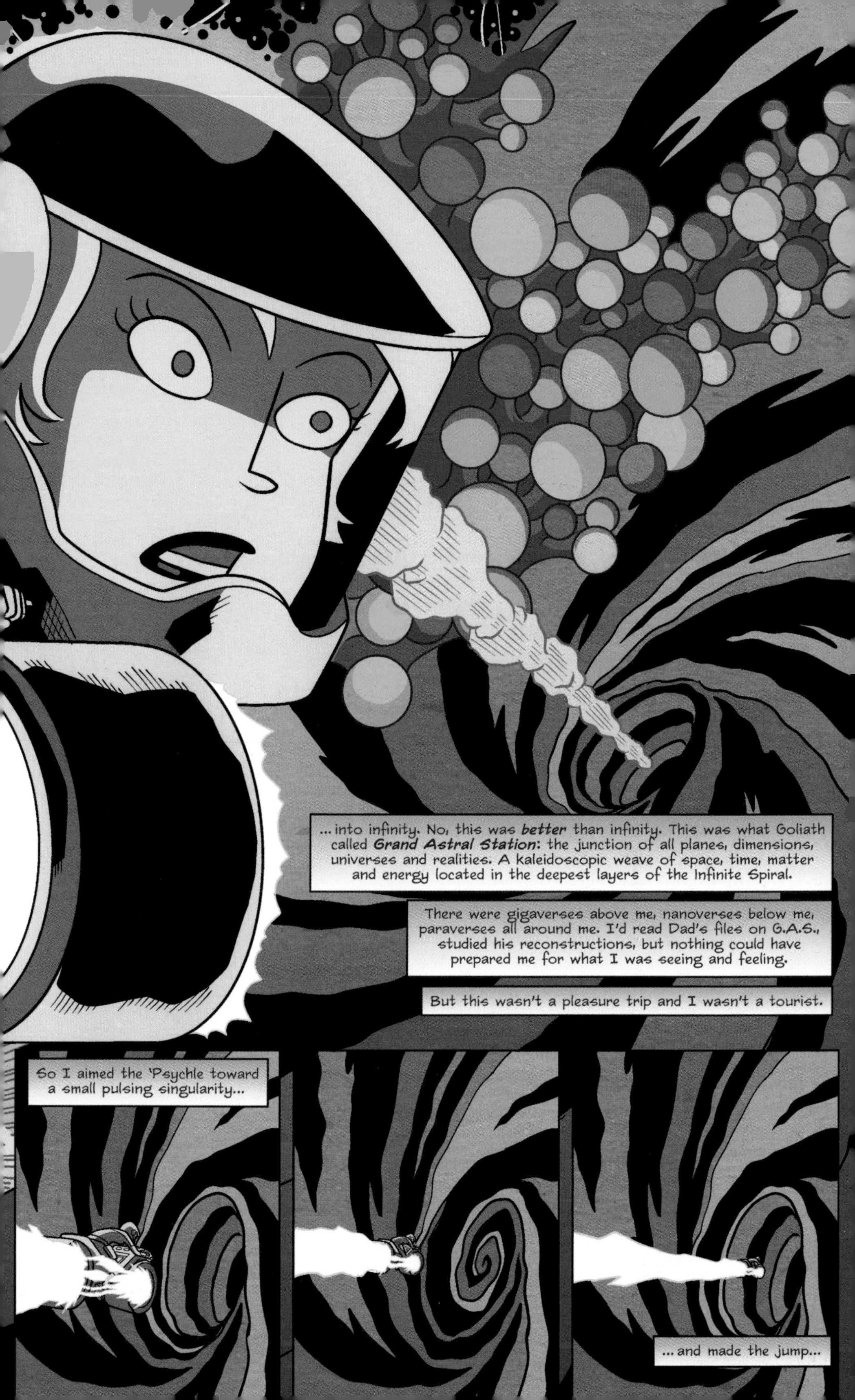
...into infinity. No, this was better than infinity. This was what Goliath called Grand Astral Station: the junction of all planes, dimensions, universes and realities. A kaleidoscopic weave of space, time, matter and energy located in the deepest layers of the Infinite Spiral.
There were gigaverses above me, nanoverses below me, paraverses all around me. I'd read Dad's files on G.A.S., studied his reconstructions, but nothing could have prepared me for what I was seeing and feeling.
But this wasn't a pleasure trip and I wasn't a tourist.
So I aimed the 'Psychle toward a small pulsing singularity...
...and made the jump...

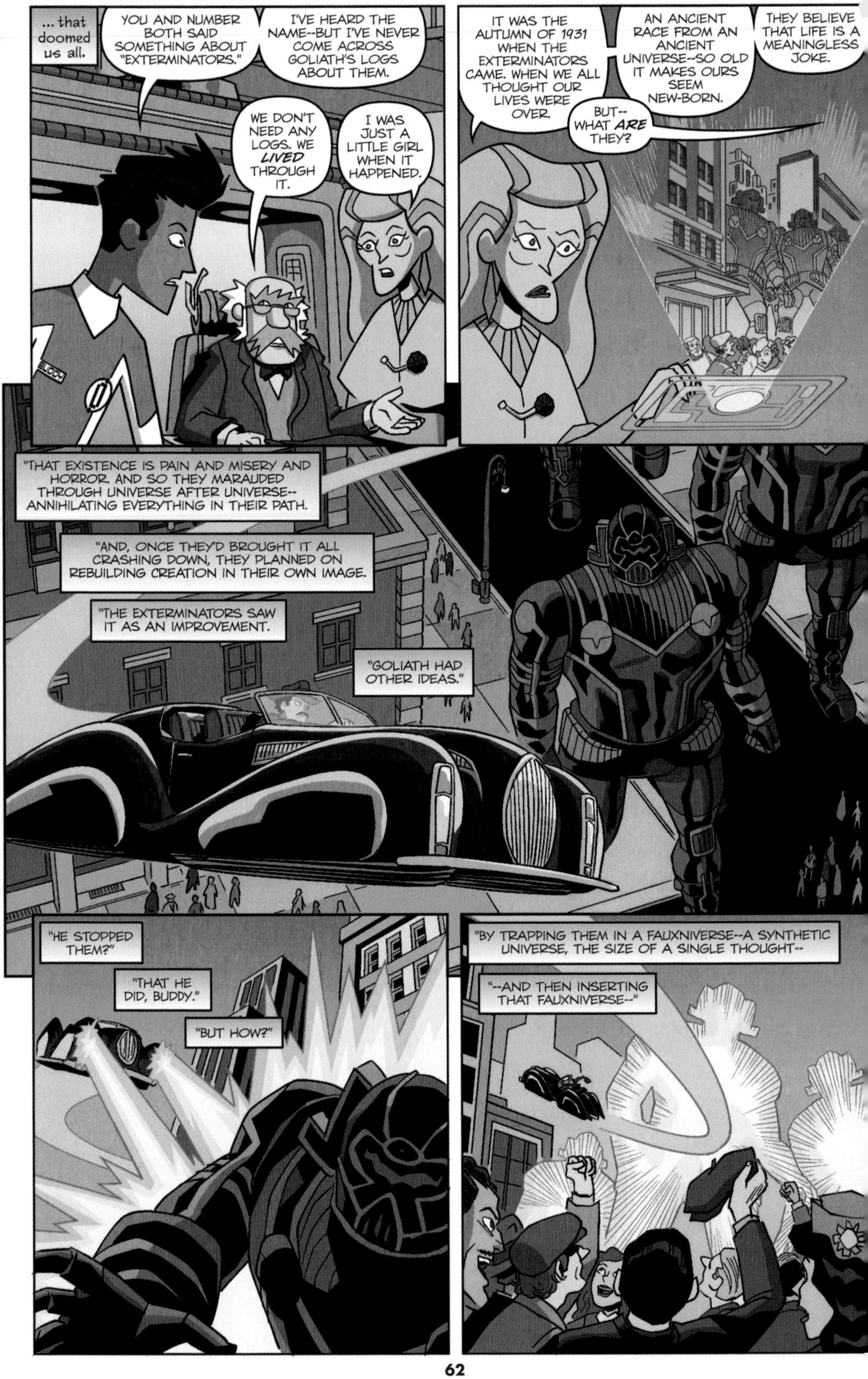
... that doomed us all.
YOU AND NUMBER BOTH SAID SOMETHING ABOUT "EXTERMINATORS."
I'VE HEARD THE NAME--BUT I'VE NEVER COME ACROSS GOLIATH'S LOGS ABOUT THEM.
WE DON'T NEED ANY LOGS. WE *LIVED* THROUGH IT.
I WAS JUST A LITTLE GIRL WHEN IT HAPPENED.
BUDDY
IT WAS THE AUTUMN OF 1931 WHEN THE EXTERMINATORS CAME. WHEN WE ALL THOUGHT OUR LIVES WERE OVER.
BUT-- WHAT *ARE* THEY?
AN ANCIENT RACE FROM AN ANCIENT UNIVERSE--SO OLD IT MAKES OURS SEEM NEW-BORN.
THEY BELIEVE THAT LIFE IS A MEANINGLESS JOKE.
"THAT EXISTENCE IS PAIN AND MISERY AND HORROR. AND SO THEY MARAUDED THROUGH UNIVERSE AFTER UNIVERSE-- ANNIHILATING EVERYTHING IN THEIR PATH.
"AND, ONCE THEY'D BROUGHT IT ALL CRASHING DOWN, THEY PLANNED ON REBUILDING CREATION IN THEIR OWN IMAGE.
"THE EXTERMINATORS SAW IT AS AN IMPROVEMENT.
"GOLIATH HAD OTHER IDEAS."
"HE STOPPED THEM?"
"THAT HE DID, BUDDY."
"BUT HOW?"
"BY TRAPPING THEM IN A FAUXNIVERSE--A SYNTHETIC UNIVERSE, THE SIZE OF A SINGLE THOUGHT--
"--AND THEN INSERTING THAT FAUXNIVERSE--"

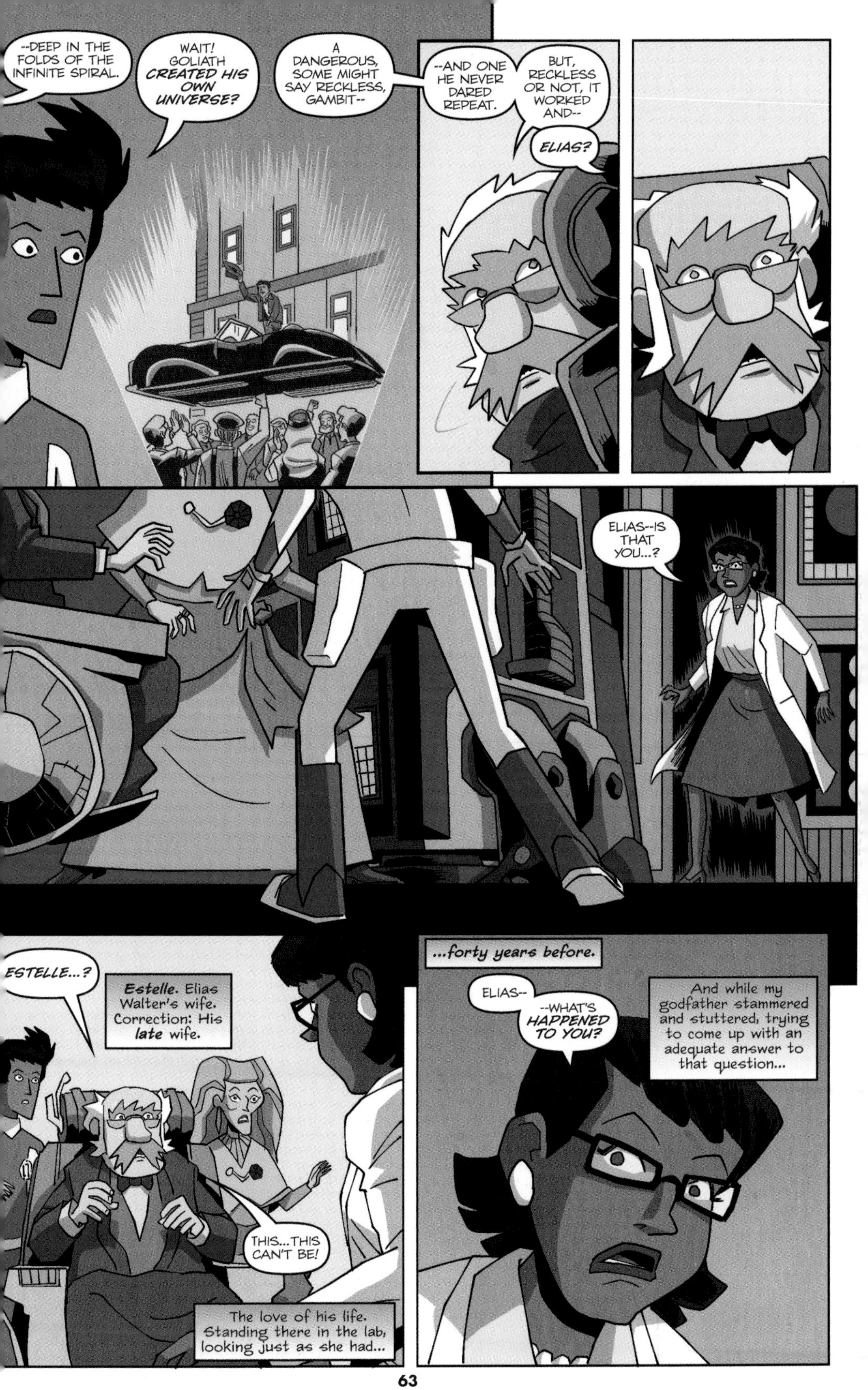
--DEEP IN THE FOLDS OF THE INFINITE SPIRAL.
WAIT! GOLIATH CREATED HIS OWN UNIVERSE?
A DANGEROUS, SOME MIGHT SAY RECKLESS, GAMBIT--
--AND ONE HE NEVER DARED REPEAT.
BUT, RECKLESS OR NOT, IT WORKED AND--
ELIAS?
ELIAS--IS THAT YOU...?
ESTELLE...?
Estelle. Elias Walter's wife. Correction: His late wife.
THIS...THIS CAN'T BE!
The love of his life. Standing there in the lab, looking just as she had...
...forty years before.
ELIAS--
--WHAT'S HAPPENED TO YOU?
And while my godfather stammered and stuttered, trying to come up with an adequate answer to that question...

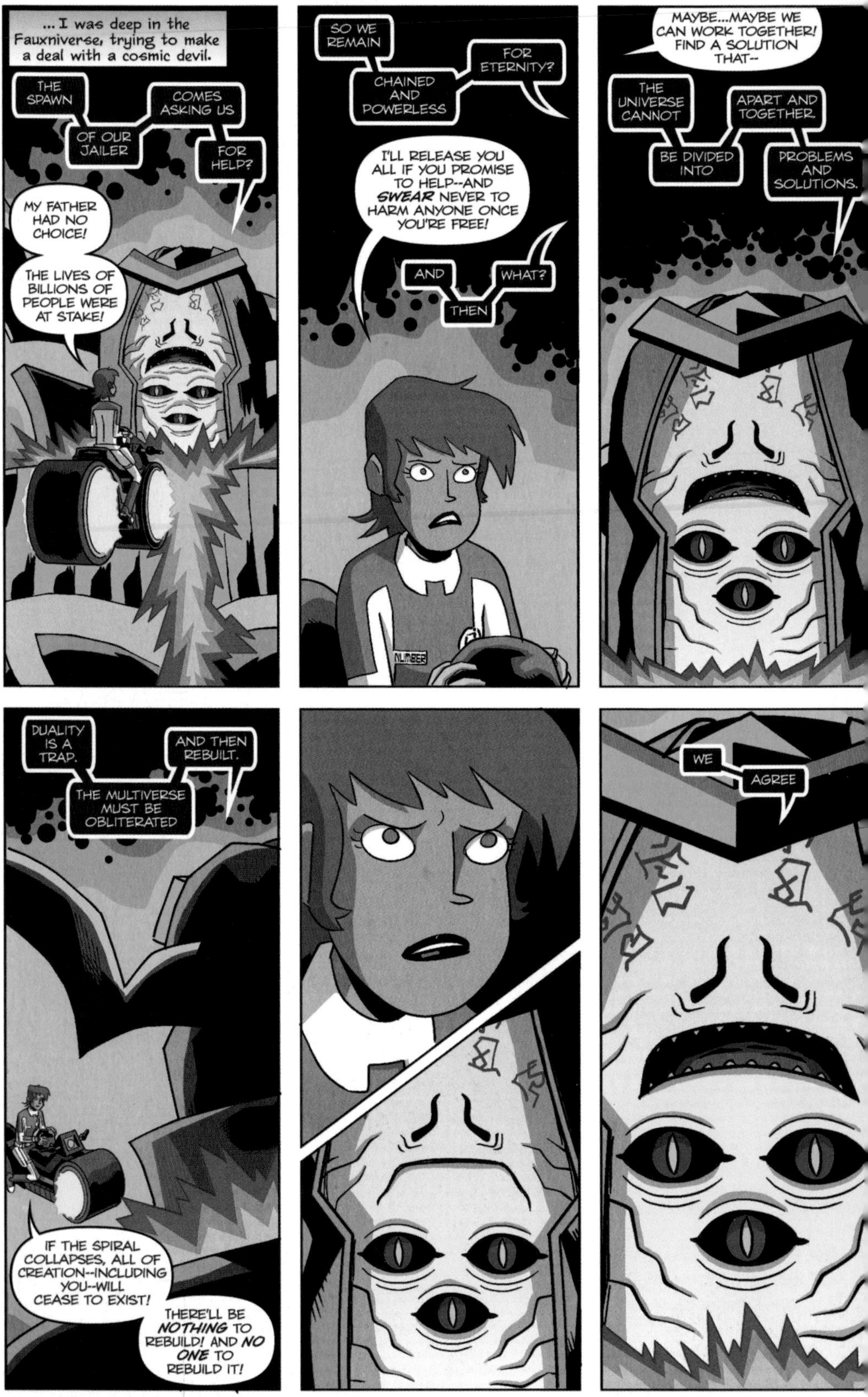

...I was deep in the Fauxniverse, trying to make a deal with a cosmic devil.
THE SPAWN
OF OUR JAILER
COMES ASKING US
FOR HELP?
MY FATHER HAD NO CHOICE!
THE LIVES OF BILLIONS OF PEOPLE WERE AT STAKE!
SO WE REMAIN
CHAINED AND POWERLESS
FOR ETERNITY?
I'LL RELEASE YOU ALL IF YOU PROMISE TO HELP--AND SWEAR NEVER TO HARM ANYONE ONCE YOU'RE FREE!
AND
THEN
WHAT?
NUMBER
MAYBE...MAYBE WE CAN WORK TOGETHER! FIND A SOLUTION THAT--
THE UNIVERSE CANNOT
BE DIVIDED INTO
APART AND TOGETHER
PROBLEMS AND SOLUTIONS.
DUALITY IS A TRAP.
THE MULTIVERSE MUST BE OBLITERATED
AND THEN REBUILT.
IF THE SPIRAL COLLAPSES, ALL OF CREATION--INCLUDING YOU--WILL CEASE TO EXIST!
THERE'LL BE NOTHING TO REBUILD! AND NO ONE TO REBUILD IT!
WE
AGREE

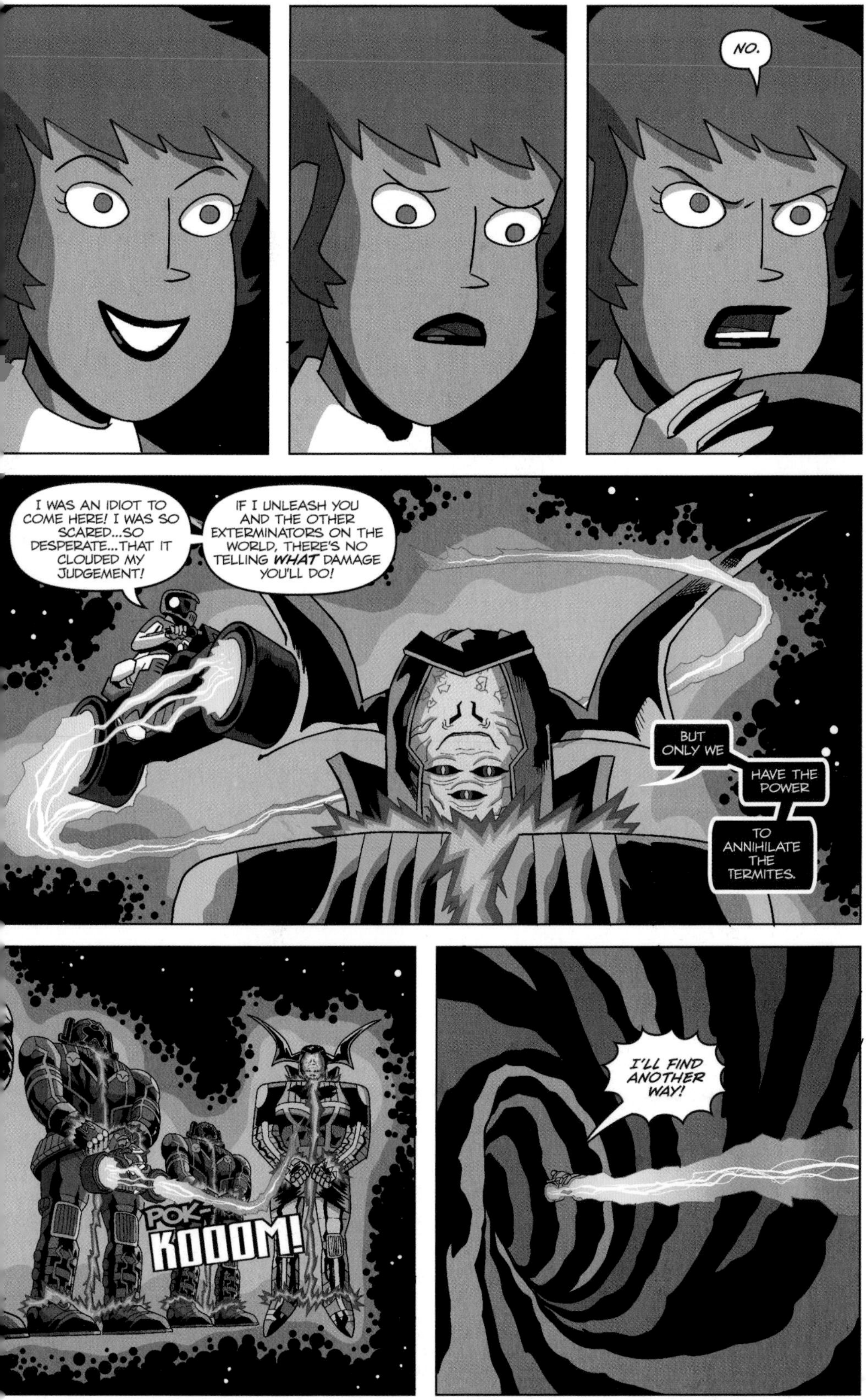
NO.
I WAS AN IDIOT TO COME HERE! I WAS SO SCARED...SO DESPERATE...THAT IT CLOUDED MY JUDGEMENT!
IF I UNLEASH YOU AND THE OTHER EXTERMINATORS ON THE WORLD, THERE'S NO TELLING WHAT DAMAGE YOU'LL DO!
BUT ONLY WE
HAVE THE POWER
TO ANNIHILATE THE TERMITES.
POK-KOOOM!
I'LL FIND ANOTHER WAY!

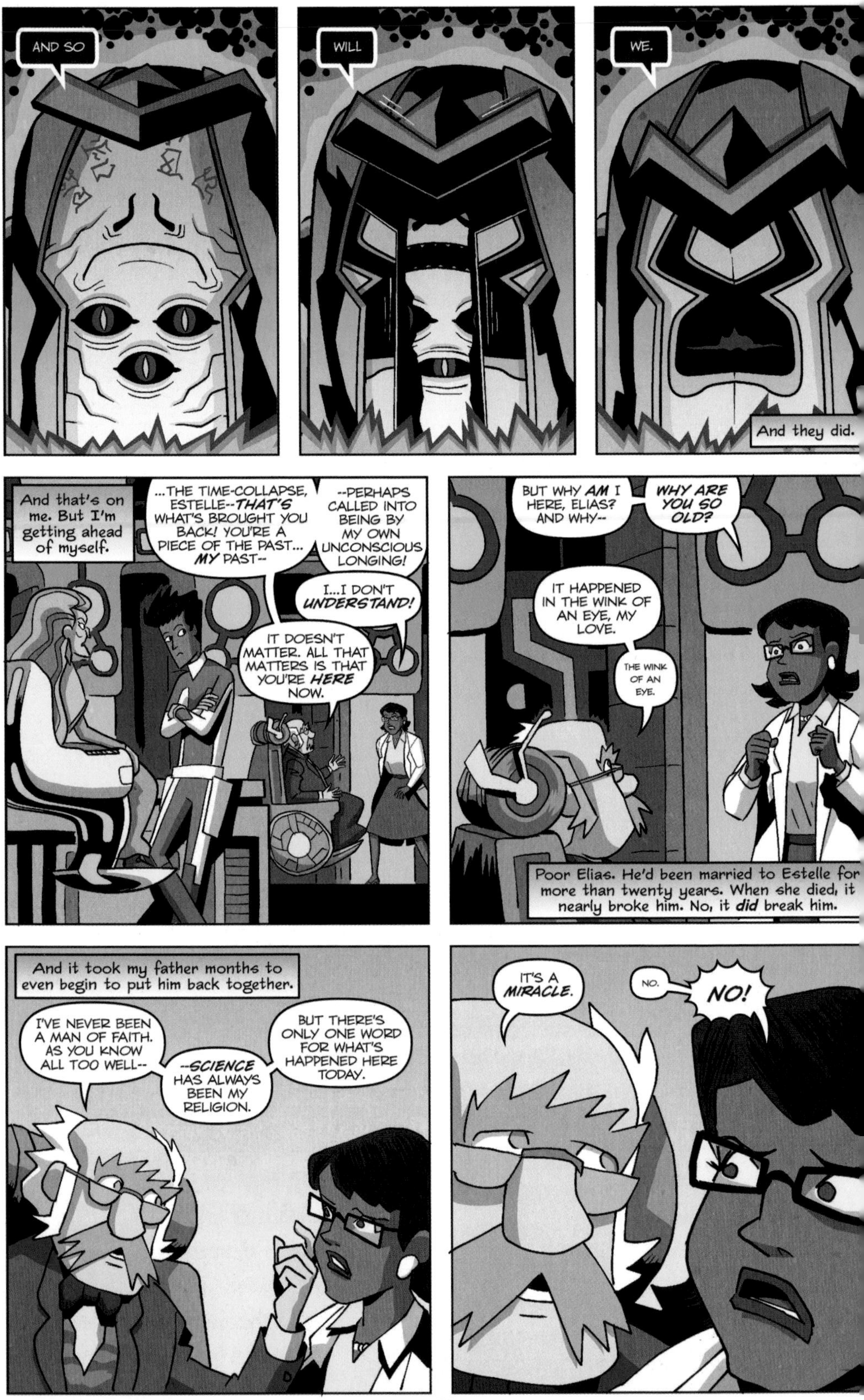
AND SO
WILL
WE.
And they did.
And that's on me. But I'm getting ahead of myself.
...THE TIME-COLLAPSE, ESTELLE--THAT'S WHAT'S BROUGHT YOU BACK! YOU'RE A PIECE OF THE PAST... MY PAST--
--PERHAPS CALLED INTO BEING BY MY OWN UNCONSCIOUS LONGING!
I...I DON'T UNDERSTAND!
IT DOESN'T MATTER. ALL THAT MATTERS IS THAT YOU'RE HERE NOW.
BUT WHY AM I HERE, ELIAS? AND WHY--
WHY ARE YOU SO OLD?
IT HAPPENED IN THE WINK OF AN EYE, MY LOVE.
THE WINK OF AN EYE.
Poor Elias. He'd been married to Estelle for more than twenty years. When she died, it nearly broke him. No, it did break him.
And it took my father months to even begin to put him back together.
I'VE NEVER BEEN A MAN OF FAITH. AS YOU KNOW ALL TOO WELL--
--SCIENCE HAS ALWAYS BEEN MY RELIGION.
BUT THERE'S ONLY ONE WORD FOR WHAT'S HAPPENED HERE TODAY.
IT'S A MIRACLE.
NO.
NO!

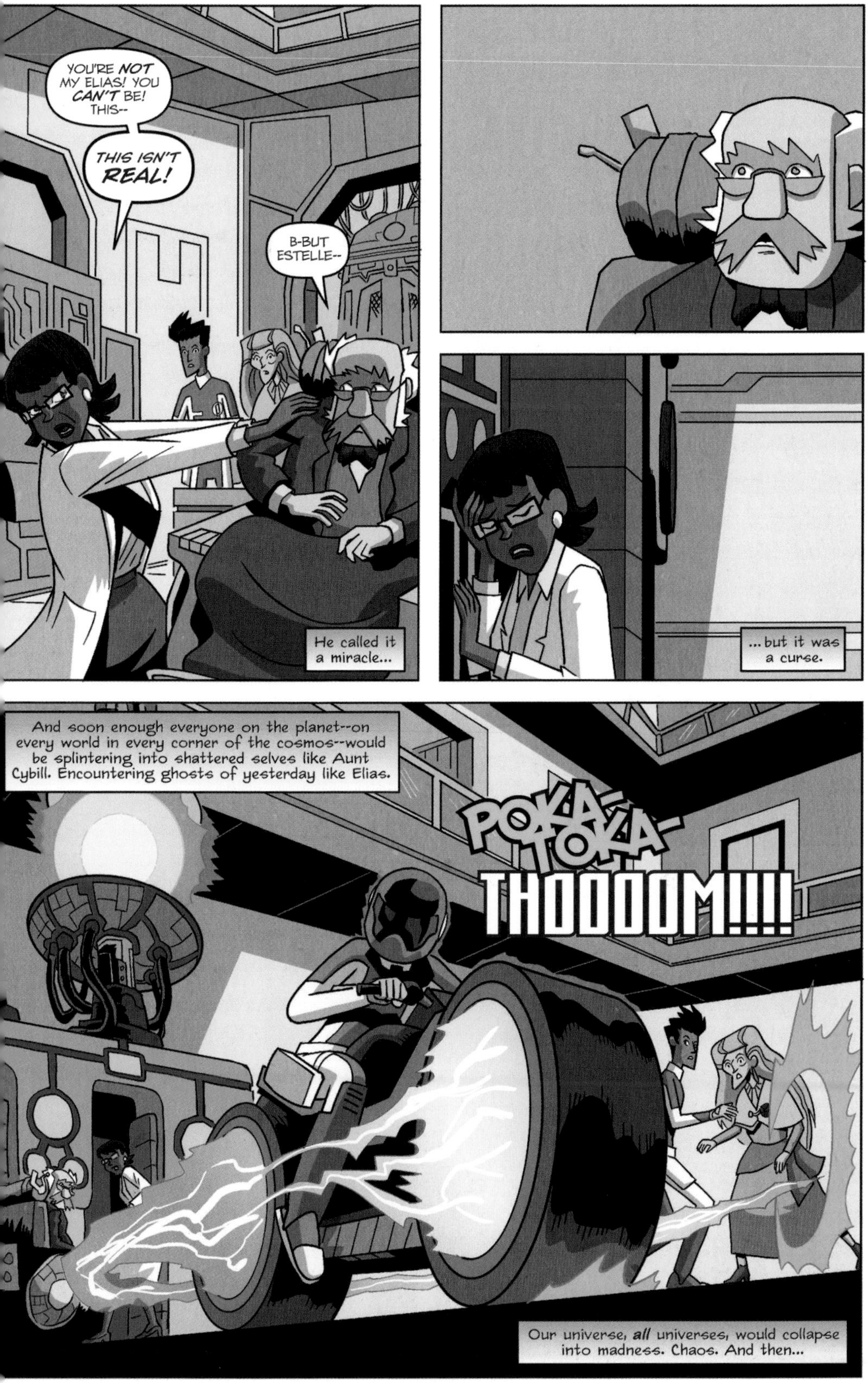
YOU'RE NOT MY ELIAS! YOU CAN'T BE! THIS--
THIS ISN'T REAL!
B-BUT ESTELLE--
He called it a miracle...
...but it was a curse.
And soon enough everyone on the planet--on every world in every corner of the cosmos--would be splintering into shattered selves like Aunt Cybill. Encountering ghosts of yesterday like Elias.
POKA-TOKA-THOOOOM!!!!
Our universe, all universes, would collapse into madness. Chaos. And then...

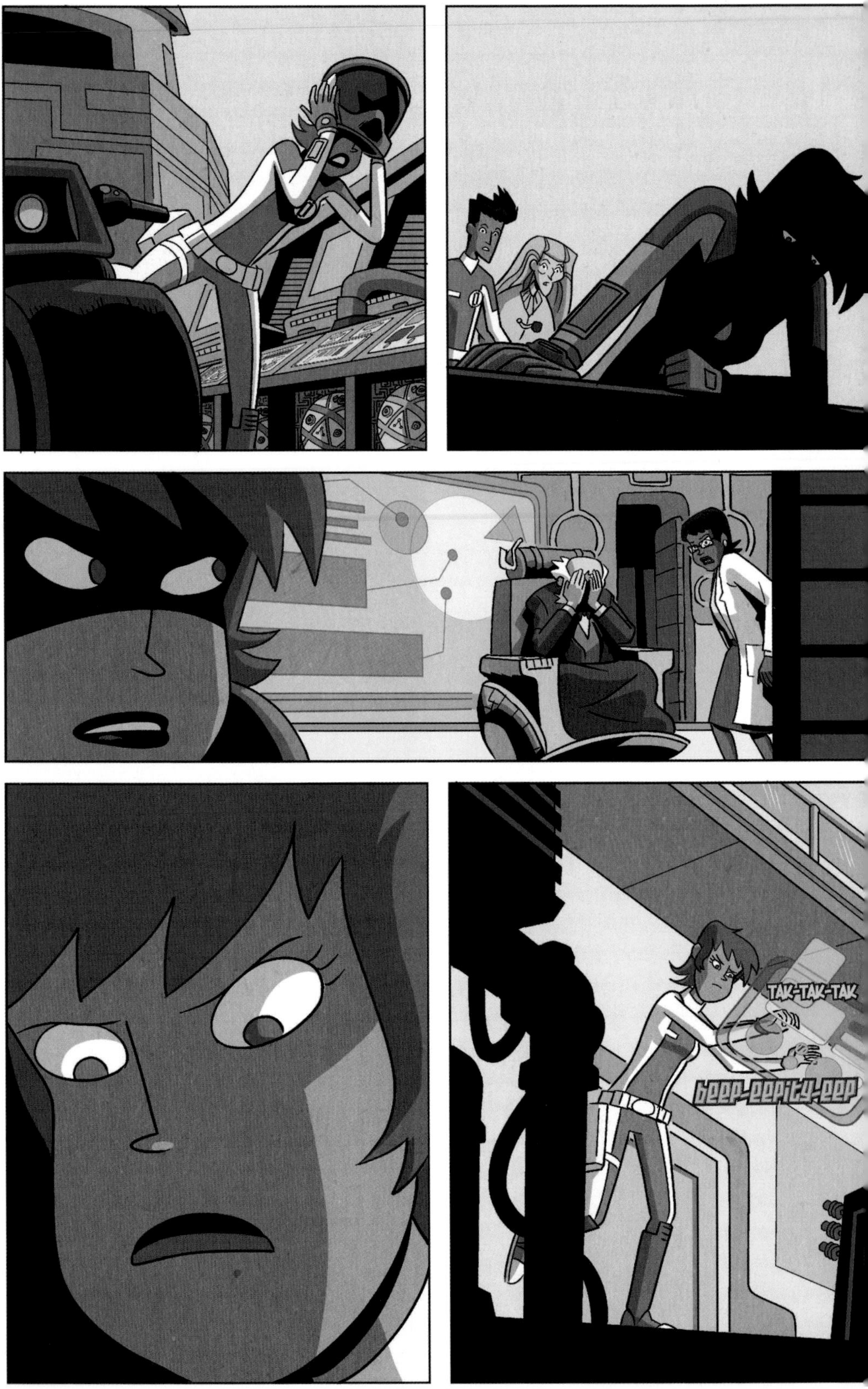
TAK-TAK-TAK
beep-eepity-eep

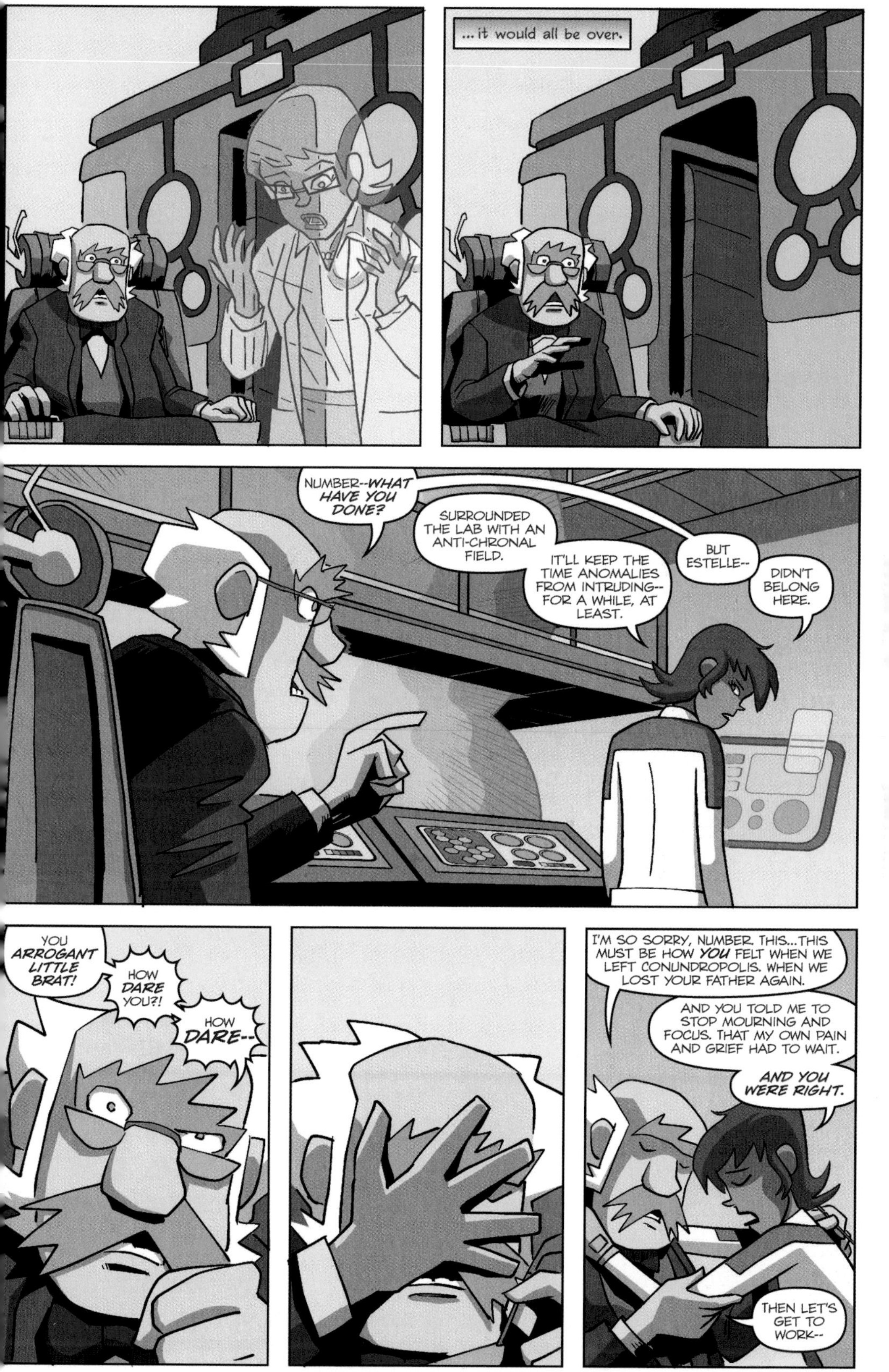
...it would all be over.
NUMBER--WHAT HAVE YOU DONE?
SURROUNDED THE LAB WITH AN ANTI-CHRONAL FIELD.
IT'LL KEEP THE TIME ANOMALIES FROM INTRUDING--FOR A WHILE, AT LEAST.
BUT ESTELLE--
DIDN'T BELONG HERE.
YOU ARROGANT LITTLE BRAT!
HOW DARE YOU?!
HOW DARE--
I'M SO SORRY, NUMBER. THIS...THIS MUST BE HOW YOU FELT WHEN WE LEFT CONUNDROPOLIS. WHEN WE LOST YOUR FATHER AGAIN.
AND YOU TOLD ME TO STOP MOURNING AND FOCUS. THAT MY OWN PAIN AND GRIEF HAD TO WAIT.
AND YOU WERE RIGHT.
THEN LET'S GET TO WORK--

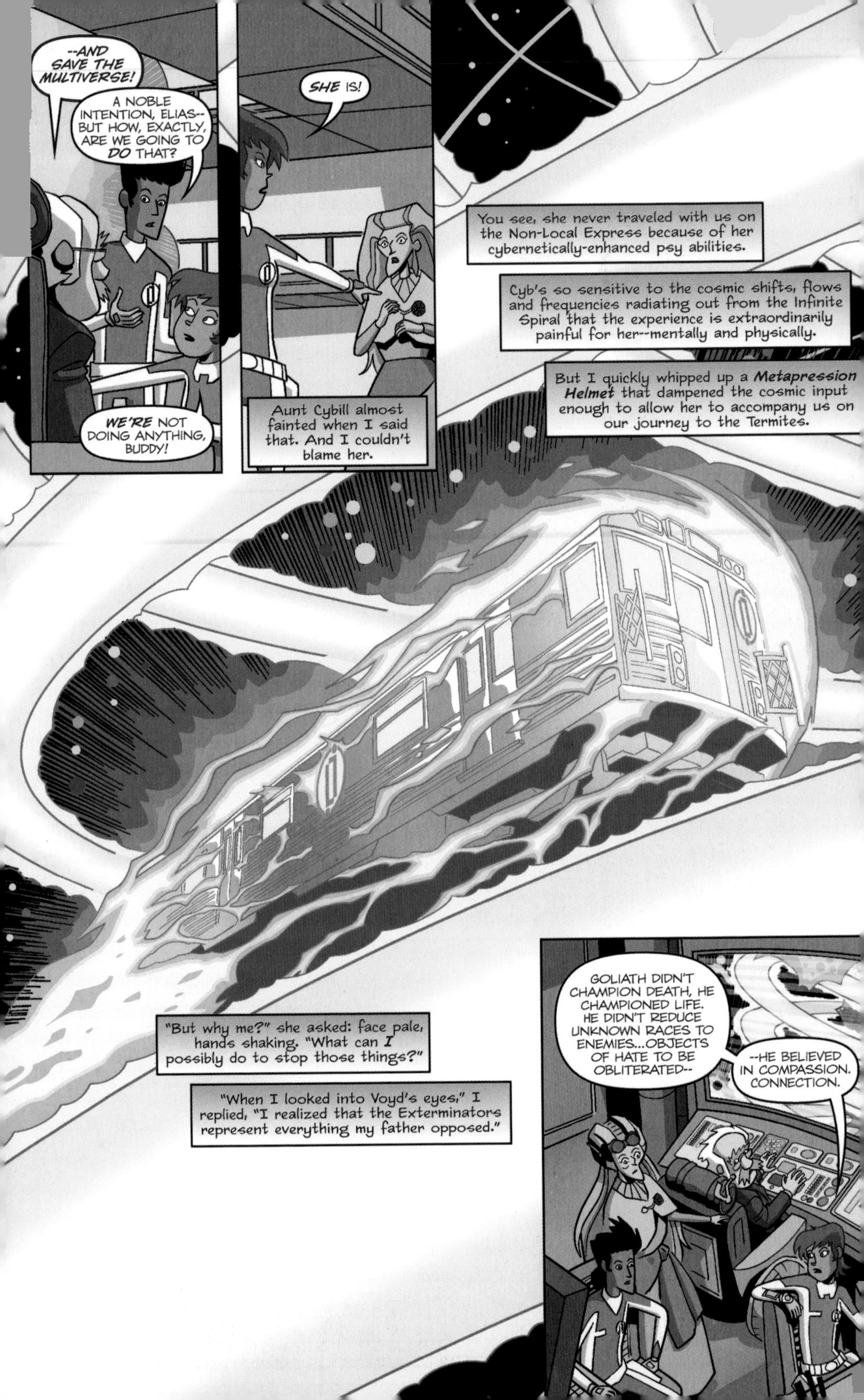
--AND SAVE THE MULTIVERSE!
A NOBLE INTENTION, ELIAS-- BUT HOW, EXACTLY, ARE WE GOING TO DO THAT?
WE'RE NOT DOING ANYTHING, BUDDY!
SHE IS!
Aunt Cybill almost fainted when I said that. And I couldn't blame her.
You see, she never traveled with us on the Non-Local Express because of her cybernetically-enhanced psy abilities.
Cyb's so sensitive to the cosmic shifts, flows and frequencies radiating out from the Infinite Spiral that the experience is extraordinarily painful for her--mentally and physically.
But I quickly whipped up a Metapression Helmet that dampened the cosmic input enough to allow her to accompany us on our journey to the Termites.
"But why me?" she asked: face pale, hands shaking. "What can I possibly do to stop those things?"
"When I looked into Voyd's eyes," I replied, "I realized that the Exterminators represent everything my father opposed."
GOLIATH DIDN'T CHAMPION DEATH, HE CHAMPIONED LIFE. HE DIDN'T REDUCE UNKNOWN RACES TO ENEMIES...OBJECTS OF HATE TO BE OBLITERATED--
--HE BELIEVED IN COMPASSION. CONNECTION.

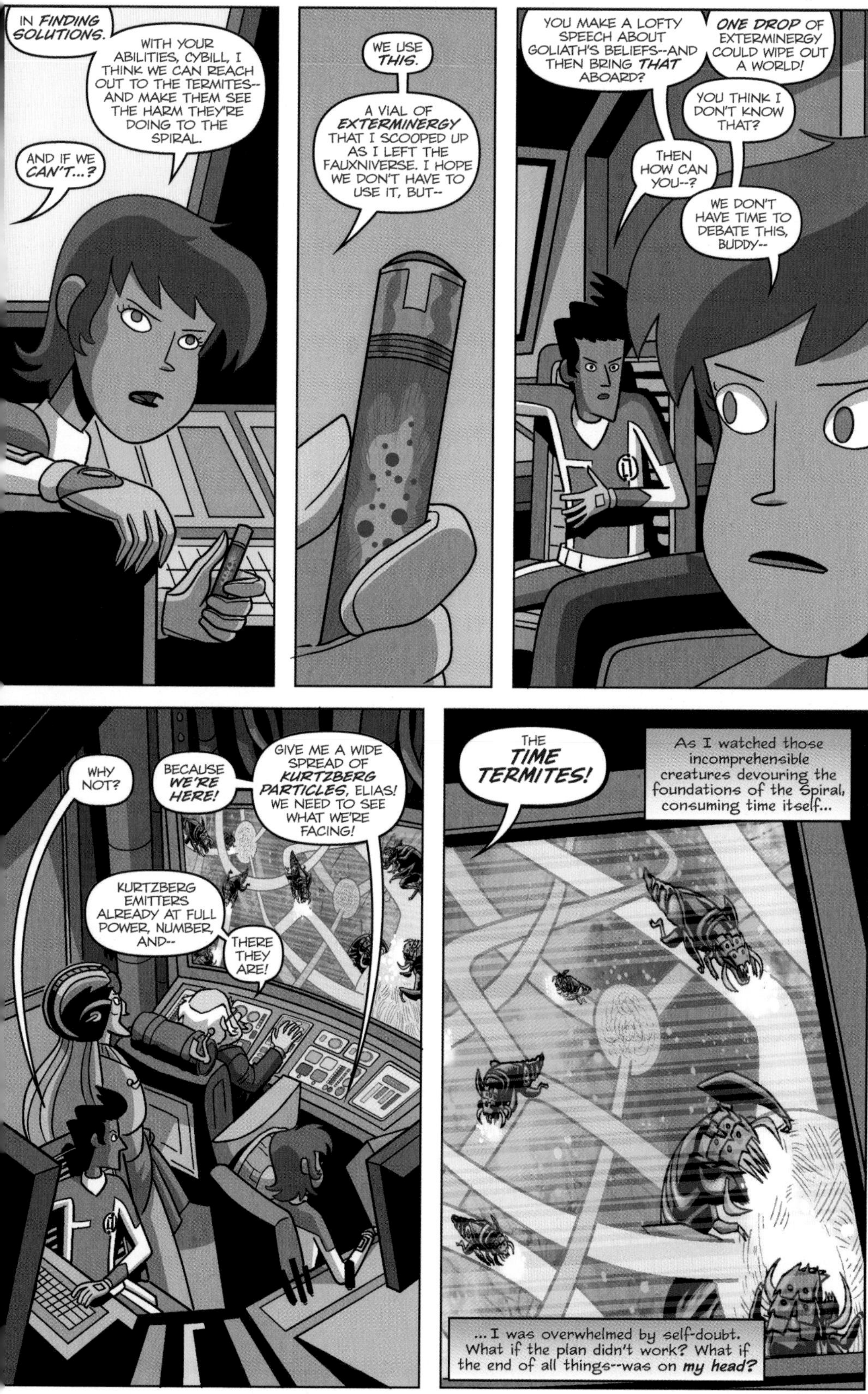
IN FINDING SOLUTIONS.
WITH YOUR ABILITIES, CYBILL, I THINK WE CAN REACH OUT TO THE TERMITES-- AND MAKE THEM SEE THE HARM THEY'RE DOING TO THE SPIRAL.
AND IF WE CAN'T...?
WE USE THIS.
A VIAL OF EXTERMINERGY THAT I SCOOPED UP AS I LEFT THE FAUXNIVERSE. I HOPE WE DON'T HAVE TO USE IT, BUT--
YOU MAKE A LOFTY SPEECH ABOUT GOLIATH'S BELIEFS--AND THEN BRING THAT ABOARD?
ONE DROP OF EXTERMINERGY COULD WIPE OUT A WORLD!
YOU THINK I DON'T KNOW THAT?
THEN HOW CAN YOU--?
WE DON'T HAVE TIME TO DEBATE THIS, BUDDY--
WHY NOT?
BECAUSE WE'RE HERE!
GIVE ME A WIDE SPREAD OF KURTZBERG PARTICLES, ELIAS! WE NEED TO SEE WHAT WE'RE FACING!
KURTZBERG EMITTERS ALREADY AT FULL POWER, NUMBER, AND--
THERE THEY ARE!
THE TIME TERMITES!
As I watched those incomprehensible creatures devouring the foundations of the Spiral, consuming time itself...
...I was overwhelmed by self-doubt. What if the plan didn't work? What if the end of all things--was on my head?

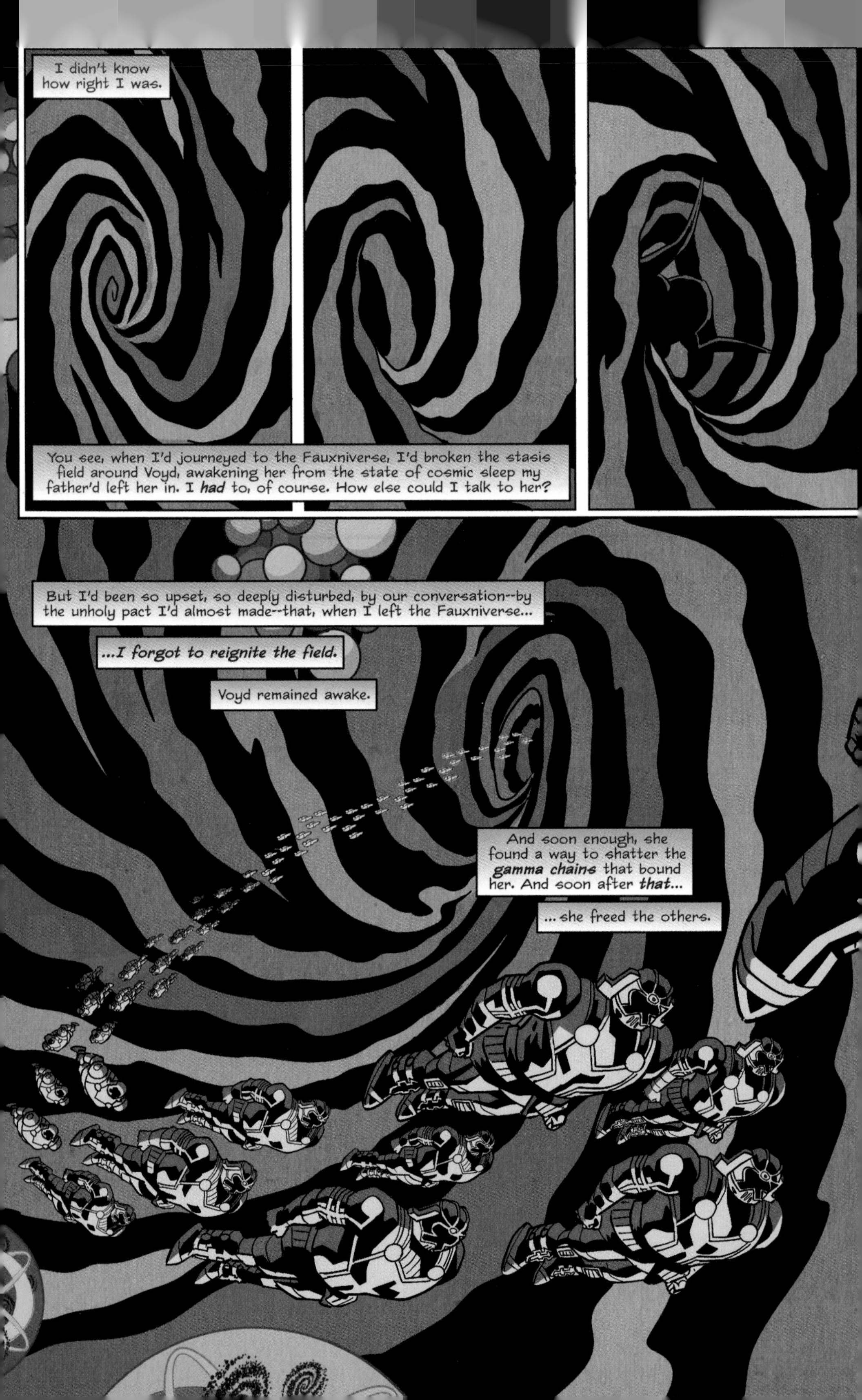
I didn't know how right I was.
You see, when I'd journeyed to the Fauxniverse, I'd broken the stasis field around Voyd, awakening her from the state of cosmic sleep my father'd left her in. I *had* to, of course. How else could I talk to her?
But I'd been so upset, so deeply disturbed, by our conversation--by the unholy pact I'd almost made--that, when I left the Fauxniverse...
...I forgot to reignite the field.
Voyd remained awake.
And soon enough, she found a way to shatter the *gamma chains* that bound her. And soon after *that*...
... she freed the others.

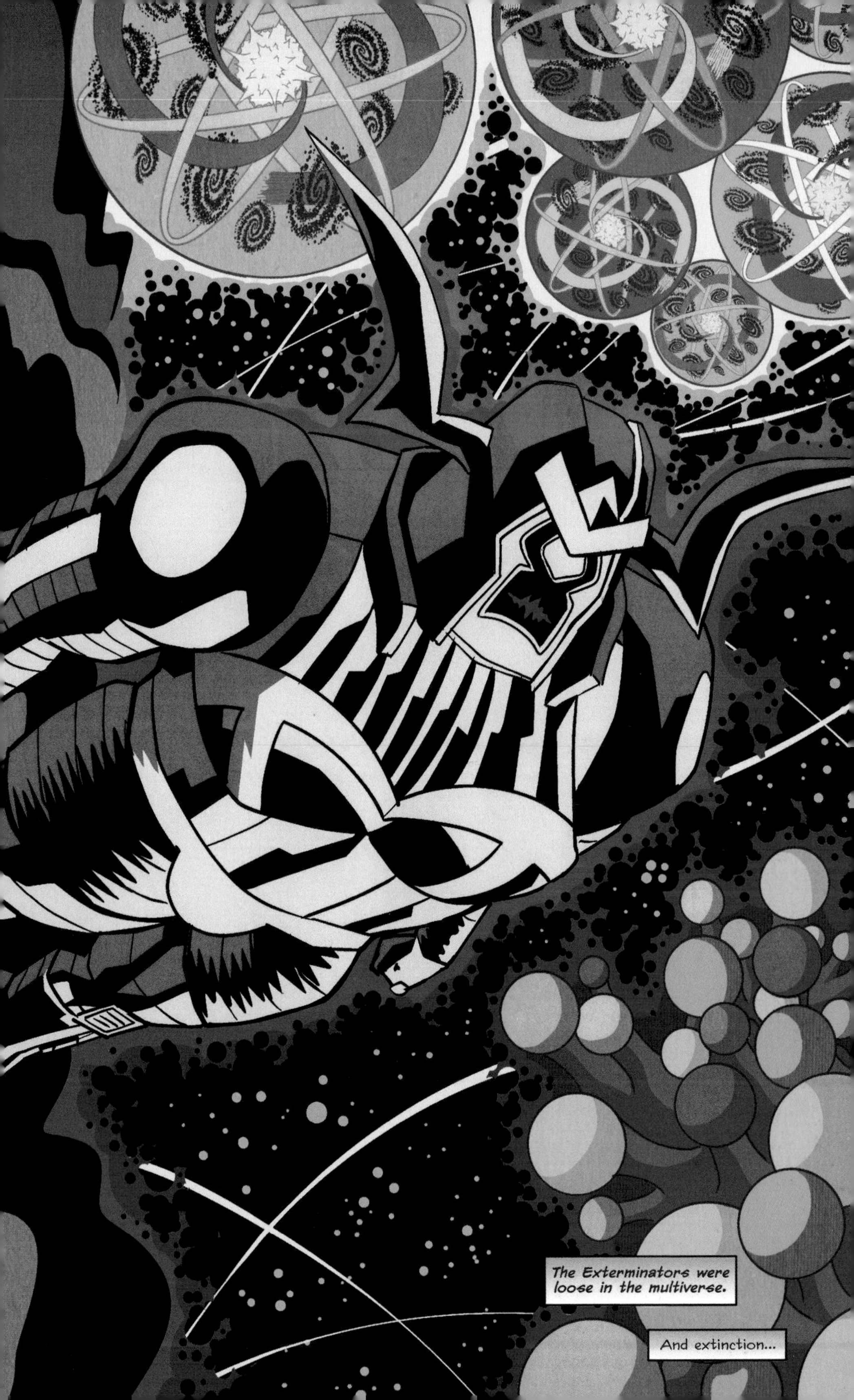
The Exterminators were loose in the multiverse.
And extinction...

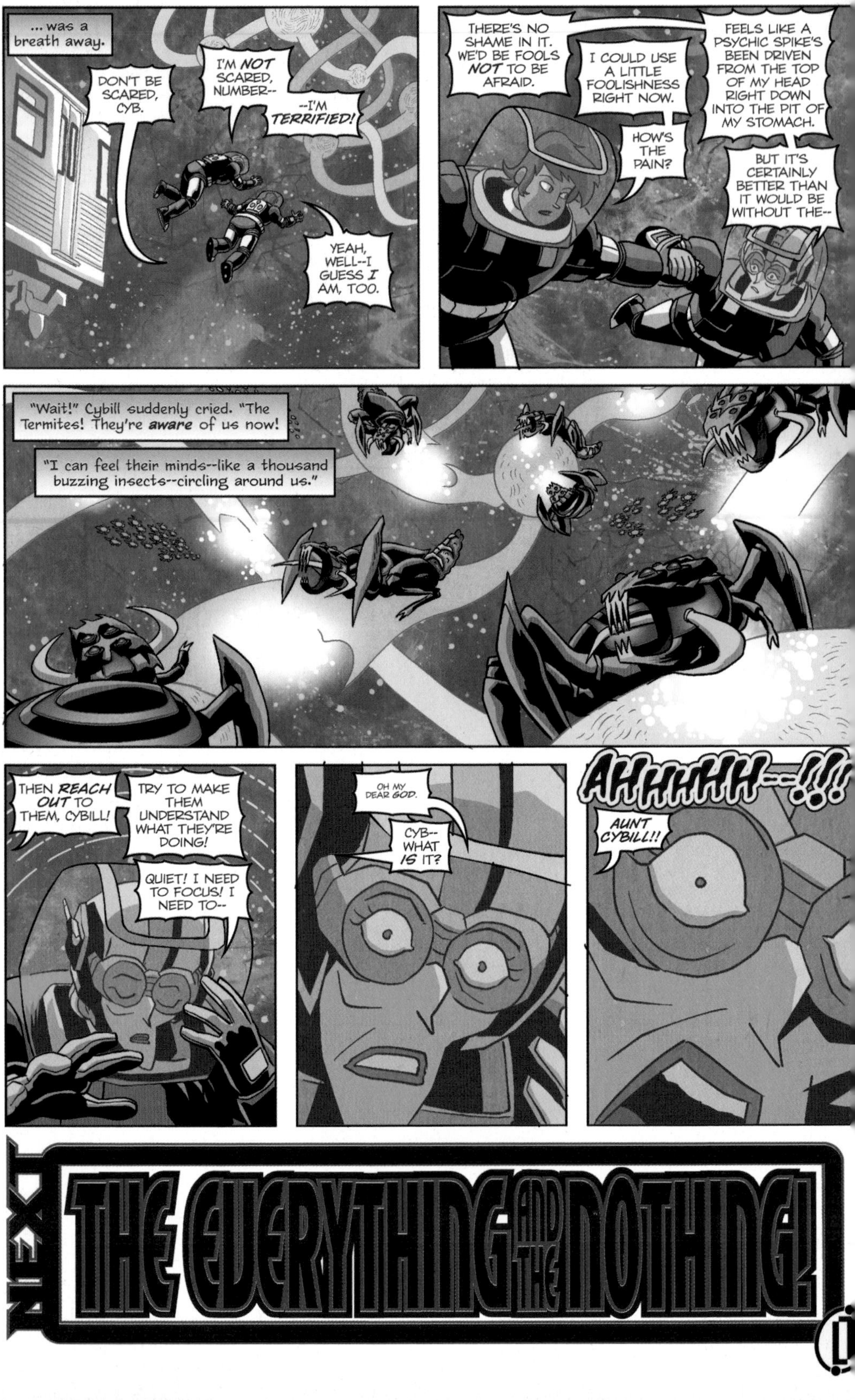
...was a breath away.
DON'T BE SCARED, CYB.
I'M NOT SCARED, NUMBER--
--I'M TERRIFIED!
YEAH, WELL--I GUESS I AM, TOO.
THERE'S NO SHAME IN IT. WE'D BE FOOLS NOT TO BE AFRAID.
I COULD USE A LITTLE FOOLISHNESS RIGHT NOW.
HOW'S THE PAIN?
FEELS LIKE A PSYCHIC SPIKE'S BEEN DRIVEN FROM THE TOP OF MY HEAD RIGHT DOWN INTO THE PIT OF MY STOMACH.
BUT IT'S CERTAINLY BETTER THAN IT WOULD BE WITHOUT THE--
"Wait!" Cybill suddenly cried. "The Termites! They're aware of us now!
"I can feel their minds--like a thousand buzzing insects--circling around us."
THEN REACH OUT TO THEM, CYBILL!
TRY TO MAKE THEM UNDERSTAND WHAT THEY'RE DOING!
QUIET! I NEED TO FOCUS! I NEED TO--
OH MY DEAR GOD.
CYB--WHAT IS IT?
AHHHHHH--!!!
AUNT CYBILL!!
NEXT
THE EVERYTHING AND THE NOTHING!

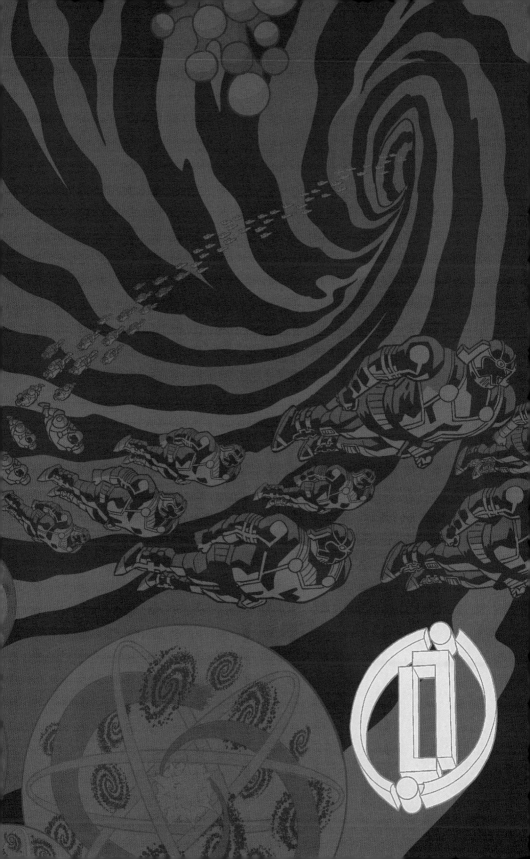

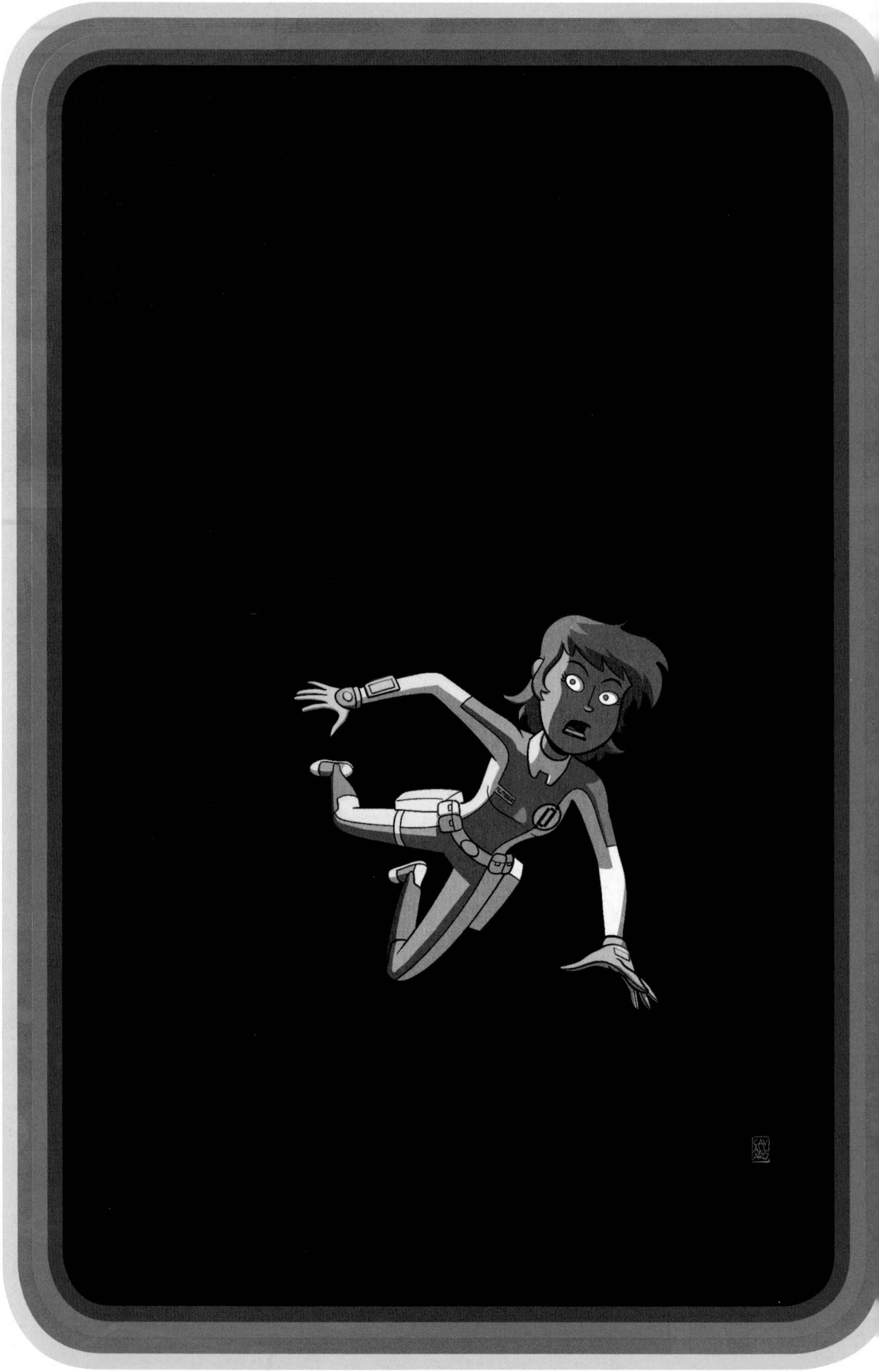

My father's family emigrated from Russia in 1912, when Dad was eight years old.

He wasn't called *Goliath* then--he was just a skinny, sickly dreamer named *Morris Horowitz.*

But soon enough that little boy's brilliance would catapult him out of the Brooklyn tenements and straight toward a destiny...

...even *he* could have never imagined.

Cassandra Caputo, on the other hand, grew up in a comfortable middle class home in Mineola, on Long Island, alongside her twin sister *Cybill.*

Cassie's life was, as she once described it, "excruciatingly normal"-- if someone with an IQ of 184 can be considered normal.

Mom's intelligence wasn't on Goliath's level (really, whose was?), but Dad always said that, when it came to matters of the heart...

...*she* was the real genius in the family.

Goliath was a legend before my mom was even born. The discoveries he'd made, the inventions he'd created, the threats he'd saved us all from...

...but across the Infinite Spiral.

...made him a hero not just in the United States, not just around the world...

In 1971, Cassie was doing graduate work in physics at MIT and Dad was a guest lecturer.

She thought he was awkward and arrogant. He thought she was self-absorbed and shallow.

Within a month they were desperately in love. Two years later they were married. And it wasn't long...

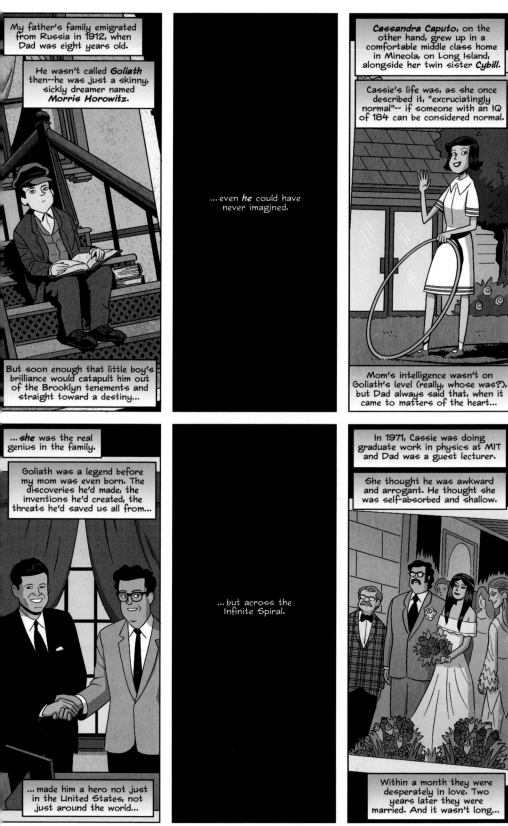

...before Mom climbed aboard the Non-Local Express and joined the **Impossible Incorporated** team.

GOLIATH

Goliath, as you may have noticed, didn't age like the rest of us. And he soon shared his secret (**whatever** it was. To this day I don't know) with my mother.

Were they immortal? No. But they came **close**.

At least for a while.

Cassie s
when **I**
that
bigges

...and
up t

Mom's plan was to be the primary parent till I was four or five, after which she'd climb back aboard the Express for a while...

...and Goliath would take over with me.

That's how it worked out, too.

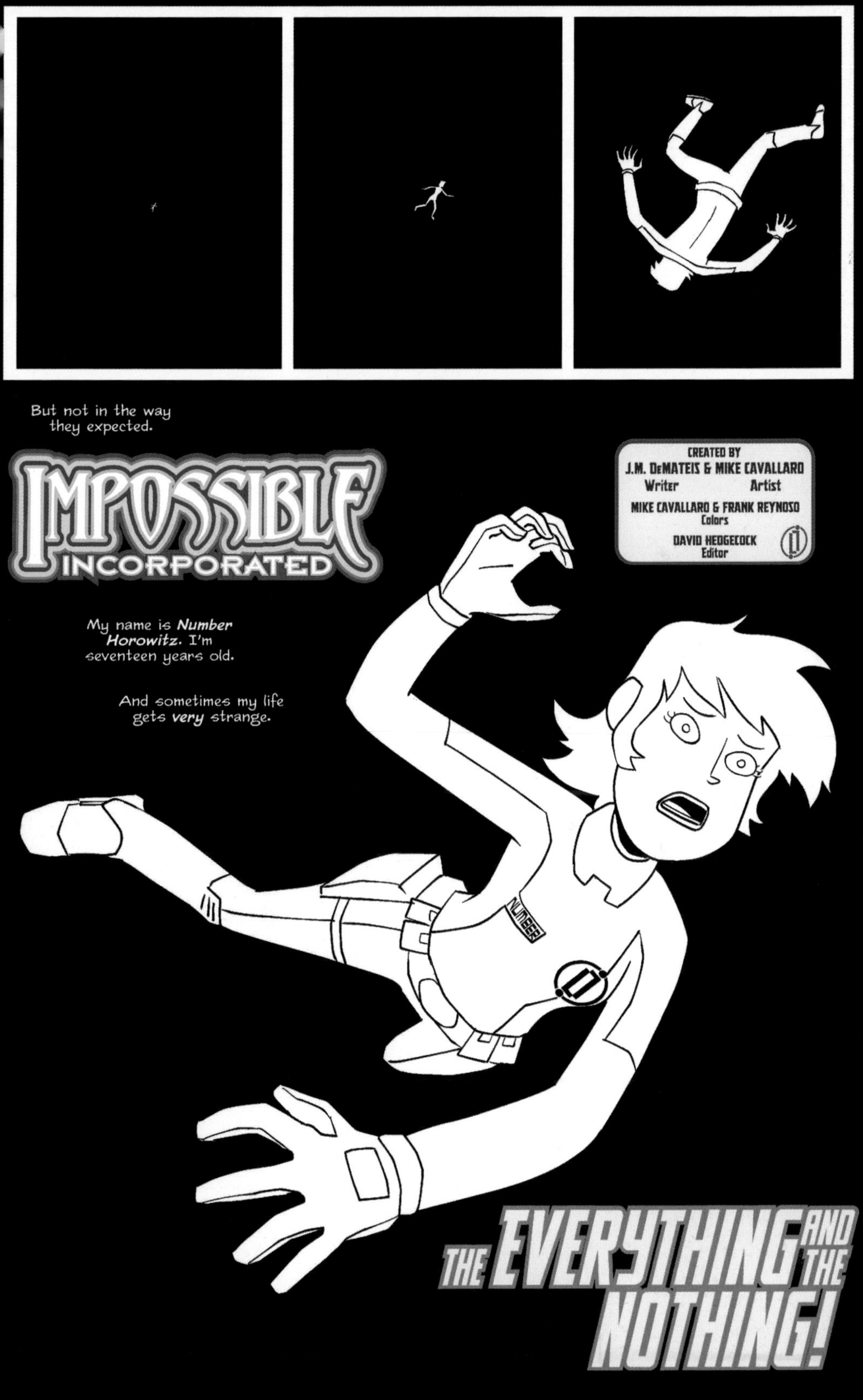

But not in the way they expected.
IMPOSSIBLE INCORPORATED
CREATED BY
J.M. DeMATEIS & MIKE CAVALLARO
Writer Artist
MIKE CAVALLARO & FRANK REYNOSO
Colors
DAVID HEDGECOCK
Editor
My name is Number Horowitz. I'm seventeen years old.
And sometimes my life gets very strange.
NUMBER
THE EVERYTHING AND THE NOTHING!

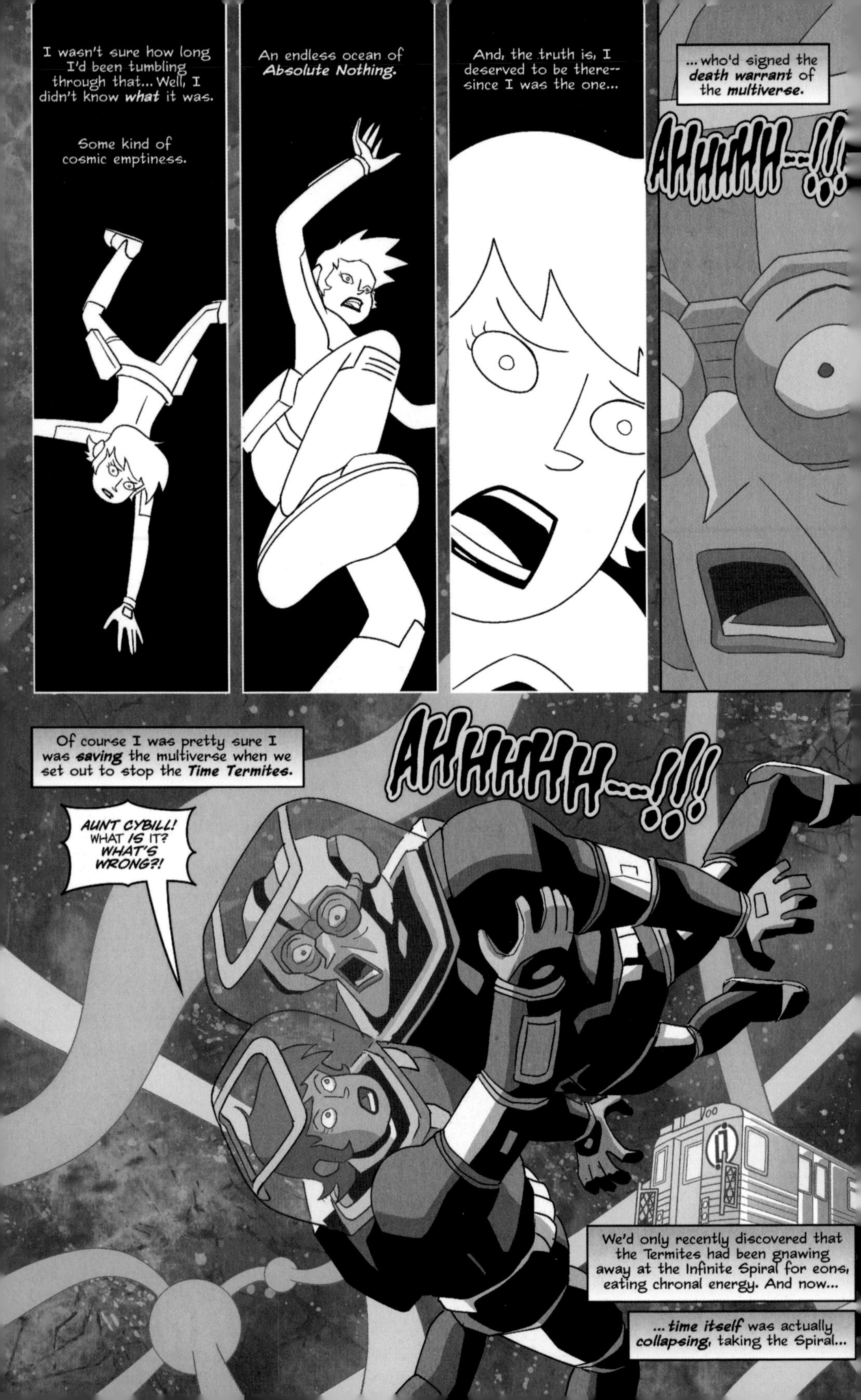
I wasn't sure how long I'd been tumbling through that... Well, I didn't know *what* it was.
Some kind of cosmic emptiness.
An endless ocean of *Absolute Nothing.*
And, the truth is, I deserved to be there--since I was the one...
...who'd signed the *death warrant* of the *multiverse.*
AHHHHH--!!!
Of course I was pretty sure I was *saving* the multiverse when we set out to stop the *Time Termites.*
AHHHHH--!!!
AUNT CYBILL! WHAT *IS* IT? *WHAT'S WRONG?!*
We'd only recently discovered that the Termites had been gnawing away at the Infinite Spiral for eons, eating chronal energy. And now...
...*time itself* was actually *collapsing*, taking the Spiral...

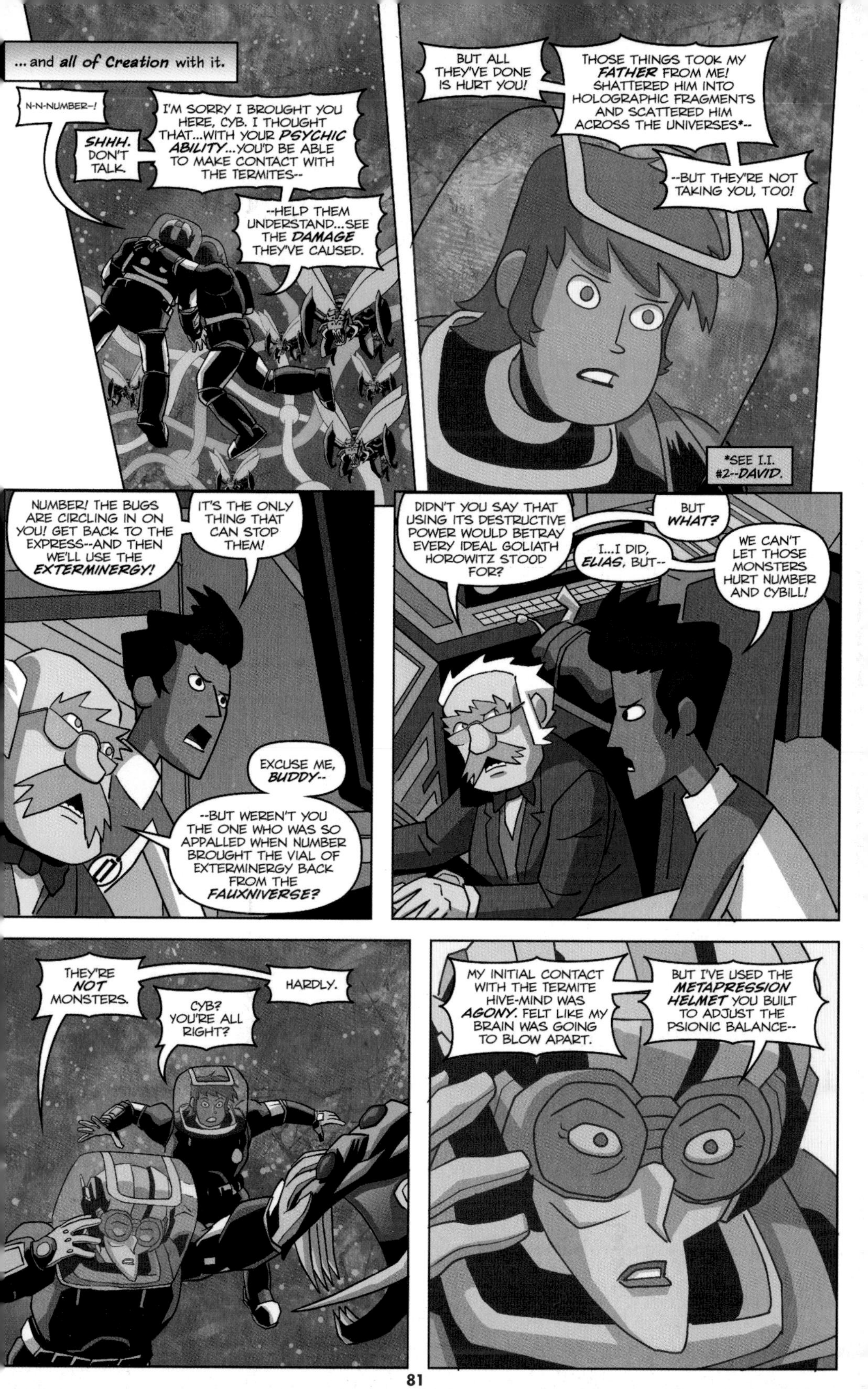
... and all of Creation with it.
N-N-NUMBER--!
SHHH. DON'T TALK.
I'M SORRY I BROUGHT YOU HERE, CYB. I THOUGHT THAT...WITH YOUR PSYCHIC ABILITY...YOU'D BE ABLE TO MAKE CONTACT WITH THE TERMITES--
--HELP THEM UNDERSTAND...SEE THE DAMAGE THEY'VE CAUSED.
BUT ALL THEY'VE DONE IS HURT YOU!
THOSE THINGS TOOK MY FATHER FROM ME! SHATTERED HIM INTO HOLOGRAPHIC FRAGMENTS AND SCATTERED HIM ACROSS THE UNIVERSES*--
--BUT THEY'RE NOT TAKING YOU, TOO!
*SEE I.I. #2--DAVID.
NUMBER! THE BUGS ARE CIRCLING IN ON YOU! GET BACK TO THE EXPRESS--AND THEN WE'LL USE THE EXTERMINERGY!
IT'S THE ONLY THING THAT CAN STOP THEM!
EXCUSE ME, BUDDY--
--BUT WEREN'T YOU THE ONE WHO WAS SO APPALLED WHEN NUMBER BROUGHT THE VIAL OF EXTERMINERGY BACK FROM THE FAUXNIVERSE?
DIDN'T YOU SAY THAT USING ITS DESTRUCTIVE POWER WOULD BETRAY EVERY IDEAL GOLIATH HOROWITZ STOOD FOR?
I...I DID, ELIAS, BUT--
BUT WHAT?
WE CAN'T LET THOSE MONSTERS HURT NUMBER AND CYBILL!
THEY'RE NOT MONSTERS.
HARDLY.
CYB? YOU'RE ALL RIGHT?
MY INITIAL CONTACT WITH THE TERMITE HIVE-MIND WAS AGONY. FELT LIKE MY BRAIN WAS GOING TO BLOW APART.
BUT I'VE USED THE METAPRESSION HELMET YOU BUILT TO ADJUST THE PSIONIC BALANCE--

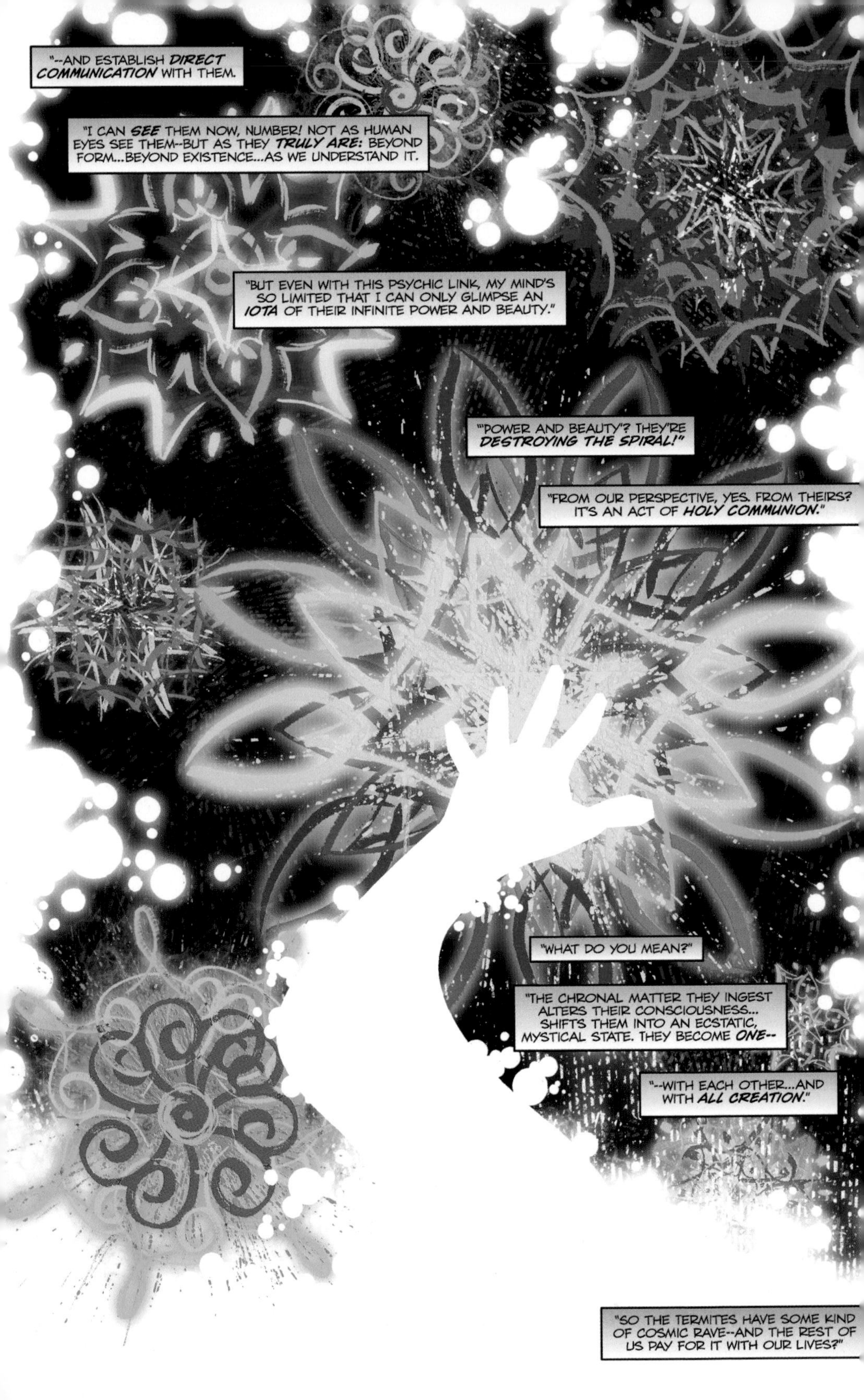
"--AND ESTABLISH DIRECT COMMUNICATION WITH THEM.
"I CAN SEE THEM NOW, NUMBER! NOT AS HUMAN EYES SEE THEM--BUT AS THEY TRULY ARE: BEYOND FORM...BEYOND EXISTENCE...AS WE UNDERSTAND IT.
"BUT EVEN WITH THIS PSYCHIC LINK, MY MIND'S SO LIMITED THAT I CAN ONLY GLIMPSE AN IOTA OF THEIR INFINITE POWER AND BEAUTY."
"'POWER AND BEAUTY'? THEY'RE DESTROYING THE SPIRAL!"
"FROM OUR PERSPECTIVE, YES. FROM THEIRS? IT'S AN ACT OF HOLY COMMUNION."
"WHAT DO YOU MEAN?"
"THE CHRONAL MATTER THEY INGEST ALTERS THEIR CONSCIOUSNESS... SHIFTS THEM INTO AN ECSTATIC, MYSTICAL STATE. THEY BECOME ONE--
"--WITH EACH OTHER...AND WITH ALL CREATION."
"SO THE TERMITES HAVE SOME KIND OF COSMIC RAVE--AND THE REST OF US PAY FOR IT WITH OUR LIVES?"

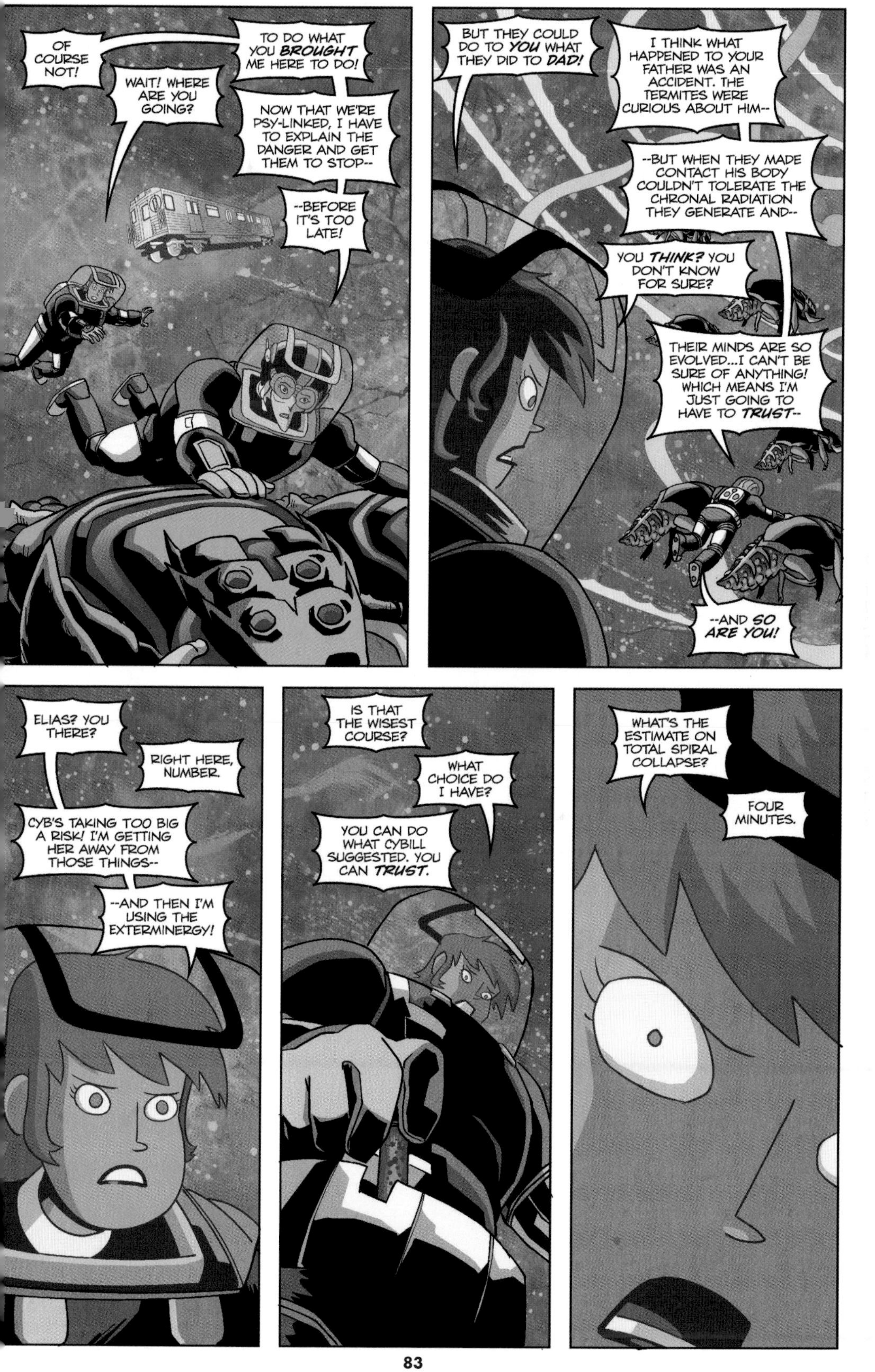
OF COURSE NOT!
TO DO WHAT YOU BROUGHT ME HERE TO DO!
WAIT! WHERE ARE YOU GOING?
NOW THAT WE'RE PSY-LINKED, I HAVE TO EXPLAIN THE DANGER AND GET THEM TO STOP--
--BEFORE IT'S TOO LATE!
BUT THEY COULD DO TO YOU WHAT THEY DID TO DAD!
I THINK WHAT HAPPENED TO YOUR FATHER WAS AN ACCIDENT. THE TERMITES WERE CURIOUS ABOUT HIM--
--BUT WHEN THEY MADE CONTACT HIS BODY COULDN'T TOLERATE THE CHRONAL RADIATION THEY GENERATE AND--
YOU THINK? YOU DON'T KNOW FOR SURE?
THEIR MINDS ARE SO EVOLVED...I CAN'T BE SURE OF ANYTHING! WHICH MEANS I'M JUST GOING TO HAVE TO TRUST--
--AND SO ARE YOU!
ELIAS? YOU THERE?
RIGHT HERE, NUMBER.
CYB'S TAKING TOO BIG A RISK! I'M GETTING HER AWAY FROM THOSE THINGS--
--AND THEN I'M USING THE EXTERMINERGY!
IS THAT THE WISEST COURSE?
WHAT CHOICE DO I HAVE?
YOU CAN DO WHAT CYBILL SUGGESTED. YOU CAN TRUST.
WHAT'S THE ESTIMATE ON TOTAL SPIRAL COLLAPSE?
FOUR MINUTES.

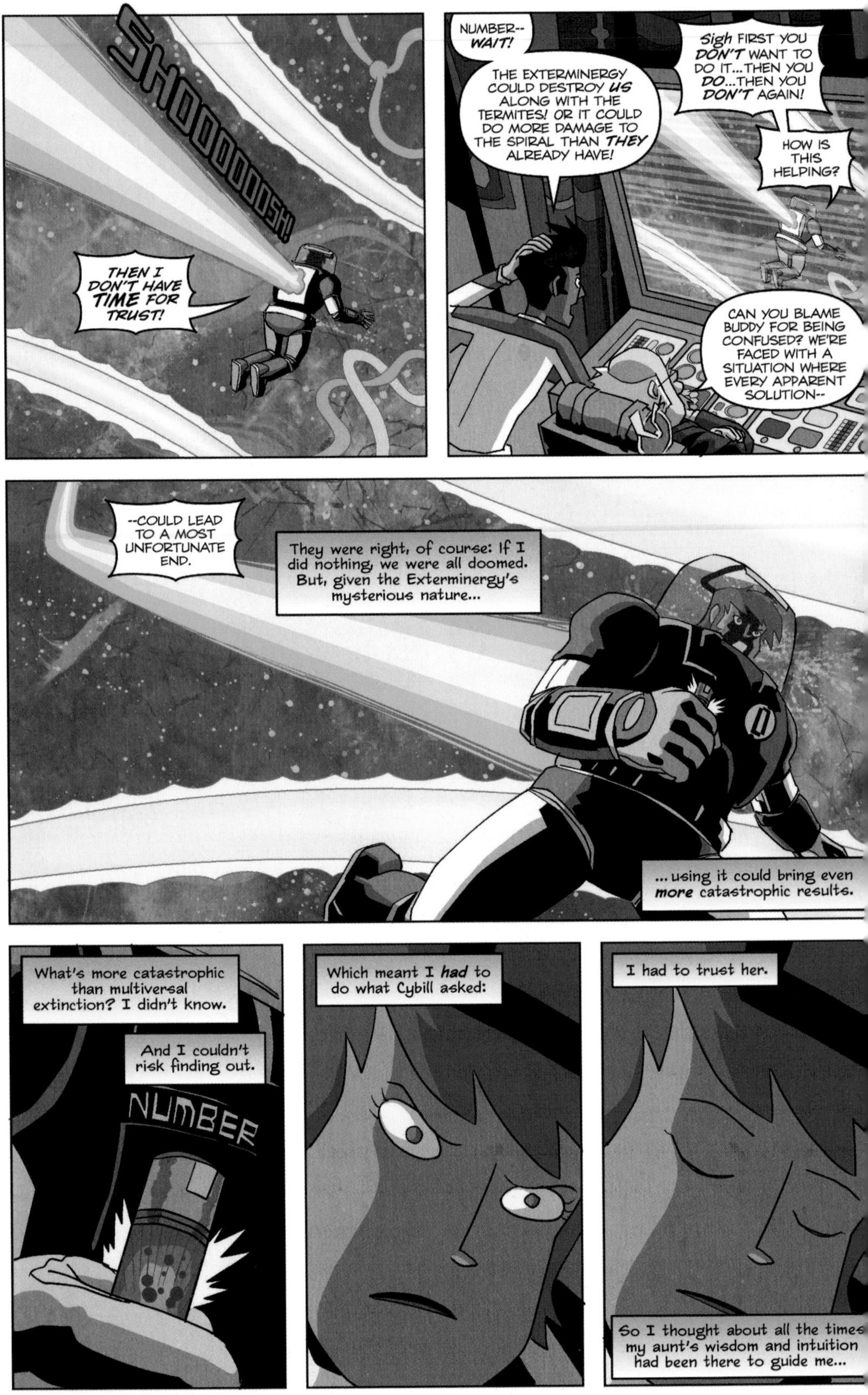
SHOOOOOOSH!
THEN I DON'T HAVE TIME FOR TRUST!
NUMBER-- WAIT!
THE EXTERMINERGY COULD DESTROY US ALONG WITH THE TERMITES! OR IT COULD DO MORE DAMAGE TO THE SPIRAL THAN THEY ALREADY HAVE!
Sigh FIRST YOU DON'T WANT TO DO IT...THEN YOU DO...THEN YOU DON'T AGAIN!
HOW IS THIS HELPING?
CAN YOU BLAME BUDDY FOR BEING CONFUSED? WE'RE FACED WITH A SITUATION WHERE EVERY APPARENT SOLUTION--
--COULD LEAD TO A MOST UNFORTUNATE END.
They were right, of course: If I did nothing, we were all doomed. But, given the Exterminergy's mysterious nature...
...using it could bring even more catastrophic results.
What's more catastrophic than multiversal extinction? I didn't know.
And I couldn't risk finding out.
NUMBER
Which meant I had to do what Cybill asked:
I had to trust her.
So I thought about all the times my aunt's wisdom and intuition had been there to guide me...

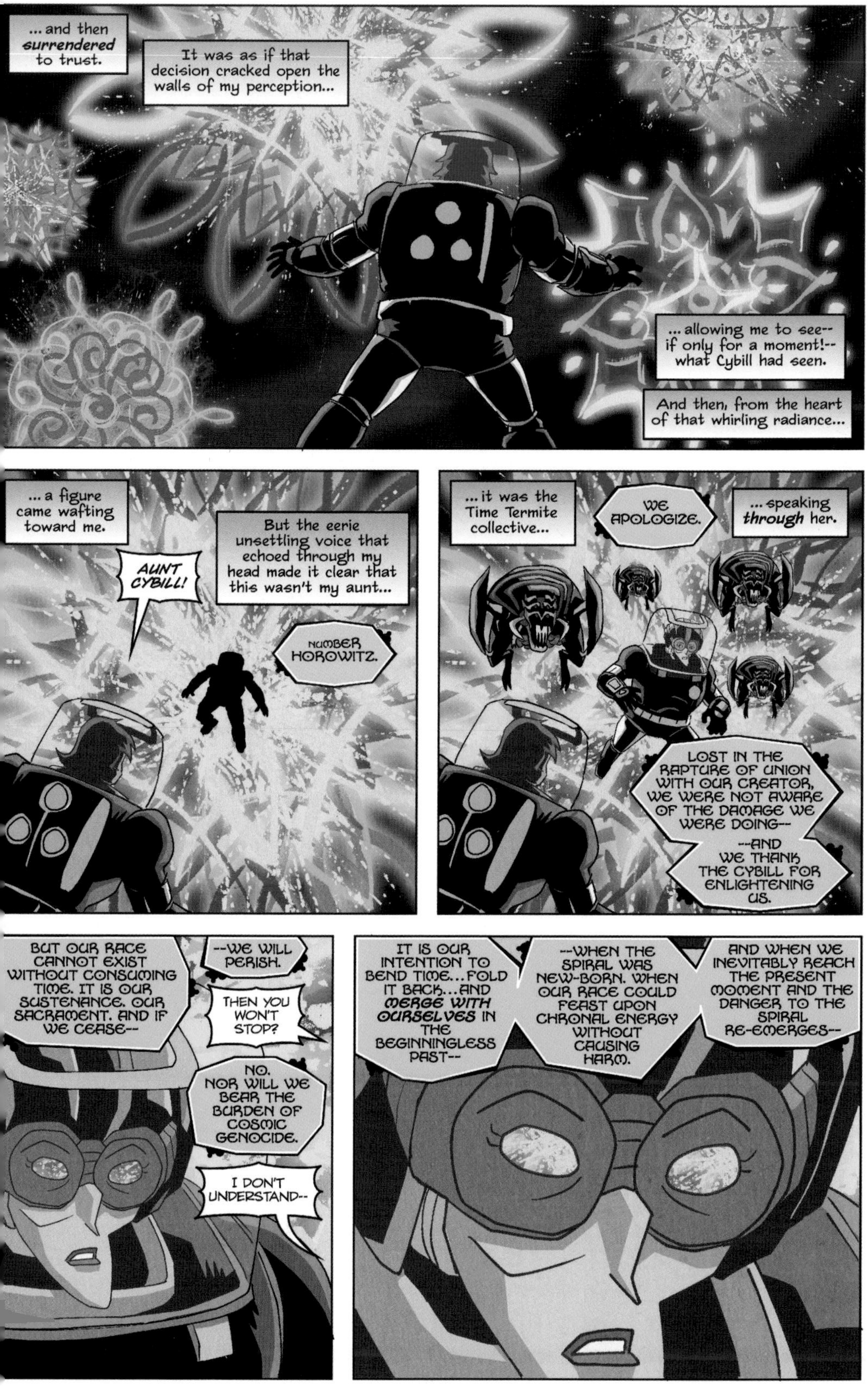
... and then **surrendered** to trust.
It was as if that decision cracked open the walls of my perception...
... allowing me to see-- if only for a moment!-- what Cybill had seen.
And then, from the heart of that whirling radiance...
... a figure came wafting toward me.
AUNT CYBILL!
But the eerie unsettling voice that echoed through my head made it clear that this wasn't my aunt...
NUMBER HOROWITZ.
... it was the Time Termite collective...
WE APOLOGIZE.
... speaking **through** her.
LOST IN THE RAPTURE OF UNION WITH OUR CREATOR, WE WERE NOT AWARE OF THE DAMAGE WE WERE DOING--
--AND WE THANK THE CYBILL FOR ENLIGHTENING US.
BUT OUR RACE CANNOT EXIST WITHOUT CONSUMING TIME. IT IS OUR SUSTENANCE. OUR SACRAMENT. AND IF WE CEASE--
--WE WILL PERISH.
THEN YOU WON'T STOP?
NO. NOR WILL WE BEAR THE BURDEN OF COSMIC GENOCIDE.
I DON'T UNDERSTAND--
IT IS OUR INTENTION TO BEND TIME... FOLD IT BACK... AND **MERGE WITH OURSELVES** IN THE BEGINNINGLESS PAST--
--WHEN THE SPIRAL WAS NEW-BORN. WHEN OUR RACE COULD FEAST UPON CHRONAL ENERGY WITHOUT CAUSING HARM.
AND WHEN WE INEVITABLY REACH THE PRESENT MOMENT AND THE DANGER TO THE SPIRAL RE-EMERGES--

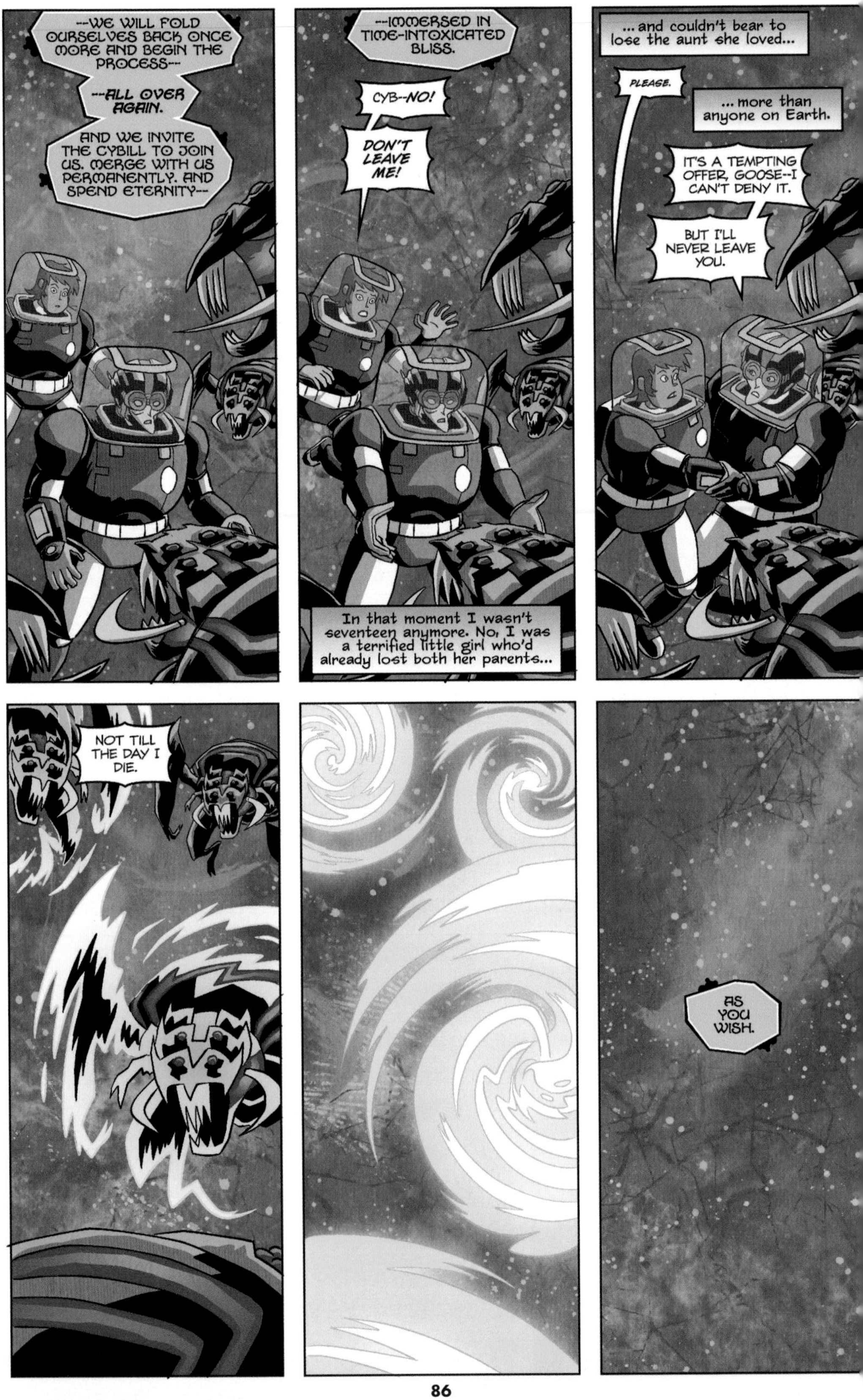
--WE WILL FOLD OURSELVES BACK ONCE MORE AND BEGIN THE PROCESS--
--ALL OVER AGAIN.
AND WE INVITE THE CYBILL TO JOIN US. MERGE WITH US PERMANENTLY. AND SPEND ETERNITY--
--IMMERSED IN TIME-INTOXICATED BLISS.
CYB--NO!
DON'T LEAVE ME!
In that moment I wasn't seventeen anymore. No, I was a terrified little girl who'd already lost both her parents...
...and couldn't bear to lose the aunt she loved...
PLEASE.
...more than anyone on Earth.
IT'S A TEMPTING OFFER, GOOSE--I CAN'T DENY IT.
BUT I'LL NEVER LEAVE YOU.
NOT TILL THE DAY I DIE.
AS YOU WISH.

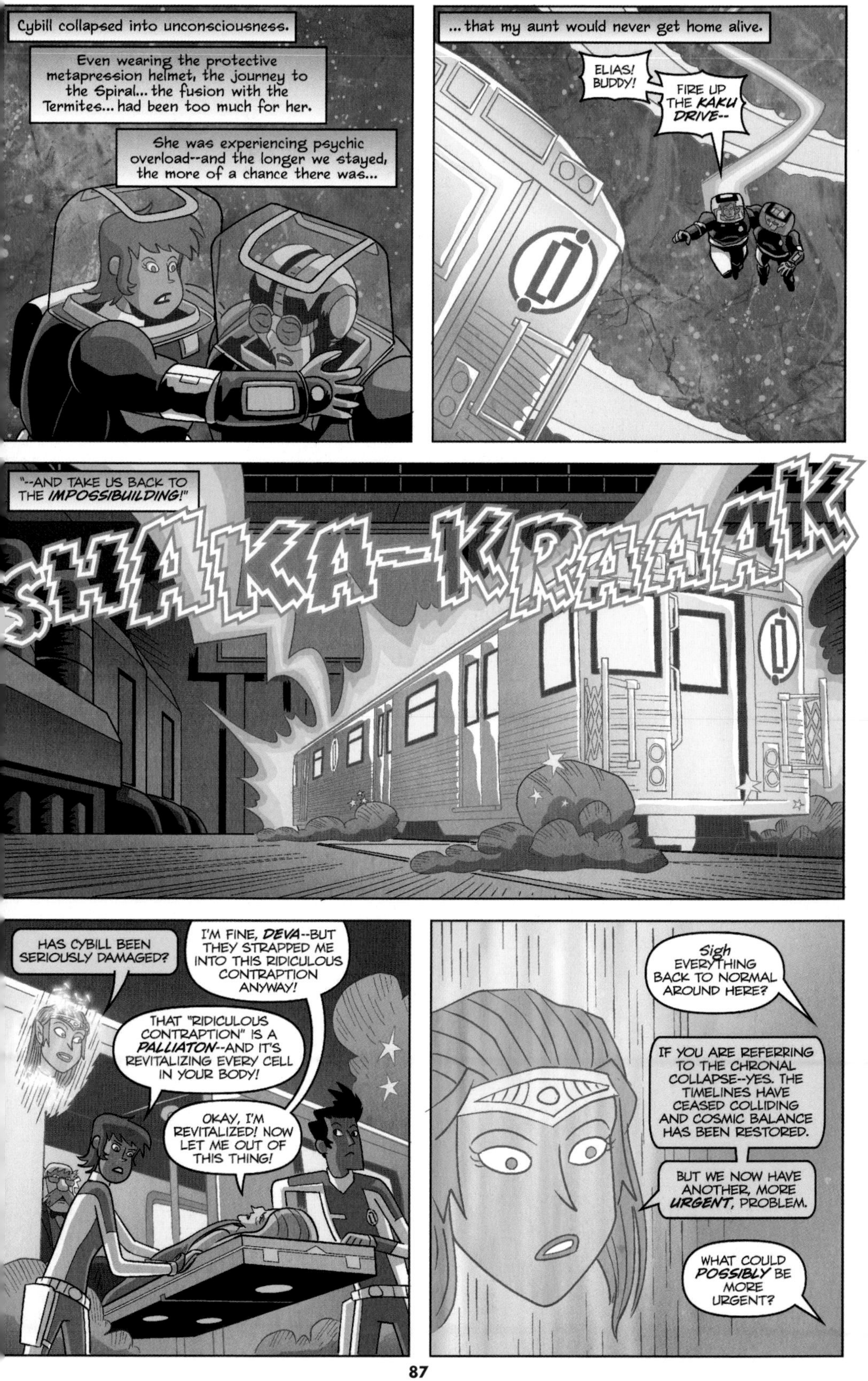
Cybill collapsed into unconsciousness.
Even wearing the protective metapression helmet, the journey to the Spiral... the fusion with the Termites... had been too much for her.
She was experiencing psychic overload--and the longer we stayed, the more of a chance there was...
... that my aunt would never get home alive.
ELIAS! BUDDY!
FIRE UP THE KAKU DRIVE--
"--AND TAKE US BACK TO THE IMPOSSIBUILDING!"
SHAKA-KRAAAK
HAS CYBILL BEEN SERIOUSLY DAMAGED?
I'M FINE, DEVA--BUT THEY STRAPPED ME INTO THIS RIDICULOUS CONTRAPTION ANYWAY!
THAT "RIDICULOUS CONTRAPTION" IS A PALLIATON--AND IT'S REVITALIZING EVERY CELL IN YOUR BODY!
OKAY, I'M REVITALIZED! NOW LET ME OUT OF THIS THING!
Sigh EVERYTHING BACK TO NORMAL AROUND HERE?
IF YOU ARE REFERRING TO THE CHRONAL COLLAPSE--YES. THE TIMELINES HAVE CEASED COLLIDING AND COSMIC BALANCE HAS BEEN RESTORED.
BUT WE NOW HAVE ANOTHER, MORE URGENT, PROBLEM.
WHAT COULD POSSIBLY BE MORE URGENT?

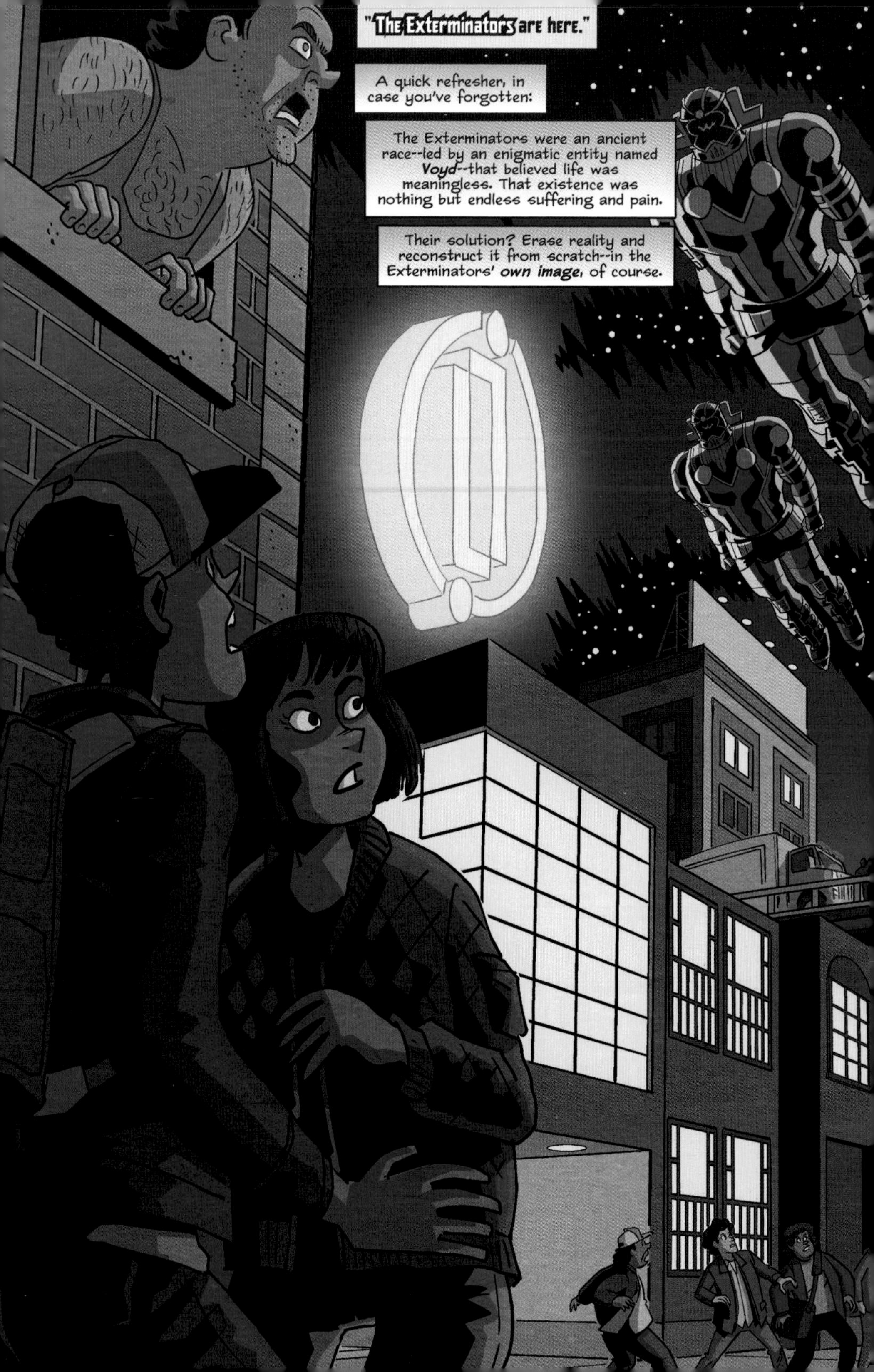
"The Exterminators are here."
A quick refresher, in case you've forgotten:
The Exterminators were an ancient race--led by an enigmatic entity named Voyd--that believed life was meaningless. That existence was nothing but endless suffering and pain.
Their solution? Erase reality and reconstruct it from scratch--in the Exterminators' own image, of course.

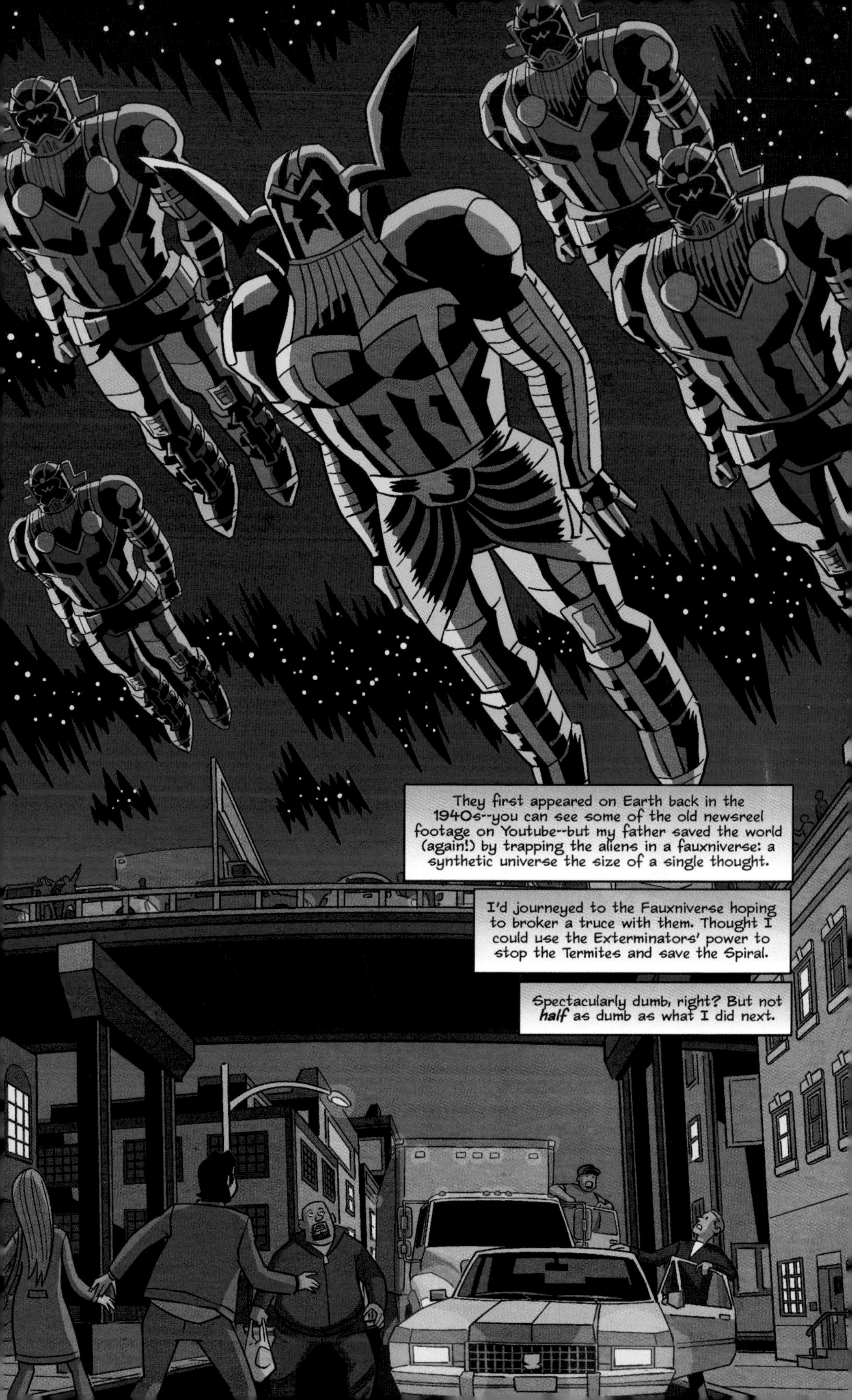
They first appeared on Earth back in the 1940s--you can see some of the old newsreel footage on Youtube--but my father saved the world (again!) by trapping the aliens in a fauxniverse: a synthetic universe the size of a single thought.
I'd journeyed to the Fauxniverse hoping to broker a truce with them. Thought I could use the Exterminators' power to stop the Termites and save the Spiral.
Spectacularly dumb, right? But not *half* as dumb as what I did next.

Goliath had contained the aliens in individual stasis fields. But in order to awaken Voyd I had to *break* the field around her. And when I left the Fauxniverse...

...*I forgot to reignite it.* (I guess "spectacularly dumb" doesn't really cover it.)

Which meant Voyd was free to release the other Exterminators...

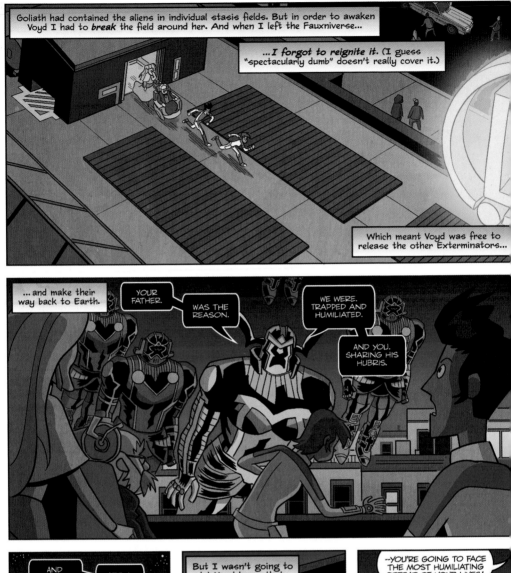

...and make their way back to Earth.

YOUR FATHER.

WAS THE REASON.

WE WERE. TRAPPED AND HUMILIATED.

AND YOU. SHARING HIS HUBRIS.

AND INTELLECT.

ARE A THREAT. TO US.

But I didn't feel like a threat. I knew I was in *way* over my head.

But I wasn't going to let Voyd know that.

MY FATHER WAS JUST *ONE MAN!* BUT WE'RE A *TEAM*--

--AND, UNLESS YOU EXTERMINATORS SURRENDER... RIGHT NOW--

--YOU'RE GOING TO FACE THE MOST HUMILIATING DEFEAT OF YOUR LIVES!

Which might have been true if I'd had access to Goliath's research on fauxniverses. Unfortunately, I didn't.

But I *was* my father's daughter, capable of formulating multiple defensive strategies simultaneously, and I hoped that as long as I kept Voyd talking.

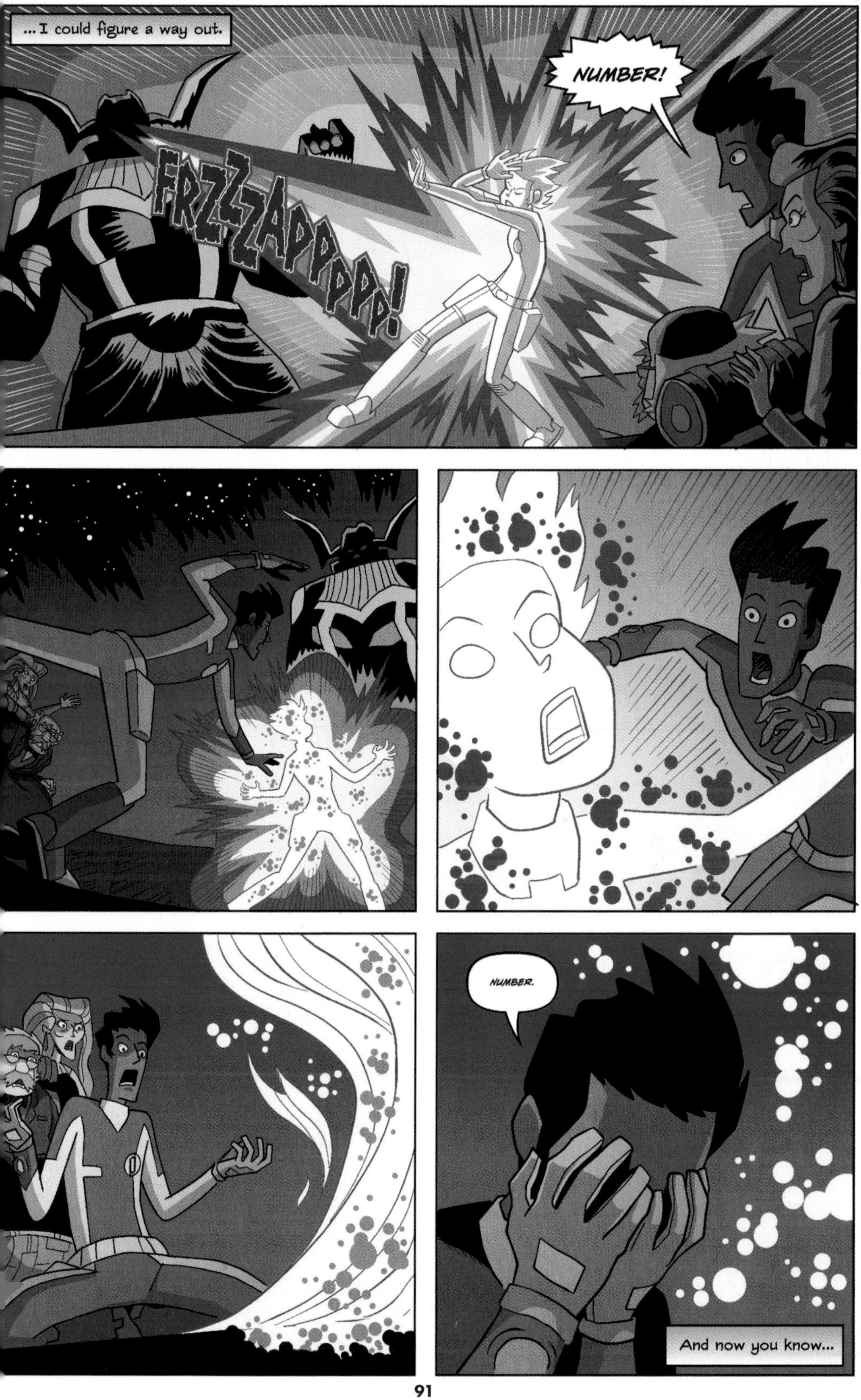
...I could figure a way out.
NUMBER!
FRZZZAPPPPP!
NUMBER.
And now you know...

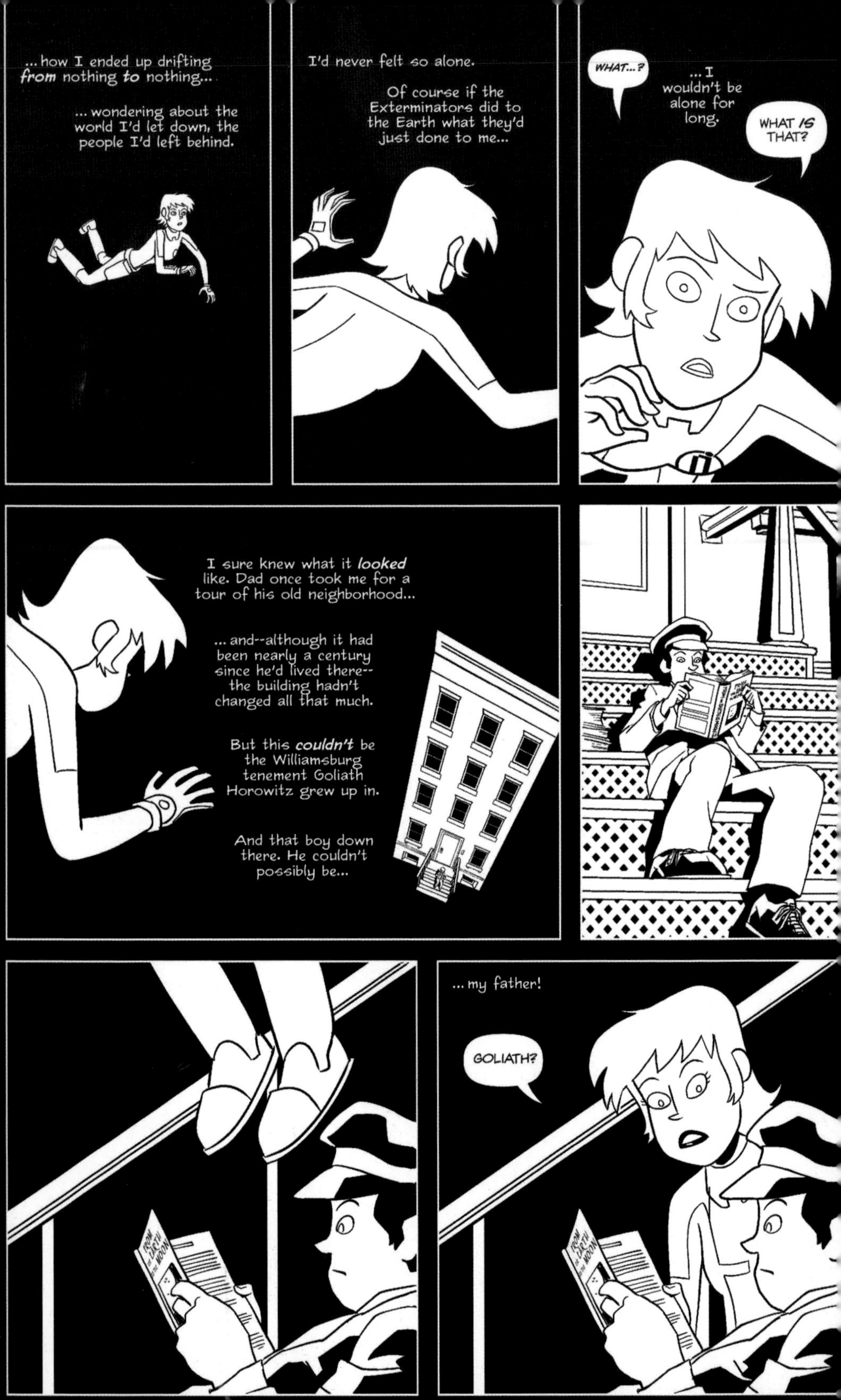
...how I ended up drifting *from* nothing *to* nothing...
...wondering about the world I'd let down, the people I'd left behind.
I'd never felt so alone.
Of course if the Exterminators did to the Earth what they'd just done to me...
WHAT...?
...I wouldn't be alone for long.
WHAT *IS* THAT?
I sure knew what it *looked* like. Dad once took me for a tour of his old neighborhood...
...and--although it had been nearly a century since he'd lived there--the building hadn't changed all that much.
But this *couldn't* be the Williamsburg tenement Goliath Horowitz grew up in.
And that boy down there. He couldn't possibly be...
...my father!
GOLIATH?

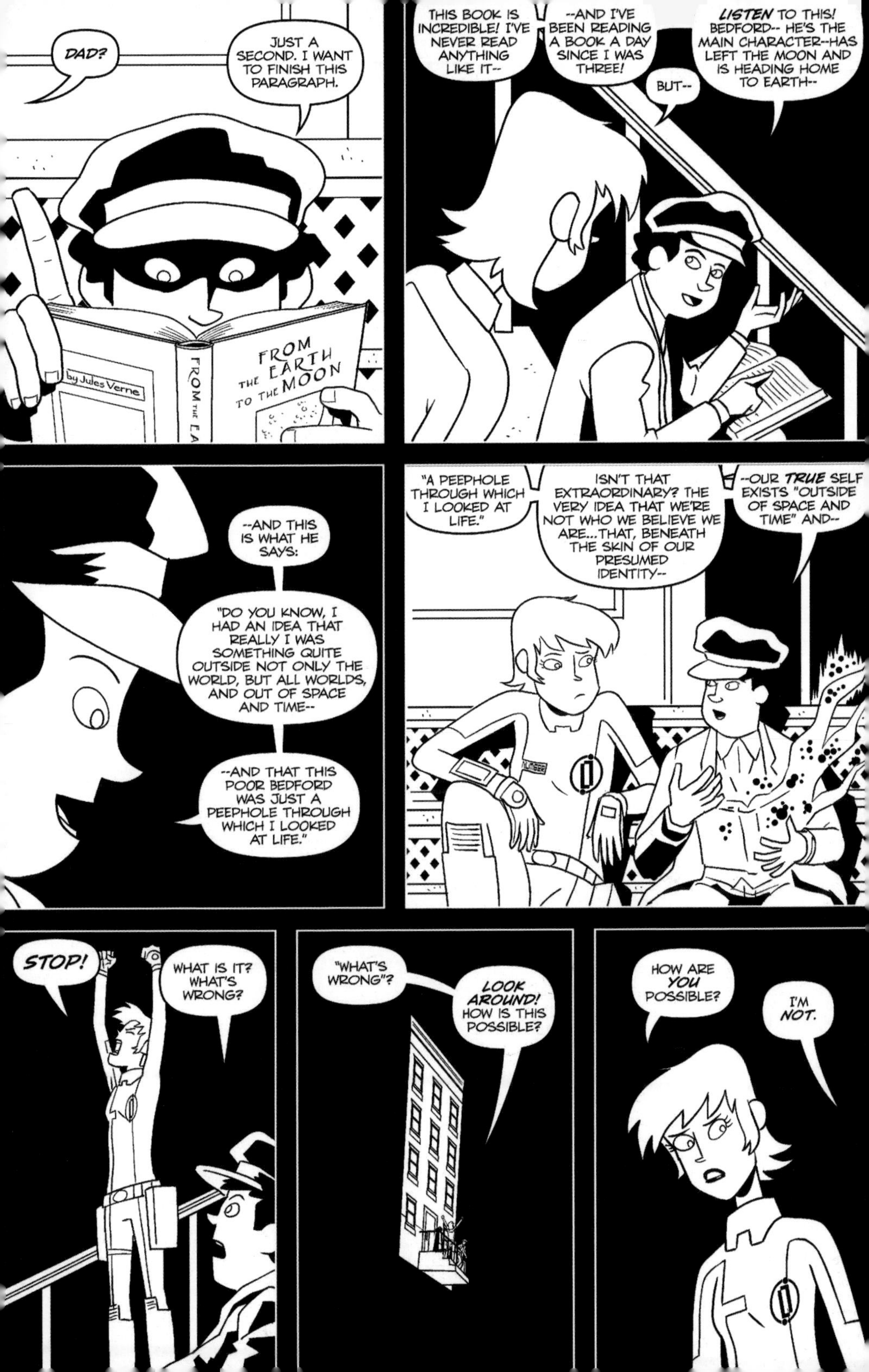
DAD?
JUST A SECOND. I WANT TO FINISH THIS PARAGRAPH.
by Jules Verne
FROM THE EARTH TO THE MOON
FROM THE EA
THIS BOOK IS INCREDIBLE! I'VE NEVER READ ANYTHING LIKE IT--
--AND I'VE BEEN READING A BOOK A DAY SINCE I WAS THREE!
BUT--
LISTEN TO THIS! BEDFORD-- HE'S THE MAIN CHARACTER--HAS LEFT THE MOON AND IS HEADING HOME TO EARTH--
--AND THIS IS WHAT HE SAYS:
"DO YOU KNOW, I HAD AN IDEA THAT REALLY I WAS SOMETHING QUITE OUTSIDE NOT ONLY THE WORLD, BUT ALL WORLDS, AND OUT OF SPACE AND TIME--
--AND THAT THIS POOR BEDFORD WAS JUST A PEEPHOLE THROUGH WHICH I LOOKED AT LIFE."
"A PEEPHOLE THROUGH WHICH I LOOKED AT LIFE."
ISN'T THAT EXTRAORDINARY? THE VERY IDEA THAT WE'RE NOT WHO WE BELIEVE WE ARE...THAT, BENEATH THE SKIN OF OUR PRESUMED IDENTITY--
--OUR TRUE SELF EXISTS "OUTSIDE OF SPACE AND TIME" AND--
STOP!
WHAT IS IT? WHAT'S WRONG?
"WHAT'S WRONG"?
LOOK AROUND! HOW IS THIS POSSIBLE?
HOW ARE YOU POSSIBLE?
I'M NOT.

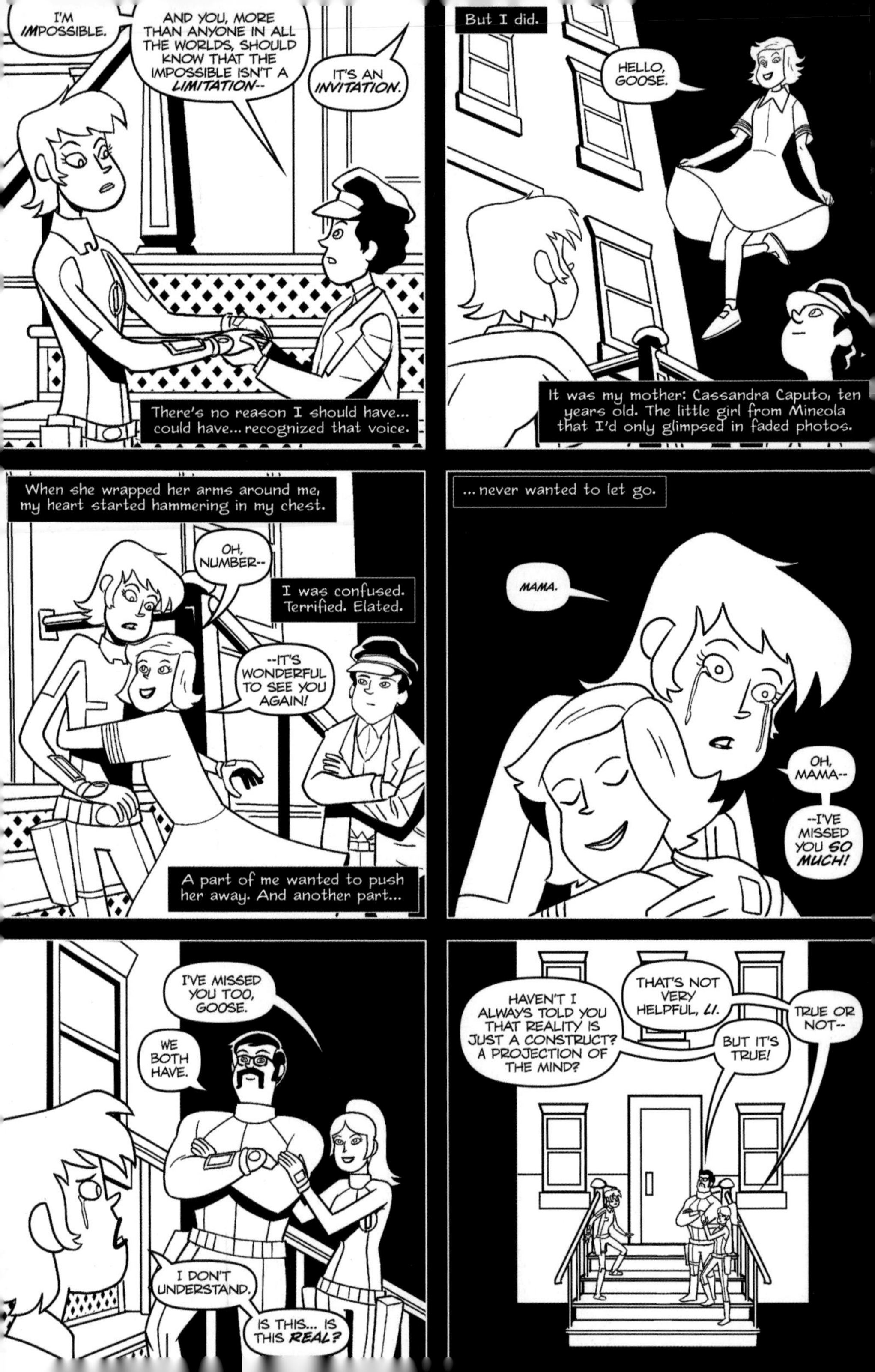
I'M IMPOSSIBLE.
AND YOU, MORE THAN ANYONE IN ALL THE WORLDS, SHOULD KNOW THAT THE IMPOSSIBLE ISN'T A LIMITATION--
IT'S AN INVITATION.
There's no reason I should have... could have... recognized that voice.
But I did.
HELLO, GOOSE.
It was my mother: Cassandra Caputo, ten years old. The little girl from Mineola that I'd only glimpsed in faded photos.
When she wrapped her arms around me, my heart started hammering in my chest.
OH, NUMBER--
I was confused. Terrified. Elated.
--IT'S WONDERFUL TO SEE YOU AGAIN!
A part of me wanted to push her away. And another part...
...never wanted to let go.
MAMA.
OH, MAMA--
--I'VE MISSED YOU SO MUCH!
I'VE MISSED YOU TOO, GOOSE.
WE BOTH HAVE.
I DON'T UNDERSTAND.
IS THIS... IS THIS REAL?
HAVEN'T I ALWAYS TOLD YOU THAT REALITY IS JUST A CONSTRUCT? A PROJECTION OF THE MIND?
THAT'S NOT VERY HELPFUL, LI.
TRUE OR NOT--
BUT IT'S TRUE!

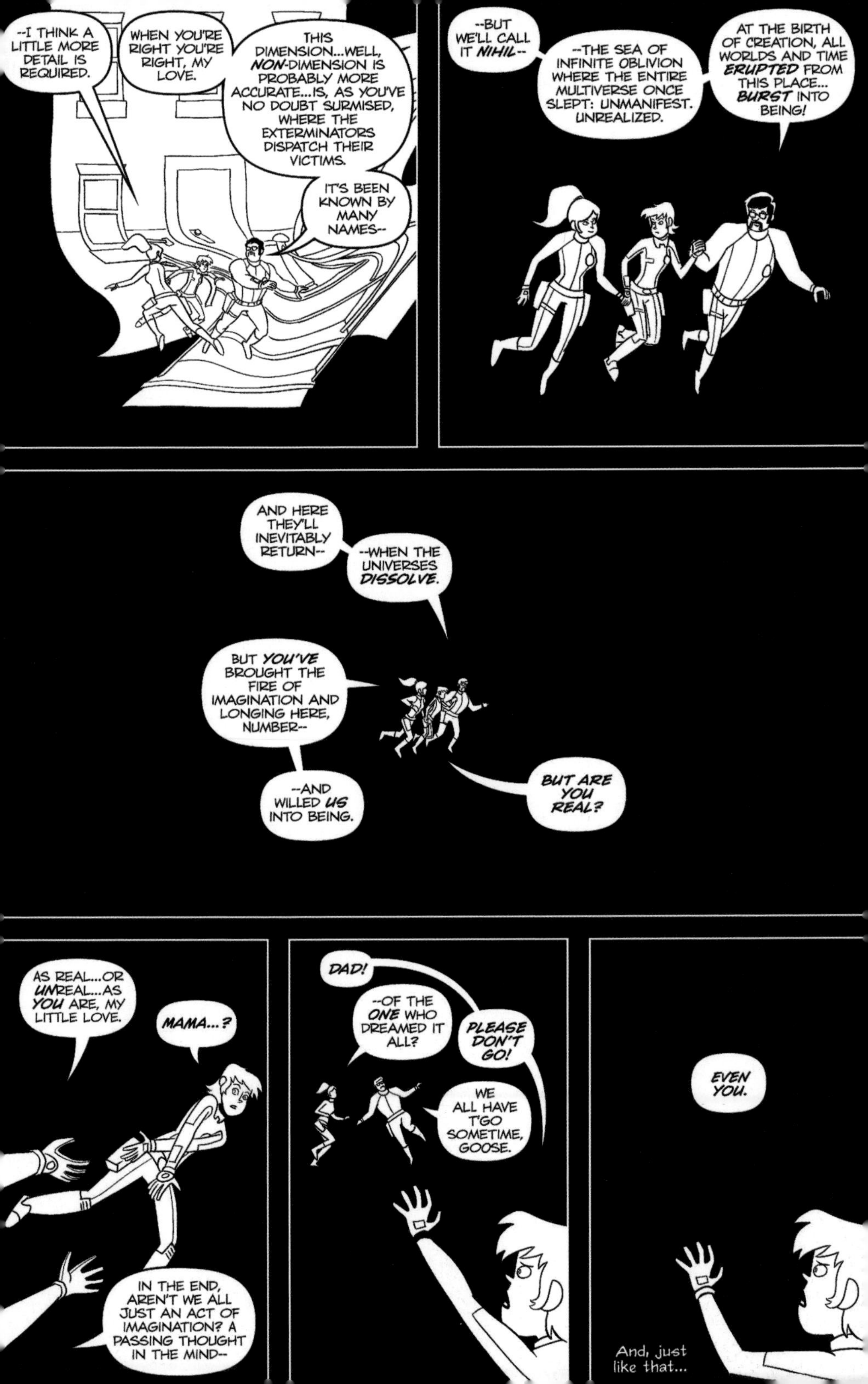
--I THINK A LITTLE MORE DETAIL IS REQUIRED.
WHEN YOU'RE RIGHT YOU'RE RIGHT, MY LOVE.
THIS DIMENSION...WELL, NON-DIMENSION IS PROBABLY MORE ACCURATE...IS, AS YOU'VE NO DOUBT SURMISED, WHERE THE EXTERMINATORS DISPATCH THEIR VICTIMS.
IT'S BEEN KNOWN BY MANY NAMES--
--BUT WE'LL CALL IT NIHIL--
--THE SEA OF INFINITE OBLIVION WHERE THE ENTIRE MULTIVERSE ONCE SLEPT: UNMANIFEST. UNREALIZED.
AT THE BIRTH OF CREATION, ALL WORLDS AND TIME ERUPTED FROM THIS PLACE... BURST INTO BEING!
AND HERE THEY'LL INEVITABLY RETURN--
--WHEN THE UNIVERSES DISSOLVE.
BUT YOU'VE BROUGHT THE FIRE OF IMAGINATION AND LONGING HERE, NUMBER--
--AND WILLED US INTO BEING.
BUT ARE YOU REAL?
AS REAL...OR UNREAL...AS YOU ARE, MY LITTLE LOVE.
MAMA...?
IN THE END, AREN'T WE ALL JUST AN ACT OF IMAGINATION? A PASSING THOUGHT IN THE MIND--
DAD!
--OF THE ONE WHO DREAMED IT ALL?
PLEASE DON'T GO!
WE ALL HAVE T'GO SOMETIME, GOOSE.
EVEN YOU.
And, just like that...

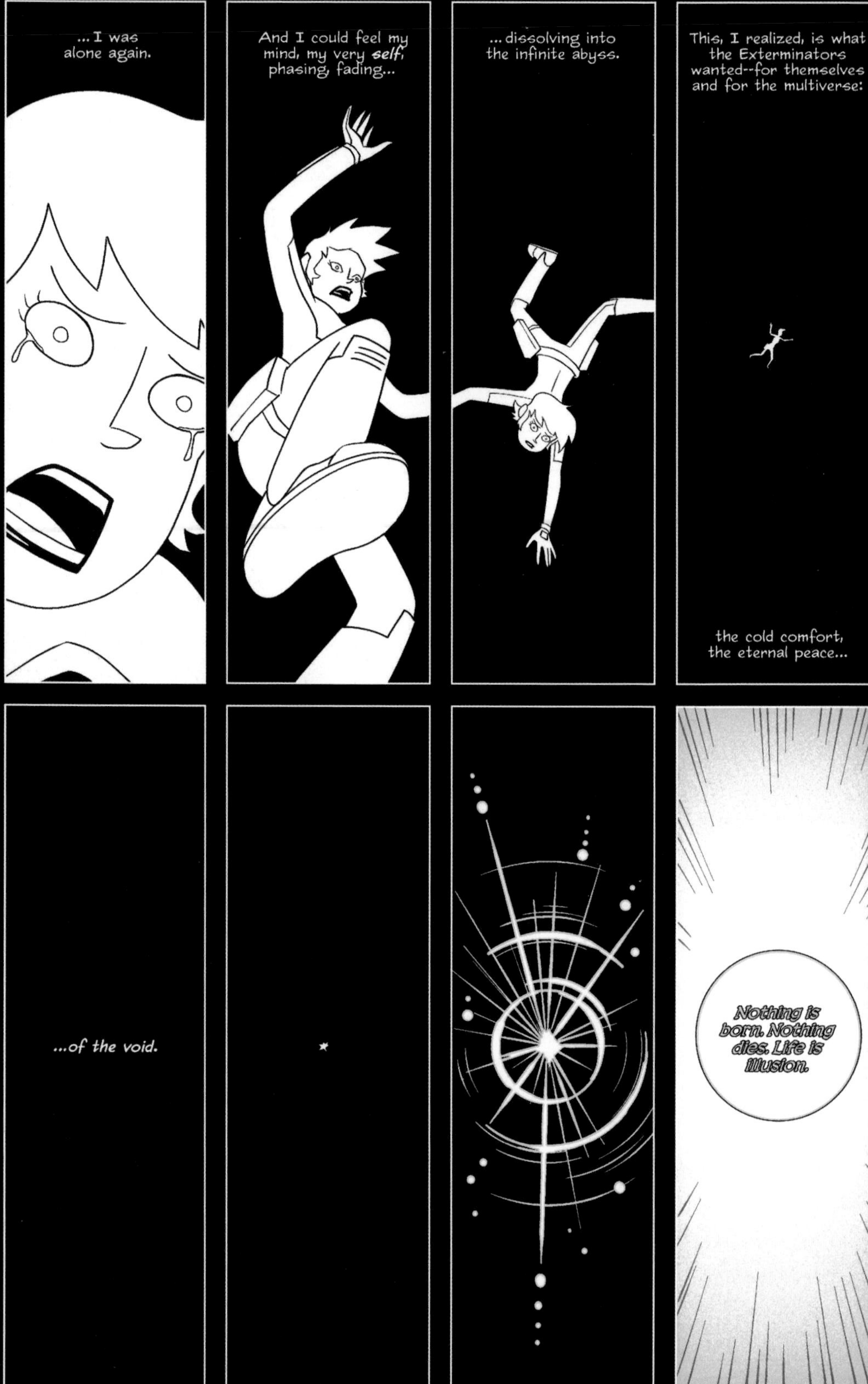
...I was
alone again.
And I could feel my
mind, my very self,
phasing, fading...
...dissolving into
the infinite abyss.
This, I realized, is what
the Exterminators
wanted--for themselves
and for the multiverse:
the cold comfort,
the eternal peace...
...of the void.
Nothing is
born. Nothing
dies. Life is
illusion.

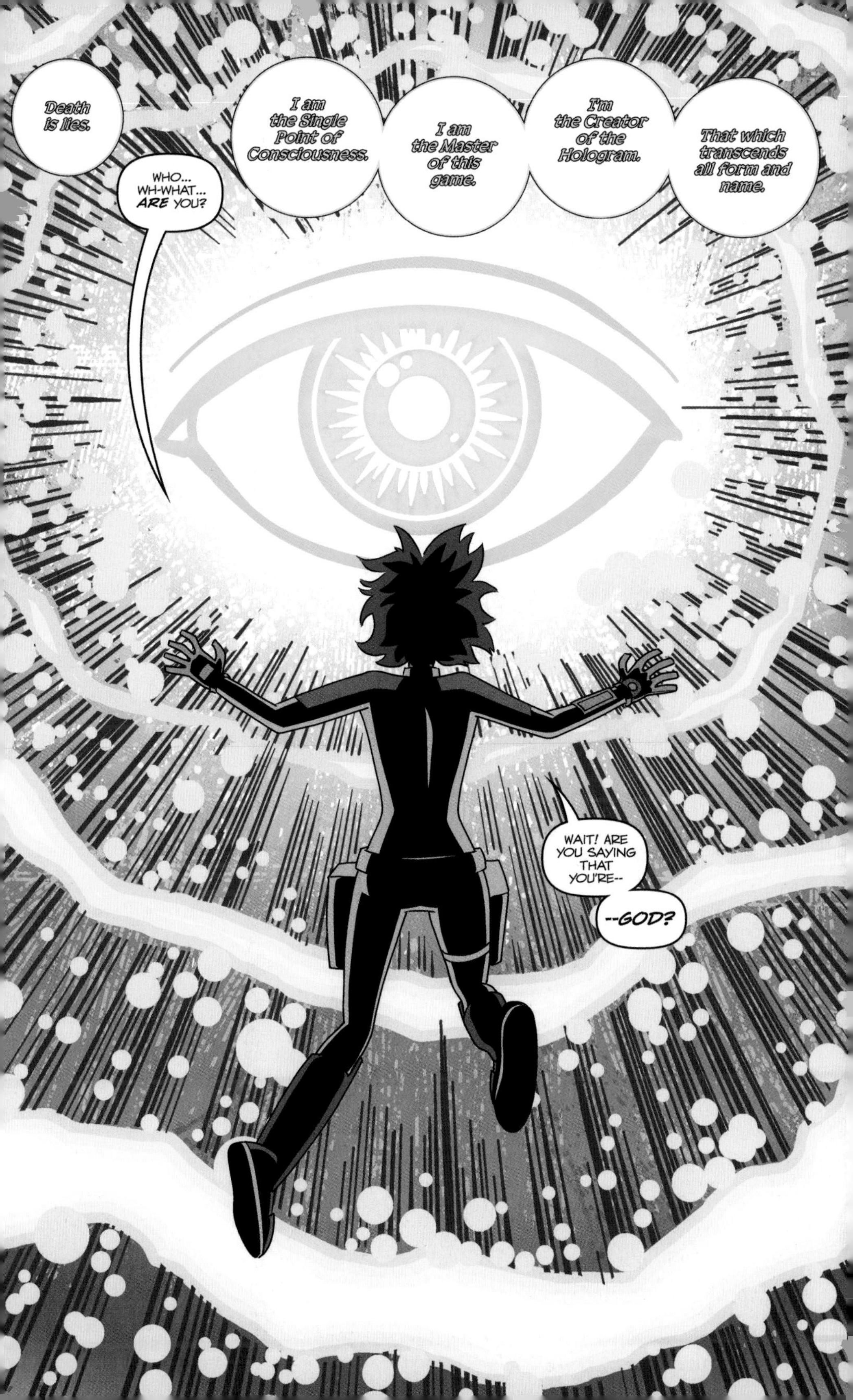
Death is lies.
WHO... WH-WHAT... ARE YOU?
I am the Single Point of Consciousness.
I am the Master of this game.
I'm the Creator of the Hologram.
That which transcends all form and name.
WAIT! ARE YOU SAYING THAT YOU'RE--
--GOD?

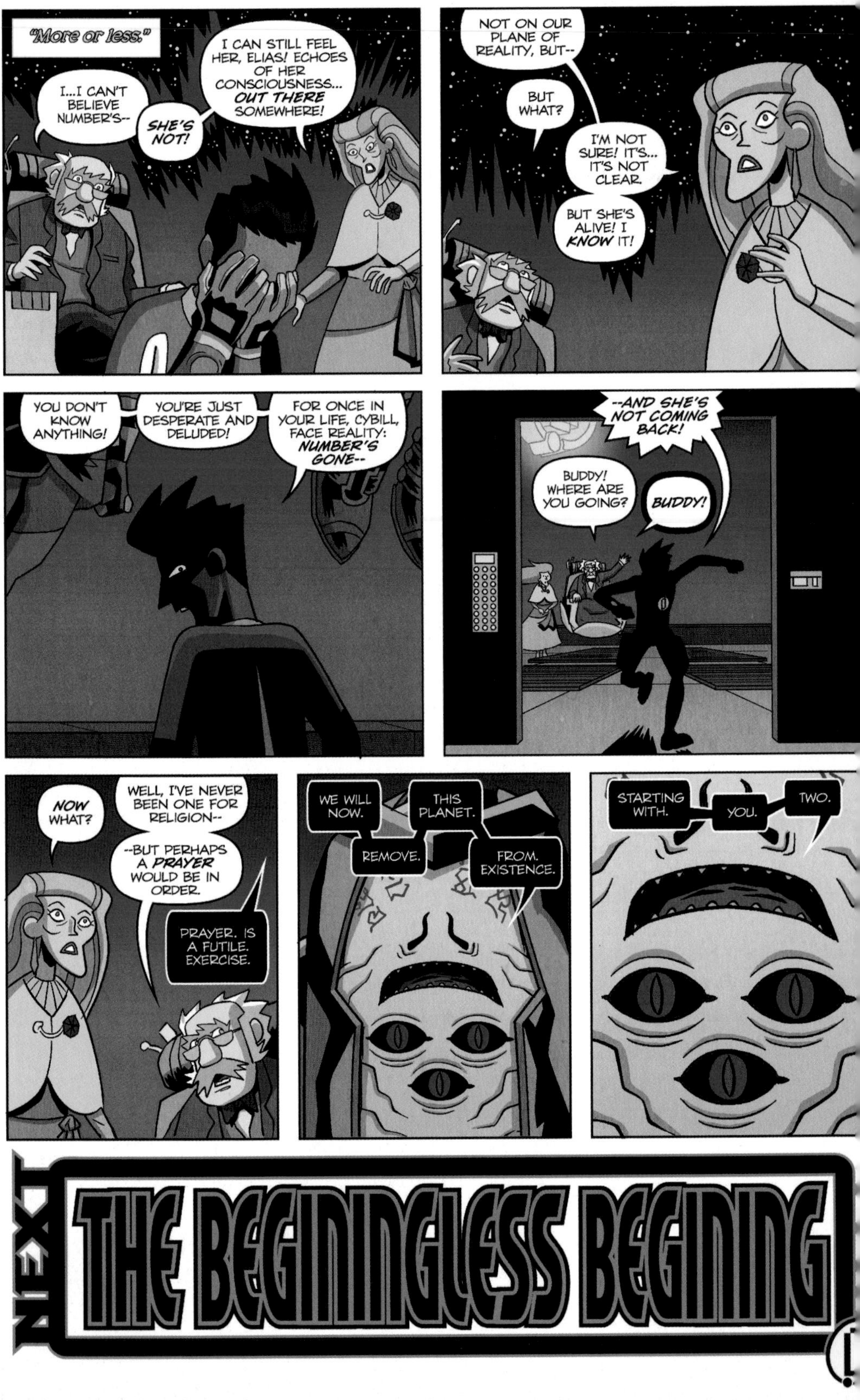
"More or less."
I...I CAN'T BELIEVE NUMBER'S--
SHE'S NOT!
I CAN STILL FEEL HER, ELIAS! ECHOES OF HER CONSCIOUSNESS... OUT THERE SOMEWHERE!
NOT ON OUR PLANE OF REALITY, BUT--
BUT WHAT?
I'M NOT SURE! IT'S... IT'S NOT CLEAR.
BUT SHE'S ALIVE! I KNOW IT!
YOU DON'T KNOW ANYTHING!
YOU'RE JUST DESPERATE AND DELUDED!
FOR ONCE IN YOUR LIFE, CYBILL, FACE REALITY: NUMBER'S GONE--
--AND SHE'S NOT COMING BACK!
BUDDY! WHERE ARE YOU GOING?
BUDDY!
NOW WHAT?
WELL, I'VE NEVER BEEN ONE FOR RELIGION--
--BUT PERHAPS A PRAYER WOULD BE IN ORDER.
PRAYER. IS A FUTILE. EXERCISE.
WE WILL NOW.
REMOVE.
THIS PLANET.
FROM. EXISTENCE.
STARTING WITH.
YOU.
TWO.
NEXT
THE BEGININGLESS BEGINING
!

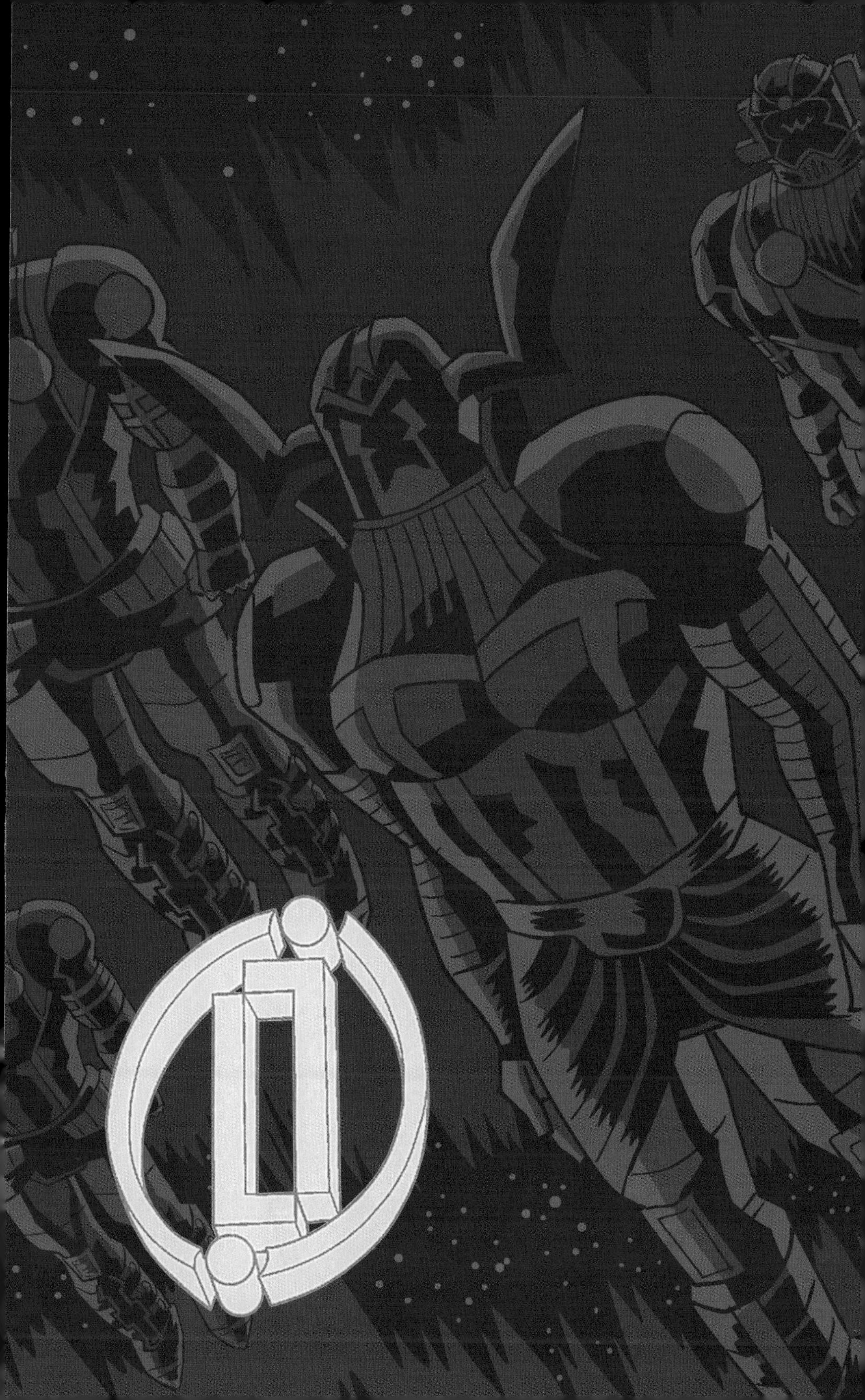

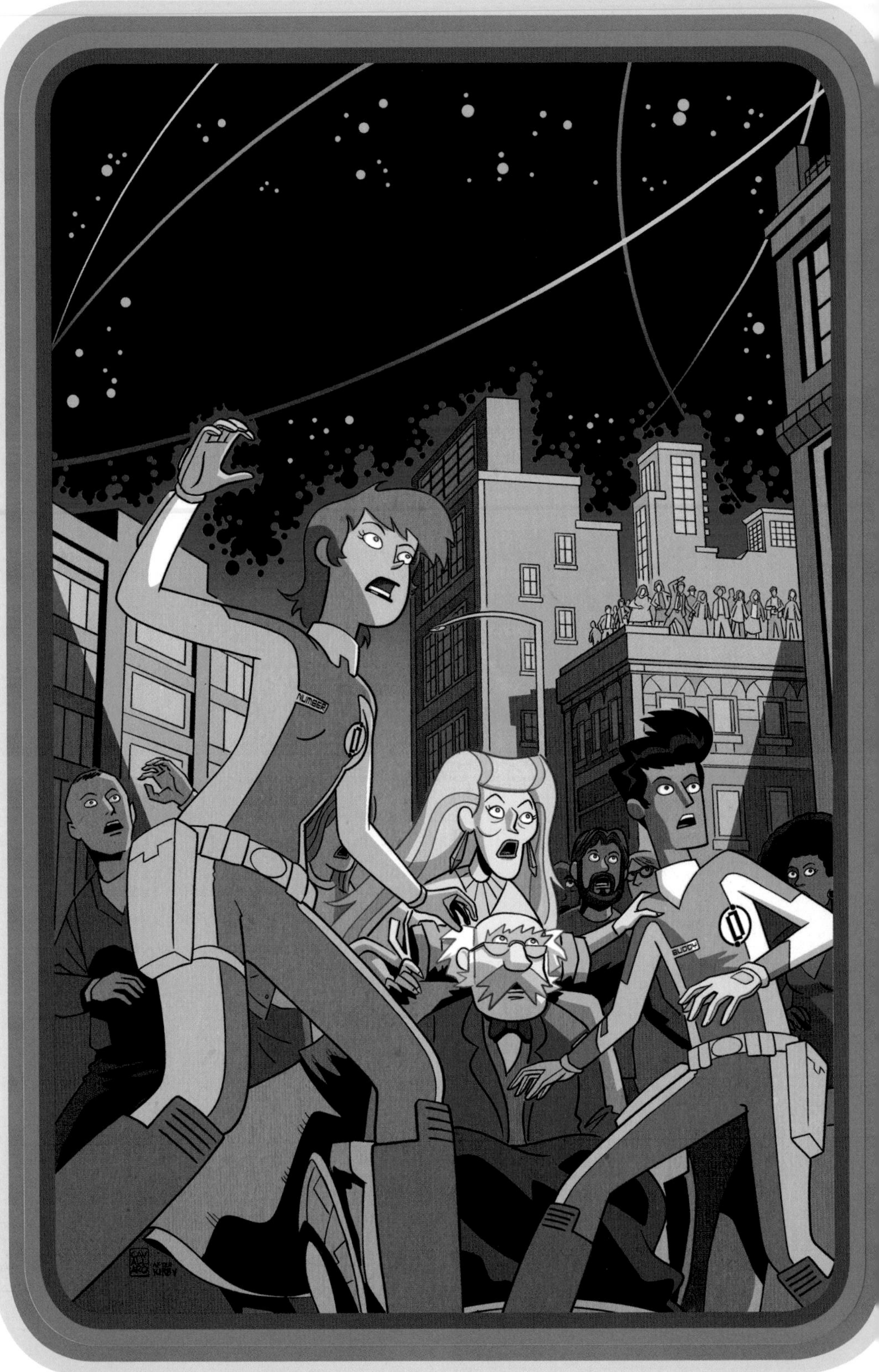
NUMBER
BUDDY
AFTER KIRBY

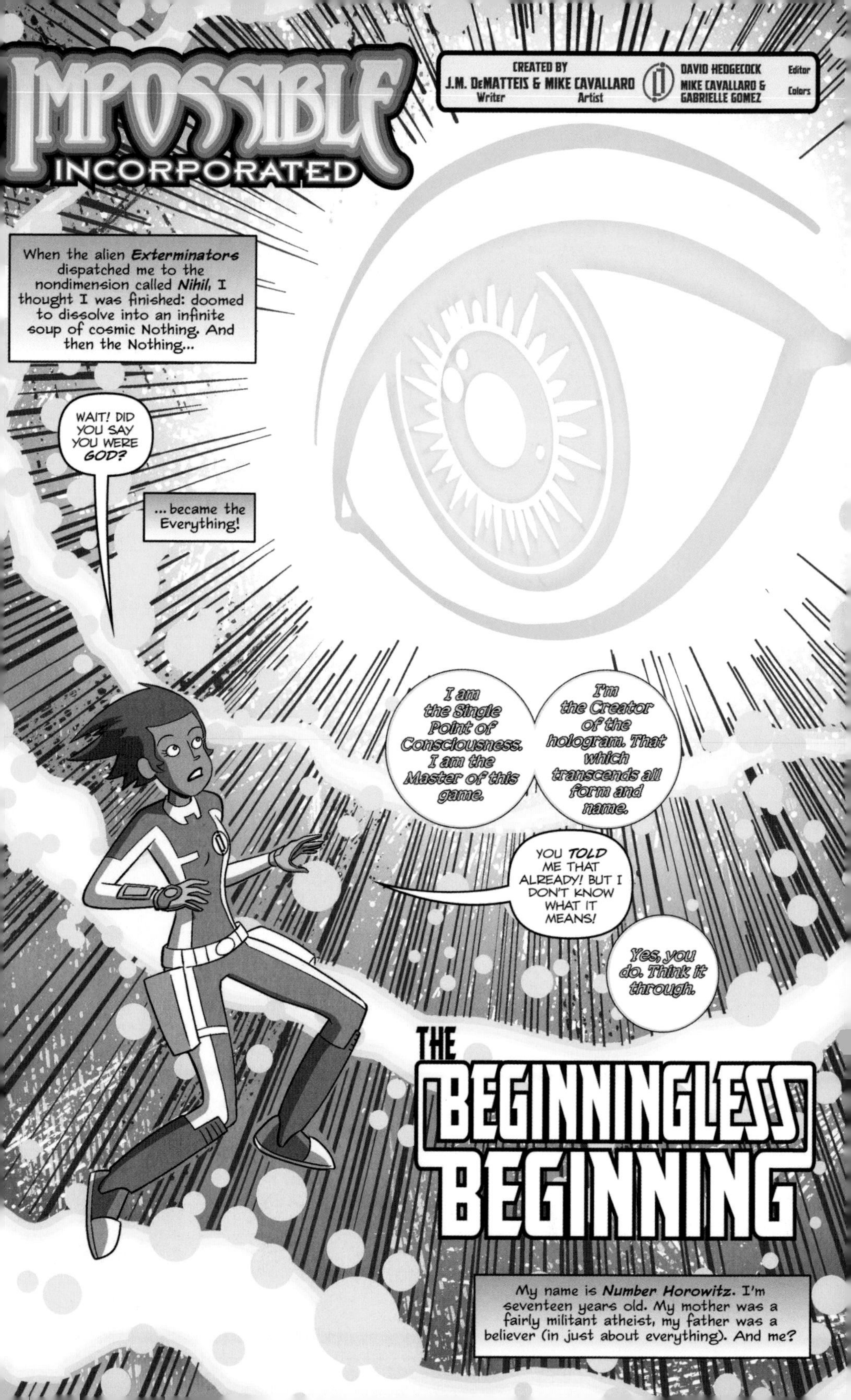
IMPOSSIBLE INCORPORATED
CREATED BY
J.M. DeMATTEIS & MIKE CAVALLARO
Writer Artist
DAVID HEDGECOCK Editor
MIKE CAVALLARO & GABRIELLE GOMEZ Colors
When the alien Exterminators dispatched me to the nondimension called Nihil, I thought I was finished: doomed to dissolve into an infinite soup of cosmic Nothing. And then the Nothing...
WAIT! DID YOU SAY YOU WERE GOD?
...became the Everything!
I am the Single Point of Consciousness. I am the Master of this game.
I'm the Creator of the hologram. That which transcends all form and name.
YOU TOLD ME THAT ALREADY! BUT I DON'T KNOW WHAT IT MEANS!
Yes, you do. Think it through.
THE BEGINNINGLESS BEGINNING
My name is Number Horowitz. I'm seventeen years old. My mother was a fairly militant atheist, my father was a believer (in just about everything). And me?

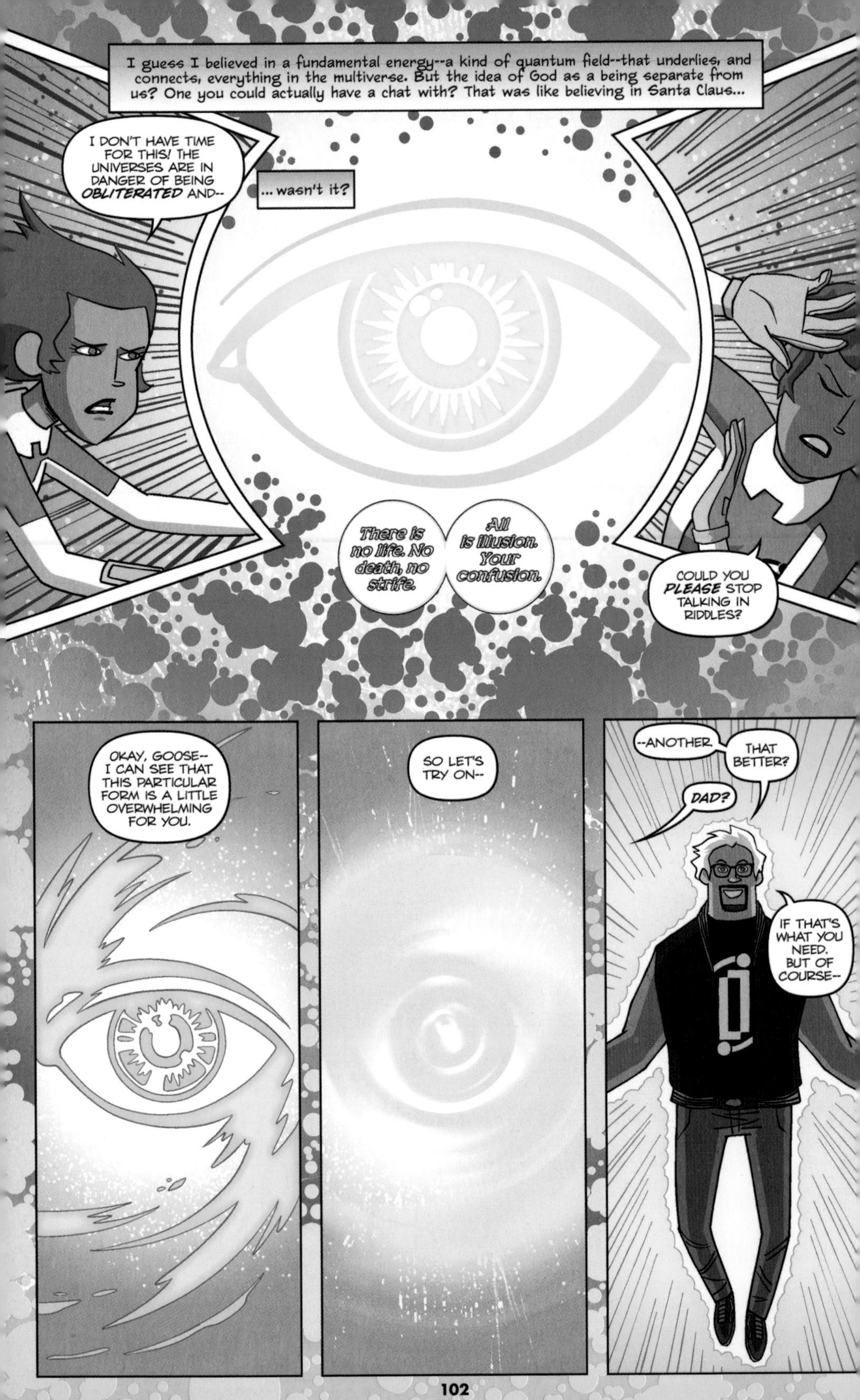

I guess I believed in a fundamental energy--a kind of quantum field--that underlies, and connects, everything in the multiverse. But the idea of God as a being separate from us? One you could actually have a chat with? That was like believing in Santa Claus...
I DON'T HAVE TIME FOR THIS! THE UNIVERSES ARE IN DANGER OF BEING OBLITERATED AND--
...wasn't it?
There is no life. No death, no strife.
All is illusion. Your confusion.
COULD YOU PLEASE STOP TALKING IN RIDDLES?
OKAY, GOOSE-- I CAN SEE THAT THIS PARTICULAR FORM IS A LITTLE OVERWHELMING FOR YOU.
SO LET'S TRY ON--
--ANOTHER.
THAT BETTER?
DAD?
IF THAT'S WHAT YOU NEED. BUT OF COURSE--

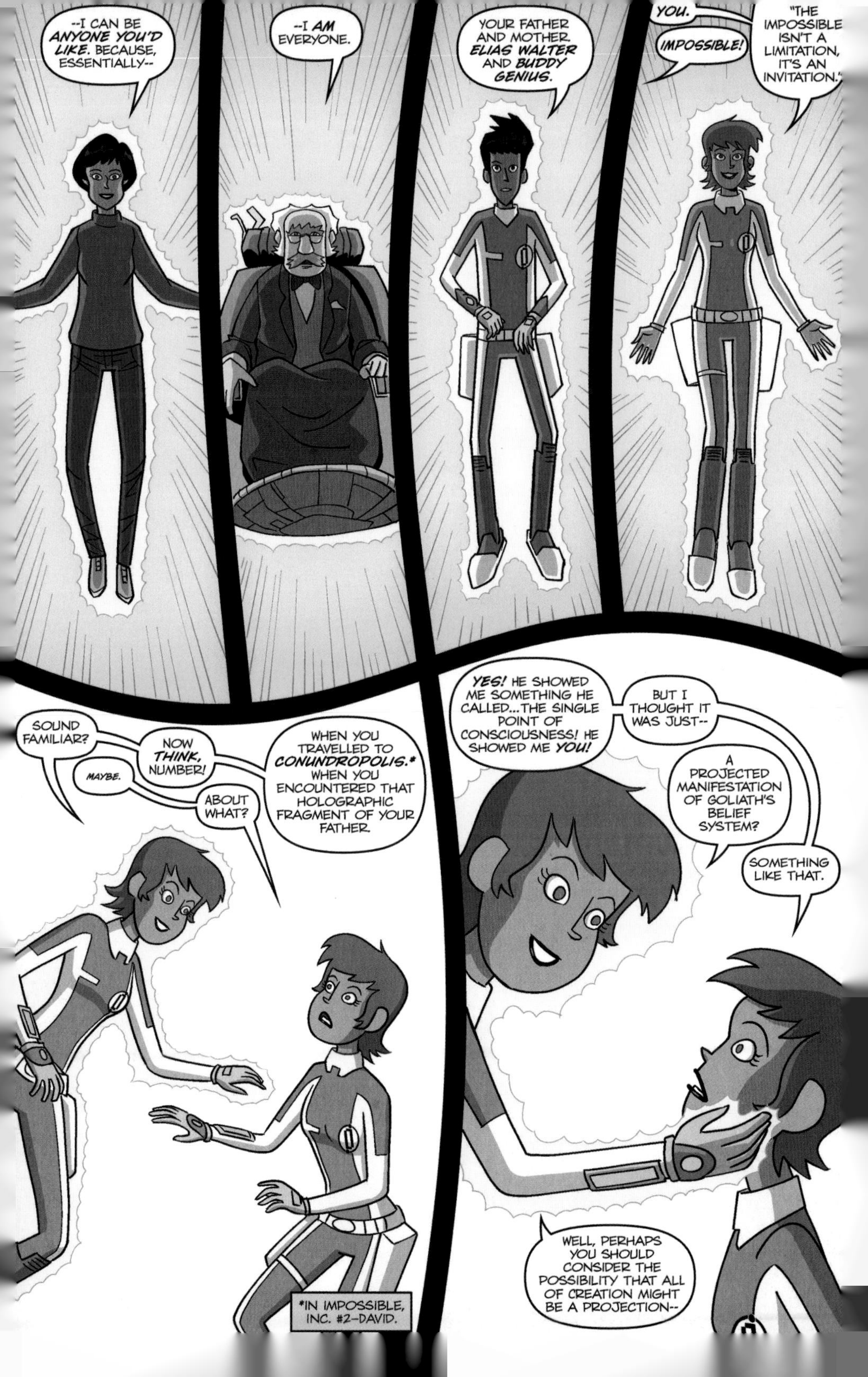
--I CAN BE ANYONE YOU'D LIKE. BECAUSE, ESSENTIALLY--
--I AM EVERYONE.
YOUR FATHER AND MOTHER. ELIAS WALTER AND BUDDY GENIUS.
YOU.
IMPOSSIBLE!
"THE IMPOSSIBLE ISN'T A LIMITATION, IT'S AN INVITATION."
SOUND FAMILIAR?
MAYBE.
NOW THINK, NUMBER!
ABOUT WHAT?
WHEN YOU TRAVELLED TO CONUNDROPOLIS.* WHEN YOU ENCOUNTERED THAT HOLOGRAPHIC FRAGMENT OF YOUR FATHER.
*IN IMPOSSIBLE, INC. #2—DAVID.
YES! HE SHOWED ME SOMETHING HE CALLED...THE SINGLE POINT OF CONSCIOUSNESS! HE SHOWED ME YOU!
BUT I THOUGHT IT WAS JUST--
A PROJECTED MANIFESTATION OF GOLIATH'S BELIEF SYSTEM?
SOMETHING LIKE THAT.
WELL, PERHAPS YOU SHOULD CONSIDER THE POSSIBILITY THAT ALL OF CREATION MIGHT BE A PROJECTION--

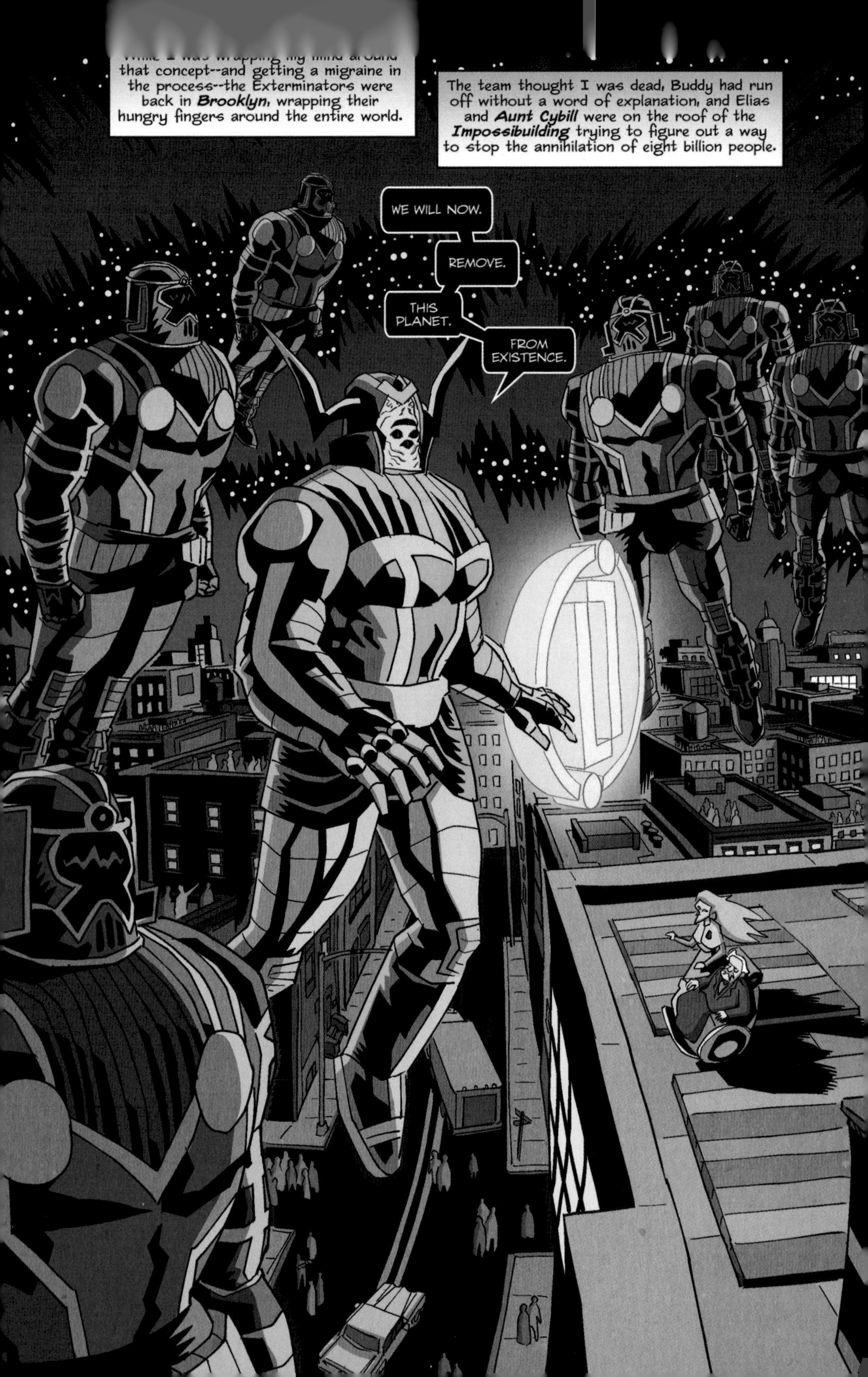
that concept--and getting a migraine in the process--the Exterminators were back in Brooklyn, wrapping their hungry fingers around the entire world.
The team thought I was dead, Buddy had run off without a word of explanation, and Elias and Aunt Cybill were on the roof of the Impossibuilding trying to figure out a way to stop the annihilation of eight billion people.
WE WILL NOW.
REMOVE.
THIS PLANET.
FROM EXISTENCE.

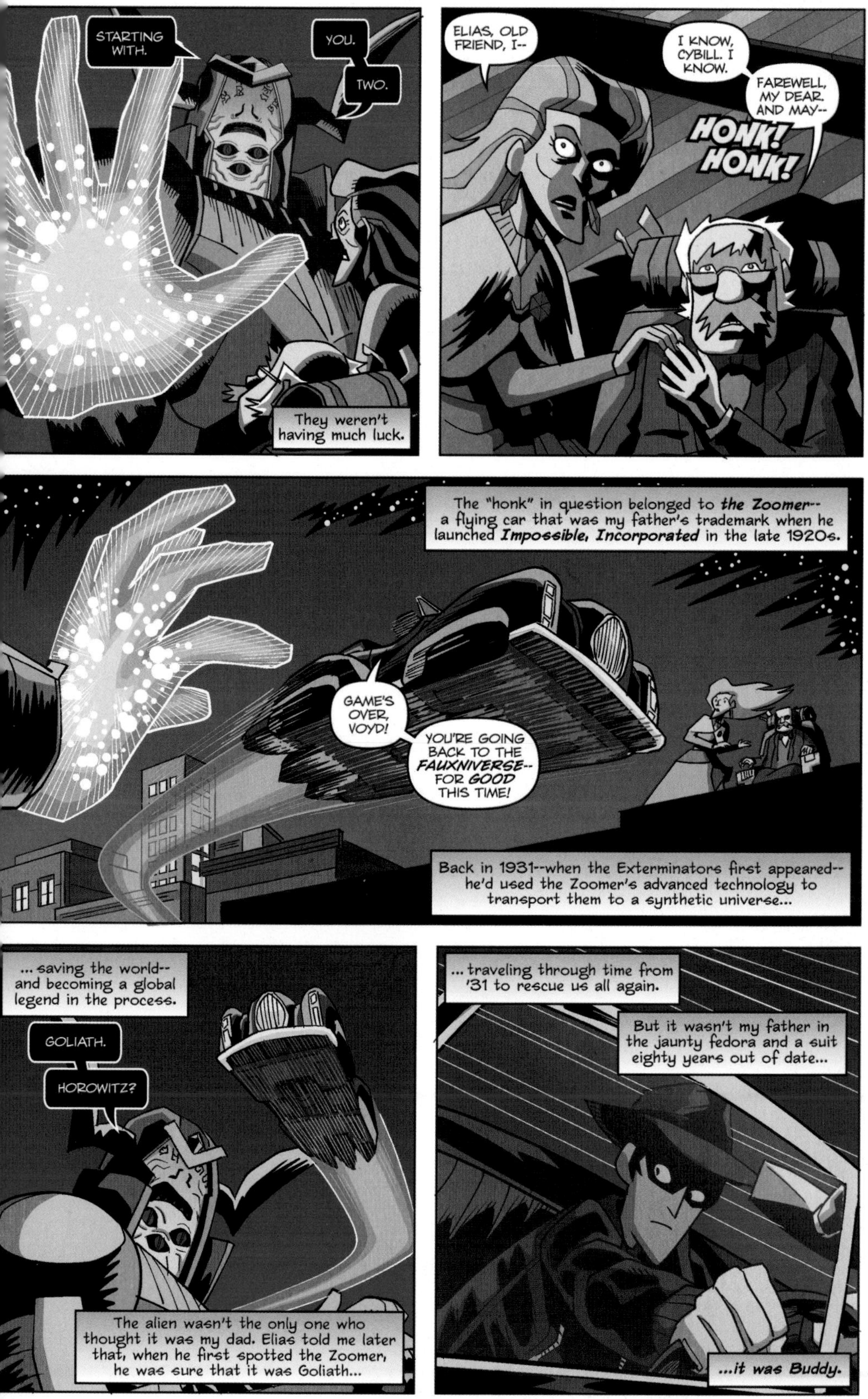

STARTING WITH.
YOU.
TWO.
They weren't having much luck.
ELIAS, OLD FRIEND, I--
I KNOW, CYBILL. I KNOW.
FAREWELL, MY DEAR. AND MAY--
HONK! HONK!
The "honk" in question belonged to *the Zoomer*-- a flying car that was my father's trademark when he launched ***Impossible, Incorporated*** in the late 1920s.
GAME'S OVER, VOYD!
YOU'RE GOING BACK TO THE ***FAUXNIVERSE***-- FOR ***GOOD*** THIS TIME!
Back in 1931--when the Exterminators first appeared-- he'd used the Zoomer's advanced technology to transport them to a synthetic universe...
... saving the world-- and becoming a global legend in the process.
GOLIATH.
HOROWITZ?
The alien wasn't the only one who thought it was my dad. Elias told me later that, when he first spotted the Zoomer, he was sure that it was Goliath...
... traveling through time from '31 to rescue us all again.
But it wasn't my father in the jaunty fedora and a suit eighty years out of date...
...it was Buddy.

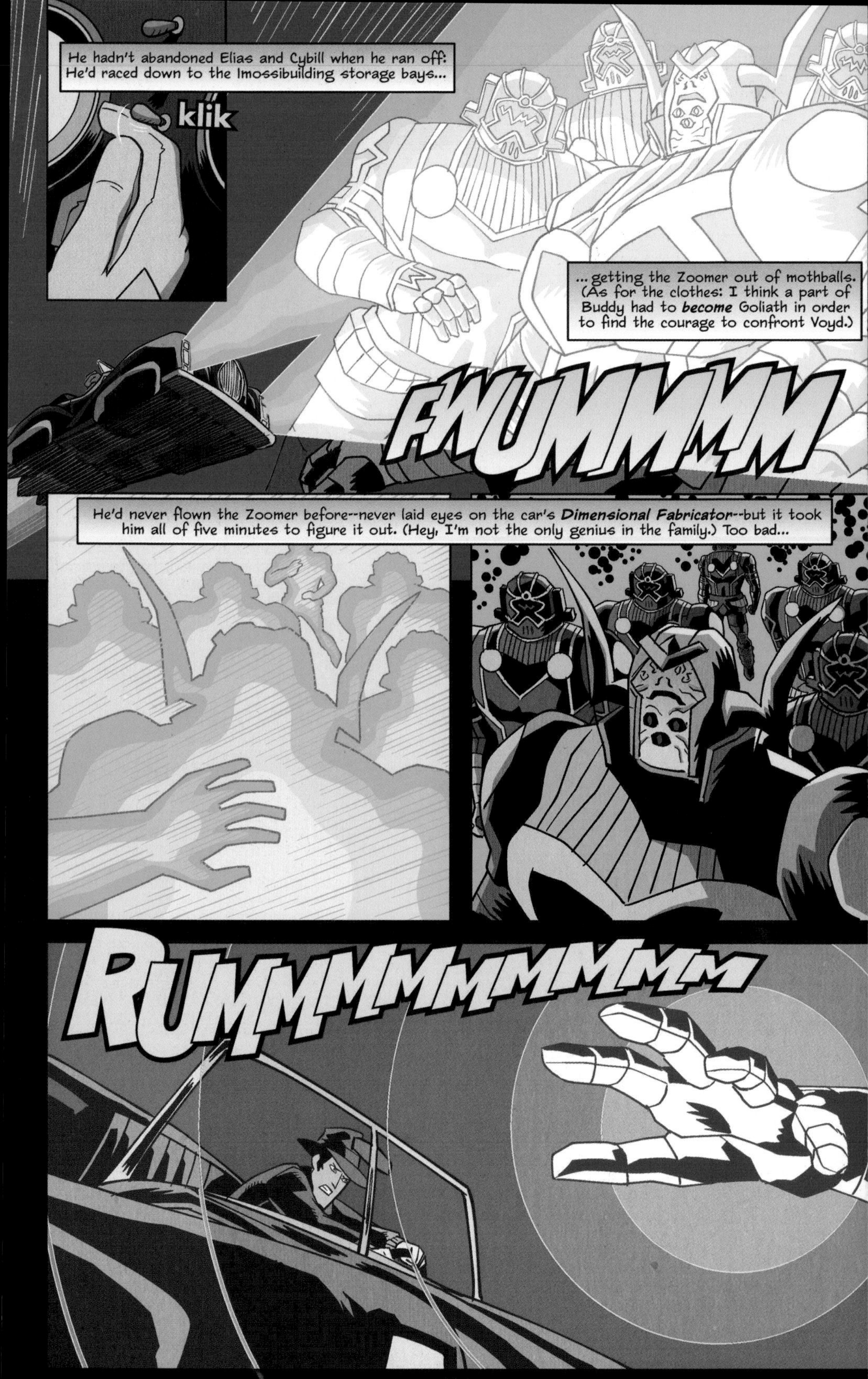
He hadn't abandoned Elias and Cybill when he ran off: He'd raced down to the Imossibuilding storage bays...
klik
...getting the Zoomer out of mothballs. (As for the clothes: I think a part of Buddy had to *become* Goliath in order to find the courage to confront Voyd.)
FNUMMMM
He'd never flown the Zoomer before--never laid eyes on the car's ***Dimensional Fabricator***--but it took him all of five minutes to figure it out. (Hey, I'm not the only genius in the family.) Too bad...
RUMMMMMMMMMM

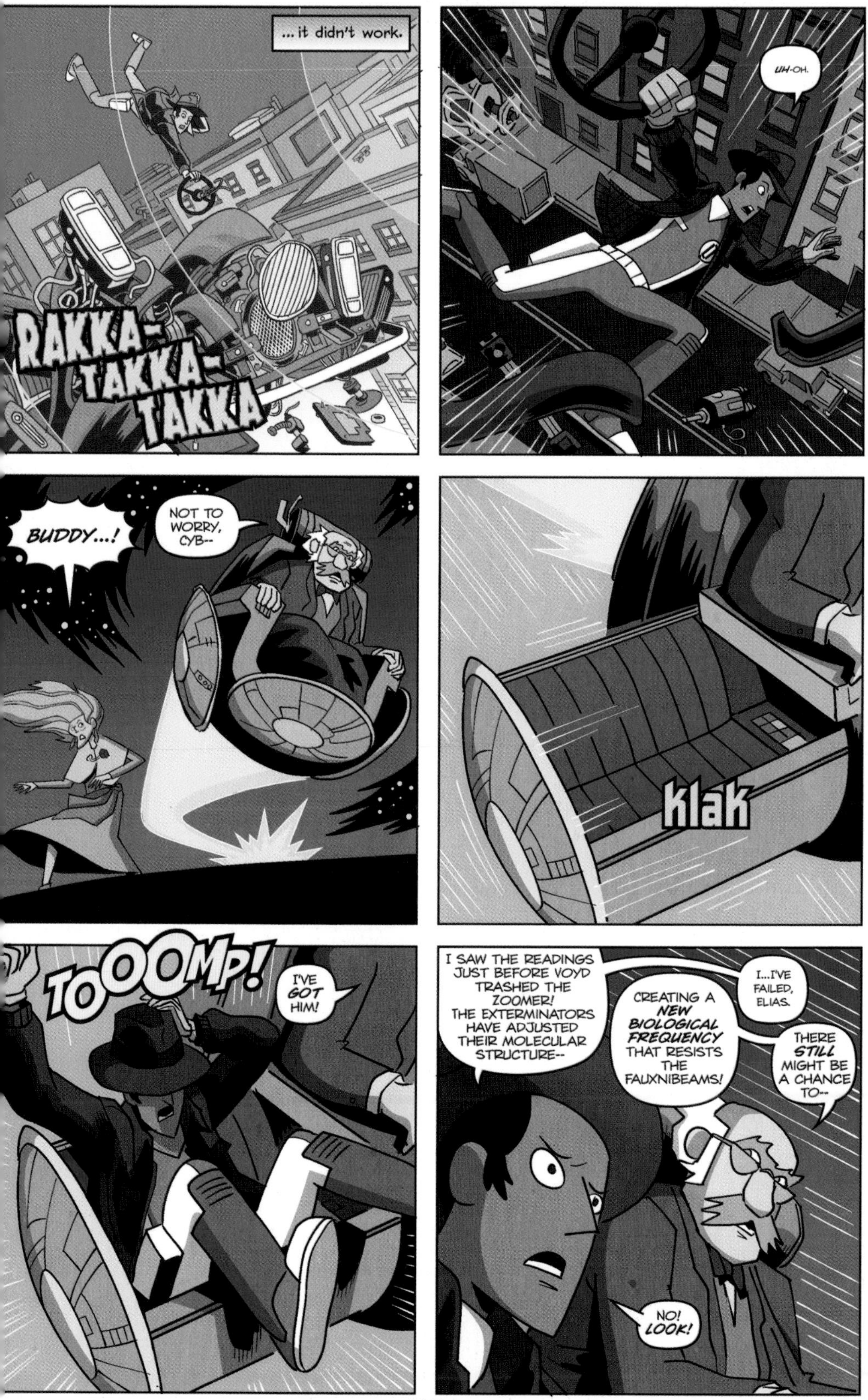
...it didn't work.
RAKKA-TAKKA-TAKKA
UH-OH.
BUDDY...!
NOT TO WORRY, CYB--
klak
TOOOOMP!
I'VE GOT HIM!
I SAW THE READINGS JUST BEFORE VOYD TRASHED THE ZOOMER! THE EXTERMINATORS HAVE ADJUSTED THEIR MOLECULAR STRUCTURE--
I...I'VE FAILED, ELIAS.
CREATING A NEW BIOLOGICAL FREQUENCY THAT RESISTS THE FAUXNIBEAMS!
THERE STILL MIGHT BE A CHANCE TO--
NO! LOOK!

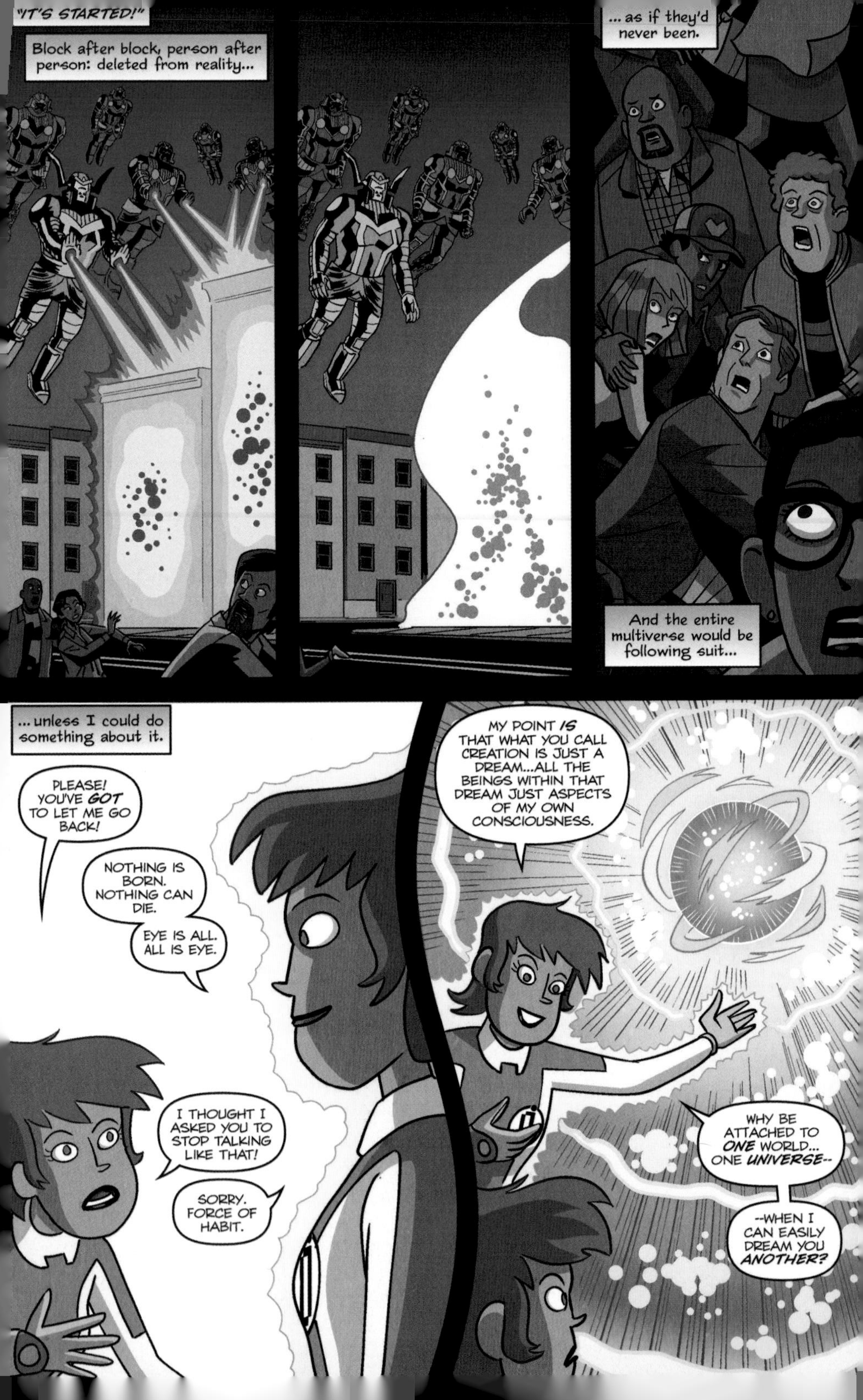
"IT'S STARTED!"
Block after block, person after person: deleted from reality...
...as if they'd never been.
And the entire multiverse would be following suit...
...unless I could do something about it.
PLEASE! YOU'VE GOT TO LET ME GO BACK!
NOTHING IS BORN. NOTHING CAN DIE.
EYE IS ALL. ALL IS EYE.
I THOUGHT I ASKED YOU TO STOP TALKING LIKE THAT!
SORRY. FORCE OF HABIT.
MY POINT IS THAT WHAT YOU CALL CREATION IS JUST A DREAM...ALL THE BEINGS WITHIN THAT DREAM JUST ASPECTS OF MY OWN CONSCIOUSNESS.
WHY BE ATTACHED TO ONE WORLD... ONE UNIVERSE--
--WHEN I CAN EASILY DREAM YOU ANOTHER?

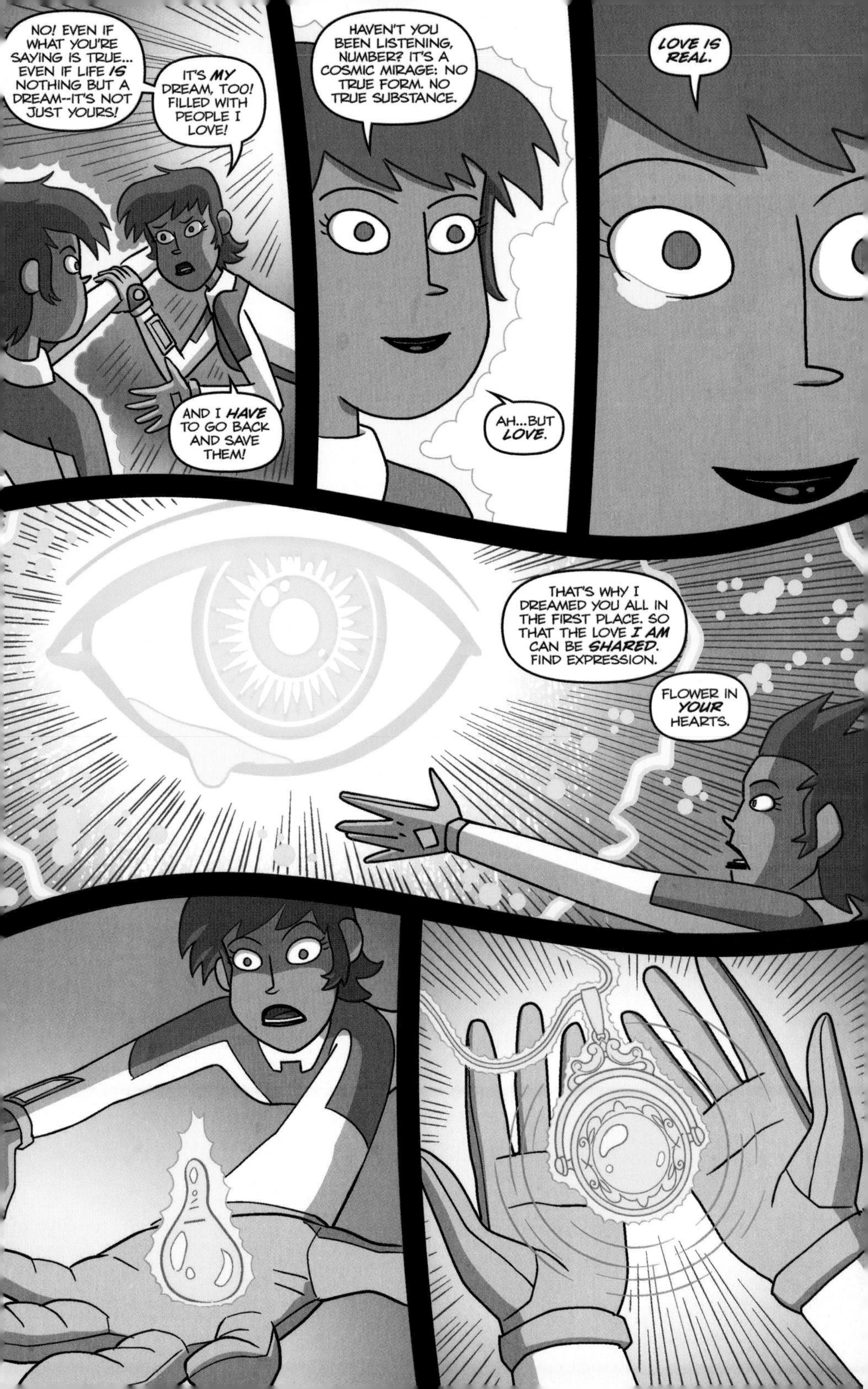
NO! EVEN IF WHAT YOU'RE SAYING IS TRUE... EVEN IF LIFE *IS* NOTHING BUT A DREAM--IT'S NOT JUST YOURS!
IT'S *MY* DREAM, TOO! FILLED WITH PEOPLE I LOVE!
AND I *HAVE* TO GO BACK AND SAVE THEM!
HAVEN'T YOU BEEN LISTENING, NUMBER? IT'S A COSMIC MIRAGE: NO TRUE FORM. NO TRUE SUBSTANCE.
AH...BUT *LOVE*.
LOVE IS REAL.
THAT'S WHY I DREAMED YOU ALL IN THE FIRST PLACE. SO THAT THE LOVE *I AM* CAN BE *SHARED*. FIND EXPRESSION.
FLOWER IN *YOUR* HEARTS.

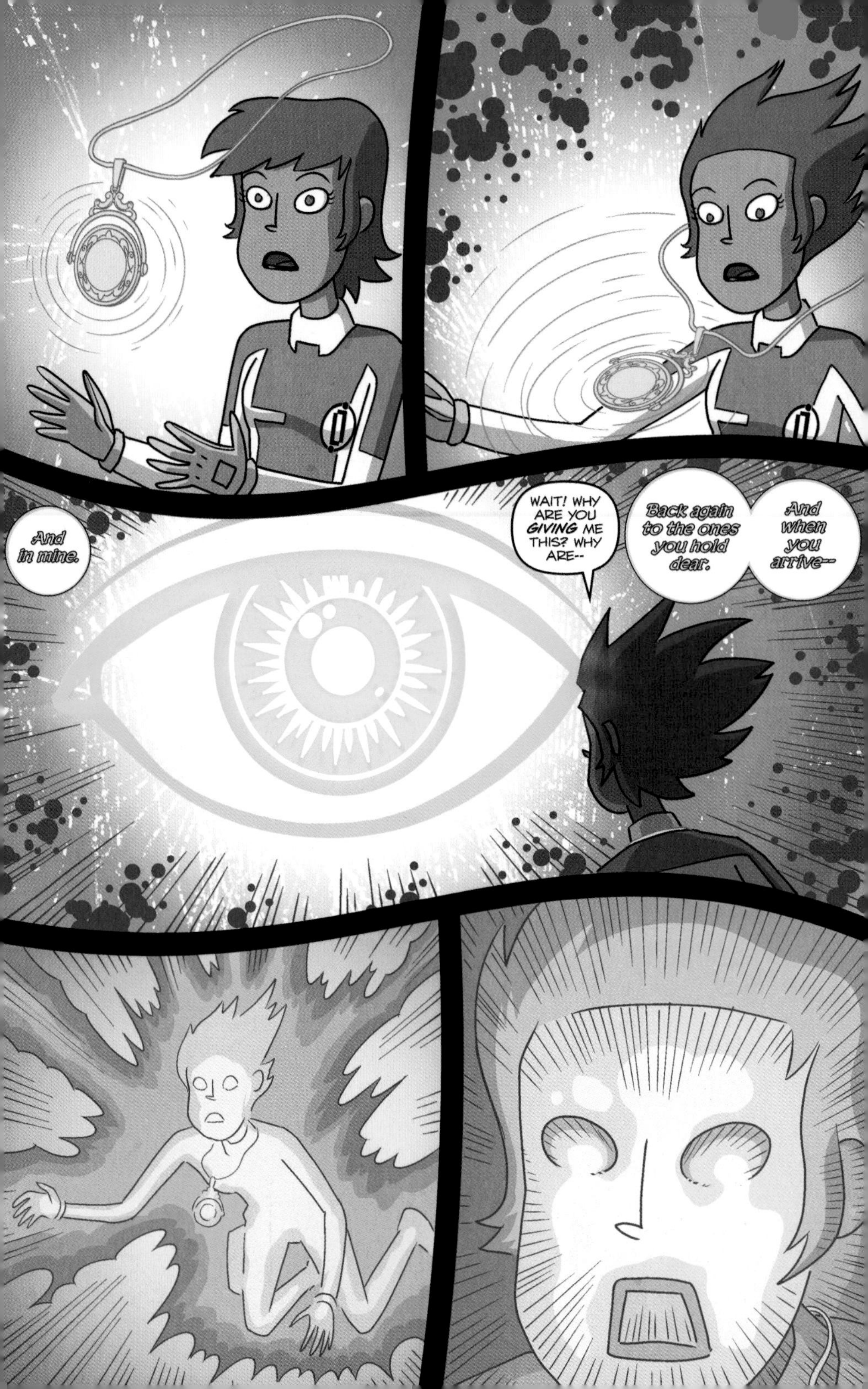
And in mine.
WAIT! WHY ARE YOU GIVING ME THIS? WHY ARE--
Back again to the ones you hold dear.
And when you arrive--

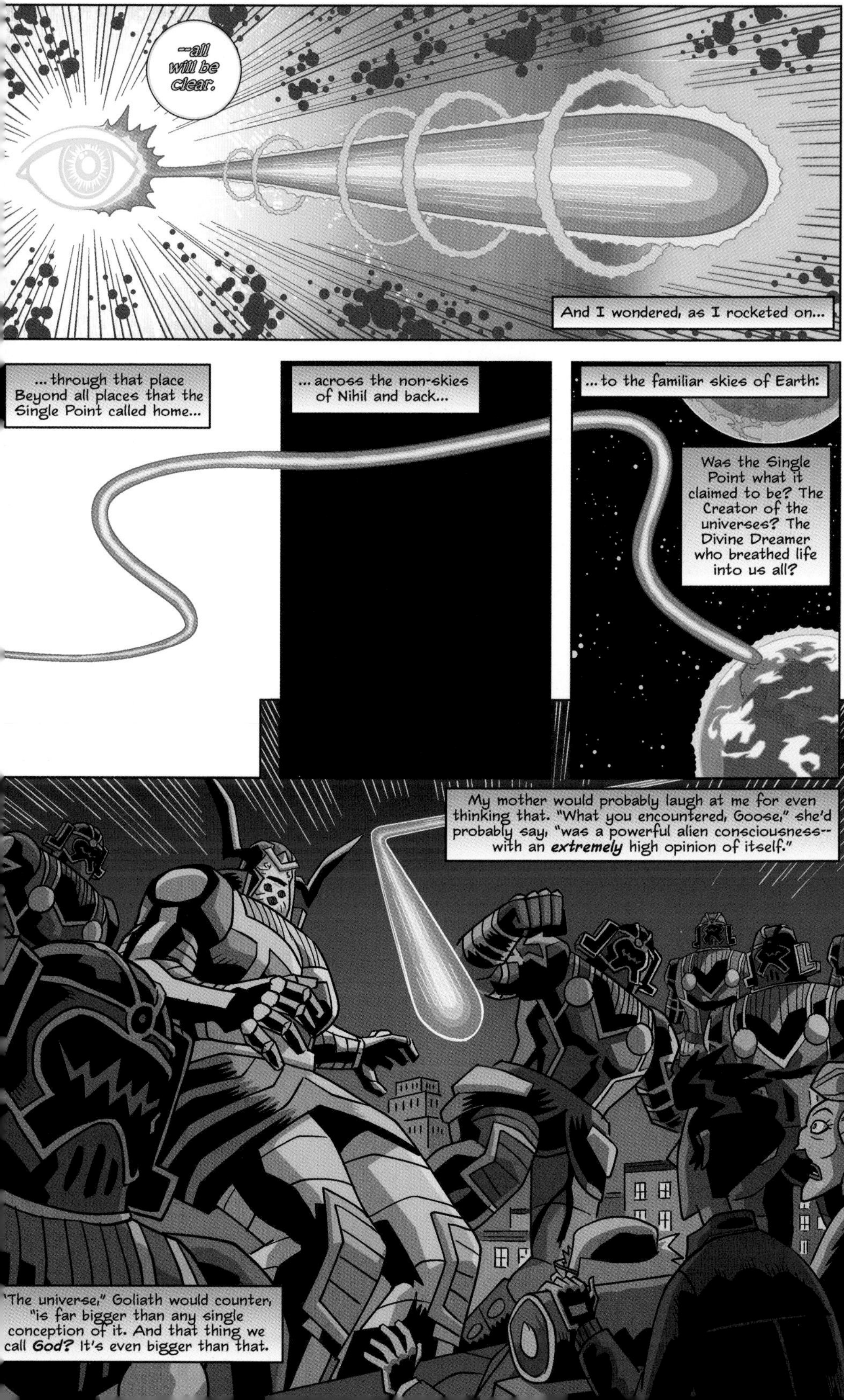
--all will be clear.
And I wondered, as I rocketed on...
...through that place Beyond all places that the Single Point called home...
...across the non-skies of Nihil and back...
...to the familiar skies of Earth:
Was the Single Point what it claimed to be? The Creator of the universes? The Divine Dreamer who breathed life into us all?
My mother would probably laugh at me for even thinking that. "What you encountered, Goose," she'd probably say, "was a powerful alien consciousness--with an *extremely* high opinion of itself."
"The universe," Goliath would counter, "is far bigger than any single conception of it. And that thing we call *God?* It's even bigger than that.

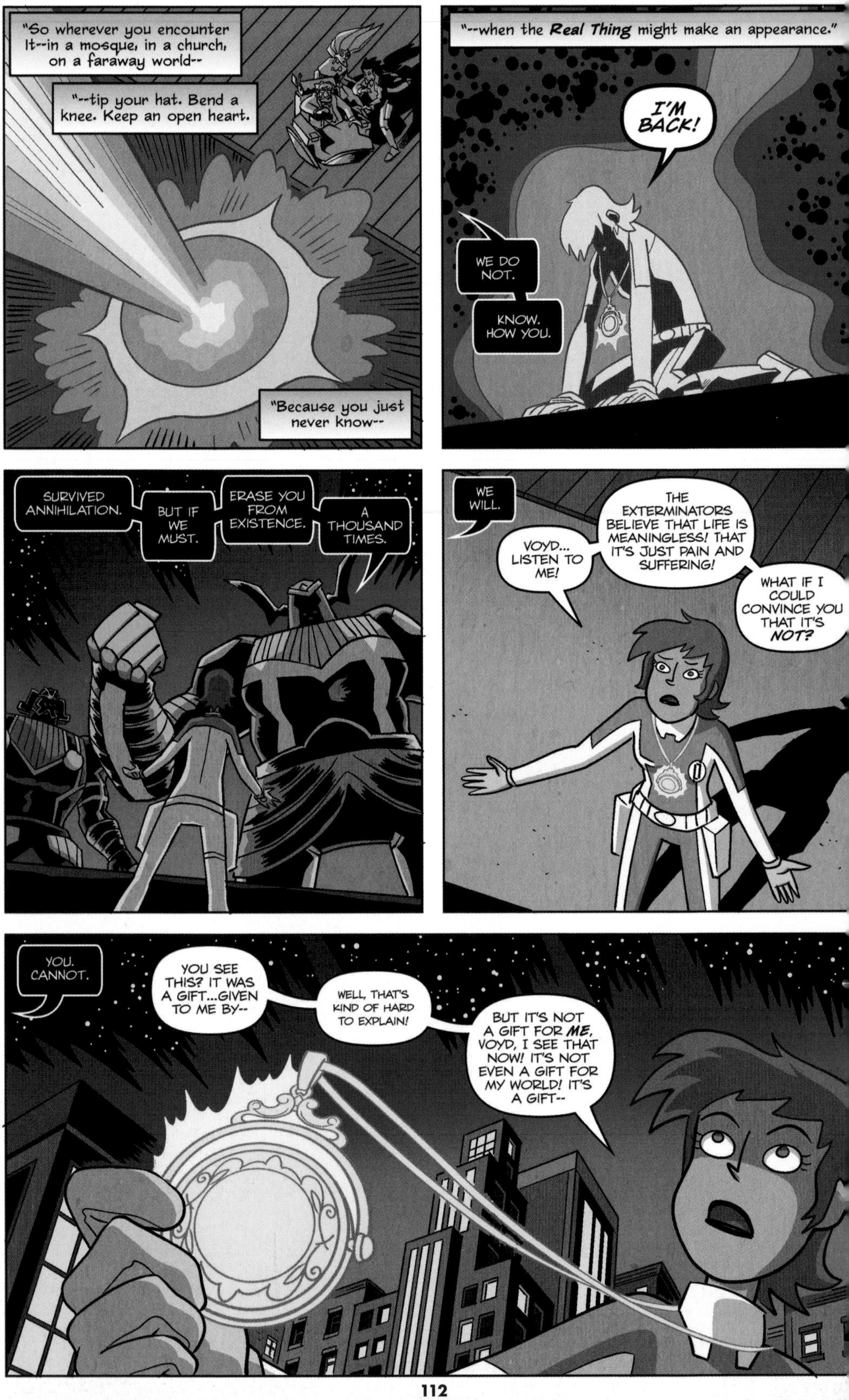
"So wherever you encounter It--in a mosque, in a church, on a faraway world--
"--tip your hat. Bend a knee. Keep an open heart.
"Because you just never know--
"--when the *Real Thing* might make an appearance."
I'M BACK!
WE DO NOT.
KNOW. HOW YOU.
SURVIVED ANNIHILATION.
BUT IF WE MUST.
ERASE YOU FROM EXISTENCE.
A THOUSAND TIMES.
WE WILL.
VOYD... LISTEN TO ME!
THE EXTERMINATORS BELIEVE THAT LIFE IS MEANINGLESS! THAT IT'S JUST PAIN AND SUFFERING!
WHAT IF I COULD CONVINCE YOU THAT IT'S *NOT?*
YOU. CANNOT.
YOU SEE THIS? IT WAS A GIFT...GIVEN TO ME BY--
WELL, THAT'S KIND OF HARD TO EXPLAIN!
BUT IT'S NOT A GIFT FOR *ME*, VOYD, I SEE THAT NOW! IT'S NOT EVEN A GIFT FOR MY WORLD! IT'S A GIFT--

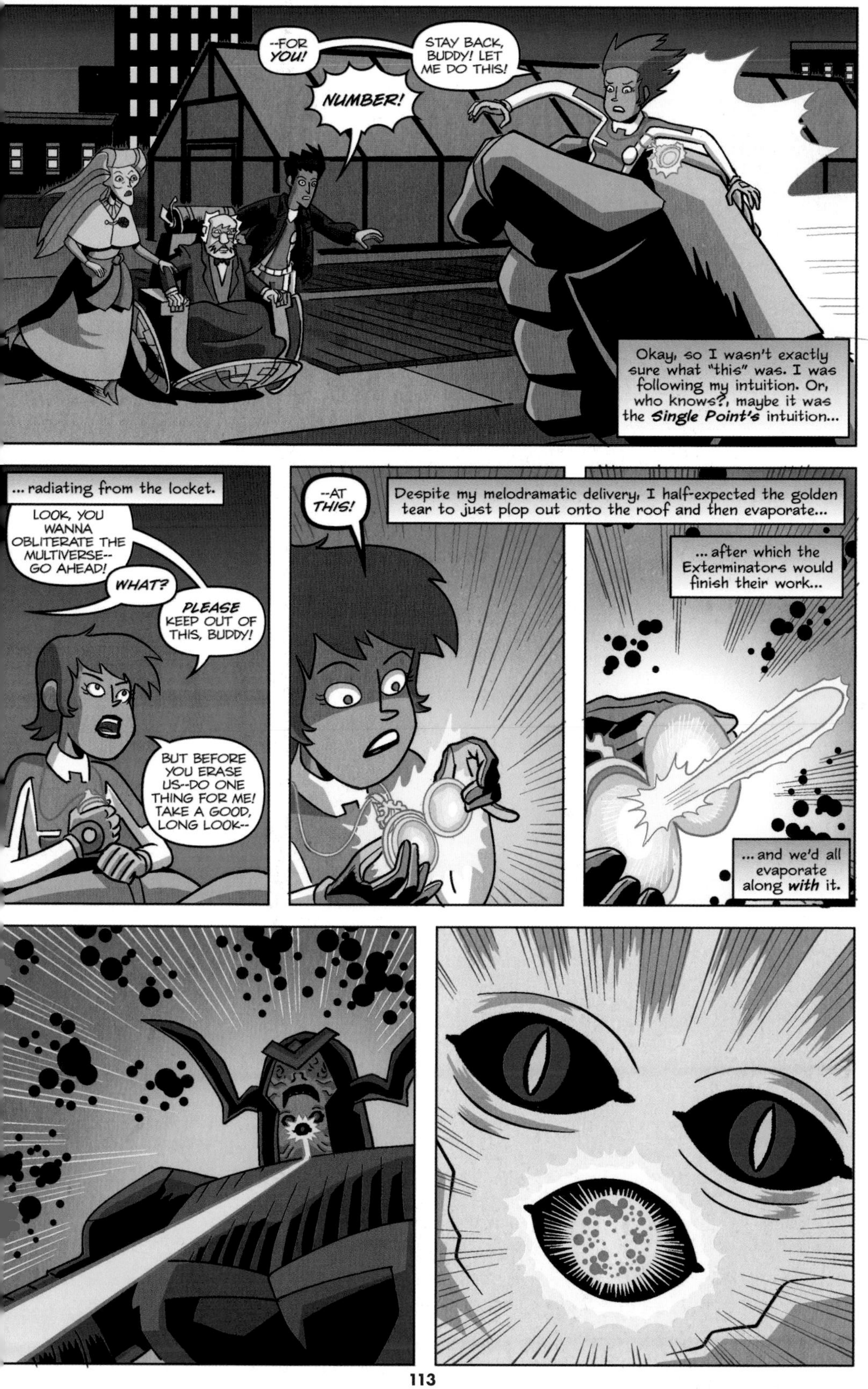
--FOR YOU!
NUMBER!
STAY BACK, BUDDY! LET ME DO THIS!
Okay, so I wasn't exactly sure what "this" was. I was following my intuition. Or, who knows?, maybe it was the Single Point's intuition...
... radiating from the locket.
LOOK, YOU WANNA OBLITERATE THE MULTIVERSE-- GO AHEAD!
WHAT?
PLEASE KEEP OUT OF THIS, BUDDY!
BUT BEFORE YOU ERASE US--DO ONE THING FOR ME! TAKE A GOOD, LONG LOOK--
--AT THIS!
Despite my melodramatic delivery, I half-expected the golden tear to just plop out onto the roof and then evaporate...
... after which the Exterminators would finish their work...
... and we'd all evaporate along with it.

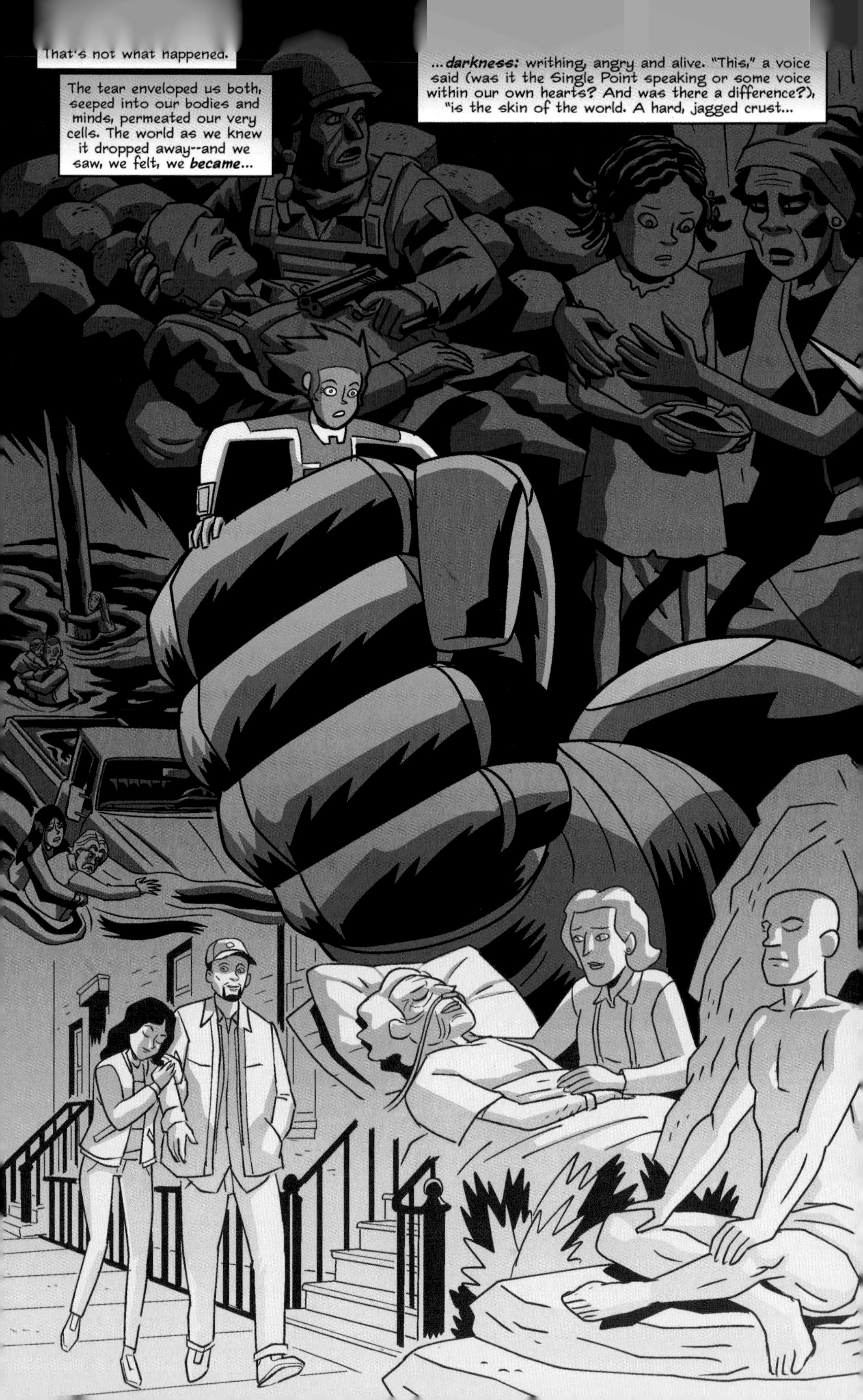

That's not what happened.
The tear enveloped us both, seeped into our bodies and minds, permeated our very cells. The world as we knew it dropped away--and we saw, we felt, we **became**...
...**darkness:** writhing, angry and alive. "This," a voice said (was it the Single Point speaking or some voice within our own hearts? And was there a difference?), "is the skin of the world. A hard, jagged crust...

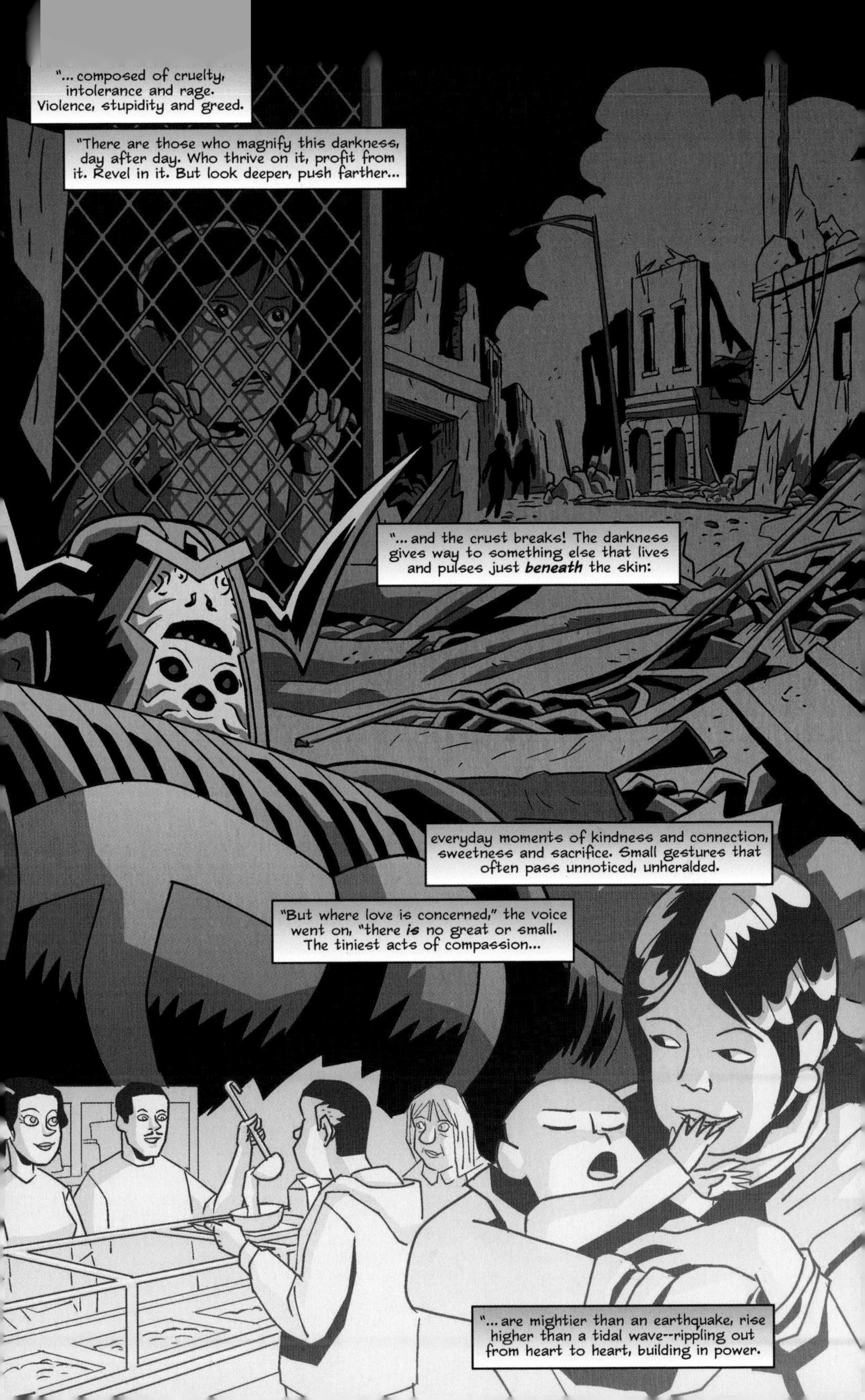
"... composed of cruelty, intolerance and rage. Violence, stupidity and greed.
"There are those who magnify this darkness, day after day. Who thrive on it, profit from it. Revel in it. But look deeper, push farther...
"... and the crust breaks! The darkness gives way to something else that lives and pulses just *beneath* the skin:
everyday moments of kindness and connection, sweetness and sacrifice. Small gestures that often pass unnoticed, unheralded.
"But where love is concerned," the voice went on, "there *is* no great or small. The tiniest acts of compassion...
"... are mightier than an earthquake, rise higher than a tidal wave--rippling out from heart to heart, building in power.

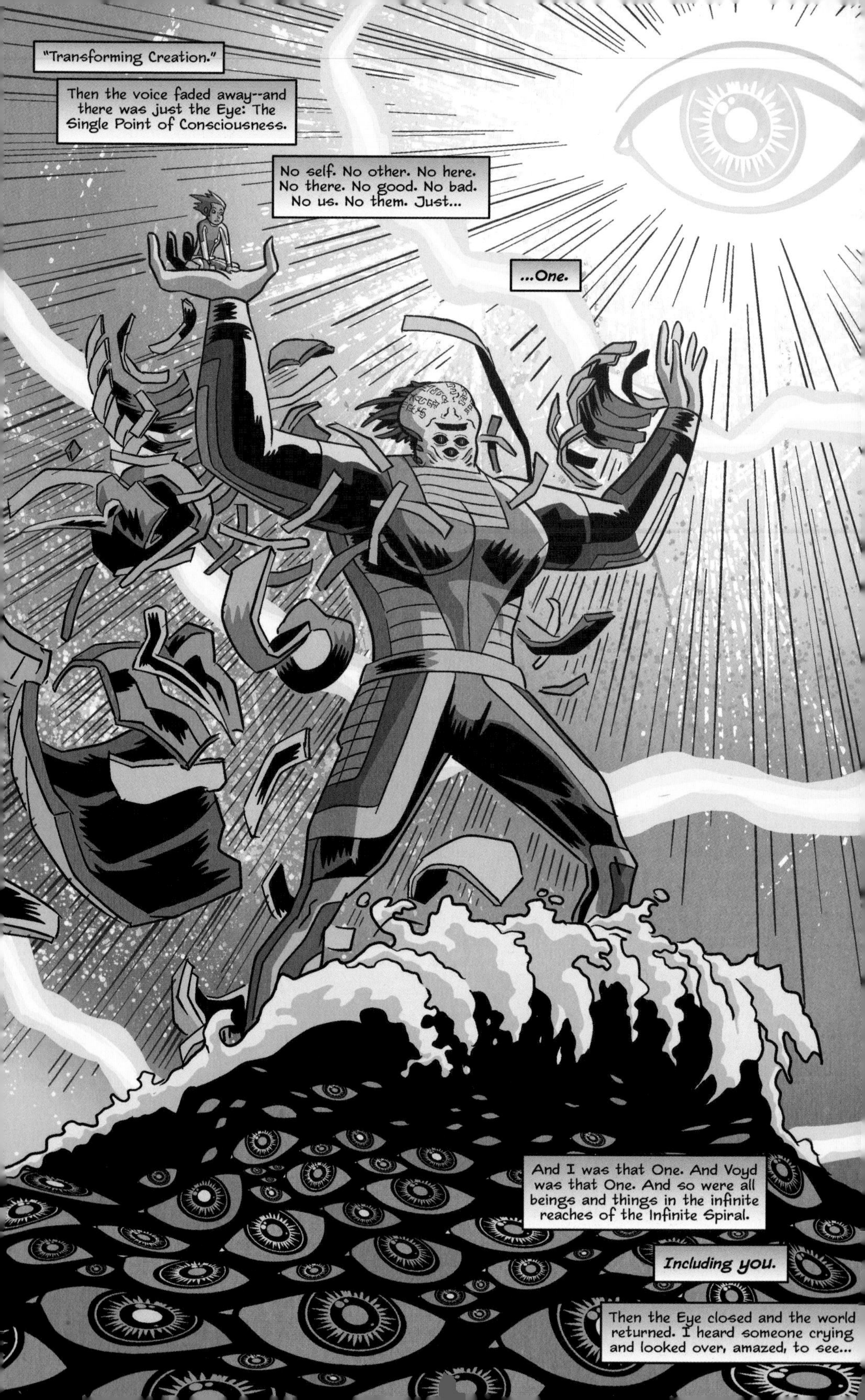
"Transforming Creation."
Then the voice faded away--and there was just the Eye: The Single Point of Consciousness.
No self. No other. No here. No there. No good. No bad. No us. No them. Just...
...One.
And I was that One. And Voyd was that One. And so were all beings and things in the infinite reaches of the Infinite Spiral.
Including you.
Then the Eye closed and the world returned. I heard someone crying and looked over, amazed, to see...

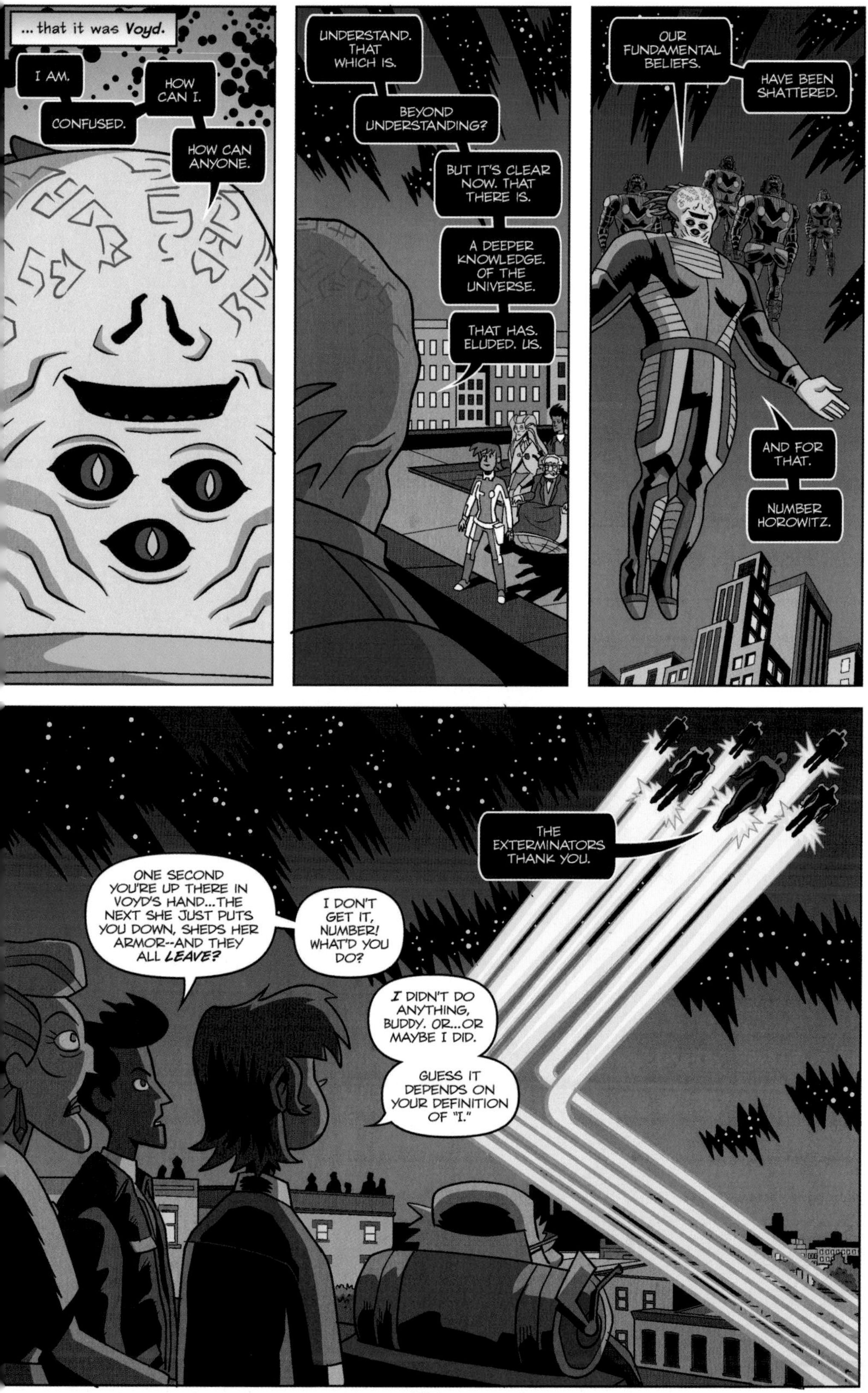
... that it was Voyd.
I AM.
CONFUSED.
HOW CAN I.
HOW CAN ANYONE.
UNDERSTAND. THAT WHICH IS.
BEYOND UNDERSTANDING?
BUT IT'S CLEAR NOW. THAT THERE IS.
A DEEPER KNOWLEDGE. OF THE UNIVERSE.
THAT HAS. ELUDED. US.
OUR FUNDAMENTAL BELIEFS.
HAVE BEEN SHATTERED.
AND FOR THAT.
NUMBER HOROWITZ.
THE EXTERMINATORS THANK YOU.
ONE SECOND YOU'RE UP THERE IN VOYD'S HAND...THE NEXT SHE JUST PUTS YOU DOWN, SHEDS HER ARMOR--AND THEY ALL LEAVE?
I DON'T GET IT, NUMBER! WHAT'D YOU DO?
I DIDN'T DO ANYTHING, BUDDY. OR...OR MAYBE I DID.
GUESS IT DEPENDS ON YOUR DEFINITION OF "I."

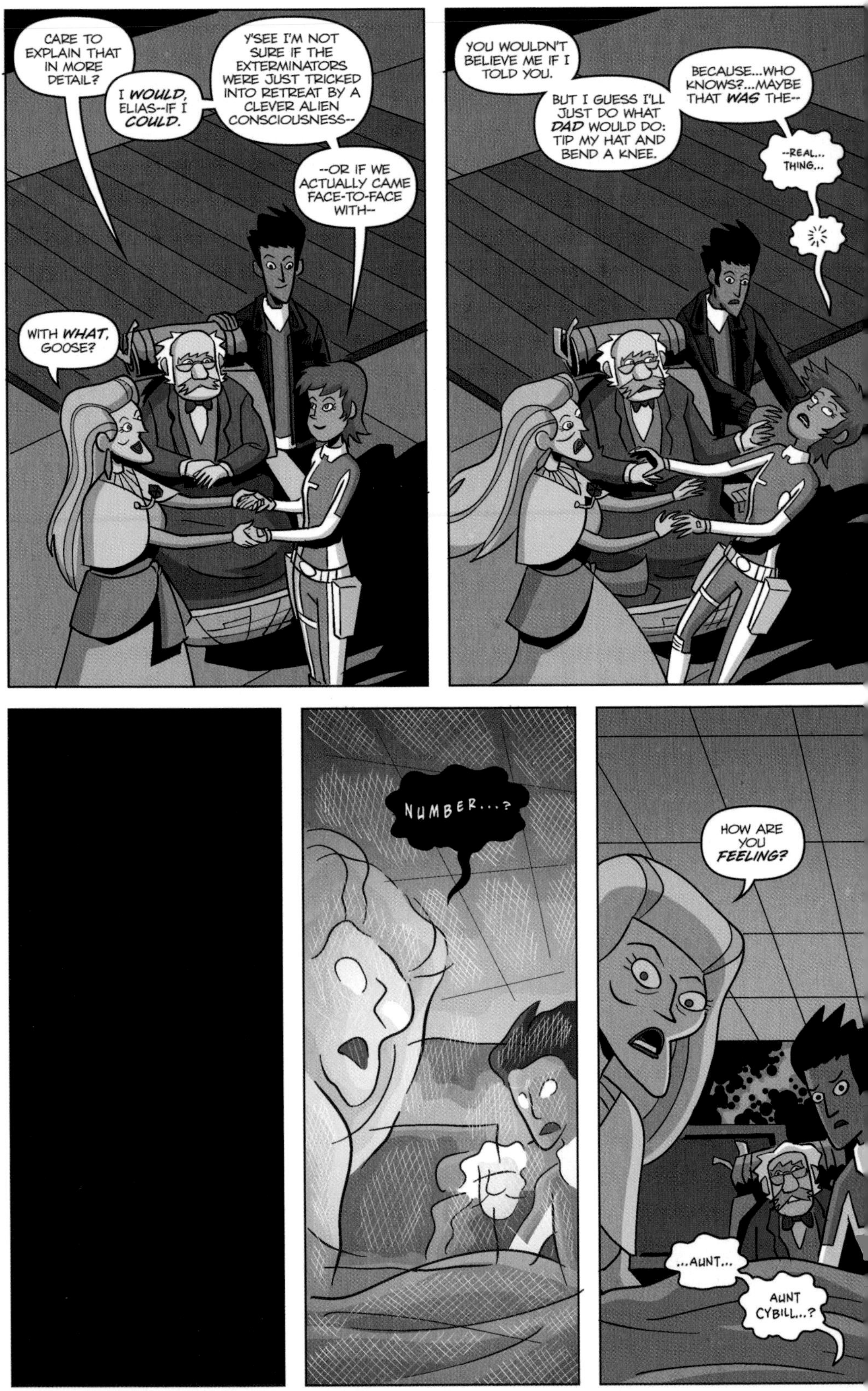
CARE TO EXPLAIN THAT IN MORE DETAIL?
I WOULD, ELIAS--IF I COULD.
Y'SEE I'M NOT SURE IF THE EXTERMINATORS WERE JUST TRICKED INTO RETREAT BY A CLEVER ALIEN CONSCIOUSNESS--
--OR IF WE ACTUALLY CAME FACE-TO-FACE WITH--
WITH WHAT, GOOSE?
YOU WOULDN'T BELIEVE ME IF I TOLD YOU.
BUT I GUESS I'LL JUST DO WHAT DAD WOULD DO: TIP MY HAT AND BEND A KNEE.
BECAUSE...WHO KNOWS?...MAYBE THAT WAS THE--
--REAL... THING...
NUMBER...?
HOW ARE YOU FEELING?
...AUNT...
AUNT CYBILL...?

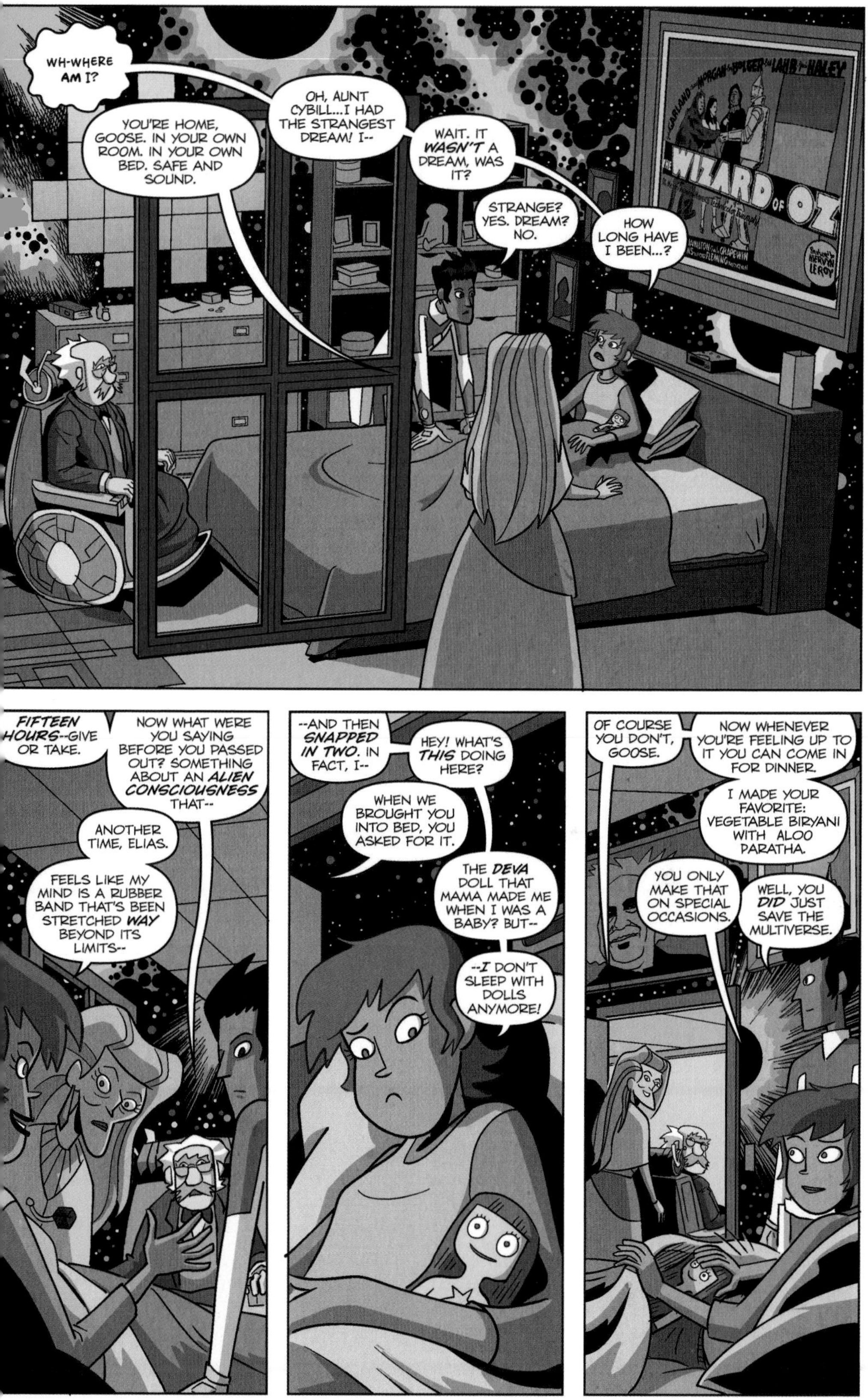
WH-WHERE AM I?
YOU'RE HOME, GOOSE. IN YOUR OWN ROOM. IN YOUR OWN BED. SAFE AND SOUND.
OH, AUNT CYBILL...I HAD THE STRANGEST DREAM! I--
WAIT. IT WASN'T A DREAM, WAS IT?
STRANGE? YES. DREAM? NO.
HOW LONG HAVE I BEEN...?
THE WIZARD OF OZ
FIFTEEN HOURS--GIVE OR TAKE.
NOW WHAT WERE YOU SAYING BEFORE YOU PASSED OUT? SOMETHING ABOUT AN ALIEN CONSCIOUSNESS THAT--
ANOTHER TIME, ELIAS.
FEELS LIKE MY MIND IS A RUBBER BAND THAT'S BEEN STRETCHED WAY BEYOND ITS LIMITS--
--AND THEN SNAPPED IN TWO. IN FACT, I--
HEY! WHAT'S THIS DOING HERE?
WHEN WE BROUGHT YOU INTO BED, YOU ASKED FOR IT.
THE DEVA DOLL THAT MAMA MADE ME WHEN I WAS A BABY? BUT--
--I DON'T SLEEP WITH DOLLS ANYMORE!
OF COURSE YOU DON'T, GOOSE.
NOW WHENEVER YOU'RE FEELING UP TO IT YOU CAN COME IN FOR DINNER.
I MADE YOUR FAVORITE: VEGETABLE BIRYANI WITH ALOO PARATHA.
YOU ONLY MAKE THAT ON SPECIAL OCCASIONS.
WELL, YOU DID JUST SAVE THE MULTIVERSE.

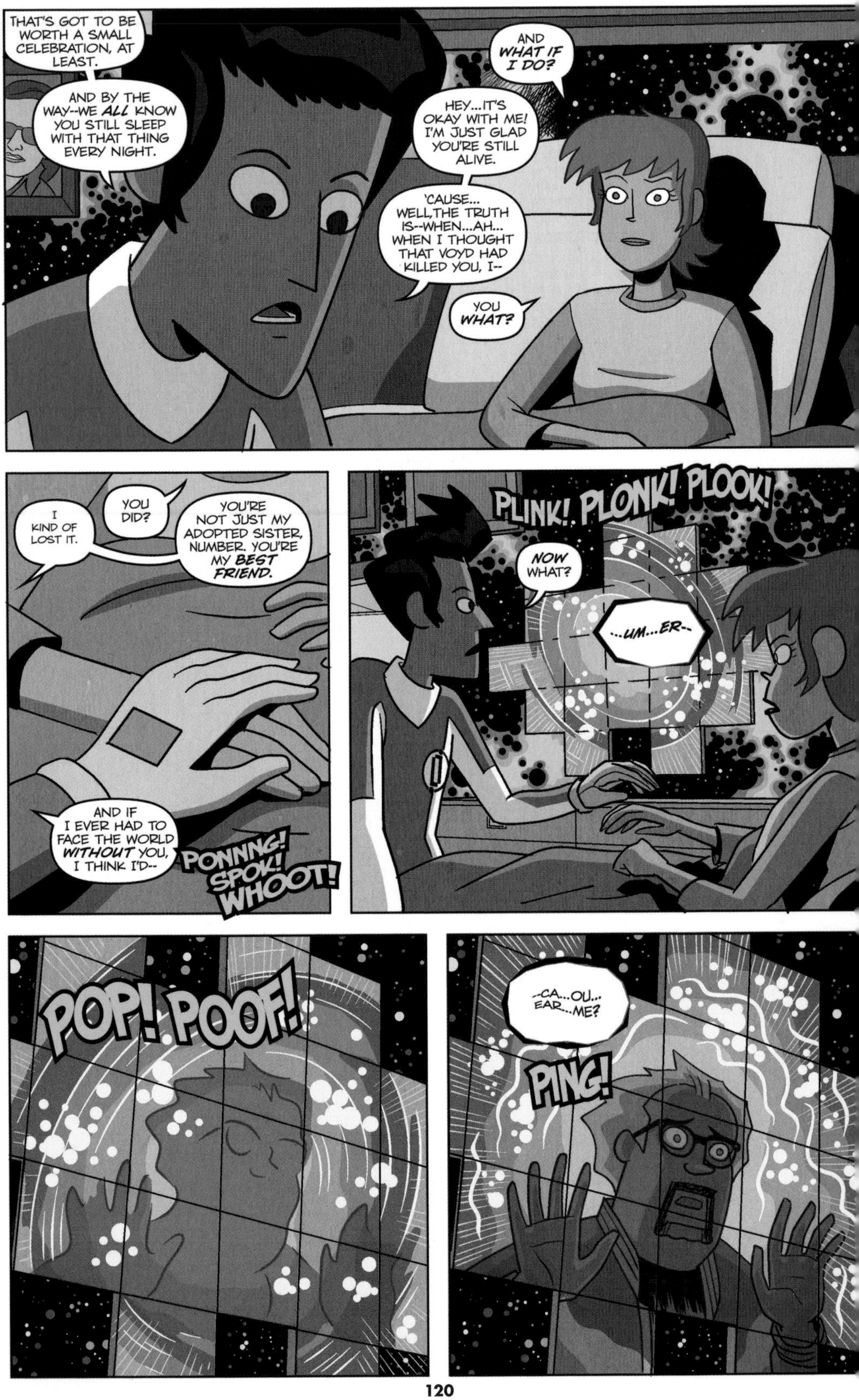
THAT'S GOT TO BE WORTH A SMALL CELEBRATION, AT LEAST.
AND BY THE WAY--WE ALL KNOW YOU STILL SLEEP WITH THAT THING EVERY NIGHT.
AND WHAT IF I DO?
HEY...IT'S OKAY WITH ME! I'M JUST GLAD YOU'RE STILL ALIVE.
'CAUSE... WELL,THE TRUTH IS--WHEN...AH... WHEN I THOUGHT THAT VOYD HAD KILLED YOU, I--
YOU WHAT?
I KIND OF LOST IT.
YOU DID?
YOU'RE NOT JUST MY ADOPTED SISTER, NUMBER. YOU'RE MY BEST FRIEND.
AND IF I EVER HAD TO FACE THE WORLD WITHOUT YOU, I THINK I'D--
PONNNG! SPOK! WHOOT!
PLINK! PLONK! PLOOK!
NOW WHAT?
...UM...ER--
POP! POOF!
--CA...OU... EAR...ME?
PING!

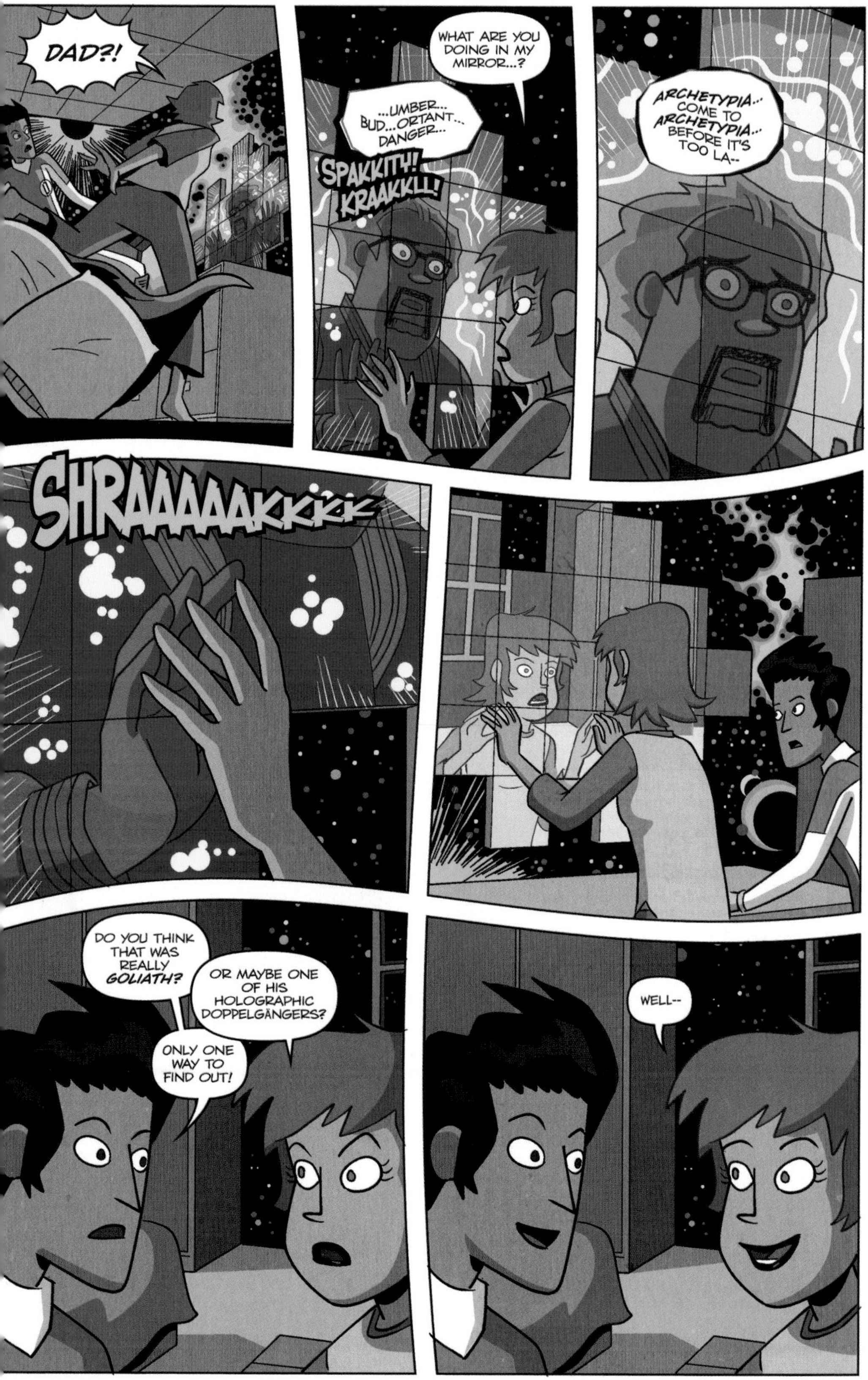
DAD?!
WHAT ARE YOU DOING IN MY MIRROR...?
...UMBER... BUD...ORTANT... DANGER...
SPAKKITY! KRAAKKLL!
ARCHETYPIA... COME TO ARCHETYPIA... BEFORE IT'S TOO LA--
SHRAAAAAKKKK
DO YOU THINK THAT WAS REALLY GOLIATH?
OR MAYBE ONE OF HIS HOLOGRAPHIC DOPPELGÄNGERS?
ONLY ONE WAY TO FIND OUT!
WELL--

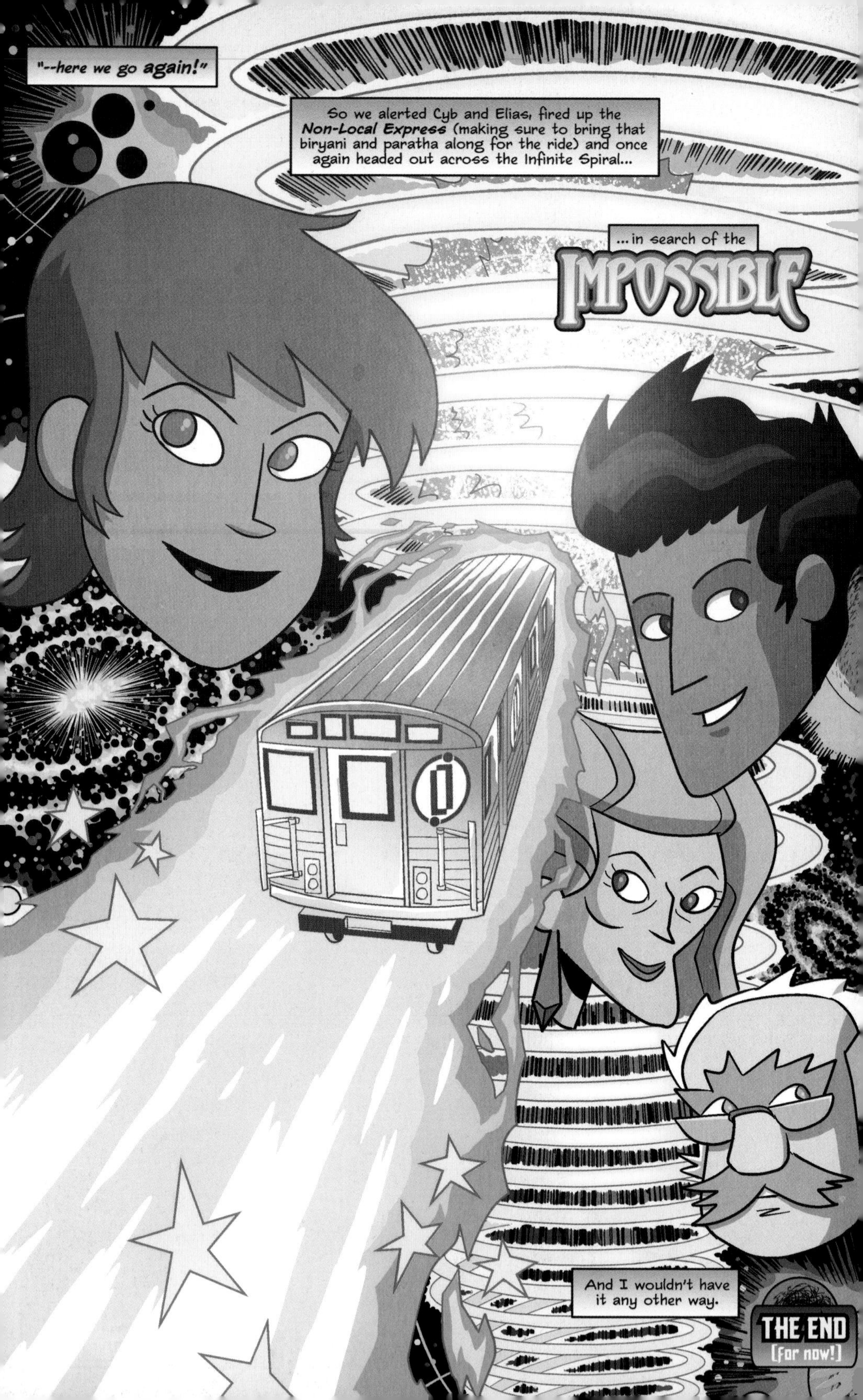
"--here we go again!"
So we alerted Cyb and Elias, fired up the Non-Local Express (making sure to bring that biryani and paratha along for the ride) and once again headed out across the Infinite Spiral...
...in search of the
IMPOSSIBLE
And I wouldn't have it any other way.
THE END
[for now!]

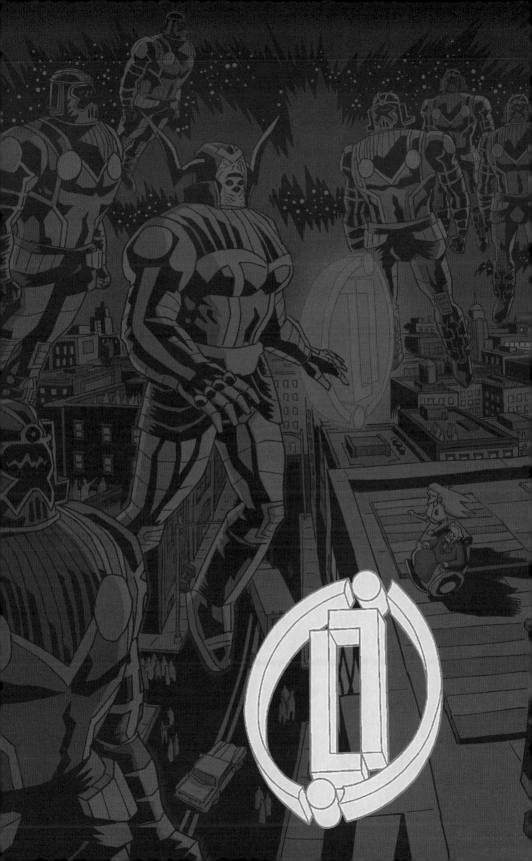

Early development sketches and excerpts from a sample story that went along with the initial *Impossible, Inc.* proposal.

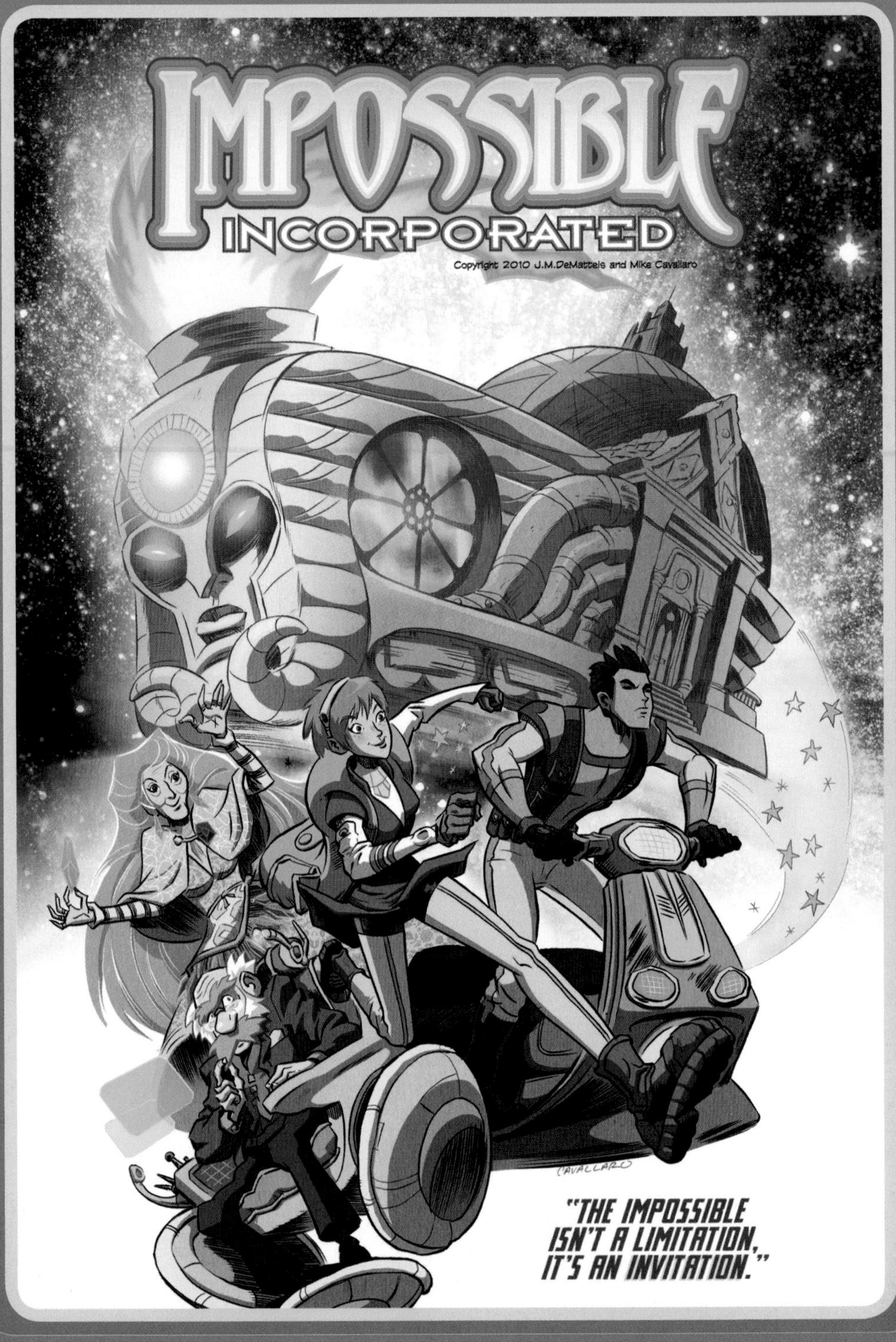

IMPOSSIBLE
INCORPORATED
Copyright 2010 J.M.DeMatteis and Mike Cavallaro
CAVALLARO
"THE IMPOSSIBLE ISN'T A LIMITATION, IT'S AN INVITATION."

ART & LETTERING BY MIKE CAVALLARO

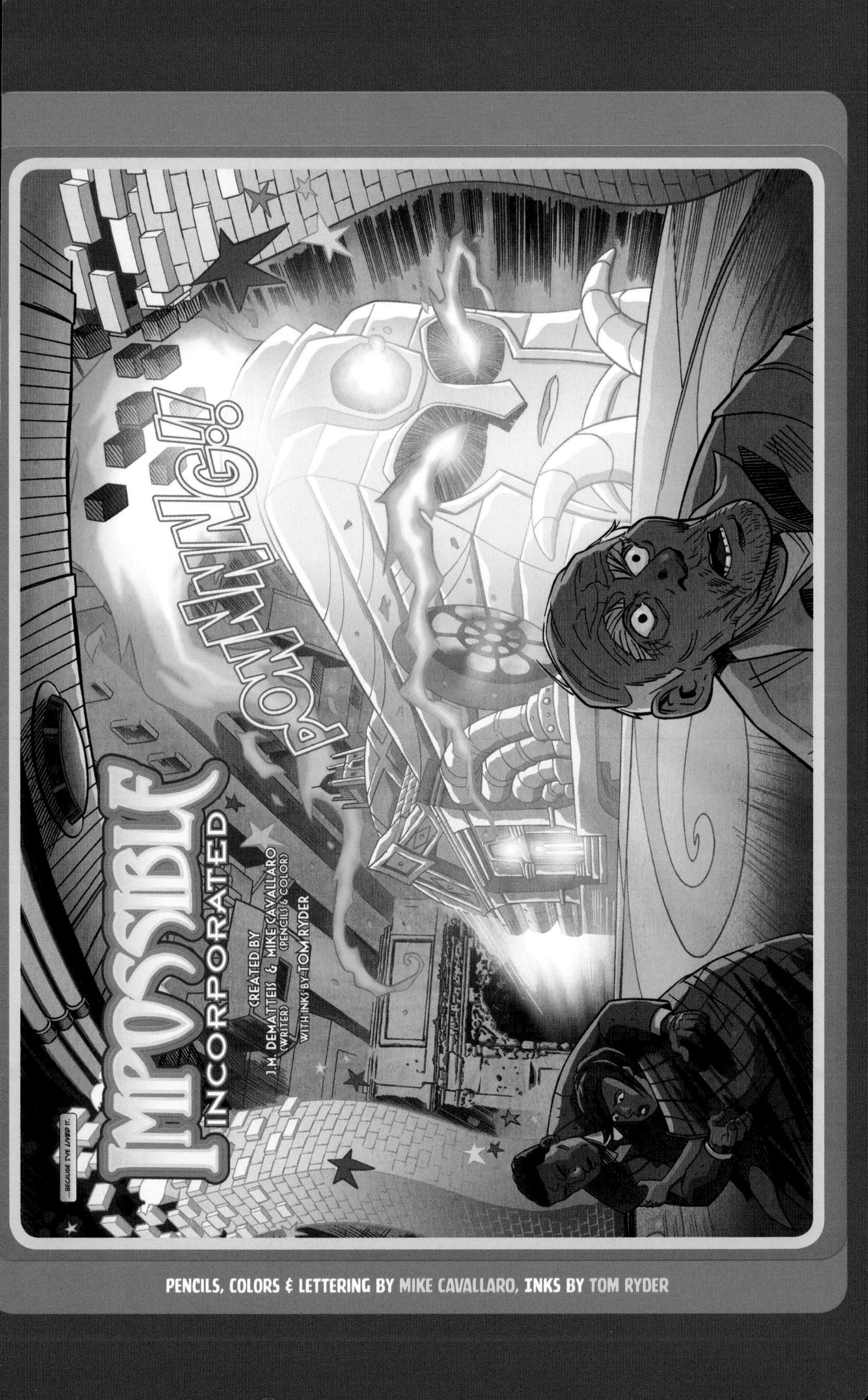
...BECAUSE I'VE LIVED IT.
IMPOSSIBLE INCORPORATED
CREATED BY
J.M. DEMATTEIS (WRITER) & MIKE CAVALLARO (PENCILS & COLOR)
WITH INKS BY TOM RYDER

PENCILS, COLORS & LETTERING BY MIKE CAVALLARO, INKS BY TOM RYDER

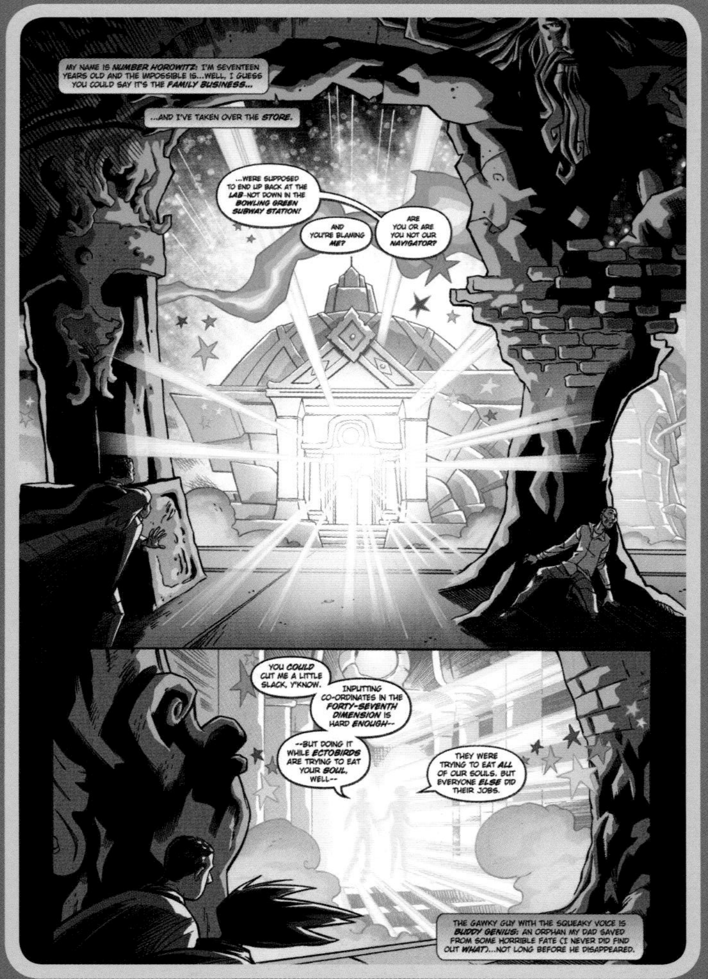
MY NAME IS NUMBER HOROWITZ: I'M SEVENTEEN YEARS OLD AND THE IMPOSSIBLE IS...WELL, I GUESS YOU COULD SAY IT'S THE FAMILY BUSINESS...
...AND I'VE TAKEN OVER THE STORE.
...WERE SUPPOSED TO END UP BACK AT THE LAB--NOT DOWN IN THE BOWLING GREEN SUBWAY STATION!
AND YOU'RE BLAMING ME?
ARE YOU OR ARE YOU NOT OUR NAVIGATOR?
YOU COULD CUT ME A LITTLE SLACK, Y'KNOW.
INPUTTING CO-ORDINATES IN THE FORTY-SEVENTH DIMENSION IS HARD ENOUGH--
--BUT DOING IT WHILE ECTOBIRDS ARE TRYING TO EAT YOUR SOUL. WELL--
THEY WERE TRYING TO EAT ALL OF OUR SOULS. BUT EVERYONE ELSE DID THEIR JOBS.
THE GAWKY GUY WITH THE SQUEAKY VOICE IS BUDDY GENIUS: AN ORPHAN MY DAD SAVED FROM SOME HORRIBLE FATE (I NEVER DID FIND OUT WHAT)...NOT LONG BEFORE HE DISAPPEARED.

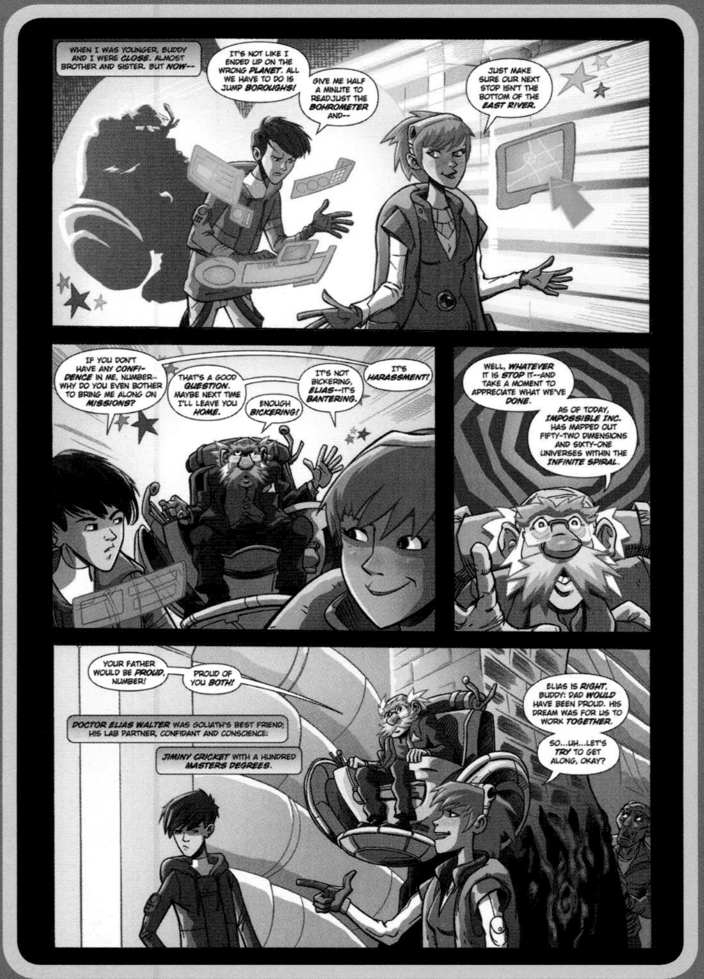
WHEN I WAS YOUNGER, BUDDY AND I WERE CLOSE. ALMOST BROTHER AND SISTER. BUT NOW--
IT'S NOT LIKE I ENDED UP ON THE WRONG PLANET. ALL WE HAVE TO DO IS JUMP BOROUGHS!
GIVE ME HALF A MINUTE TO READJUST THE BOHROMETER AND--
JUST MAKE SURE OUR NEXT STOP ISN'T THE BOTTOM OF THE EAST RIVER.
IF YOU DON'T HAVE ANY CONFI-DENCE IN ME, NUMBER--WHY DO YOU EVEN BOTHER TO BRING ME ALONG ON MISSIONS?
THAT'S A GOOD QUESTION. MAYBE NEXT TIME I'LL LEAVE YOU HOME.
ENOUGH BICKERING!
IT'S NOT BICKERING, ELIAS--IT'S BANTERING.
IT'S HARASSMENT!
WELL, WHATEVER IT IS STOP IT--AND TAKE A MOMENT TO APPRECIATE WHAT WE'VE DONE.
AS OF TODAY, IMPOSSIBLE INC. HAS MAPPED OUT FIFTY-TWO DIMENSIONS AND SIXTY-ONE UNIVERSES WITHIN THE INFINITE SPIRAL.
YOUR FATHER WOULD BE PROUD, NUMBER!
PROUD OF YOU BOTH!
DOCTOR ELIAS WALTER WAS GOLIATH'S BEST FRIEND; HIS LAB PARTNER, CONFIDANT AND CONSCIENCE:
JIMINY CRICKET WITH A HUNDRED MASTERS DEGREES.
ELIAS IS RIGHT, BUDDY: DAD WOULD HAVE BEEN PROUD. HIS DREAM WAS FOR US TO WORK TOGETHER.
SO...UH...LET'S TRY TO GET ALONG, OKAY?

PENCILS, COLORS & LETTERING BY MIKE CAVALLARO, INKS BY TOM RYDER

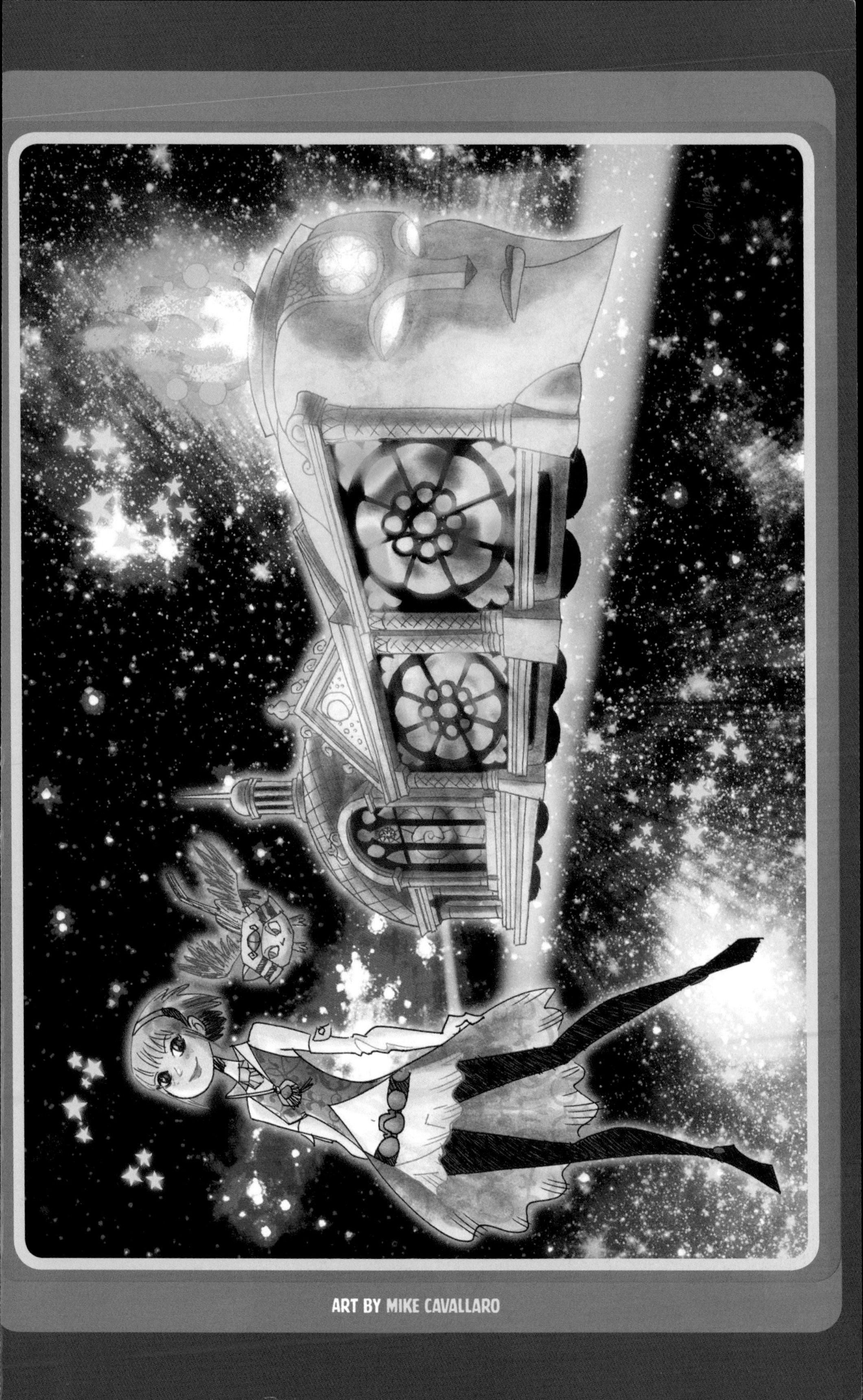

ART BY MIKE CAVALLARO

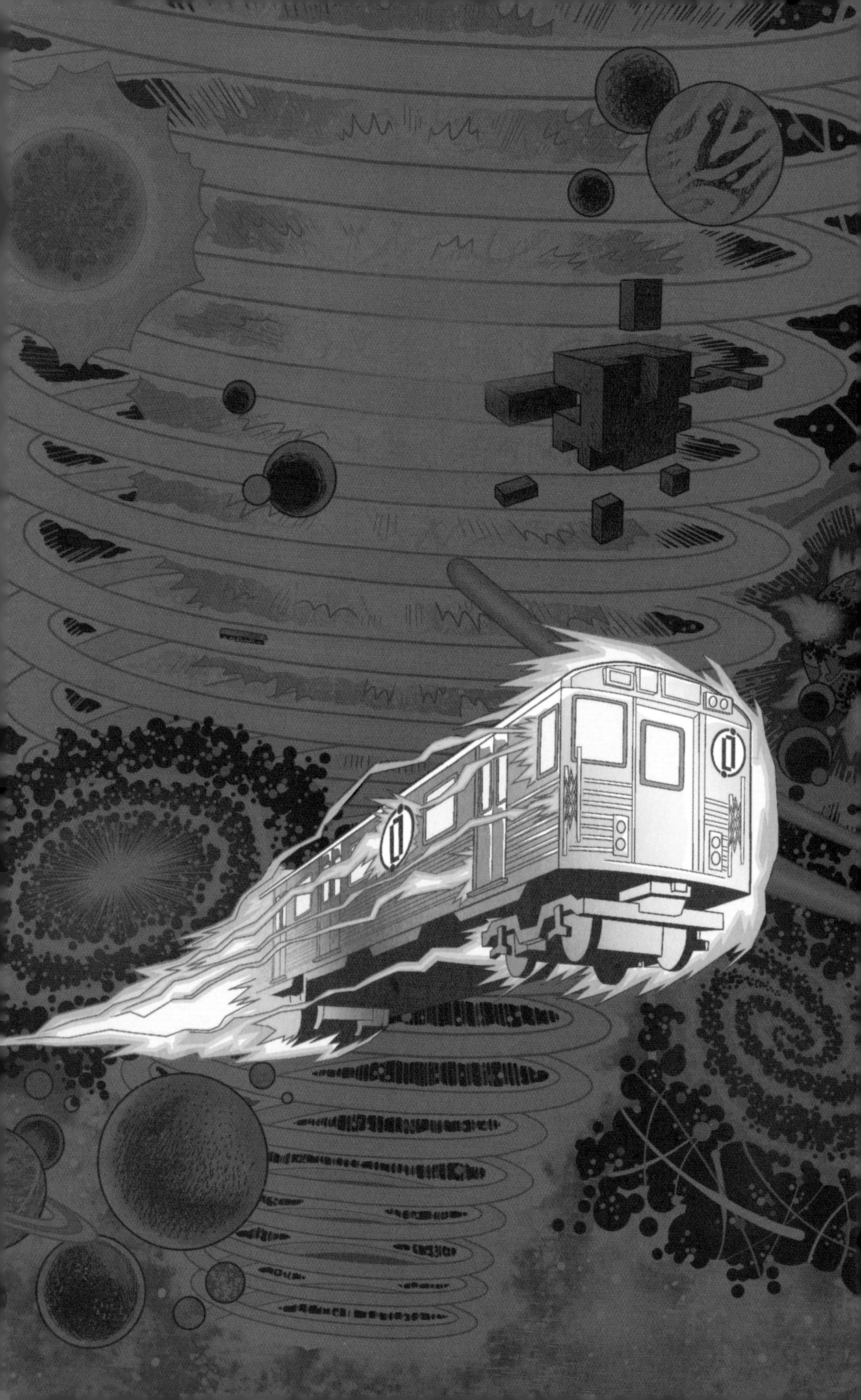